PRAISE FROM EARLY READERS

Alter is a gripping and intricate tale of conspiracy, mad scientists and broken lives. A multiverse of blurry lines, lies, and deceit where we are confronted with the best of humankind... and its very worst.
-Lucie Ataya, Author: *No Pain, No Game*

"It got me thinking, wondering, second guessing and every time I thought I'd figured it out, the story took me by surprise and took me on another ride."

"I have legitimately not read or seen a story like this before. It's unique, and I loved it."

"Twists right to the end!"

ALTER

Book I

H. R. Truelove

Midnight Tide
PUBLISHING

Published by Midnight Tide Publishing

www.midnighttidepublishing.com

Book Title/H. R. Truelove- 1st ed.

Paperback ISBN: 978-0-578995-99-4

Hardcover ISBN: 978-0-578995-56-1

For the family that planted the seed,
and the family that helped me grow.

"They're my friends. So what if they're in my head?"

Part One

CAGED

1–Lennox

The Dark World — 2035: The Evernight

My eyes were weak, but I heard every heartbeat in the Hollow. Every thud had a signature as unique as each of the countless snowflakes piled outside.

The chilly air stung my eyes and lips. My ears curled from the cold and the tips of my fingers were burned black.

We didn't even have a word for frostbite in the Dark World. Many Shadows who slept in the Hollow had missing fingers, hands, or entire arms and legs. Some limbs were taken in battle, others lost to the cold, but not one of them was a lesser fighter for it. We were born fighting, thrashing our way into the frosted wasteland of the Dark World with nothing but the voice in our heads.

I'd named mine Wisdom.

My conscience. The angel on my shoulder. The Devil.

An imaginary friend—who wasn't imaginary.

A visitor in my head, whose thoughts were a plague on my mind.

Do it now, Lennox. While Helectra's sleeping. Her death will be quick and easy. You'll be out of the Hollow before anyone knows you're responsible.

What if you're wrong? I asked, my words heard by Wisdom alone.

Helectra's a spy! I went through the Crawlers' records myself. Would you like to see them? Wisdom's tone was far more threatening than helpful.

No. I trust you. It was a two-week hike to the closest computer I'd be able to verify the information on, anyway.

You should trust me. I've never been wrong. About anything. Wisdom's irritation was so strong, a bitter taste settled on my tongue. *We need to deal with Helectra before the Crawlers come after her. End her, Lennox. And don't hurt anyone else this time.*

Wisdom's memories threatened to pierce my mind. I focused my thoughts, pitting my will against hers like a shield. I only wanted her words. I couldn't handle her feelings.

Helectra wouldn't end my life quietly. Crawler or not, I owe her a fight. I can do this. The pain will stay with me.

Wisdom's doubt broke my shield and tore through my body.

Of course, Lennox. As always, you'll do what you think is best. No matter what happens.

Wisdom slipped from my mind, nothing but the jerk at my scalp to remind me a visitor was here. There was no time to celebrate the relief her quiet brought because once my visitor left, her voice was replaced with a new sound.

Thump, thump, thump.

Even a heartbeat sounded different when it belonged to a traitor. I followed the traitorous beat through the series of caves I'd sought refuge in with nearly thirty others. The children born during the Evernight were called Shadows, and the Crawlers hunted them mercilessly.

Many slept, though it was late morning, but for every seemingly peaceful snore, there were plenty more screams of night terrors. No one slept well in the Hollow. Hell, no one slept well in the Dark World. It was too cold and too miserable. And why would we enjoy sleep? A Shadow's dreams are as dark as the Evernight outside.

Homemade weapons forged from rock were heaped in piles alongside the high-tech laser guns and night-vision equipment we'd collected over the years. Every inch of the cave floor was covered with furs, bones, and leathers stained with blood.

Ice was thick beneath the spiked soles of my boots and thick on the walls. The scent of crude fuels cut the air as a pair of teenage girls thawed the ice with flamethrowers, the blasts of flame the only light in the cave.

No sun shone outside; it was lost behind the gray that blanketed all of the Dark World. We lived like animals, surviving on wild game—on luck—or with the help of a visitor like Wisdom.

She was the light in my desolate world. Her home was beautiful, fantastical, a living dream. A place my mind had visited so many times I smelled the sweet air still.

But she was gone, and I remained in the dark, standing before one of the few friends I had outside my head. The one Wisdom had revealed to be a liar.

Helectra slept on a worn hide that still stank of the animal it came from. The arm that poked from her fur covering was riddled with jagged scars. They reminded me of my own scars and the experiments that had earned them.

I remembered Malicious telling me what a good little girl I was. "Unbreakable." The echo of my tormentor's words brought back the long-lost memory of fear.

My heart pounded as I watched Helectra sleep. She belonged to him. Unlike the Shadows, Helectra didn't hide from Malicious. She crawled toward him, serving him—bringing him new kids to break. I didn't want it to be true. I didn't want to lose anyone else.

"Wake up," I growled.

"Lennox?" Helectra sat up, pushing aside the tuft of hair that fell over her lavender eyes. Though only seventeen like me, her black hair, too, was flecked with gray. "Is something wrong?" The rhythm of her heart quickened. You only woke a Shadow in an emergency.

The unease I'd experienced seconds before vanished as I remembered Wisdom's warning. Helectra's no friend. She's one of them. A Crawler, the reason the Shadows run. And here she was, pretending she needed me to give her intel.

"I got a message from Wisdom." My killer instinct flared, and I struggled not to give in, as my hands longed to wrap around her neck. *What am I doing?* I wondered, hating the turmoil stewing in my gut. Why didn't I just tell the others about Helectra now? We'd have the Hollow evacuated long before the Crawlers breached the mountains.

I needed to give Helectra a chance to explain herself. To convince me that Wisdom was wrong and she was still one of us. "Come play, and I'll tell you what I know."

Relaxing, a grin spread across Helectra's lips as she rose from her hide.

We slipped through the narrow opening in the ice that separated the caves. Here, Shadows trained, practicing hand-to-hand combat or taking turns catching another's thrown blade from the air.

We weaved through the Shadows as they danced in faux battle. Tall, lean teens with gray hair and aching bones threw punches alongside pairs of toddlers who wrestled mercilessly, driving one another into the ice, from which they reemerged, faces streaked with blood. All innocent, playful really, compared to what the Crawlers did to us.

A space formed as the others took their sparring to the edges of the cave. Helectra and I were elders here, the only shepherds these kids had. Like me, many of them had been left at the Hollow as a last resort, a desperate bid by their parents before the Crawlers came for them.

They gave us space out of respect and out of fear. Only killers survived in the Dark World as long as we had.

Helectra pulled off her gloves, stuffing them into a pouch at her side and revealing a crude tattoo, though it was hard to make out beneath her scars. "Thanks for inviting me. My muscles are getting stiff."

I tossed aside my own gloves. The spikes sewn into the palm of them were as sharp as claws, but every Shadow preferred to fight without weapons. "Me too. I'm growing frail without my daily run." The Crawlers' heat-seeking weapons had patrolled all week, and being cooped up wasn't good for my body or my mind.

"So, what did you have to tell me?" Helectra lunged, hoping to surprise me with a strike on the right.

I caught her wrist, pulling her weight into a spin that made her slide a few inches on the ice. Then, I delivered a jab to her side, quickly followed by a punch that connected with Helectra's cheekbone.

"Testy, are we?" She rubbed the offended cheek.

"Got stuff on my mind," I muttered, wishing I could ask her outside instead. It was distracting in the noisy cave, but it was foolish to fight in the valley where the Crawlers' heat-seekers could sense us from miles away. I wasn't afraid to take on the Crawlers alone, but it wasn't worth putting the others at risk.

Helectra watched me expectantly. Reading me. Listening to the sound of my heart. A Shadow's eyes were dim thanks to the Evernight, but on a still day, we could hear for miles.

She dropped, ankle hooking my boot in a sweep that knocked me into the pair who fought beside us.

They shoved me back with feral hisses, and I spun into a roundhouse, the spikes on my heel stopping an inch from Helectra's face.

She grabbed the boot, thrusting my foot upward and throwing me onto my back. Blood soaked my gums as my head bounced against the ice.

"You're distracted," Helectra said, offering me a hand.

Leaping to my feet, I smacked the offensive offer aside.

I didn't like this. Sparring. Playing. I was as deadly as the bears locked in the depths of the Abyss. Like them, I didn't toy with my victims.

My uppercut met the soft flesh beneath Helectra's jaw. Teeth clashed, and red spittle sprayed from her lips. She'd barely uttered a groan before I landed another slew of punches to her ear.

Helectra squirmed, struggling to raise her hands high enough to protect her most vulnerable parts. There were no rules in the Hollow. No fight was said to be clean. My hands wrapped tightly around Helectra's coarse locks and her fingers wiggled through mine. We tore ropes of hair from one another's scalp, spiked heels scraping shins as we gouged at anything that might hurt.

Blood covered one of Helectra's eyes, but her lips still held a grin. She thought we were bonding. Playing a game old friends in the Hollow often played. Helectra had won as many fights against me as I had against her. But the truth was, I'd always held back. Tapered my punches. For as deadly as the Crawlers made me, it would never be easy for me to end a life.

I was a superior fighter, but Helectra was far more graceful. She looked like she belonged in an ancient music box, twirling on the ice, using the smooth ground to propel her body as she landed a series of kicks to my chest and gut. Watching her spin was harder on me than the fight. The way she moved was so quick, the world around her distorted. Even Helectra looked different when she was fighting. Her face was smoother, her hair still dark.

Thump, thump, thump. The traitorous tempo of her heartbeat was my soundtrack as I lashed out, hammering her face with blow after blow.

As every hit landed, I remembered that face.

Age eight, welcoming me to the Hollow and then slicing the throat of the Crawler who followed me to the door.

Twelve, at the hot springs, soaking our weary bodies after a battle where we'd watched many of our friends die.

Fifteen, face beatific as she lay on a bed of ice to soothe the burns the heat-seekers had left.

Now, I pummeled that face without restraint, only stopping when she whispered, "mercy."

I paused, recognizing the safe word, but all I heard was the feeble and erratic song of Helectra's heart.

Thump. Thu-ump. Thump.

Wisdom had to be wrong. No way Helectra was a Crawler.

The word of the friend in my head against the one quivering beneath my fist.

I faltered, and in that moment, Helectra changed.

Her raggedy hair became a sleek braid.

Her suit of leathers and furs changed to linens the color of snow.

She wasn't Helectra—I was looking at someone else. From somewhere else.

The icy Hollow, filled with the cries of children and the smell of blood, transformed into another world, but the place I glimpsed was not the dreamland Wisdom came from.

"No, no, no," I said, scrambling off Helectra and climbing to my feet. I couldn't be seeing Earth. I hadn't visited in ten years.

My head spun. I was still in the Hollow, where the cold air burned every sense. But the fringes of my mind threatened to pull me somewhere . . . else.

Helectra's purple eyes turned black beneath her swollen lids, signaling she was now the one with a visitor in her mind.

And that visitor would tell her what I knew.

She jumped up, a new strength coursing through her as she delivered a left-hook, followed by an uppercut that brought another wave of iron to my tongue. She swung her head back before slamming it into mine. Dark shapes swirled through my vision, and a rush of dizziness traveled from my skull to my gut.

The Hollow was spinning.

And my mind was spinning with it.

Helectra leaped on top of me, fists working my face as she ground her knee into my stomach.

"Mercy," I muttered, unable to keep my focus. The lines of Helectra's face were changing rapidly. Her skin was scarred, then smooth. Her look, her clothing, her smell—everything about Helectra was different.

"Mercy!" I cried again, but Helectra didn't let up.

Wisdom, I need you! Something's wrong! My technique was flawless as ever, but my hard muscles seemed soft, and my movements lagged, almost like I'd been drugged.

Had I? Could Helectra have slipped me something? Maybe taking me out had been a part of her plan all along.

The din of training was replaced by the deafening roar of heartbeats. The Shadows had stopped their practice fight, sensing a real one.

"What do you know?" Helectra hissed, climbing to her feet and pulling me upright.

The betrayal was still coursing through me. The lies, the deceit. Helectra was my friend! There weren't many of those in my life.

"You're a traitor."

The purple returned to her eyes.

"How did you find out?" she asked, knee bending ever so slightly as she steadied herself, body tensing for its most important battle. No questions. No denial. Helectra made no effort to deflect my accusation.

"Wisdom intercepted a message from the Crawlers. Your new mission. I guess you should've been more careful."

"Damn," she whispered, a hint of regret in her voice. "I was hoping I'd be the one to tell you."

She pulled a dagger from the pouch at her side.

I swung a hand to knock the dagger from her grip, but my fist barely moved two inches before locking in place, like an invisible chain had clamped down on my wrist. My body felt stiff and rigid, my movements forced as if someone else controlled them.

Helectra's raised blade glinted in the torchlight. Not my friend but an executioner.

Wisdom! She's going to kill me! My head was full, but if I had a visitor, she wasn't revealing herself.

Why couldn't she hear me? If I couldn't pull it together, the effects would be devastating. And not just here in the Dark World.

Helectra pounced, sinking the dagger into the flesh of my thigh. I howled as the fiery pain radiated through my leg. The heartbeats of the Shadows were different now, seeming to echo. I shook my head, willing the sound to shut up so I could concentrate.

Helectra tore the blade from my thigh, and I doubled over, palm catching the fresh blood that poured from the wound. Helectra circled, her predator eyes fixed on me—her injured prey. Her breathing was heavy, but her heart was excited. She couldn't wait to destroy the infamous Lennox, because she had never been my friend. She'd always belonged to the Crawlers. With that realization, I sliced a stiffened hand through the air, smacking the dagger from Helectra's grip.

The dagger spun across the icy floor, coming to a stop against the boot of a young girl. I ran for the dagger, scooping it up, and turning the blade on Helectra before she had a chance to recover.

All my strength poured into the blade. But I couldn't do it alone.

Wisdom, please. I tried a final time, begging her to save me from myself. From what I was.

I lurched toward Helectra, with the handle of the dagger grasped firmly in my hand, and watched the world around me change. I saw color for the first time in months. The icy walls came alive with reds, blues, and other hues I couldn't even name. Colors swirled into rainbows, clouds, forests, and rivers until I was surrounded by a dreamlike world complete with fantastical animals and candy-bearing trees.

Wisdom's world.

I tried to ground myself, but before I could, the colors swirled into a tornado, blending all the hues into the blandest brown, which settled into a barren desert, the air so hot I longed to lick the ice back home. A red and purple sky was draped over mounds of sand and scorched black earth.

Clouds gathered above me, and warm drops of rain pounded the desert into an ocean.

I was moving, but only in my mind. In reality, the spikes

of my boots remained on the ice, and the dagger was still in my hand.

As the dagger pierced Helectra's heart, my world shifted again.

I'm not supposed to be here.

The hospital walls I saw were white. So white my weak eyes slammed shut at the sight of them. All I heard was a failing heart.

Thump, thump, thu—

2 - Laura

Earth (The Green World) — 2035

If not for the goldfish swimming around the fish tank in the corner, I'd wonder if there was any life in this place. I was surrounded by bodies, all still, all quiet. Eager to jump through whatever hoops Dr. Zahara put in front of them. Just like me.

"What about you, Laura?" Dr. Z asked. "What do you want to share today?"

I cleared my throat, going over the mental script in my head one last time. "I've dreamed of Aquarius for as long as I can remember. I guess you'd call them dreams. Sometimes, I was asleep. But other times, I'd slip away in the middle of the day. A certain smell or memory was all it took to see this new place, where everyone was miserable because it was raining all the time." I stopped, glancing around the circle of folding chairs that held both my fellow patients and a jury of my peers.

Group therapy had become a trial. No one at Clover Center listened when I talked about my dream visits or the voices I heard when I closed my eyes. They only wanted to judge me for the things I couldn't control. The things they thought I was imagining.

"Can you see Aquarius now, Laura?" asked a girl with a long braid and soulful green eyes. She wore a hoodie three times too big for her, and the shadows covering her face looked like bruises. "When you look at Dr. Z, who do you see?"

"Haily, stop that," Dr. Z said. "Let Laura speak."

Haily retreated into her hoodie, her excited grin turning to disappointment.

The others in the circle hid smirks and giggles. If Dr. Z turned her back, they'd be gossiping and making faces. They'd witnessed the real me. The one I'd worked so hard to hide from the doctors.

A few lucky girls seemed disinterested. They were busy counting ceiling tiles or picking at their nails. Clover Center was nothing but a brief stop in their lives. But for ten years now, these white walls had been my home. Only two weeks until my eighteenth birthday, and nothing was keeping me from leaving then.

Dr. Z trained her dark eyes on mine. The other patients didn't know it, but a secret conversation was taking place between my longtime therapist and me. A test. A little game of Truth or Dare, where either choice could lead to my freedom or more years of confinement.

I took a deep breath, daring myself to give my best performance yet. I didn't need an award; all I needed was to get out of Clover Center.

"—But now I know those were only dreams. I wasn't seeing another reality where me and my family live a bizarro life on some war-torn island. I was coping." Dr. Z gave me an encouraging smile. "And now that I've learned new tools, I can find a better way to cope."

I paused, almost expecting the room to break out in applause over my success story. But they ignored me, only peeking up for long enough to see if I was still talking. They didn't like it when I was well; I was so much more interesting when I did things like threaten to jump off the roof or stay up all night screaming.

Dr. Z scribbled something in her notebook. "Wonderful, Laura."

Dr. Z was a peacock floating in a sea of beige. Fierce. Beautiful. Everything I wished I could be. She was my parents' age but had that cool, youthful vibe most adults her age lacked.

"I'm so proud of you." She clapped her hands and addressed the group. "I want all of you to take notice of Laura. No matter how many setbacks you have, anything is possible if you work hard and remember your goals."

Once, when I was a kid, I'd asked Dr. Z if I could be a cool Black woman, too. She laughed and said that although I could be almost anything I wanted, that one probably wouldn't happen. That was the first time I ever really grasped that other people couldn't change who they were.

Not like I could.

I shivered, as a chill settled in. Seattle was known for being on the cooler side but usually not in June and definitely not during the infamous heatwave of 2035. This entire year felt like someone left the thermostat turned up to 'Hell.'

Was the AC broken again?

Struggling not to shiver, I squirmed as I attempted to get warm, stifling a yelp when the cool metal of the folding chair brushed my back. Why was it so freaking cold in here?

Thump, thump, thump. My heart started to race like it was running with the bulls. The sound of my heart thumping in my ears was so loud it drowned out the conversation Dr. Z was having. Heart pounding, I tried to focus on the chilly room, but heavy darkness covered my eyes. Had someone turned off the lights?

My temples pounded in an aching throb. The smell of gasoline hung in the air, and I glimpsed flames.

The light slowly returned, and as my eyes adjusted, the stark white walls of Clover Center's cafeteria came into view. The ring of folding chairs. The round tables shoved up against the wall. I knew that nurse's stations, pictureless ivory halls, and more barred windows hid on the other side.

I'm still here, I told myself, wishing the thought was more reassuring. My hands clasped the thin fabric of my uniform as I waited for the nausea to subside. It was always disorienting to slip away. But where had I slipped to? This cold, dark place was nothing like the water-covered world I'd visited all my life.

The other patients fidgeted in their seats, all eager to hurry through our weekly group therapy session so they could get back to the distractions the library and rec room offered. Clover Center helped them, but this hospital was nothing but a cage to me. If anything was good for nausea, it was fresh air. But the White Coats kept me from it like I was allergic.

"Can I share next?" Haily asked, oblivious to the ice-cold room, my spinning head, and the flame-lit cave I'd seen. It was so surreal slipping from one reality to another. Chaos to tranquility. No one but me knew the horrors I saw when I closed my eyes.

Dr. Z bobbed her head enthusiastically, leaning in to hear about Haily's morning like she was talking about her trip to Paris.

Dr. Z enjoyed these simple meetings. She didn't really want to know what I saw. My parents had been the same way. Once, I'd tried telling my father the details of a dream I'd had about the Wet World. Afterward, I'd spent the day and night locked in the hall closet. I was exactly three when I stopped calling Dawson "Dad."

"Haily, how was the phone call with your mother?" Dr. Z asked, concern etched across her brow.

"Horrible." Haily ran her pale hand down the length of her braid. "That woman is so cruel!" She lowered her eyes to her lap. "I skipped a meal."

Haily had arrived the week before. Her mother stormed through the door frosted in pearls, speakerphone blaring to remind all of Clover Center she was far too busy to deal with her daughter's problems. She spent five minutes telling Haily how much prettier she'd be with "the tiniest bit of padding"

15

while she bounced her own bony leg and complained about the fact Haily hadn't bothered to put on any makeup.

The woman almost made my family seem nurturing.

"She only wants what's best for you," Dr. Z lied. "Your mother thinks Clover Center is the safest place for you right now."

I'd been given the same line. Dr. Z and the doctors at Clover Center were all the family I'd had in the ten years I'd lived here.

"I hid my lunch," Haily continued. "Snuck it out in my shoe so no one would see." She shivered, sinking deeper into her oversized sweatshirt until all I saw were her bulging eyes.

Dr. Z was like a peacock—proud and majestic. If Haily were a bird, she'd be a pigeon, living off of scraps and hardly thriving. I imagined her pecking at the wad of gum crusted in the ugly gray linoleum at my feet. She'd probably be happier as a bird.

Dr. Z took Haily's hands in hers and told her she wasn't allowed to skip meals or smuggle food. And then, Dr. Z hugged Haily so tight, I pretended she was hugging me instead.

It was reassuring to see people care about each other here. Dr. Z had a way of making us feel special. If I imagined hard enough, this group almost made up for not having any friends and being abandoned by my family.

Almost.

I'd sat through thousands of these meetings over the course of my childhood and knew how Dr. Z would handle anything from anxiety to zebra-stripe fetishes. Seriously, I'd heard so much, I thought I deserved a doctorate. Not exactly wanting to be a psychiatrist myself, I couldn't help but tune her out.

Ten years inside these white walls—zero answers.

I'd barely entered third grade when my parents brought me to Clover Center. Security wheeled me in, tied down, muzzle over my face like Hannibal Lector. I couldn't recall the hours leading up to my admittance, but the doctors said I'd injured three paramedics and thrown a chair through a window before they could sedate me.

I'd spent the last decade trying to undo that day.

My body was a vehicle out of my control. A vessel in which my dream visitor could take the steering wheel whenever she wished. If only the dreams would go away, so no one would look at me the way the people in this room did.

No more whispers, no more rumors. Maybe a chance to make an actual friend. Those things were only possible outside Clover Center.

"Laura, are you listening?"

With a nod, I forced my attention on Dr. Z. "Sorry."

Haily was still talking, but her voice had taken on a thick accent, her words slurred together as if her tongue doubled in size. "Zera said we'll probably have to move to another island if we want anything other than pigeon for supper."

"What did you say?" I jumped to my feet and stormed toward Haily, finger pointed like a dagger.

Dr. Z's stilettos clacked against the linoleum as she crossed to me. "Laura, what's gotten into you? Get back in your seat."

"You heard that, didn't you?" I spun to face her. "Haily just called you Zera! That's the woman from—" I stopped, Dr. Z's disappointed look assuring me she hadn't heard anything out of the ordinary.

"The woman from Aquarius, the Wet World you dream about?" Dr. Z finished.

"Yeah."

Dr. Z scribbled something in her notebook. "You understand this is very confusing for me, don't you, Laura?" She flipped through several pages of the notebook. "For months now, you've been telling me this was an act. That you were making up Erris and Zera and everyone else on Aquarius. But now you're implying you are hearing things, and what's more concerning is, you're pulling Haily into this."

I was distracted by the two golden hoops hanging from Dr. Z's ears. The light glinted from them like the sun reflecting off the ocean. It was so real, I felt moisture in the air.

It was the most peculiar sensation.

Not *déjà vu*, not a memory . . .

My mind started to slide. I was daydreaming, picturing a life outside of Clover Center. A life on the beach.

No! I thought, panic setting in as I realized I wasn't daydreaming at all. I was losing control. Please, not in front of Dr. Z.

I opened my mouth, but the voice that came out belonged to someone else. I spoke in a slow drawl, my accent from another person, another place. "I ain't moving islands." Erris' words slipped through my lips as if I were nothing but a radio. I tried to speak, but her frequency was stronger, her words drowning mine out. "I'll join the Gleaners before I leave Fox Island."

Giggles broke out around the room as the other patients realized what was going on. They loved it when I slipped and the stranger in the back of my mind took control.

My head tilted unnaturally toward Haily. Her eyes were wide and scared.

She flickered, her body changing forms. Haily's braid turned gray and then withered into a buzz-cut. Her green eyes darkened to brown, and a messy tattoo appeared on her wrist.

Reality was blurring, if only for me. The rocky beach and nearby ocean stretched out, so real I wanted to dunk my feet in the surf, but I was afraid of what would happen if I moved. A foul scent filled the hot, muggy air, and I closed my eyes as a few drops of rain brushed my hairline.

"Laura, stop!" Dr. Z demanded, her voice a distant echo. I wanted to stop, but I couldn't. I tried to keep my mental visitor away, but I'd never been able to do much to keep the others from taking over. Helpless, my limbs grew heavy. Dr. Z's beautiful skirt turned to rags and her golden hoops became discs that filled her earlobes.

I watched Dr. Z's mouth move as she called for assistance, but the sounds in the room were drowned out as my mind shifted and all traces of Clover Center's sterile white walls melted into an endless sea.

A long and smooth object was clasped in my hands, but what was it?

An arrow?

A dagger?

Before I could figure it out, something sharp struck the back of my head. I tasted blood before everything turned black.

***

"Laura."

My arms were bound tightly to my sides. My eyes fluttered open, heavy with the remains of the tranquilizer I'd been tagged with. I was strapped to a cot, looking up at Dr. Z. Her face was different from how I remembered. She'd always been stern, but there had always been love there, too. Dr. Z truly cared about the girls she worked with. Now she looked at me like I was a rabid animal known to bite.

"Dr. Z?" I asked. Only, I said it 'Dr. Zeee.' "Where am I?" There were no vaulted ceilings or calming fish tanks here—only white walls.

"You're in Clover Center's medical ward," Dr. Z said. "I had to sedate you. There was . . . an accident." Her glance was uncomfortable as she adjusted her crisp ivory blazer. "You had an episode, and someone was hurt."

The room spun in slow motion as Dr. Z's words hit me. "What do you mean?" My heart was already racing, but now it pounded in my ears. "I haven't had an outburst in months. And no one's been hurt in years."

Dr. Z's dark eyes landed on mine. When she spoke, her voice was frail, timid. Nothing like the strong and sure timbre I knew so well. "Laura, there's no easy way to say this. You killed a girl from our group—Haily."

As the words bounced through my mind, a sickening horror crept up inside me, causing my stomach to revolt.

Dr. Z acted quickly, shoving my head to the side before I choked on my vomit.

A cold, sick feeling settled in my gut, and I wondered if I would ever feel warmth again. Despair screamed through me, pulling at every sense like it was tearing stitches. Horror, denial, anger. Each jostled for their place but only left me with confusion.

As the sick feeling subsided, I swallowed down the bitter lump. "What happened? I . . . I don't remember . . ."

She watched the floor, unwilling to look my way. "A butter knife," she whispered. "It was left on the table following the faculty luncheon. I guess the cleaning crew missed it."

Oh. *Oh, God.*

A deep and primal wail escaped my lips. Sobs racked through me, and I started convulsing wildly against the thick straps that covered the length of my body.

What had I done?

My hands felt alien. Strangers who'd betrayed me. Cursed me.

Dr. Z's expression softened, offering me the tiniest bit of empathy despite her fear.

A door burst open on the other side of the room, and my mother's shrill voice sent Dr. Z scurrying back.

"Oh my God, what are you doing to Laura? Why is she strapped down like that?"

"Carol, calm down," said Dawson, close behind her. "What do you expect? She killed someone for goodness' sake."

I was pretty sure my father had never said the word *goodness* in his life, but Dr. Z taught me to filter out the bad, and every word out of Dawson's mouth belonged in a garbage heap.

It was hard to see my parents from where I lay, but I didn't need to. Mom's clothes would be rumpled and her frizzy hair piled in a nest on her head. Dawson always played the business executive perfectly in his ironed suit, and no doubt my stepmother Amanda was lurking silently in the doorway, watching my mother like a hungry raven, ready to pick up her scraps.

I could feel my mother's scowl as she swung to face Dawson. "I expect our daughter to be treated like a human being. What's going on here, Dr. Zahara?" Mom bent over me, her tired eyes filled with worry. "Oh, Laura, what have they done to you now?"

"Carol, we can't talk like that," Dr. Z reminded her. "Laura needs to take responsibility for her own actions."

My own actions? My stomach rolled. *It wasn't me,* I wanted to say, but all that came out were frustrated tears.

Mom huffed. "Are you kidding me? Laura would never hurt someone like that. She's sweet as a mouse." She snuggled close, forcing me to recoil from the fresh cigarette smoke that hung on her shirt. "It's this hospital, Dawson. I told you what these places do."

"Oh, not this again!" Dawson said, massaging his eyes. "Enough with the conspiracies, Carol. They have her on video stabbing that girl. Now there's proof of what she's capable of." His voice dropped low. "You haven't forgotten about her 'invisible' friends, have you?"

My invisible friends.

I fought against the fog, desperate to recall the hours before. What had I done to Haily? Was it me? Or one of the others . . .

My body was a traitor. A thief had stolen my hands and used them to murder an innocent girl. No matter how hard I'd tried to convince Dr. Z otherwise, I was dangerous.

I felt queasy again and swallowed down a nasty lump of the wholegrain pancake I'd had for breakfast. I thought of the places I visited in my dreams and the people I became while I was there. People so much like me.

My eyes scrunched tight. I tried to ease the last of the tranquilizer from my system, but it would be hours before my blood was clean. And by then, they'd have new seds for me.

The conversation between my parents and Dr. Z faded to the back of the room. The parts I did hear included words like "trouble," "dangerous," and more than one, "I can't do this anymore!"

Do what? I wondered, trying to figure out which words belonged to whom. They only allowed Mom to visit once a year, and Dawson and Amanda visited even less often than that. It had been Dr. Z and the other White Coats who raised me.

From across the room, I heard, "What about Haily?"

The name snapped me back to reality like a palm across the face. Haily. Fellow patient, almost-friend, and the girl I killed.

I tried picturing her, but I couldn't remember what she looked like. Every time I thought of Haily, she looked . . . different. Her hair was a graying black one second and then buzzed short the next. A new name came to me. *Helectra.*

What happened? When did I grab a knife? No matter how hard I tried, all I remembered was the icy cave I'd been dreaming about. There'd been a fight . . .

My thoughts were interrupted by my parent's bickering. My family was finally here, but even this couldn't make them get along.

Shut up! I tried. *Quit arguing long enough for me to get my head straight!* I was trapped on the cot, my own words muffled, while someone else forced their way into my mind, pushing me aside. My head pounded, and an intense pressure built behind my eyes.

The heavy scent of bleach that dripped from every surface in Clover Center was replaced by the stench of gunpowder and rotten fish. The air-conditioned room felt so muggy, I expected it to start raining at any second.

"Is the raid over?" Erris asked, her foreign accent dripping from my tongue like thick syrup. "Are the Gleaners gone?"

Dr. Z flew to my side, a look of great concern on her face. "Laura, your eyes!"

Her makeup was flawless, from her high-arched brows to her maroon-lined lips. But then, the makeup faded away and wrinkled, leathery skin aged by the sun took its place. Her slick black bun shrunk back, revealing a scalp buzzed so short I saw bugs crawling across it. Dr. Z's ivory jacket and silk skirt turned to rags, and her hoop earrings became two golden discs.

I was slipping again, teetering dangerously close to stumbling into Aquarius. Why couldn't I stop seeing the Wet World? Maybe it was the sedatives. Dr. Z must have given me the dose they reserved for circus animals.

Clover Center's white walls faded, and I glimpsed an island in the middle of an endless sea. There were ships in the distance, a few with black sails that matched the smoke pouring from the vessels.

Boom!

The cannon blasts were so loud, I was sure they'd rattle the windows. But they weren't here on Earth. The sound echoed from the place I'd dreamed of all my life.

3—ERRIS

Aquarius (The Wet World) — 10 A.F

Erris, get down!"

I ducked, Zera's words reaching my ear a millisecond before the tip of her arrow did.

The arrow struck its target, a burly soldier in a black Gleaners' uniform who'd been climbing up the cliffside. He tumbled backward, joining the pile of bodies scattered across the beach. It was easy to see who was winning, even from a distance, even in the rain. Compared to our side, there were very few black uniforms lying in the mud.

The trail of bodies littering the beach led to shore, where Holdouts waited to meet the black-sailed boats.

Gleaners. Thieves, robbers, kidnappers—Military. The Gleaners served the man who'd named himself President of Aquarius, and they came damn near weekly to do his will.

We were staked out on Fox Island's only bluff. The heavy gray clouds overhead were a reminder of the rain that plagued Aquarius. A rocky path leading through sparse foliage wound around lopsided shanties made of rotten plywood and rusted storage containers, and mosquitoes as hungry as me hovered around them in droves.

A slender girl with a shaved head crouched in the brush at my side, hands pressed tight to her ears. A hand-carved tattoo showed on Hale's wrist, black tally marks symbolizing ten years passed since the flood. Every Holdout had the tattoo, even me, though I was a lousy fighter.

A Gleaner was close behind the one Zera had taken out. Hale watched the battle being waged along the shoreline, oblivious to the man who reached for her leg, eager to take her and turn her into his boss for a prize. The Gleaner's black glove crept closer. He'd grab Hale and yank her down the cliffside before Zera realized he was there.

I was a terrible fighter, but being a soldier was about more than the fight. Sometimes, it was your other skills that made you valuable.

I closed my eyes, squeezing my fists tight and digging my nails into my palms until the Gleaner vanished. For a second, I glimpsed white walls, but I didn't linger on them. *Thump, thump, thump.* The sound of Lennox's heartbeat hit my ears as the air grew cold.

My head was pounding, making it hard to remember my training.

I tried to separate Lennox's thoughts from her pain, but something jerked me back to Fox Island before I could settle in.

"Erris! What were you thinking?" Zera grabbed me by the shoulders and gave me a rough shake. "How many times have I warned you about slipping off during a raid? You almost got us killed!"

The Gleaner was slumped in the thorny bushes that climbed up the bluff, Zera's arrow poking from his side.

"I wanted to borrow Lennox's strength," I said. The rags Zera wore for clothing stank like the fish she'd netted for yesterday's breakfast, and I shrank back from the stench.

"Get it together," Zera hissed. "It's time to fall back."

I scooped up my bow and followed the others further uphill. Our rubber boots were clunky, but the Gleaners' heavy suits had no chance of trailing us up a steep hike. "Lennox could've ripped that guy's head off!"

Hale stopped just long enough to sock me in the arm.

"Or she might've ripped *my* head off! You can't control what she does. It's stupid to try to visit that girl, Erris. Leave your dreamworlds be like the rest of us. Find one of them crooked Gleaners who'll make you a trade for some medicine so you can get a decent sleep for once."

"I ain't got nothin' to trade," I reminded her. "The Gleaners will just put me in a cage. Out here, at least, I can hunt."

No Gleaners were around, so I lifted the bow from my side, my arrow following a scrawny pigeon as it hopped from branch to branch in a nearby elm tree. Mother Elm, we called her, one of the last few trees standing on Fox Island.

Ignoring the dirty golden dread hanging in front of my face, I tugged the string back in rhythm with my slow-drawn breath. My body tensed as the arrow whipped loose from my bow and rattled the leaves of Mother Elm. "Dammit!" I muttered, watching the pigeon flap toward the ships battling on the ocean.

The President's Gleaners were ever-present, always waiting off the coast of our little island, hoping we'd slip up so they could take this land, too. The military had already stolen half of our boats and several of our people, laying claim to every rock poking from the ocean here to Rat Island.

For now, they followed their orders. They weren't all bad. Many of the soldiers were known to make trades, and the produce and medication they brought had even created a few alliances between the warring groups. But I would never make a trade like that. I'd watched my folks leave on one of those Gleaner boats the year before, and I'd sink every ship in their fleet before I touched their food or their medicine.

Grasping my bow firmly, I hurried down the path after Zera and Hale. A wall of rusted sheet metal provided cover for the Holdout archers lying belly-deep in the mud, arrows following the black uniforms spilling over the beach.

A few *thunks* peppered the air, but most of the archers remained patient, knowing their flimsy arrows wouldn't puncture the Gleaner's combat wear from this range.

Zera slipped through the door of the first shanty we reached, which happened to be Fox Island's only schoolhouse. Inside was nothing but a sad ring of folding chairs.

All the glass on Fox Island had been broken by cannons, and to keep out the murderous mosquitoes, large sheets of screen enveloped the shanties instead.

Boom! I dropped, hands firm to my ears. Easing to my knees, I crept toward the window.

Boom!

I stopped, the cannon fire startling me from my thoughts. But it did more than that. The few stooped palms and ancient conifers I glimpsed through the window disappeared. Even Mother Elm. For a second, the island vanished entirely. I was in a room with white walls brighter than the sunlight that graced Aquarius.

"Erris, get down!" Zera hissed, practically tackling me away from the window. "Someone will see you!"

Boom! The cannons were getting closer. I tried not to think of the Gleaners' black sails or the prisoners they'd be taking with them. The bodies they'd leave behind.

Boom!

The walls had been brown once, but the rain had left large patches that looked like bloodstains. Black mold speckled the walls, ceiling, and even the floor, which squished beneath my feet.

I squinted, sure my sleepy eyes were fooling me. I could've sworn something about the room had changed. Hale transformed before my eyes. Her bristled scalp grew into a long, dark braid, her raggedy smock and trousers became a shapeless ivory top, and for the briefest moment, the room had white walls.

"Ugh, I wish the Gleaners would haul off already," I

muttered, cradling my head in my hands. "I need to eat something."

"You almost got that pigeon back there," Hale offered.

"Thanks," I said, disappointed. "But I missed. If I don't find something besides fish, my belly's gonna revolt!"

"I know." Hale gestured toward the dark-skinned woman who kept watch by the window. "Zera said we'll probably have to move to another island if we want anything other than pigeon for supper."

"I ain't moving islands." I shook my head. "I'll join the Gleaners before I leave Fox Island." I was staying right here until my folks came back.

"Shut your mouth," Zera whispered over her shoulder, "or they will take you."

Boom!

A cannon echoed in the distance, reminding me the battle was far from over.

Boom!

A wave of dizziness washed over me. I dug my bare feet into the floorboards, eyes squeezed tight as I struggled to stay upright. My senses ran wild, causing me to smell colors and taste sounds. My guts sloshed as if I were out on the open sea instead of in the schoolhouse. The scent of mildew flirted with something that made my nostrils burn, and the room flickered in and out of focus. Every blast of the cannons rattled me from reality. I was slip-sliding in and out of my mind. In and out of another world.

I gagged as antiseptic infiltrated my senses, stinging my nose, mouth, and eyes. Where was that smell coming from?

I felt cold metal in my palm, but before I could make sense of what it was, my hand was in the air and I was lunging toward Hale. She was flickering, too. I couldn't really be sure if it was her standing there or someone else.

***

"Erris, wake up!" Zera's eyes were wide, her expression horrified.

I lay face-up on the floor of Zera's schoolhouse, the taste of salt so thick on my tongue I begged for a drink.

How did I get here? "Is the raid over?" I asked, confused. "Are the Gleaners gone?" The sound of panicked screams and cannon fire assured me the Gleaners were still on Fox Island.

A migraine set up camp in the back of my skull, and I grimaced when my head brushed the uneven floorboards. My hand crept back, finding a sticky mess in my dreadlocked hair.

Zera crouched beside me. "I had to hurt you. I couldn't get you to stop." A tattoo of an emerald peacock covered most of her shoulder.

"Stop what?" I wondered. "I ain't had a blackout like that in a while." Hadn't missed them either. I brought my hand in front of my face, groaning at the sight of fingers painted in blood. What had I done? As I gazed upon my maroon-stained clothing, my breath caught, and my chest squeezed in on itself as if trapped in a vice. That was a lot of red. "This ain't just my blood, is it?"

"I'm so sorry." Zera's hands gripped tightly around mine, fear in her eyes flickering like candlelight. In the ten years I'd lived on Fox Island, I'd never seen Zera scared like that. "You lost control, Erris!" She helped me to my feet, and I fought to stay upright.

"Did you drug me?" I felt like I could faint again at any second. My mind spun, and I saw glimpses of white walls.

Zera gaped. "No, I didn't drug you. You, me, and Hale were waitin' out the Gleaners, and all of a sudden you just . . . you—" Her dark complexion paled.

"What, Zera?"

"You stabbed Hale. You took that bowie knife from your pocket and started hacking at her with it."

My eyes followed her pointed finger toward a bloody knife lying by my feet, and my stomach churned at the horrible realization.

Zera let out a shaky sob. "You were on her like an animal! You didn't just lose control; you . . ." She shook her head. "I've never seen nobody attack a person like that."

"No," I whispered. "I was waiting out the Gleaners . . ." I turned toward the door, stopping short when I saw the maroon spray circling Hale's cold, still body.

My free hand shot to my mouth. I'd done *that?*

Every good feeling drained from me at the sight of her, and I wanted nothing more than to curl up at her side and die. The way the girl's limbs twisted was . . . wrong. Her face was bloodied, and stab wounds peppered her arms and legs. Zera was right. I was an animal.

I scanned the ground, finding my bow smashed to pieces. Flashes came back to my aching skull as I remembered Zera beating me with my own weapon.

I fell to my knees, not caring when they slammed into the hard floor. My face smashed against the splintery wood, sending black spots fluttering through my vision. The taste of old fish surged in the back of my throat. I felt cold despite the muggy air. I wanted to lie there and never get back up again.

Boom!

"It's the Gleaners," Zera said. "They got another boat in." She stared out the window for a moment. "Move it now, Erris." She pulled me to my feet again, nearly yanking my arm from the socket as she dragged me out the door and into the drizzling rain. She was leading me down the trail, but it wasn't toward the gallows, it was toward the Gleaners.

"Yer gonna send me off instead?" I wiggled my arm, trying to pull it from her grasp. "What are you doing, Zera? It was an accident!"

I took a step away from Zera, and a searing hot pain tore through me like I'd been caught by a bullet. My hand trailed to my thigh, finding a fresh cut. Where'd that come from? The skin around the wound was hot and tender, and the cut felt like it was already well on its way to infection.

Screams sounded up and down the shoreline as the Gleaners pulled people from the shanties and tried to corral them on the beach.

"You gotta go, Erris!" Zera said, yanking me toward the beach. "Yer too dangerous to stay here. The Holdouts will kill you."

"Let 'em!"

I thought of Hale's body splayed across the floorboards of the schoolhouse.

"Please!" I cried, wincing every time my right foot touched the ground. "Don't send me to Rat Island! I deserve to die, Zera!" I looked down at my ripped shorts, half-expecting to see an arrow poking from my thigh. Why did my leg hurt so damn much? "I'd rather die!"

I'd heard horrid stories about Rat Island over the years. Sometimes, the Gleaners left you to rot at Prisoner's Point. But other times—

Boom!

Zera ducked at the sound of a cannon blasting in the distance.

She straightened up, but she no longer looked like my schoolteacher. Her coat was clean and white, her silk skirt covered in flowers . . .

Boom! Dr. Z was gone, and Zera stood there again.

"Erris!"

I stumbled after Zera as if a strong breeze were pushing me. Was I even moving my legs? They felt numb, stilted, almost locked in place.

Lennox, you there? My head pounded from both the wound on the back of my skull and the presence in my mind. *Lennox, I can't concentrate!*

Zera changed with every cannon blast. One second, she was my old schoolteacher. Then, she would become the doctor in the fancy white coat.

Gleaner boats cluttered the shore, everything from schooners fitted with cannons to tiny rowboats cast aside on the beach like they had plenty to spare.

Boom!

Filthy, no-good Gleaners, would you knock off that noise? Every blast threatened to push me out of my world and into another. I didn't like that white-walled place Laura came from. I didn't like feeling trapped.

There were bodies now. Crumpled up in piles on either side of me. Stuck with arrows or daggers, mostly as the gunpowder was reserved for the cannons. I was thankful the smell of salt and rain covered up the blood. But I'd been given clean-up duty on the beach many times. I knew the smells and unspoken rituals of body disposal too well.

There wasn't room for a cemetery on Fox Island, and throwing bodies in the ocean brought the sharks dangerously close to shore. We needed the fish too badly. So, most of the deceased were surrendered to Rat Island. I wonder if anyone ever asked why they'd want them.

Boom!

My eyes scanned each body. It was my own personal ritual. I was making sure none of them were my folks, though I hadn't seen them in over a year. If I ever did find them, I sure wouldn't be handing their bodies over to the Gleaners.

Zera kept her bow raised, following the trail of bodies all the way to shore.

"Why are you turning me in now?" I yelled, ducking in rhythm with arrow fire and cannon blasts. "You could've any of the other times I messed up."

"This wasn't no mess, Erris. It's a sign. The Gleaners were gonna come for you eventually. You're valuable."

Zera hung back, looking me up and down from my torn-up shorts and holey top to my size-too-big rubber boots. She was appraising me, guessing my worth.

Zera waved an arm over her head like she was flagging down an old friend. But it wasn't no friend she waved to—it was a Gleaner.

Guess I was worth something after all.

Spotting her, the man pulled an arrow from the quiver at his side.

"I got one!" Zera said, tossing me toward the Gleaner without a care. Zera wasn't my schoolteacher no more. She wasn't even a Holdout anymore. I realized she was one of them. A Gleaner. An opportunist eager to cash me in for a prize.

Aiming his bow our way, the Gleaner hissed, "You got what?" Big and tall, with rolling hills of muscles that filled out his dark jacket, his whole appearance suggested that the Gleaners were plenty well-fed. "We already got enough kids."

"Not like this one." Zera hooked a thumb over her shoulder. "Go look in the schoolhouse if you need to see for yourself." Her voice lowered. "She's strong. She's one of the ones the President's after."

The Gleaner's eyebrows lifted, and he gave a nasty smile full of broken teeth. "Is she?"

Zera nodded excitedly. "So, what can I have for her? Meat? Oranges?" She got real quiet. "Antibiotics?"

The Gleaner's expression shifted. "Must think she's special, expecting somethin' like that." His fingers went slack. My ears had barely registered the whistle in the wind before I heard the thwack! as the Gleaner's arrow struck Zera through the throat. There was a sickening gurgle, and then her body was on the ground.

"Zera!" I shrieked, crawling toward the place she had slumped in the mud. The Gleaner stopped me with a kick to the side.

"What's so special 'bout you?" he asked, nocking another arrow.

My chest heaved, panic rising as my head swung from Zera's body to the Gleaner ship waiting on the shore. Squinting against the warm rain, I scanned each Holdout as they were loaded onto the boat, knowing none were my ma or pa. I swallowed down the fish-flavored panic rising in my throat. Zera wasn't wrong. The Holdouts would kill me once they knew what I'd done. The closest thing I'd had to family here was dead at my feet. Who knew when my folks were coming back from Rat Island? Maybe it was time I went after them.

I deserved it after what I'd done to Hale.

"My name is Erris," I said, each word shaking out of me. "And I see other worlds."

4—Laura

I was ripped back to Clover Center, the smell of sea salt replaced by bleach and something else—something bitter and tangy and foul. The scent of Haily's blood was crusted in my gown. My parents and Dr. Z had left, leaving me alone with a thin man I'd never seen before. His face was ghostly white and his mouth was frozen in an "O" like the man from *The Scream*. I'd always loved that painting. I felt I could relate.

"Erris?" he asked as he shined a penlight in my eyes. A grinding headache flared, and I winced under the light's assault.

"What did you call me?" I squeezed my eyes tight, forcing the light out.

The man pulled a lever next to the cot, allowing it to fold forward so I could sit up.

He took a seat on a rolling desk chair. My arms were secured tightly at my sides, but he pushed his chair out of my reach, anyway.

"You said your name was Erris, just a few moments ago."

"I did?" I remembered nothing after my parents arrived. "Where did my mom go?"

The man pressed his lips together beneath his thick mustache. "Your father and stepmother are in Dr. Zahara's office discussing your transfer. Your mother seemed pretty rattled by your outburst. I think she was asked to return home."

"Home?" I was used to being confused after a blackout, but nothing was making sense now.

"But she drove all this way . . ."

"Yes, well, it appears your mother is no longer responsible for your legal or medical decisions, and Dr. Z didn't think it appropriate for her to stay. You'll have to ask your father about it when he comes in to say goodbye."

Goodbye? "Dawson's leaving too?" What was going on? My pounding skull was keeping me from thinking straight.

The man bit his lip and leaned forward. His breath smelled sterile, like mouthwash, and it made my eyes sting to be so close to him.

"Are you with the police?" I asked.

He shook his head. "I'm Dr. Nikola Venkin. I'm a specialist of sorts."

"They said I hurt someone." I struggled with the words. Saying them out loud put a burden of responsibility behind them I wasn't ready for.

The man met my eyes with his own lumps of coal. He was looking right through me, searching me. And even I didn't know what he might find.

"Yes, you did." His chin dropped in a nod. "And because of that, you can't stay at Clover Center. This serves as a hospital for perfectionism and eating disorders. Not issues like yours."

An unsettling realization drifted over me. I'd heard about the kind of places they sent murderers to. Places where they blocked the daylight out so tight you couldn't even guess what season it was. A chill ran through me. My birthday. It was only a couple of weeks away . . .

The fantasy I'd harbored about being released soon felt a lifetime past. I realized now, I would finally be leaving Clover Center, but like when I arrived, it would be in straps.

The chill I felt brought shivers as Haily's face returned to haunt my thoughts. What did I expect? I'd killed someone. I deserved to be locked up.

"You specialize in dissociative disorders?" I asked, desperate to flee her image.

My right thigh itched, and I longed for the straps to loosen enough for me to scratch it.

"Not exactly," Dr. Venkin replied. "But I think we both know that's not what we're dealing with here. My institute specializes in a myriad of things, and I always say, my doctors are some of the best in the universe."

"Nothing like that's ever happened before," I said. "I usually don't . . . stab people. How did I do that, anyway? I don't even remember a weapon."

Dr. Venkin readjusted in his chair, crossing one leg over the other and resting his elbow on his knee as he leaned toward me. "Nothing at all?" he asked. "Your memory is totally gone?"

I nodded. "But that's not unusual. I black out a lot."

"I know, Laura. I've read your files. In fact, I've been reading them for months. I find your case fascinating."

My eyebrows scrunched together. "Were you waiting around for me to hurt somebody? How'd you get a hold of my records, anyway?"

He cleared his throat and adjusted his lapel. The lines of his suit were crisp and the fit perfect. I understood now. Venkin stunk of my father's money.

"I want to speak to Dawson," I demanded with all the authority I could scrape from my place on the cot.

"I told you, there's some paperwork he needs to fill out now. There's a short window of time before Haily's parents arrive, and it's best we get you out of here before then."

Haily. The stir in my gut returned. My heartbeat quickened from a canter to a gallop. *I killed someone?* I killed someone! How? It had been so long since I'd hurt anyone but myself.

All I saw was Haily. Who was responsible for her death? Was it Erris? Growing up, I never knew what she might do while in my body, but I'd never worried about her being a murderer before. A sinking feeling settled in. If it wasn't her, then who? I hadn't been visited by anyone else since I was a child.

"Will they take me to jail first?" I asked. "To wait out the trial?"

"Trial?" Dr. Venkin gave me a confused look. "Laura, I think you misunderstand . . ."

There was a knock at the door, and Dr. Z poked her head inside. "We're all done in here."

Dawson and Amanda entered behind her, none of the three willing to meet my eye.

"I'll give you a moment." Dr. Venkin stood from the chair. He leaned in and whispered something in Dawson's ear before he slipped out the door with Dr. Z.

Come back, I thought, dreading being left alone with these two.

"It was an accident," I said when the door was shut. "I don't even . . . I can't remember it. I blacked out. It—It wasn't me. I didn't hurt her."

Tears burned in my eyes. No matter what I remembered, I was at fault here. Even so, I was desperate for the tiniest bit of sympathy, and I hated that this was who I wanted it from.

Please, believe me. For once.

"It was one of the others," I said, wishing I could take the words back as soon as I'd admitted them.

Dawson's eyes stayed glued to the floor, but Amanda's beady stare was full of terror and disgust. I focused on the place where her navy blouse bunched around her midsection.

Dawson inhaled. "Laura, there's no easy way to say this. I can't deal with you anymore. Your mom can't either. Your outbursts are getting more dangerous, and now you've . . ." He sighed, finally catching my eye. As he swallowed, I watched the large mole that rested on his Adam's apple rise and fall. If Dawson was a bird, he'd be a vulture.

He exchanged a sideways look with Amanda before he spoke again. "Your stepmom's pregnant." My gaze flew back to her belly. "You're too dangerous to stay here, and you know you can't come home. I started that new job for the EPA, and I need to focus on my own life now. You're going to be moving on from Clover Center, and someone else will pay your way from now on." Dawson drew in a deep breath before he dropped the sword. "I'm afraid this is going to be goodbye for us."

Dawson wouldn't be visiting me anymore? Not that he did that often, anyway. I tried not to care, doing my best to push the pain down, but all I could think of was Amanda's unborn baby. The perfect addition to Dawson's replacement family. Why didn't the asshole just put me out front with a "Free Puppies" sign? "Where's Mom?" I finally asked, refusing to give him another thought.

"She was escorted home. The court decided she shouldn't be able to decide for you a while ago, and I'm not sure she was strong enough to say goodbye, honestly. They've got her on some interesting meds these days . . ."

Mom was cutting me off too? Now there was no stopping the tears.

For the first time, I wished someone else would take my place. I didn't even care what happened while she was here. I'd gladly wake up with a new injury as opposed to living through this horrible conversation.

The door opened again, and Dawson and Amanda gave Dr. Venkin a grateful smile for the interruption. Dr. Z hung by her office door; arms crossed. She changed her jacket, I realized, cold and sick feeling returning as I remembered the other one was covered in Haily's blood.

Dawson gestured to the thin man who was watching me as if I were going to win him first prize at the science fair. "Dr. Venkin will be your new guardian."

"You're giving me away?" I blurted, hating the disloyal tears that snuck from the corners of my eyes.

Dawson had given me away long ago—when he sent me away and left my mother. He'd run from us as fast as he could, straight into Amanda's arms. It had only been a matter of time before he made it official.

Still, the sinking despair of abandonment washed over me. They may have been a crummy family, but they were mine.

A shrill voice sounded from the corner. "It's the only way to keep you out of prison, Laura. They'll try you as an adult!" It was the first thing Amanda said, and my hatred for her surged at the words. I guess I couldn't blame her for never speaking to me.

"I'm not giving you away," Dawson clarified. "It's too close to your birthday; you'll have to volunteer. But this is better than the alternative. You'd be going somewhere safe. For you and everyone else. Dr. Venkin runs an institute that specializes in personality disorders like yours. We worked together many years ago. He's a good man; he'll treat you well."

My glare shifted to Dr. Venkin. What kind of bird would he be? Definitely one of the early kind. Quick to snatch up the worm—or someone else's murderous daughter.

"They already told us it's not a personality disorder," I said. "Remember, like five thousand tests ago?" The doctors had been tossing my diagnosis around for years. Was I crazy or not? Was I making it up or not? Every time a specialist decided on a name for what was wrong with me, they would change their mind the next day. I suspected a few of them even retired afterward, convinced they'd failed at their jobs.

"I don't know what's going on." Dawson leaned in, patting my shoulder with all the emotion of a vending machine. "But I hope Dr. Venkin can help you."

Left alone with me, Amanda flashed a forced smile. Stupid Bird. "Good luck!" she cawed, hot on Dawson's heels as they marched out of Clover Center and out of my life.

The sound of my beating heart made its way to my ears. Freedom, so close I'd been picking out parkas, was now being torn away from me in the cruelest way. I couldn't even remember my crime. Could barely feel it.

I stared at the door, thinking of Dr. Venkin on the other side. Would his hospital be like Clover Center? Would the doctors be nice?

Did it matter?

My pounding heart reminded me of the life I'd taken from Haily. I didn't want to be dangerous anymore. I couldn't handle losing anyone else because of the others.

If I wanted freedom, I needed to get rid of the visitors. Which meant I needed Venkin.

5 – Laura

The ride to Dr. Venkin's institution was cramped, and the van smelled horrible—like the hygiene-phobic driver, but I wasn't strapped to a cot, so I guess it wasn't all bad. I saw rolling cow fields through the window and thanked God for every Holstein that pulled my thoughts away from Haily.

What would her parents be going through now? Who had called them? Dr. Z? I slammed my head back into the seat, welcoming the physical pain that released the mental one. Dr. Z would have warned me that was an unhealthy coping mechanism, but it had been her, not me, who ended our doctor-patient relationship.

The warm breeze blowing from the driver's cracked window turned my attention back to the cows. It felt incredible to be outside. The White Coats walked me through the courtyard in the middle of Clover Center on days it was warm enough, but it had been years since I'd been allowed in a wide-open space. Apparently, there'd been "outbursts."

We left the suburbs on a winding road. Rural homes were separated by drooping barbed-wire fences helpless against the encroaching blackberries. As we neared Seattle's city limits, the houses started to bunch together again, and we turned down a long, paved driveway lined by tall shrubs that stood like soldiers in formation.

We were waved through a gate by a security guard in a bulging black jacket. The van wound around a driveway, and pulled to a stop in front of a sprawling ivory building. I looked for the familiar barred windows, but there were no windows at all.

The Tomlinson Institute of Research, or TIR, as Dr. Venkin called it, appeared as cold and soulless as the goodbyes at Clover Center had been. So much for family. Even Dr. Z barely said a word as they whisked my cot out the door. *She didn't love me anymore, either. If she ever did,* I thought, biting hard on my lip and forcing the tears to retreat before they overtook me again. The demons in my mind had severed my relationship with everyone in my life, leaving me with no one except Dr. Venkin.

A fresh group of white-coated attendants arrived with a wheelchair, and I was thankful when Dr. Venkin waved the flock away, insisting I was capable of walking. It was my first strap-free escort in a very long time.

I reveled in the sun, savoring the feeling of the dry air on my face. I took a hefty breath of fresh air before following Dr. Venkin through the set of glass doors in front. *Please don't let me ruin this. Another slip and I may never see the sun again.*

"Every patient here is one of my children," Dr. Venkin said, the corners of his mouth relaxing into a kind smile. "I can afford to give them all better lives because of my research. I hope you appreciate what a magnificent opportunity this is."

I gave an obedient nod. "Sure. Thanks," I muttered. I knew I deserved worse, and since Haily's death, nothing waited for me at Clover Center but lifetime isolation or a sentence in a psych ward—also isolated.

A series of watercolors broke up the modest lobby. A splash of a red sunset behind the welcome desk. A calming blue ocean over a set of matching chairs arranged in the waiting area. Green fields and violet flower prints assaulted my eyes from every wall. The paintings were fine but loud, so I kept my eyes on my feet instead.

TIR was the largest building I'd ever had the privilege of being imprisoned in. The floor echoed with every step, and the hum of lights provided a steady rhythm from the ceiling. Clover Center's halls had been filled with the chatter of nurses and patients, but aside from the humming lights, the hallways in TIR were eerily silent.

There was no missing the biggest difference here: black-shirted security guards lurking beneath every exit sign. Their hands twitched at their sides as I passed, hovering over the tasers holstered there. I didn't linger on the weapons long. I'd been on the receiving end of their jolts a few times at Clover Center.

"A lot of Black Coats here."

"There are a lot of dangerous people here," said Dr. Venkin. "But it's only a precaution. TIR is as safe a place as any. I want you to feel comfortable here, Laura."

I was pretty sure that was impossible, but I nodded anyway.

Dr. Venkin stopped at a counter where a frumpy woman peered at me through plexiglass. "This is where we part," he said. "I'm afraid my skills are more on the administrative side. Think of me as a recruiter. Now that you're here, we can get you set up with some real help." He gestured toward the woman on the other side of the plexiglass. "After Sandra fits you for a uniform, the attendants will show you to your room. I know you're going to do great here, Laura." He reached over to give my shoulder a squeeze. I flinched, revolted by his touch. Why had I done that? Sure, I wasn't used to being physical, but I'd never had a body part spontaneously flee someone before.

Venkin's hand hovered in the air. "Welcome to TIR, Laura. We want you to feel at home here."

His words settled in as I watched him walk away. For ten years, I'd held hope that I would go home with my parents someday. As the years went on and that became increasingly unlikely, the hope had changed to something else. The idea of finding my own family. But now that hope was gone, and I had a new group of strangers to be my pretend family.

I followed Sandra into a walk-in closet where she fit me for a top and helped me pull a shapeless smock over my head. Branded with the letters TIR, the smocks were all the same size and came pre-stained. I assumed Venkin had gotten a deal on used hospital sheets and it had been someone's bright idea to call them "uniforms."

Sandra gave me a hideous pair of pants to match and sent me on my way. My next stop was at the medical office, where a pudgy-faced nurse checked my vitals and asked about my health history.

"All clear," she said, giving me an almost genuine smile.

A pair of attendants in white coats waited for me outside the door to the nurse's office. A man with a salt-and-pepper mustache handed me a laminated card that showed my daily schedule and room number.

"Who's Dr. Morris?" I asked, reading the name off the schedule. "It looks like I'm supposed to see him every day." *Sometimes twice a day*, I noted, wondering why that was. Psychiatrist visits only happened once a week at Clover Center.

"You can see for yourself soon." Mr. Mustache gestured down the hall. "He wanted to meet you right away."

"Where is everyone?" I whispered, afraid each word out of my mouth was going to amplify through these sleeping halls. "Where are all the other kids?"

The White Coats stayed silent, leaving me with the sound of screaming fluorescent lights, and even worse, my own thoughts.

TIR sure didn't feel like a home. The boxes mounted on the walls containing blue plastic gloves and hand sanitizer dispensers reminded me TIR was technically a hospital, but it didn't feel like that either.

Maybe TIR was only an illusion. Maybe Dr. Venkin had brought me to a prison after all.

We reached a door that read "Dr. Morris—Psychotherapy," and Lady White Coat gave a rapt knock before shoving me inside.

Dr. Morris' office was painted in the same drab ivory. Mostly empty, all I saw were a couple of leather chairs and a tall metal filing cabinet.

I was greeted by an older doctor with a ring of white hair around the crown of his head and a pair of oval glasses taking over his face. I wondered what kind of bird he would be. "Hello, Laura," he said, offering a limp handshake.

"Hello," I mumbled, eyes glued to the comfortable-looking chair in front of me. Was that a cushion? No cot. No straps. And where were the inkblots? "What do we do here?"

Dr. Morris laughed. He smiled at me in a way I imagined someone's grandfather would. My own grandparents never bothered to meet me, too off-put by the trouble I caused my parents early in life. "We talk here. About whatever you want."

I shrugged. It didn't sound so bad. He motioned for me to sit down before taking his own seat and snatching a stylus from a crystal pen cup. He watched me, twirling the stylus between his fingers like a baton.

"Tell me, Laura, how are you feeling?"

I thought about the familiar question. "Itchy," I said, studying the juice stain at my feet.

"Itchy?" he asked, surprised.

"Yeah, just below my right hip, it's been driving me nuts all day."

Dr. Morris nodded. "How are you feeling about the death you're responsible for?"

Ah, that. I knew someone would ask me about it eventually, but I still wasn't sure how to answer.

Guilt stabbed at every thought of Haily. I strained, trying to remember the hours before. I was in my regular morning group with Dr. Z; then, it was like I was hit by a Mack truck that knocked me all the way into Aquarius.

I let out a frustrated sigh.

Usually, when I slipped away from my mind, I woke up

in the Wet World. But I wasn't so sure that was what happened this time. I thought maybe I could remember. Just maybe, I could figure out what had happened to Haily, but my memory was a gaping hole.

Besides, it wasn't like Dr. Morris was going to believe me. This was a game I knew too well.

First, he'd lay out the bait.

"It's normal to have difficulty processing death," Dr. Morris said. He opened the top drawer of his desk and rummaged around. "Do you know what's in here?" he asked. "Contraband." He gave me a wink. "Little knick-knacks a few wily patients tried to sneak in over the years. What would you like, Laura? A Yo-Yo? Chewing gum? Friendship bracelets?"

"I don't have any friends."

"Yet," Dr. Morris said, sliding the door shut. "But that's only because you just arrived at TIR. Our patients have developed some truly remarkable friendships here, and I'm sure you will, too."

"How's that supposed to happen? I couldn't even share a table in the cafeteria at Clover Center."

"Well, you're no longer at Clover Center. At TIR, you'll be able to share a table, interact with other patients. You'll even have a roommate."

"I get a roommate?" I asked in surprise.

"Even after . . . ?"

I'd never had a roommate. I was an only child, and the White Coats at Clover Center sure weren't looking to take on another liability. I'd assumed I was destined for solitary confinement here, too.

Dr. Morris cocked his head to the side. "We believe in giving everyone the chance to show us who they are. I'd like to assume you're safe to be here. You won't prove me wrong, will you, Laura?"

"No." He had me on the hook before I realized what was happening.

Where was the judgment in his eyes? The cold calculation I was used to seeing in white-walled offices like this?

"Why aren't you worried about me?" I asked, knowing it had to be too good to be true.

"Oh, I'm absolutely worried about you," he said, nodding his head. "I'm concerned about your well-being and your health. But the policy stands. You won't be given any extra restrictions here unless you show us that you need them."

"So," he said, drumming his fingers on the desktop. "Do you want to at least *try* talking to me?"

I did. I wanted Dr. Morris to be a friend, or a father, or even that wise old grandpa who sends me loud and expensive toys every Christmas.

But I'd never had those things. All I'd ever had was White Coats. Doctors, nurses, attendants who ushered me around between chores.

"How are you feeling, Laura?" he asked again. He grabbed his stylus and poised it over a silver tablet on his desk.

What would happen if I told him? If he labeled me too hot or too cold? If I shared that the reason I was so detached was because I couldn't handle the weight of my emotion. Every hurt I caused was piled like a stone on my back.

It hurt enough to live with the things I'd done, let alone the things I felt in my dreams.

Would his trust be gone once I started sharing things like that? Once he got to know the real me?

There was only one way to find out. Doctor Morris was the barrier between me and freedom. And maybe he would be different than all the others.

"Honestly? I'm feeling a little numb. I feel terrible for Haily and her family, and for the other girls in the group I suppose, but I don't really remember the . . . incident . . . and because of that, I don't think it's quite sunk in yet."

Dr. Morris scribbled something on his tablet and gave the stylus a twirl. "What do you remember?"

"About Haily? Not much. I wasn't angry at her or anything—"

"Not her," Dr. Morris interrupted. "What's the last thing you remember happening before you lost control?"

"Huh?" I gave him a puzzled look. "You don't want to know why I hurt her?"

"It was an accident, wasn't it?"

"Well, yeah, but—"

"I just thought you'd rather not dwell on the unpleasant details. If you didn't intend to injure that girl, maybe we can focus on *why* you blacked out in the first place."

I wasn't sure if I was relieved. Although I was grateful he wasn't asking me to share, it didn't really seem fair to Haily the way she was being swept aside like that.

I'm sure he'd press me more about it later.

"The last thing I remember is thinking that the room was cold. Noticeably cold, you know? Because of the heat wave?"

Dr. Morris scooted closer.

"I got really dizzy," I said, examining the various shades of black, brown, and red that created a gross camouflage around my feet. "Everything sort of went dark, and then—"

"You blacked out?"

I'd been asked this question a thousand times and given the same answer, but I tried again in the hopes it would mean something different to Dr. Morris.

"Not exactly."

He edged closer until his hot, garlicky breath was right on my face. Although he was a teensy less creepy than Dr. Venkin, I missed the other man's mouthwash.

I shoved my chair back.

"You didn't lose consciousness?" he asked.

I shook my head.

When Dr. Morris spoke, his voice was reassuring and calm. "It's okay, Laura. You can tell me."

Could I? Everything in me screamed to keep my secrets.

He won't believe you, anyway.

But what if he did?

"The room . . . changed," I said, goosebumps rising as I remembered the cold air I'd felt in the cave. "Everything went dark as if I'd fainted, and then it was light again, but I wasn't at Clover Center anymore."

I pushed back my chair, as eager to escape his judgment as I was his breath. "I'm not making it up."

The toe of my slipper circled the largest red stain. Who drinks Kool-Aid in their psychiatrist's office?

"Where did you go?" he asked.

My eyebrows shot up. I studied his gaze, but it didn't look like the judgment and disbelief had moved in yet. If anything, Dr. Morris seemed genuinely curious. It was a refreshing change from what I was used to in these interrogations.

"Somewhere else. Like another world."

"With aliens?"

"No." I shook my head. "It looks like Earth, but the ocean covers most of its surface."

"You've visited this place before?" Dr. Morris asked.

I looked up. Still no judgment. In fact, Dr. Morris' eyes looked brighter than ever.

"I've dreamed of that place as long as I can remember. Usually, I see the Wet World, but I've visited other places too."

"You have?" His face lit up. "What are they like?"

I considered lying. Maybe this was my chance to start a whole new narrative with the White Coats, but what if I had another outburst and hurt someone else?

I decided to indulge Dr. Morris for now. I came to TIR because I wanted help. If I was looking for a lonely room and a chance to spin a new web of lies, I could have had that in prison.

"I've seen places where everything is desert or I'm in this dark cave."

Dr. Morris was taking notes on his tablet so fast I was afraid the stylus was going to fly across the room like a ballistic missile. "Fascinating," he said. "Do you pass out? Go catatonic? Laura, tell me, what happens to your body while you're seeing these other places?"

My jaw nearly hit the floor. He was actually listening to me? I'd had similar conversations with many doctors over the years, but they usually never lasted this long. Most of the time, I'd be interrupted with a theory or potential diagnosis.

The way Dr. Morris spoke was different—more open-minded. Almost like he wanted me to be telling the truth.

"That's the part that's hard to explain. All I know is that I go into this kind of trance. According to the kids at Clover Center, I usually look like I'm sleeping, but sometimes I go wild. I'll start screaming, throwing stuff, trying to climb the walls. When it's like that, I don't remember much."

Dr. Morris grabbed a video camera from his desk and set it on top of a filing cabinet so that it pointed at me. It was a boxy old camcorder like every 80s home movie had been recorded on. "I'd like to tape this, Laura. Is that alright?"

"What for?" I asked suspiciously. "I told you, it's out of my control. Can't you just write down my answers?"

"Yes, but this will allow me to record other things. What factors might lead to you having one of these *experiences*. Triggers and what not."

I shrugged. "I'm just saying, don't be disappointed if you end up with a bunch of footage of me sitting here looking silly."

Dr. Morris grinned. "Humor me."

"Where do you go?" he asked when a green light blinked from the camcorder. "What's the weather like there?"

I gave him a puzzled look. "Why are you interested in a weather report?"

He was busy writing notes.

I lay my head back, studying the ceiling tiles instead of the carpet. "The place I see most often is Aquarius, but I call it the Wet World because it's always raining. The area is ruled by these military police called Gleaners, and everyone lives on these islands . . ."

My breathing shallowed as I remembered Fox Island. A shiver crawled across my skin, and I glanced over my shoulder, sure that Gleaners were near.

My head spun. Dr. Morris' office disappeared, and I stood facing the open sea. I smelled sea salt and felt the muggy air. There was another smell here, too. Blood. It came from the bodies piled in the mud all around me. I only caught a whiff before the rain washed the scent away, and I was back at Dr. Morris' desk. The old man's cheeks were flushed, his mouth hanging open.

"You're gonna eat a fly," I warned.

His mouth snapped shut. Dr. Morris pushed back in his chair and watched me with his fingers laced together. "Thank you, Laura, you can leave now."

"That's all?" We'd barely talked for five minutes.

"Yes," Dr. Morris said, his tense expression relaxing into a smile. "You spend some time getting settled in. I'll be in touch."

I got up, wondering what Dr. Morris had seen. Dr. Z had recorded me once and then played the video back at another meeting. It was eerie watching my eyes go slack as my body tilted over ever so slowly and I fell out of the chair. I started to jerk back and forth. I was screaming. Sobbing. Trying to dig into my flesh with my fingernails. Dr. Z had stopped recording then, but the moment stuck with me. Not because of the scene I'd watched play out but because I couldn't remember the events of that day. I'd left my body, but I hadn't gone to Aquarius. I don't know where I went.

I shivered at the memory. It scared me to think my mind might be sneaking out on me.

The White Coats who waited outside Dr. Morris' office didn't say a word as they led me down the hall. The attendants here were cold, but even this stroll was a freedom I wasn't used to. How long would that last? Security guards roamed through the halls, but even the Black Coats barely cast a glance my way. Where were the straps? Didn't they know what I'd done?

Cameras blinked from the ceiling like lurking gargoyles, keeping watch should a patient step out of the Black Coats' sight. It seemed unlikely with so many guards, but who knew what dangers hid in these halls?

Along the way, the White Coats pointed out places like the reading room and craft center, and a teensy flare of excitement ignited at the thought I may actually be allowed hobbies here. Clover Center had been ever-focused on getting 'better' but everything at TIR suggested these doctors liked people exactly as they were. With that, the little flare extinguished.

I caught a glimpse of my face in the chrome of a water fountain. My skin was smooth and unblemished at seventeen years old, but my mind felt full and weary. In a couple of weeks, I would finally be eighteen, which was the maximum age a patient could be made to stay at Clover Center. I'd accepted that I may become a legal adult before I ever understood the weird things that happened to me, but I now realized that my stay at TIR was just getting started. My gaze lingered on the rows of books I could see through the propped-open door to the reading room. Guess I'd need those hobbies after all.

The White Coats told me my room was being cleaned, so I was afforded a surprise trip to the rec room.

The door to the rec room was left open because a security guard in an undersized black coat blocked the opening, his outline taking up most of the frame. The tag on the guard's jacket labeled him "Rowan" and he hovered behind the white-coated attendant like the smaller man's eclipse.

"Hands to yourself," the guard warned as I squeezed past.

A haunting quiet hung over the room despite the plethora of bodies. Board games and magazines were left ignored on the wooden tables.

I stumbled through the crowd of blank-faced teenagers clad in yellowed smocks that matched the walls they stared at.

Clover Center had only allowed female patients, but at TIR, I saw boys my age for the first time. They were ugly, and the ones I got close to smelled like old onion stew, but at least I could mark 'meet a boy' off of the list of life events I'd missed out on.

A girl with bright red hair tickling her jaw watched me from a folding chair on the far side of the room. Beside her sat two girls wearing the same sedated smiles that had been common after lunchtime at Clover Center as well. The girl with the red bob was different. Her eyes still showed signs of life.

I picked at the tabletop, noticing it was covered in scratches like Dr. Morris' desk had been. I slipped the tip of one fingernail in, stretching my fingers to fit into the neighboring trenches.

I glanced toward the girl with the red bob, but she was gone, leaving her two zombified friends behind. Where was she? I scanned the room. A sizeable group had gathered around a TV mounted on the wall behind a protective shield. The screen was blank but they were fascinated by it nonetheless.

She wasn't there. Not over by the table full of coloring books, either.

"Hey, I'm Jessica."

I jumped, slamming my knee into the underside of the table and biting my lip to keep from cussing.

The girl with the red bob was sitting across the table from me but turned toward the wall so her back faced my way. "Are they watching?" she whispered. "The White Coats?"

I checked, verifying the attendants were busy dealing out medication.

She turned toward me and waved to her companions. "Sorry about them. They'll be more fun in a while."

I laughed. "Sometimes I skip my seds, too. If I have to be crazy, then I at least want to feel it."

Jessica's smile drooped.

"Oh, I'm sorry, I shouldn't have said—"

"No. You shouldn't. But I understand you're stressed, so I'll give you a pass." She stood and waved for me to follow her to a round table in a secluded corner of the room. She lowered her voice. "Besides, mental health isn't what this place is about." Jessica tapped a slender finger against her temple. "We have something else—something in our brains the White Coats want."

I gave her a skeptical look. "Like what?"

Jessica shrugged. "I don't know. I guess they haven't found it yet."

My eyes flicked around the room, taking in the bird

sanctuary Dawson had sold me to. I saw a long-necked heron and an unfortunate boy whose beak nose made him resemble a toucan. I turned back to Jessica. With her red bob, she made a good cardinal.

"So, what's the deal here?"

She leaned in, as excited about the gossip as I was. "What do you go by?" she asked.

"Laura."

"Laura, do you know what the 'R' in TIR stands for?"

"Research? They study brain disorders, don't they?"

"Yes"—Jessica paused—"and no. They study brains, but the doctors sure aren't looking to fix them. They're . . ." She trailed off, noticing the Black Coat guarding the door.

"So, who did they give you?" she asked. "You know, as your primary?"

"I just got back from Dr. Morris' office."

She raised her eyebrows. "They sent you to Morris?"

"Sure, he was nice." Nice enough anyway.

Jessica scoffed. "Well, he should be, as rich as our parents have made him. This place is a gold mine for a guy like Morris."

"What do you mean?" I felt like I'd brushed up against an inside joke. I was no stranger to the sensation, as I was often hijacked from my body and left with no memory of what had happened, but my imaginary antennae pricked up, eager to be in on a secret.

Jessica glanced around, confirming the White Coats were out of earshot. "Dr. Morris does these experiments. Venkin may write the checks, but Morris is the one you need to be careful of. He's the one who'll break you."

Break me? That little old man I'd just visited? "I don't buy it."

Jessica gave me a sweet smile. "I'm only trying to look out for you. You ought to be careful of Morris. Dr. Venkin, not so much. It's more important to him we stay alive."

"Dr. Morris has killed patients?" I asked, doubtful. "He really doesn't seem the mad scientist type." I tried not to dwell on the fingernail scratches. They could have been from anything.

Jessica placed her hand on my shoulder and leaned close, the intimate gesture sending goosebumps down my spine. "You're new here, Laura. But just you wait."

6-Lennox

The Hollow was in chaos. Like a beacon, Helectra's death had raised an army. The Shadows never killed their own.

As I was no longer their shepherd, my flock descended on me blade-first. My limbs were a clumsy flurry of kicks and punches. My head felt dizzy and wrong, and my escape was powered by instinct alone.

Crunch, crunch, crunch. The clash of boots on snow was close at my back, and I felt the flames of their weapons licking at the leathers I wore. Seven, eight, nine heartbeats followed me now, with more coming.

A young boy gained on me, and a yelp escaped my lips as I felt the tip of his blade pierce my leathers and cut into the flesh of my shoulder. Beside him, a teenage girl wielded a flamethrower. I smelled frying hair and wondered if was coming from me or my furs.

Hisses. Shrieks. Wild, mourning screams. The Shadows cast aside their weapons in favor of carnal bloodlust. They wanted to tear me to shreds with their bare hands.

Flames taunted my back as I struggled through the tiny opening in the ice, fleeing the Hollow in favor of the wide-open valley outside.

Once I reached it, the pursuit stopped.

I looked back, chest heaving as I watched the Shadows retreat inside. I was in Crawler territory now.

Hidden deep in the mountains, the location was perfect for avoiding the heat-seekers' detection. Lookouts posted at every peak would give us plenty of warning should the Crawlers find their way here.

The Hollow was great for hiding, but it was a lousy place to run from.

I'd barely made it out with Helectra's gloves, my own spikes having been lost somewhere on the cavern floor. Spikes were as necessary as furs in the Dark World, and it hadn't been worth the seconds I'd wasted ripping Helectra's pouch free from her body. Inside, I'd found the gloves and a tiny device with a blinking red light.

A tracker.

I pulled the tracker from Helectra's pouch, dropped it into the snow, and crushed it with the heel of my boot.

Wisdom! I was so frustrated I wanted to scream her name out loud. If not for the Crawlers, I would have taken the chance. *Where are you?*

I needed to know what went wrong inside the cave. All my life I'd had the ability to jump between worlds, so why was I struggling now? And why had I seen *that* world? Earth had been off-limits to me for a decade now. Wisdom had made sure of it.

I shivered, pulling my furs snug as I trudged through the snow. The path was well-worn in my mind though there was nothing to see.

Anxiety nipped at my thoughts. My dry nostrils picked up the scent of rain and death. The sensation of taut hairs spread across my scalp as Erris tried to slide into my mind, but I kept her out, locking my thoughts against hers. Her presence came with a glimmer of light, and for a second, I saw the snowy route before me.

I didn't have the time or desire for any visitor but Wisdom. Erris considered me a weapon, but she would have to learn to use her own. I pushed her away, exorcising all the light from my life until I was left in a darkness that could only exist when the sun hadn't shone in a very long time. Eighteen years, in fact. A blanket of snow and ice covered the surface of my world, killing every living thing that wasn't sheltered in the Abyss when the ice age came.

In all my days on this cruel, ice-ridden planet, I'd never once seen the sun. Or the moon. Or even the stars. A different light could be seen on days such as this. It was a shade called green; I'd been told by those who had the benefit of living in a world where color still showed.

Not me. My world was black, and on these green-lit days, I sometimes even saw gray.

If I wanted colors, I'd have to go somewhere else.

Wisdom! I focused my thoughts, but I saw no sign of her colorful home.

Helectra's death, no matter how necessary, haunted me, and I hated being alone. A chill had settled in despite my numbness to the cold, and my stomach boiled with burning acid.

Crunch, crunch, crunch. Every step echoed in my ears, though the frost-covered bluffs would keep the sound from carrying. My ears strained, desperate to hear past the crunching and the sound of my hammering heart. The valley was booby trapped both by us and the enemy. Animal traps lay buried in the snow, their deadly jaws eager to catch a hare or the leg of an unsuspecting Crawler.

The eastern end of the valley was a minefield, a precaution the Crawlers took in any open piece of land. We'd lost more than a few kids traveling through here and although I wasn't afraid of mines, I didn't much look forward to tearing my own leg from one of the traps.

The Hollow was a part of my past now. Helectra was gone, leaving me a sole ally in the Dark World. The journey to Fade's cave would be arduous by foot, as I'd be exposed to the elements for no less than a fortnight.

Thinking of Fade brought in a new set of worries, but I

shook them off, needing a distraction so I wouldn't drown in self-loathing before I escaped the valley alive.

I stopped, finding a spot in the snow by instinct. It was a grave, though no rock or tombstone had been left to mark it. For ten years, I'd visited this spot as often as I could to pay respects to my mother.

"I'm not coming back," I said, kneeling briefly and running my glove over the spot where my mother had died. "I know I haven't made good on my promise yet, but I will. I'm going to fix this. I'll make sure your sacrifice was worth it." I closed my eyes, though I wasn't afraid of tears coming. I'd only cried once since infanthood, and even the death of my mother didn't make me as sad as I'd been then.

I got up. There was nothing else to say.

The air was warm and held a sweet scent. *Wisdom?* I asked, knowing she was the only thing that could make me feel this way.

The blackness of the Dark World melted away as if the air really were hot, and the arctic wasteland transformed. Usually, Wisdom's world would be filled with colorful trees and plants, stocked with fantastical animals ripped straight out of storybooks. But today, her world was dark and miserable, just like mine.

"Are you here?" I asked, struggling to see her. Someone stood on the far end of the field, but from here, I couldn't tell if she was eight or eighteen.

I told you that fighting Helectra was a bad idea.

Wisdom! I saw Laura. I saw everyone!

Our worlds are getting closer. Time is running out.

Fade said we have longer, I reminded her. *Years even.*

Fade is wrong.

Wisdom's usually sweet voice was cold and soulless, devoid of all compassion.

There's enough time, I told her. *I'll make things better.*

Wisdom's disappointment was suffocating. *For whom?* she asked, all of her warmth and light locked away. All I could feel was her rage.

My world's already dying. Can you fix that? Will you bring back what you've taken from me? I've spent my days alone, Lennox. Because of you, I haven't seen my best friend in ten years.

Me neither! Didn't she know I'd lost people too?

Whose fault is that? asked Wisdom. *You never listen to me, do you? And look how we all got hurt!*

The sound of an erratic heartbeat thumped in the distance. *Wisdom, calm down.*

Anger flowed through me, Wisdom's hatred seeping into my pores with such force that I dropped to my knees and drove a fist into the hard snow.

The snow grew warm beneath my glove, and for a brief moment, I saw a glimpse of green grass, a splash of blue in the sky . . . but Wisdom cruelly pulled every image of her world away.

No, Lennox. You belong in the dark. Lest you forget what you are, what you're capable of, the things you did to Laura . . .

"Stop it, Wisdom!" I screamed. *You won't let me forget.*

Why should I? she asked, her voice booming in my ears even though the girl across the field hadn't moved any closer.

I peered into the dark, desperate to glimpse her face, but instead, I saw Helectra's shocked expression the moment I'd plunged the dagger into her chest. The memory replayed over and over, but every time the blade sank into Helectra's flesh, her face looked a little different, and I knew I was seeing my victims from every world.

How? I asked, the word a gravelly whisper barely willing to leave my tongue. *How did I kill them?*

Our worlds are bleeding together, Wisdom said. *Something's wrong with the machine. My world will only be the first.* Another icy shiver brushed my neck.

Wisdom was quiet, but I heard the rattle of her ventilator. *It's time for you to go home, Lennox.*

All the warmth was sucked from the air as Wisdom spat me back into the cold and lonely Dark World. I opened my eyes, finding my face already dusted with a thin layer of snow.

It was a good thing, too. As my senses sharpened to my surroundings, I realized what had pulled me back.

A loud hum erupted overhead, the frost-covered wasteland of the Dark World muffling any warning of the heat-seekers' arrival.

I kneeled in the snow, heart pounding in my chest as the hum grew louder. They were mapping the valley, scanning for my body heat. A roar sounded overhead as they bore down on me.

"Not today," I told the hum, dropping to my belly and burrowing further into the snow. The thick balaclava wrapped around my face kept the icy snow from cutting my already-scarred flesh as I forced myself as deep as the frost would allow me.

After a few minutes, the hum moved west. I stayed in my snow-tomb, listening to the sound grow faint. When I was sure the heat-seekers were gone, I crawled out of my hiding place and turned north, the compass in my body setting my course without the need of a moon or stars. The sky was suffocatingly black, the snow blocking out even the green light now, and if the heat-seekers were any indication, I was the only thing breathing for miles and miles.

If something was wrong in the Abyss, Fade was the only one who could help me. In the Dark World, anyway. I still hoped to keep the others out of it.

Remembering the white walls I'd seen the moment my dagger plunged into Helectra's heart, my mission cemented itself in my mind.

I would do whatever it took to protect the Shadows. I'd even protect Laura.

7-Laura

After my conversation with Jessica, the White Coats led me to my room so I could sleep off my sedatives. My roommate was already gone when I finally woke midafternoon the next day, and a fresh pair of white-coated attendants were waiting to escort me to the only activity I hadn't slept through: group therapy. The joy.

"Laura, stop scratching yourself!"

My new group leader was a plump lady named Becky who had a long neck. Her hair was nearly pink and cut into a pixie hairdo. She'd make a decent flamingo, but she was no Dr. Z. I missed her, even if she was quick to boot me out the door.

My hand paused above my right thigh. I glanced around the circle, counting twelve pairs of eyes fixated on me. A brand-new jury.

"Sorry," I mumbled, returning my hands to my lap. I'd looked the sore spot over several times already, only finding the blotchy red rash from where I'd obsessively scratched.

The room stunk of black coffee that had likely sat on the burner all morning. The same stench had met my nostrils every day at Clover Center. Instead of the cafeteria, TIR had a special room reserved for group meetings. Paintings of vibrant seascapes decorated the walls. Nothing about the paintings gave the illusion of freedom. If anything, they only served to remind me the walls were rapidly closing in.

At least Jessica was here. She sat across from me, slumped with her chin in her palm as she watched me curiously.

"It's your turn, Laura." Becky had already forced the rest of the group to introduce themselves.

"Hi." I waved, scanning the ring of misfits. Greasy-haired finches, drooling swallows, and a few potoos looked back. "I transferred from Clover Center; I've been there since I was eight."

"Welcome, Laura," Becky said. "Why do you think you're with us?"

The question made me flinch. Why'd she think I was here? To enjoy the lively music and stunning artwork? Years of equally awkward introductions from groups past came flooding back to me.

Gritting my teeth so my usual sarcasm wouldn't slip through, I considered my answer. One minute I'm seeing other worlds, and next thing you know, I'm assaulting people.

"I have outbursts," came out instead.

Becky tapped the open folder in her lap, chewing her lower lip as she skimmed Dr. Z's notes about my many issues. "Your file says you were involved in a traumatic event recently?"

That was one way of putting it. How had I even gotten my hands on a butter knife? Of all the days for the cleaning crew to miss a weapon.

I released a slow breath. "I stabbed someone in my group . . . and she died."

Gasps traveled around the circle like a shock wave. *Ugh.* I gave myself a mental kick, realizing how callous I'd sounded. What other secrets were going to slip out of me? Even if I didn't deserve it, I was desperate to fit in. Perhaps if I showed the doctors they could trust me around other patients, they'd see that I wasn't dangerous. Maybe, someday, I'd see the sun again.

Becky watched me expectantly. She wasn't the only one.

"You did *what?*" squealed Shannon, the tall strawberry blonde who sat next to Jessica. The shaggy-haired boy beside her looked just as nervous—as did every other wide-eyed soul in the group.

They needed answers—reassurances—I wasn't dangerous, but Haily's death still felt alien to me, like a story I'd heard from someone else. The memory was buried too deep.

The dark-haired girl on Jessica's other side moved closer. Her haircut was identical to Jessica's but looked like someone had hacked it off with a dull blade.

"What happened?" Gina asked, nibbling her fingertips.

"I don't know. I blacked out in my last group and attacked a girl. I don't remember any of it."

I tried to remember, if only for Haily and not myself. We may not have been besties at Clover Center, but she deserved to have the person who ended her life feel remorse about it. I owed her that.

Unfortunately, I'd always been terrible at empathy. I stuffed away the bad things I'd done, shoving their memories into boxes I refused to take out. Of course, I was sorry, but it was hard to regret something you didn't do. I gritted my teeth, doing my best to look sad.

The others watched me nervously, unconvinced by my act. I'd marked myself. No way would I be making any friends at TIR.

At least there was Jessica.

"I don't think you're dangerous," she said from across the room. The other patients turned their heads to her like she was magnetic. She sparkled here, in a world so dim.

"I don't think so either." I gave her a thankful smile. "But my file says differently."

Jessica grinned. "My file doesn't know half of what I've

done."

Becky cleared her throat. "Thank you, Laura." She let the folder fall closed and turned her attention to the lanky teen at her side. "What about you, Terrance?"

"Wait a minute," Jessica interrupted. "I want to hear more about Laura." She beamed, and so did I because her happiness was so contagious.

"Jessica, you know there will be plenty of time for sharing. We have other things to go over now."

Jessica slumped back with her lip jutted out in disappointment.

I laughed, earning an irritated look from Becky, who turned back to Terrance. "So, Terrance, how have you been feeling?"

"I keep having seizures," he said, watching the knobby knee that stuck from the cuff of his ivory shorts. "When I wake up, I don't remember who I am."

"Do you use the checklist?" Becky asked. She raised a finger to the air, marking invisible check boxes as she spoke. "Name," she said, finger swishing. "Safety of surroundings," she said with another check. "Location."

I was never a fan of group meetings. It was too hard to concentrate. If I wasn't daydreaming, I was busy obsessing over the air conditioning being too low or too high. Even now, all I could think about was the freezing air blowing from the vent.

Why was it so cold? Seattle was going through a ridiculous drought that had lasted from late February through mid-June. Venkin had to be paying a fortune to cover these power bills. Or my parents were, I thought, remembering what Jessica had said.

Were Dawson and Amanda feeling guilty about dumping me?

Did my mom miss me?

My nails dug deeper, raking my skin as I thought of Haily's face. Her dark braid, her troubled green eyes . . . Already, her memory was leaving me, drifting away into blackness.

It felt like falling asleep, drifting between reality and a dream.

My aching limbs were locked in place as the cold air bit ferociously at every inch of exposed skin. The sickening, familiar smell of death wafted up from my clothing. My head felt full, like someone was trying to stuff a second brain into my skull.

A hoarse voice sounded in the back of my mind. It was familiar. Maybe I knew it from my dreams because I couldn't place it anywhere in my world. *Wisdom!* she cried.

Wisdom? Was that a name I knew?

I couldn't remember.

The entire time I'd lived at Clover Center, Erris and her war-ridden Wet World had been the only place I'd seen. Until the icy cave. But before that, there had been others.

The voice faded and mercifully, the air grew warmer, the darkness replaced by heavy rain clouds.

The smell of salt wafted through the air. It was fresh, like the ocean I visited when I was twelve. It was one of the few Clover Center field trips they had invited me on. One of the girls had gotten overwhelmed and tried to throw herself into the water. We had to go home early, and I always wished I could've stayed long enough to feel the chilly water on my feet. On Aquarius, I had as much ocean as I could want.

In a rush of cool, salty air, I was there again. I expected to see the fog-draped ocean and the rocky shoreline of Fox Island. But when I opened my eyes, I found Erris was no longer a Holdout. She was a prisoner.

8—ERRIS

The boat smelled of sweat, ale, and shit. The Gleaners howled a curse-filled tune about a lady named Sadie, who they all knew well. Their drunken ballad was only drowned out by the wails of Holdout children lamenting the loss of their families.

I'd said so many prayers, they started looping in the back of my mind. Sometimes, I thought I wasn't the only one praying. I wasn't sure, but I thought maybe someone else was in there praying for me too.

Hanging lamps illuminated the rows of Holdouts shackled in the belly of the ship. The oldest in the bunch couldn't have been over twenty, and I wondered how long it might be before I found my folks.

"Have you seen any grumps?" I asked a fuzzy-haired girl beside me. Tears had plowed thick streaks through the grime on her face, making it look like she had whiskers.

"The Gleaners don't take no grownups," she said, letting out a quiet sob.

"They do, too." I shifted toward the boy on my left.

"Have you seen any of the grumps?" I asked him.

"The only grumps are up there," he said, lifting his shackles toward the Gleaners still carrying on with their gross song.

The wound on my leg alternated between a nagging ache and a deep itch. When I touched the spot, dried blood stuck to my fingers. It may have come from an arrow or a knife. The sides of the cut were angry and hot, and the cut's serrated edge didn't resemble any blade wound I'd seen.

Lennox? I asked, thinking my warrior's name for the thousandth time since I'd been loaded on this boat.

I felt no breeze—saw no dark caves. When I closed my eyes, all I saw was Earth and its stupid white walls. Lennox had always been there, as long as I could remember. Her voice in my mind was one of the only things that had kept me from throwing myself into the ocean in the last ten years.

Is this because I killed Hale?

I squished myself into the rotting boards of the hull, pretending they were the arms of my mother.

The sun was setting on Aquarius as we reached Rat Island, and by the time we finally docked, most of the kids had cried themselves to sleep. A shiver hung in the damp air as the Gleaners hauled me off the ship. Cages cluttered Prisoner's Point, and the nude prisoners inside tried to stay warm by burying themselves in the mud.

The buildings on Rat Island stuck from the mud like rusty knives, and I was careful to watch my step, not wanting to scrape my skin on a jagged piece of metal or have my feet sink into the rotten boards of the dock.

We were split into lines. A piece of wood was stuck in the mud, and anyone shorter than the red mark on top was sent to line one. They put me in line two, and I finally saw some adults in line three. There was a fourth line, but only a few people stood in it, and they were too far away for me to see who they were.

The throbbing wound in my leg burned hot as fire, and I bit hard into my lip to keep from howling. Recognizing a handful of folks from Fox Island, my breath caught.

Where were Daddy and Ma?

My heart raced as I scanned the rotten boards of the dock, the muddy shore, and the line of prisoners marching from the boat. My folks were here somewhere. It was the only reason I'd come.

My heart was beating so hard, I was surprised I couldn't hear it over the moans that rang through Prisoner's Point.

Now that I was here, everything looked different. Whatever illness I'd experienced back on Fox Island—whatever possession made me attack Hale and turn myself in—was gone now.

A rush of terror washed over me for the first time since I'd woken up in the schoolhouse. All I thought about was what I'd taken from Hale, her family, her friends.

I'd steal a boat and pick a place to hide until I found Daddy and Ma. The Gleaners' black-sailed ships were docked nearby, but I'd need help to sail. That had always been my folks' thing, as most Holdout kids were expected to stay close to shore. Besides, there were more than just Gleaners hiding in the waters. Aquarius was rife with thieves, and the Raiders had whole floating cities out there. I'd be no match for their well-armed ships.

That was another problem. I'd need a weapon. My bow had been reduced to a heap of scraps back on Fox Island, so I'd have to keep an eye out for a Gleaner weapon to steal.

My escape plan was interrupted by a jab in my backside. I turned around, yelping when the Gleaner gave me another prod with the baton. "Where you from?" he hissed.

"Fox Island," I said, feeling exposed by the man's probing stare.

His eyebrows lifted. "A little fox, huh?" He looked pleased as he rubbed his finger over his zit-covered chin. "Yes, yes, you are indeed." He gave a satisfied nod, reaching out a hand, and the turquoise wave embroidered on his shirt rippled as he ran his fingers down the length of my arm and over my tally mark tattoo.

"I want to see the President," I said, knowing that

following orders was the only thing Gleaners knew how to do.

"We all want to see the President. You'll have to wait your turn like everybody else." Nudging me forward, he whispered, "Looks like it's your turn now."

I winced as I limped toward the processing desk. An even larger Gleaner sat on a crate, scratching symbols into a thick ledger with a quill. "Name?" he asked, shoving a filthy finger into one of his gaping nostrils.

"Erris," I said, hoping I wouldn't have to watch him eat whatever he found in there.

"Erris from Fox Island," added the Gleaner, who'd accompanied me.

Nosepicker scratched a symbol in the ledger. "Where's she going?"

The Gleaner cupped my shoulder. "She'd like to meet the President."

Nosepicker scoffed. "Wouldn't we all? Let me guess, she's hoping to make a deal with him?"

I glared. "Eff you. I don't make deals."

The Gleaners laughed. "You *are* foxy, aren't you?"

"I'd rather be a fox, than a Gleaner. It's only you lot that makes deals and claims prizes."

"What prizes?" asked the Gleaner at my side, his grip tightening into the flesh of my shoulder.

"Prizes for kids. It's well known you get treated for bringing us in."

Nosepicker ran the nib of the quill down the ledger. "Hmm, I don't see no prizes here. Last I heard, it was the Holdouts who got paid to give up their kids."

"Me too," agreed the zit-faced Gleaner at my side. He winked at the other man. "But our prizes come after dark, don't they?"

The Gleaners shared another greasy laugh.

"You're lying," I said. "I'm valuable."

"Yer not valuable," hissed the man beside me. "The President's dog just likes to have lots of toys to play with. Every time he breaks a kid, us Gleaners get sent for a new one."

Stupid, lying Gleaners.

Nosepicker scrawled something else in his ledger before slamming it shut. "Put her on the beach." His lips curled up. "Good luck getting your meeting with the President."

The Gleaner with the baton led me down the shore, and my leg threatened to give out with every step. He stopped when he noticed I was struggling to keep up.

"Let me help you," he said, hand snaking around my waist and squeezing into the flesh of my hip. His hand continued roving down my backside ...

"I've killed before," I warned him, "and I'll do it again."

His hungry grin vanished. He dropped his hand to his side, coming up again with the baton. "Move," he said, words punctuated by another jab.

There was hardly room to walk through the cages. None were empty, and some were crowded so full I saw arms and legs sticking through the bars. Colorful birds perched under every ledge, desperate to escape the rain. Everything from muted sparrows to vibrant cardinals and dagger-nosed herons could be seen fluttering in the shadows, their presence creating a strange dystopia. Kids watched the birds through the bars, their sunken eyes full of hunger.

We reached the last cage on the path, which was large and unoccupied but still piled with the feces and bones of the last animal the Gleaners had kept in it.

My host snarled. "A fitting home for a killer like you."

He shoved me down, giving a hard kick to my already tender ribs. A shot of bile erupted from my throat. It was too dark to make out colors in the night, but I tasted the copper on my tongue.

The Gleaner tore the shreds of cloth from my body until I was naked and shivering in the night. It was an initiation—a reminder we were Gleaner property, no longer human.

He pulled my limbs taut, fastening my wrists to the top of the cage and tying each ankle to the ground, my body on display for all of Rat Island to see, should anyone have the humanity left in them to care.

They wouldn't, though. It was obvious the people pinned around me were much closer to death than I was.

"This is how the President treats his guests?"

"You want a meeting with the President?" the Gleaner asked. "Then you have to pass a test. All the kids have to take it before they get on his list."

"What kinda test?"

The Gleaner stepped closer, his stare helping itself to my shame.

I thought of Lennox, hoping she'd break through and beat this guy to a pulp. But when I closed my eyes, I was still alone. She was shunning me. Forsaking me.

"The doctor's test. He'll come for you when it's time."

People in ivory pantsuits were checking in on a few of the cages. Like the Gleaners, the doctors here were thick and their outfits clean. "One of *them?*" I asked, hoping I could convince someone to look at my leg. Before I could wave a doctor down, though, I saw something that made me forget all about the leering Gleaner and the pain in my thigh.

A man only a few inches taller than me, with long dirty blonde braids pulled back with a band. I'd know that crooked smile anywhere. If it were light, his eyes would be the same shade as mine.

"Daddy!" I screamed, shaking my shackled wrists. "Daddy, that you? You gotta help me!"

9 –Laura

L aura!" I snapped back to Earth, where I was greeted by the cruel stench of wasted caffeine. Becky was shaking me and obviously had been for a few minutes. The kids in the group were split. Some appeared horrified, while others wore looks of great amusement on their faces. People always loved a show. I found Jessica, but she wouldn't meet my eye.

"Get me a nurse!" Becky called.

Someone cleared their throat from the door. How long had Dr. Morris been standing there? "That won't be necessary, Becky. Thank you." He tilted his head my way. "Laura, would you come with me?" His tone was polite but urgent.

I stood, doing my best to ignore the stares. Jessica studied the shadows on the wall as she pretended not to see me pass. One snap and there go our friendship bracelets.

Still on sea legs, I fought vertigo with each step and struggled not to trip as I walked. Part of me felt like it was back on Rat Island.

Dr. Morris' office seemed larger somehow after being in the cramped cage. I collapsed in the chair, thankful that the queasy feeling had passed.

"What happened in there?" I asked when he was seated.

He fished the stylus out of the crystal pen cup before answering. "It looks like you dozed off, and then you started screaming for your Daddy."

Yikes. "Sounds embarrassing," I mumbled, cheeks growing hot. I hadn't called Dawson "Daddy" once in this life.

I twirled a strand of golden blonde hair—the same color as Dawson's—around my finger. I dropped the strand with disgust, the memory of his face too fresh. Maybe I'd cut my hair too? I wondered what Gina used . . . craft scissors? A kitchen knife? Didn't seem likely they'd let her near one of those.

"What you experienced just now . . . did you go to the same place as before?"

I looked into Dr. Morris' eyes. Green like the wallpaper in my childhood bedroom. In the middle of the night, I'd woken and tried to shred the wallpaper with my fingers. My parents had found me screaming, my fingertips bloody, green wallpaper all over my mouth.

"I didn't go anywhere," I said. "I was just dreaming."

Giving me a doubtful look, Dr. Morris pointed the stylus my way. "Laura, I can't help you if you're going to lie to me."

"What good will the truth do?"

He dipped the tip of the stylus into one of the tiny scratches on the desktop. He studied it for a moment, like he was waiting for the stylus to answer for him. "There aren't many options. You can try working with me—see if my process does anything to help manage your visions . . . or you can serve out your sentence in the prison across town. The choice is really up to you," he said as if I truly had options.

For a second, I remembered Jessica's warning about Dr. Morris. Was he really planning to break me? Or could he do the thing every other doctor had failed at? He seemed to believe me, which already put him in a different category than the other doctors I'd met with. What if he could help me, too? I'd never know if I didn't tell him what I saw. It's not like he was wrong. My only other option was prison.

"I was somewhere else," I admitted. "Aquarius. Erris, the

girl I visit there, was moved to a new place called Rat Island. I don't know much about it except that everyone in the Wet World is afraid of that place."

"Any idea why?"

"No." I kicked the red stain at my feet. "But when I fell asleep in Becky's group, I woke up in a cage. There were these doctors, wearing white coats like you are. I don't know what they were up to, but one of them looked just like Dawson."

Dr. Morris uttered a "hmm" and scrawled something on the tablet before him. "Who's Dawson?" he asked, adjusting his glasses over his bushy white eyebrows. Clearly, he resembled an owl. It was so obvious I couldn't believe I hadn't seen it before.

"Dawson is my father," I mumbled, the key word barely audible.

A look of extraordinary interest spread across Dr. Morris' face and he nodded. "Yes, I remember now. And he's on Aquarius as well?"

"Yeah, him and Dr. Z; she's a teacher called Zera there. Oh, and my mom."

"You've seen your mother in Aquarius?"

"Yes, as far as I know, she's on Rat Island, too."

Dr. Morris laced his fingers together and peered at me. This was when he would suggest I was experiencing a break from reality and placing people from real life in my fantasy.

"Have you ever tried to visit Aquarius on purpose?"

I shook my head in disbelief. "You really don't think I'm making it up?"

Dr. Morris' eyebrows raised. "Are you?"

"Of course not. It's just . . . nobody's ever taken me seriously before. Usually, this is the part where my therapist writes me a new prescription."

"Do you want more medication?" he asked.

"No, definitely not. I hate the meds I already have."

"Then stop taking them."

"Really?"

He shrugged. "You don't need them." He slid back in his chair. "I mean, you should probably keep your sleeping aids. A good night's sleep is vital to one's health. But I see no reason for daily anti-psychotics."

"You don't?" I nearly stood up in my chair. "Even after my freak-out in group?" I lowered my voice. "What I did to Haily?"

Dr. Morris picked up his stylus and spun it in a slow cartwheel. "I don't think medication will stop what's going on with you." He paused. "If stopping these outbursts is what you want to do."

I nodded. "Yes. I definitely want them to stop."

He smiled. "Wonderful. Then can we proceed like you're telling the truth?"

Seriously? I'd waited eighteen years for someone to ask me a question like that. I didn't know whether to laugh, cry, or perform some hysterical combination of the two.

For once, I wasn't being treated like a liar. Dr. Morris would never know what a gift he'd given me.

I nodded, still speechless.

"Do you always feel out of control when you have these experiences, or have you ever tried getting to Aquarius on your own?"

"Usually, it's out of my control. Except once." Now that I was speaking, the memories poured from me, eager to be heard by someone, anyone. "When I was a kid. I'd only ever dreamed of the Wet World before, but one day, I visited it while I was getting ready to take a bath. My parents were fighting a lot at home, but when I went to Aquarius, they loved each other there. They loved *me*. They thought I was extraordinary there. So, I thought really, really hard about the water as my mom was filling up the tub and suddenly, I was in the Wet World. My parents—the ones in Aquarius anyway—were giving me a diving lesson. We were looking for stuff under the water. The floods had come recently and there was this house at the bottom of the ocean . . ."

Later, I learned that I'd kept plunging my head into the water that day. My mother thought I was trying to drown myself. By the time I left Aquarius, I was tied to a cot.

Dr. Morris caught my eye. He reached under his desk and emerged with a plastic bowl of foil-wrapped candy. Nudging the bowl toward me, he asked, "Would you like a chocolate?"

The words had barely registered before I plucked a candy from the dish. "Thanks." I gobbled down the bittersweet morsel, feeling no shame as it smeared across my lips. Dr. Z never let us have candy.

"I know it's hard," Dr. Morris said, offering me a napkin. "I'm sure you feel like you've been abandoned. Your parents really were acting in your best interest by sending you here, though."

I nodded, and my eyes fixed on the desk. "Because of Haily," I whispered.

He extended a hand, letting it hover over mine, our skin never quite touching. "We can protect you here. That girl's parents would demand justice for their daughter's death. I'm sure you know that."

I did. I remembered my own mother's outrage when she found me tied down at Clover Center.

Dr. Morris was patient, his face kind. The words Jessica had said earlier in the rec room had been bouncing back and forth in my mind, but I couldn't see it. This sweet old barn owl was no killer.

Then again, neither was I.

Studying the spiderweb in the corner so I wouldn't lose my nerve, I asked a question I'd been dreading. "Do you believe me when I say I didn't mean to hurt Haily?"

Dr. Morris didn't blink. His voice was steady. "Whatever happened, whatever I believe . . . you are still responsible for her death."

That was a reality I was starting to realize there was no escape from.

My voice breaking, I asked, "Can you help me find out why I'm so dangerous?"

A smile crept across Dr. Morris' face as he leaned toward me. "I know why. Because it's not you at all."

"If that's true, then why am I here? Go tell my parents,

Venkin, all of them. Let everybody know I'm cured and free to go."

Dr. Morris sighed. "You know I can't do that. It's not up to me. All I can do is help you harness your gifts."

"What gifts? All I have is an illness that makes me hurt people." My eyes fell to his desk. "Isolates me from people. It's no gift. It's a curse I need to be set free from."

Dr. Morris gave me one of those kind smiles I was starting to get used to. "At TIR, *you* are very much a gift. And what you do makes you extraordinary. Let us be your family, Laura."

A hurricane of emotions was building in me, and my eyelids felt like failing levees. "What will I have to do?"

Dr. Morris pushed his tablet aside and pulled out a large square object from under his desk. It was a medicine cabinet with a trifold mirror.

"Laura, there may be a way for you to help us make things right and undo some of the hurt you've caused."

"How? I can't undo anything." Dr. Morris' words were obviously too good to be true. How was a mirror going to help me?

"Look at your reflection," Dr. Morris ordered.

I sighed and leaned over the cabinet. A fuzzy ponytail and tired eyes stared back. "There I am."

Dr. Morris opened the left cabinet door, and my reflection doubled. Next, he lifted the right mirror. The reflections bounced off of each other, creating the illusion of hundreds of Lauras watching each other.

I remembered playing this same trick with the mirror that hung over my parent's bathroom sink. Dr. Morris was looking for the same thing I had been all those years before.

At first, every reflection was a clone of the one beside it. But I noticed a few started to change. My eyes were darker in one reflection, my hair a lighter blonde in another.

I gasped when a single reflection winked back at me.

"You see them, don't you?" Dr. Morris asked. He chuckled. "You are special."

"Who are they?"

"We're not sure yet, but we're working to find out."

"Are they dangerous?" I asked. I squinted to find every reflection that differed from mine, but the longer I stared, the blurrier my face looked until I couldn't tell one reflection from another.

"Some, yes, but maybe not all. We're hoping you'll help us find the friendly ones."

"What if they find me first?" I asked, but Dr. Morris was too busy setting up his camcorder.

***

At dinner, a wall of quiet chatter met me at the cafeteria door. Food had been a major source of stress for a lot of girls at Clover Center, but the kids here ate with voracious appetites. High on the chocolate Dr. Morris had given me, I hurried through the line, surprised at how edible the food on my plate looked when I got my tray.

The attendant wielding the ladle on the other side of the sneeze guard looked straight out of Special Ops. Who is this guy? A quick scan of the cafeteria confirmed every White Coat in the room had arms like G.I. Joe.

"Thank you for your service," I mumbled, earning a confused look from Sergeant Ladle.

The cafeteria only provided plastic spoons; forks and knives were considered far too dangerous. White Coats stood at the end of every table, ready to collect the trays and utensils as soon as we were done and dispose of them before anyone had the chance to carve a shank.

Jessica was sandwiched between her friends, watching me. I smiled, but her face never changed. My heart sunk. Maybe I'd misread her all along.

I ate alone at a table full of people. They all stared at the blank wall, pretending I didn't exist, so I did the same, but every blank wall showed Haily's face.

I stabbed my spoon into a lumpy meatball. What had I done? Two weeks! I was two weeks from my eighteenth birthday, and then I would have been free as a bird. Dr. Z probably would have gotten me a cake on my last day.

Instead, a decade at Clover Center had been rewarded by narrowly avoiding a murder charge and an indefinite lockup within TIR's white walls.

I was so sick of walls. Hopefully, Dr. Morris would help me figure out what was going on soon.

Needing a distraction, I turned to the girl beside me, a willowy songbird who was humming a tune.

When we made eye contact, the humming girl scooted away, and I swung back to my wall. No new friends for me. It wasn't exactly surprising that no one wanted to hang out with me, knowing what I'd done the day before.

I considered Dr. Morris' offer instead. Could he really make the visits stop? It seemed impossible after a lifetime filled with intrusive thoughts, blackouts, and outbursts.

What I would give to never smell the stench of Aquarius again.

My gaze lifted as I sensed someone watching me. It was hard to figure out who'd given me the jeebies, as it seemed half the room was staring. Jessica still faced my way, but her eyes were glazy and lost. The broad-shouldered Black Coat who greeted me in the rec room was watching me from the door.

I kept my eyes on the table, doing my best to ignore his stare, though the feeling of unease never went away.

After dinner, the White Coats ushered us down the hall to the rec room. On occasion, someone would hold up the line to voice a complaint to the staff, but the people at TIR were far more serene than I'd expected. I was starting to worry I was the most helpless patient here.

People lined up in the rec room to receive night meds, and I was relieved to reach my favorite part of the day. The only medication I was excited to take, as it was guaranteed to help me sleep through the night. Where I went in my dreams? *That* I wasn't always so sure of.

When someone bumped me in line, I glanced back, surprised to see Jessica. "What's your room number?" she whispered.

"Twenty-four," I mumbled back, ignoring a boy who was leering at me over his shoulder. His stare made me feel x-rayed. Probed. I hated the attention and made a point of scratching the invisible itch on my leg, hoping he'd think I was harboring some sort of contagious rash.

"Why do you want to know?" I turned around, but Jessica was already gone.

***

At bedtime, I crawled onto my hard mattress, dreading the uncertainty the night was sure to offer. An attendant dropped off two pillows, one for me and another for my roommate—a squirrely girl named Ruth who had yet to talk —before locking us in for the night.

I handed Ruth a pillow, which she snatched up with a yelp before diving into her bed.

"Goodnight then," I muttered, climbing into my own bed.

I'd barely settled under the thin blanket when the room lights went off. Within minutes, Ruth was snoring.

I lay there staring at the ceiling and listening to the attendants in the hall. I hadn't slept outside Clover Center in ten years. Even with the night meds, I doubted I'd get much sleep tonight, which meant I'd be slipping soon. When I heard a whisper from under my bed, I thought I already had.

"Is she asleep?"

I leaped from my covers and dropped to the floor. "Jessica? What are you doing here?"

She grinned. "I wanted to chat. Alone."

"Really?" My cheeks felt hot. She was interested in me? "Why?"

Jessica slid out from under the bed and dropped onto the mattress. She glanced at Ruth, who was still fast asleep. "Can I tell you a secret?" she asked, twirling a red curl around the end of her finger.

My heart was racing. She wanted to confide in me? I

dialed back my excitement, not wanting to chase her away. Jessica was always surrounded by friends. She couldn't possibly understand what it was like to feel alone the way I did.

"Sure. I mean, yeah, of course."

She leaned close, and I took a deep breath of the lavender detergent in her top. It was the most glorious perfume I'd smelled outside of Dr. Z's Love Spell. Everything at Clover Center was washed in bleach, and I'd thought the chlorine scent had been permanently burned into my nostrils.

"My sister and I are planning to escape," she whispered, watching Ruth out of the corner of her eye. "She's staying on the other side of the building. We already found a guard who's willing to help. He's one of the nice ones, you know? We were going to take Gina and Shannon along, but I don't think they're ready. They actually need this place. Not like you and me."

I was flattered she'd used "you and me" in a sentence, but I wasn't as confident about the other part. As badly as I wanted out, I was pretty sure I needed this place, too.

I wrung my hands in my lap. "I don't have anywhere to go. My family doesn't want me."

Jessica gave my leg a gentle pat. "You'll stay with me. My family doesn't want me either. All I have is my sister. She's my best friend. The only one who's ever looked out for me."

"She sounds great."

"You'll love her." Jessica glanced around, her gaze lingering on Ruth's slumbering form. "Hey, what was that about in group today?" she asked.

"Oh." I stared at the floor; glad she couldn't see how red my face was. "I have these—"

"Breaks?"

"Kind of. But not really. It's like, I visit this place . . ." I sighed, wondering how much to share. Like Dr. Morris, something about Jessica made her easy to talk to. Besides, Jessica was a patient here, too. She probably had her own secrets. "When I was really little, I used to hear voices, like imaginary friends, but they were so real, you know? I knew their families, what their homes looked like. I only remember a couple, but the closest was—" I paused. I didn't like to talk about her.

Jessica gave me a reassuring smile, urging me to continue.

"They were all my age. Like we were sisters. But the places they came from weren't anything like ours. They were scary. When I dreamed about those places, I'd always be running or hiding. Someone was always chasing me."

Jessica stared at her lap. "People chase me in my dreams, too." Her frail voice cracked. "Sometimes, they catch me."

"What happens when they do?"

Jessica grinned, swatting at the air like it was silly to be afraid of your dreams. "I wake up, duh!"

Too bad it still felt like someone was looking over my shoulder while I was awake.

"My parents were afraid I would hurt myself, so they took me to the hospital," I said, changing the subject.

Jessica's jaw tensed. I couldn't tell whether she was fascinated or desperate for an excuse to escape me. Ruth let out a snore, startling Jessica to her feet. "I better go, but we'll talk more later, okay?" She started toward the door.

"Hey, wait!" I whispered. "Are you afraid of me?"

She grinned again. "Because of what happened today?"

I nodded, scratching at the phantom itch on my leg. "Don't you think I'm dangerous?"

Jessica cupped her chin with her palm as she thought about it. "Nope."

"You don't?"

"Of course not. I've faked bigger tantrums than that to get out of group lots of times." She waved and disappeared into the hall.

Hadn't that door been locked?

I stared after her, the happiest I'd ever felt. I was making a friend. I was sure of it now. And Dr. Morris? Maybe he really could help me.

But that would only happen if I stayed.

10-Laura

I never knew if I was dreaming. Coming out of my sedated sleep was like emerging from the depths of a warm and heavy sleeping bag. Most days, nothing in my real life was interesting enough to inspire dreams.

Instead of dreaming, I visited other worlds.

My eyes opened to a field. A young girl stood in a meadow dotted with the magenta, yellow, and cream hues of pansies. Her golden hair hung in neat ringlets, and a wide-brimmed hat shielded her eyes from the sun.

A majestic pink mare stood at her side with a long golden tail. The tail swished, knocking aside dragonflies that sparkled like diamonds. The girl was brushing the unicorn, humming a tune I recognized as a lullaby my mother used to sing me.

"Blessed children roving every land, Come heal together, hand-in-hand."

The unicorn vanished from the girl's side, and the meadow dissolved into grains of sand.

My skin grew hot as the air turned muggy and drops of rain started to fall.

"Laura!" she cried, dropping her brush. "Help me!"

Something about this girl was so familiar. I knew her from long ago. I thought she was one of my visitors, but I hadn't seen her in a very long time.

"What is it?" I asked. "What do you need?"

"He's coming!"

I bolted upright in my bed with a hand to my pounding heart. My sheets were soaked with sweat, and the little girl's voice was still ringing in my ears.

Ruth stood over me, pillow held in front of her like a shield. She let out a chirp and scurried back to her bed, where she hid beneath the covers.

"Sorry about that," I mumbled, wondering what I'd done to frighten her. "I was just dreaming."

Wasn't I?

It sure didn't feel like a dream.

When I finally fell back asleep, the field from my dream was replaced by the muddy shores of the Wet World.

This was definitely not a dream. I opened Erris' eyes and flexed, feeling her fingertips wiggle.

I didn't know where Erris went while I took her place. Maybe she was still with me, but I didn't think so, because when I made these sleep visits I had more control than usual. There wasn't the slow, dragging sensation I'd experienced in the moments leading up to Haily's death. No, in my dreams, I had full use of her hands and mind. Unfortunately, it didn't seem that would do me much good tonight, as Erris had nowhere to go.

The sound of sobs rose over the crashing waves. I was surrounded by the smell of rotten earth and human feces. Whatever happened on this island, I didn't want to be here.

Rat Island was unlike any place I'd visited on Aquarius before. Instead of scraggly trees and rocky beaches, cages covered the island, each brimming with fugitives. The Gleaners had taken Erris' clothing and left her no bucket, so her body was sticky and patterned with dirt that clung to her urine-soaked legs like stockings.

"Erris!"

I heard someone call her name just before dawn. I looked over and saw Jessica.

She stepped out from behind a cage full of slumbering prisoners. She wore a makeshift dress made from a fishing net, and a chunk of rope was tied around her waist like a belt. This Jessica was thinner and far dirtier than the one I knew on Earth, but the glint in her eyes was the same. I needed that glint. It was life. It was hope.

"I heard you tell the Gleaner you killed someone," she said, taking a step toward me.

I wanted to ask if she remembered me from another world, but I didn't want to draw any attention from the Gleaners.

I tried to play it cool, despite the horror of my situation. "I can't remember," I answered honestly.

"I think you did," said Jessica, coming closer. "It's nothing to be ashamed of. I've killed too. It's how I ended up here."

She was free. Maybe she could help me. Help Erris.

I think my parents are here," I whispered. "Somewhere with the adults."

"My folks are Raiders." Jessica stood out in the open. It was like she didn't fear the Gleaners. "Our ship is nearby. It's hidden on this little island that still grows fruit trees. The Gleaners never patrol there."

I'd never heard of a place the Gleaners didn't patrol. From what I'd learned during my time in the Wet World, they especially liked places that still grew food.

Jessica stepped closer. "I have a plan to get back, but I need some help."

I glanced at my bound wrists. "I need help too."

Jessica pulled a dagger from her ratty dress. "Watch for Gleaners." She smacked the handle against the rusted padlock on my cage until the lock broke apart and fell to the ground in chunks of wasted metal. When the door was open, she stood on her tiptoes and sliced through my ropes with the curved blade.

I scurried into the shadows on weary legs. "Where did you get that?" I hissed.

"A Gleaner left it for me. We made a deal. He does favors for me sometimes." She held out a hand, and I noticed a flame tattoo on her wrist. "Name's Jackie. Pleasure to meet you."

"Jackie, huh?" She was Jessica's clone; give her gnarled red curls a wash and they were one and the same. "I'm . . ." I caught myself, noticing the black tally marks etched across my wrist when I held out my own hand. ". . . Erris."

Jackie opened her mouth, but her voice came out as no more than a squeak. Her eyes grew wide, and a pale finger pointed over my shoulder. "It's too late."

I turned to see a man whose face was shrouded in shadows, leaving his oversized eyewear to float in the night like two glittering moons. "Morris found you."

11–ERRIS

M orris?"
I looked back, but Jackie was gone. Who was that girl, and how had she gotten a knife in here?

"Hello, Erris. Welcome to Rat Island." Morris stepped from the shadows, and I felt a hard rock form in the bottom of my belly.

I glanced over my shoulder, scanning the cages for Jackie's red mane. Raider coward.

Shivering in the cool night, I wrapped my hands around myself, which did nothing to cover my humiliation. The cut on my leg was burning hot and throbbed in rhythm with my heart. It hurt to stand upright for too long, so I shifted my feet to juggle the weight.

I turned back to the old man in the shadows. He wore a white hooded jacket and a pair of penfocals, binoculars that doubled as goggles. The penfocals oozed green pus and looked like they'd been sewn directly into his skin, which was an unnatural gray pallor noticeable even in the night.

I'd been warned about Morris, the President's second-in-command. He was who the Holdouts protected us from—the man Zera had been teaching me to be strong against. Rat Island wasn't just a prison. It was a laboratory built to destroy kids with powers like mine.

Everything in me screamed that I'd made the wrong choice coming here, but nothing waited for me on Fox Island. Besides, my folks were here. I was sure of it now. Daddy hadn't heard me calling for him, but he was alive, and that was all that mattered. The only thing left to do was get away from the Gleaners.

"I'm impressed," Morris said. "It didn't take you long at all to escape. That's good. It means you're sturdy." His lips twisted into a grin as if I should be pleased by the compliment. "I'd like you to come with me. My office is close by."

Shutters at the end of his penfocals blinked like eyelashes.

"I ain't going nowhere," I said, searching for an escape. Where had that Raider Jackie gone? Who let her out of a cage? I crossed my arms. "I'm waiting to see the President. Are you here to do my test?"

Morris grinned. "You're a wild one, aren't you?"

You're a survivor, said a voice in the back of my mind. For a second, I thought it was Zera's voice, but it couldn't be. She'd always known that I wouldn't survive—and so had I. The children of Aquarius quickly learned not to believe in happy endings.

Lennox?

My nagging skull and the echoing heartbeat let me know she was there.

Be brave, Erris.

"You plannin' to hurt me?" I asked Morris, the ache in my ribs reminding me of what the black-coated Gleaners were capable of.

But Morris' coat wasn't black. It was white.

"Of course not. I'm going to help you, Erris. Teach you. Together, you and I can save Aquarius."

"What do I get for helping?" I asked.

Morris pulled a foil-wrapped square from his pocket.

"Chocolate?"

I snatched the chocolate from him. I tossed the foil into the mud and inspected the speckled white candy before popping it into my mouth. Sure, I'd been taught not to take candy from strangers, but I'd never met a stranger with candy before. "Old chocolate's not good enough," I said between bites. The chocolate was bland and chalky . . . but tasty as birthday cake. "How about a meeting with the President?"

"Sure," he said, handing over another chocolate. "What else do you want?"

"Can I see my folks?"

He tilted his head as he considered it. "I'm sure that can be arranged. After a time."

I stepped toward him, although my thoughts were still screaming to run the other way.

Tales of Morris swept through Fox Island like lice. Warnings mostly aimed at the young. No one was sure what he did on Rat Island, as the few people who'd ever seen his face refused to talk about their experience.

I considered making a run for the shore, but there was no chance of escape. The Gleaners knew these waters like their own bodies. Even if I managed to get a boat, I wouldn't be able to do much more than a couple of sad circles, if the Gleaners or Raiders didn't get me first. Besides, I wasn't going anywhere without my family.

Morris pulled a bunched-up cloth from the lining of his jacket. Then, he shook the cloth out to reveal the remains of an oversized sweater.

"Thanks," I mumbled, a tinge of gratefulness in my voice as I ripped the gown from his hands and covered myself.

The fabric was scratchy and smelled of rot, but it did the job of maintaining whatever dignity I had left.

"How am I supposed to save Aquarius?" I asked, shivering in the chilly rain. "I suck at fighting. I'm not good with numbers or anything. I don't know what you think I can do."

Morris ran his scaly palm down the length of my cheek.

"Your mind, Erris. That's what's going to save Aquarius."

Morris changed the moment his skin touched mine. The barely-human man with the oozing eyewear became a doctor in a clean white coat.

I shuddered free of his nasty hand, disappointed to see the old Morris back again.

What was that? I'd seen Zera turn to Dr. Z before and watched Hale become others, but I always thought that was because we were Holdouts.

Something curious awoke in me. Could Morris have visitors, too?

He turned toward the row of warehouses at the end of the path. "My office is just over there."

Squinting toward the buildings, I wondered what might be inside. Were my folks there? Did they know I was here yet?

"What do you do there?" I asked, hopping on my good leg to relieve the pain in my thigh.

"Various things, but mostly I'll try to harness your singular talents."

"You know what I can do?"

"Of course. I think you're incredibly valuable, Erris."

"You do?"

He nodded, penfocal lenses fluttering. "Let's go. The sooner we get started, the sooner you can see your parents."

I hobbled down the trail after Morris, doing my best to ignore the wailing prisoners we passed. I thought I recognized a few kids from Fox Island, but the ones who were awake stared into the night with glazed expressions, showing no sign they remembered who I was.

Every once in a while, one of the kids would change, and for a second, I would see them in stained yellow smocks instead of their naked shame. Rat Island made me appreciate the rain, as everything around me looked like it desperately needed a bath.

Sand fleas danced over my bare feet, and I crinkled my nose at the thought of crunching them between my toes.

Laura had been here. I knew because I could still smell

the fresh, fruity scent of her shampoo in my dreadlocked hair. If only Laura did me any good. All she'd ever done was take from me.

Lennox, you still here? Her silence only added to my punishment. Lennox was the source of my strength. Without her, I was nothing.

I deserved to be punished for what I'd done to Hale, but growing up knowing there was only one unbreakable law had made me sure I'd never break it. Never in my years had I expected to live with such a sin.

I hated myself—loathed the very body I was trapped in. Squeezing myself tight, I tried hard to think of home. *Do what Morris says, and you'll get to see your folks.*

They'd be so happy to see me. The first thing Ma would say was how much I'd grown. And Daddy—he'd squeeze me so tight I wouldn't ever want him to let go.

The ground on Rat Island was barren, except for a few tufts of brush that teemed with the rats the island was known for. The island was impossibly flat thanks to the hard grating that reinforced the ground, and if not for the square building I saw on the horizon, I would have thought it possible to see all the way to Mother Elm. I knew that wasn't really true, but it brought me some small bit of peace to think I might see Fox Island again someday.

I counted my steps as I walked, mind churning over my escape plan. First, I'd find Daddy and Ma. Then, I'd get hold of a couple of bows, and we'd steal a boat . . .

My eyes scanned the ocean. Sails bobbed on the water, their passengers' cries signaling the people on board were destined for the cages and not the guard shacks.

The night played a song of crickets and snores, moans and screams. The prisoners looked wasted, and I wondered what there was to eat here. Fox Island held a forest, and although I'd never seen the namesake foxes, a few deer had survived the flood, only to be hunted to extinction within the year. After that, we'd been left to feast on fish and whatever birds were stupid enough to stick around the island. It didn't look like that would be changing here.

A massive white building sat in the middle of Rat Island. Sheet metal covered most of the lower story, but I could see a few small windows above.

"Is this a hospital?" I asked. "I thought they were all flooded."

"We were fortunate this one was built on a hill," Morris said.

We reached an entrance. Rust had eaten sizable holes in the walls, and I could see lamplight inside.

Above the door read: RAT — Research and Technology.

Morris shoved the door aside so I could enter. Sheet metal walls separated Morris' office from the rest of the hospital. The small room held a desk with two chairs and a metal bookshelf. A strange circular object like a mirror was mounted on the wall.

Morris nudged me into a seat and took his own across the desk. His eyes were humorously magnified through the lens of his penfocals, and the shutters on the ends never stopped blinking.

"What do you think of Rat Island, Erris?"

"Are you serious?" I asked him. "It's a shithole. All I've got going for me is the fact I ain't dead yet."

He chuckled. "I have no intention of killing you. That wouldn't benefit either of us."

My mind drifted to the prisoners outside; many of them looked like they would have much preferred death.

The large glass ring mounted on the wall behind him skeeved me out. It looked like a giant eye staring at me. "What is that thing?"

Morris swung his head to look. "This is the Ocular." He drummed his fingers on the crooked desk. "I'm glad you asked me about it because I have a question for *you*, now."

What could Morris want to know? What did he suspect I saw when I closed my eyes? *Be brave*, I told myself. You're only here to see your folks. Whatever he's curious about, I'm sure he'll figure it out soon.

There was a hum as the Ocular came alive. Bright violet light filled the room and fire spread through my limbs as my nerves protested the Ocular's cruel probe. It was searching me, and I felt its examination so solidly, it was like little fingers wiggling around in my brain.

I heard screams . . . so loud and so afraid I didn't even know if they belonged to me.

Morris leaned close, a bitter stench filling his hot breath. "Tell me, Erris. Who is Laura?"

12 - Laura

At breakfast, Jessica never looked my way. I felt like I'd dreamed about her, but if I had, the memory was all but gone the next day.

Every morning started with the White Coats handing out medication. Dr. Morris had written me a note excusing me from the pills, and I already felt closer to freedom than I ever had at Clover Center.

We were split into age groups and the White Coats would read excerpts from old textbooks. They called these "lessons," but the time seemed to be mostly used for napping.

After lunch, I was sent to the kitchen to help with chores. Tall metal refrigerators lined the walls alongside shelves of cans. A metal door took up a big chunk of one wall, and I watched as a few White Coats snuck inside the walk-in freezer to escape the heat.

I watched Jessica out of the corner of my eye as I sprayed down the stainless-steel countertop and wiped it clean with a holey rag. The way Shannon and Gina swept the floors made me wonder if this was their first attempt at doing the chore, but Jessica hummed as she scrubbed pots and pans before passing them off to another patient who'd dry them.

"It's so hot," Shannon complained.

"Warmer outside every day," Gina agreed. "Dr. Venkin should buy some better ACs."

"He can't. He's spending too much money buying off parents," Jessica said.

"And lawyers, doctors, government officials," the boy with the rag added.

They all laughed.

"Shut it!" snapped the Black Coat on watch.

Jessica blew him a kiss and went back to her dishes. How did she do that? Everything was so easy for her. She even made life at TIR seem bearable. So why did she want out so badly?

She rinsed off a pot and handed it to the boy with the towel. "The Gleaners can get you some if you need it," he mumbled, rubbing the towel across the outside of the pot. "They can find whatever you need."

Jessica grinned. "Watch yourself, Carl. You're slipping again."

The boy shook his head. "I ain't slippin'." His eyes looked wild. "You know what I'm talking about J—"

"Wrap it up!" the Black Coat barked.

I jumped, dropping the rag and squeezing my eyes shut to avoid an eyeful of liquid cleaner.

Carl was already hanging his apron on the hook by the door, and Shannon and Gina's brooms were leaning against the wall.

"You slipping too, Laura?" Jessica winked.

Honestly, I had no idea. I returned my rag to the bucket and followed them out the door, sure my ears were playing tricks on me.

Next was my daily visit with Dr. Morris, which was turning out to be my favorite part of the day.

He passed me a chocolate before running through the usual questions about my thoughts and feelings. Did I think about hurting myself? Did I think about hurting anyone else?

Then, he turned to questions about Aquarius. When was my first visit? How did I get there? Did it happen more in the mornings or at night? What about after I ate?

He marked my answers on his tablet before dropping his stylus into the crystal pen cup. "Any strange dreams?" he asked, palms propped under his chin.

I shrugged. "Probably, but the seds usually keep me from remembering them."

Dr. Morris nodded, and I had to blink my eyes, sure his face changed. But when I looked again, it was just the owl-like old man watching me from the other side of the desk. He wore his simple frames, not the strange eyewear I'd imagined him in a moment before.

"What do you think is happening to me?" I asked, studying the scratches on his desk. They'd probably been made by a pen, I told myself, nonetheless wondering why there were so many of them.

Dr. Morris raised a single bushy eyebrow. "I'm sure you know I don't have an answer for you yet. You'll have to let me get to know you a bit more, Laura."

A sticky lump formed in my throat, and I swallowed it down.

He turned on the video camera. "Close your eyes and picture Aquarius."

My eyelids fell shut. I squeezed them tighter, seeing only pink light filtering through. "Nothing." I sighed. "I haven't seen anything since yesterday." Hopes rising, I shrugged. "That's good, isn't it? Sounds like I'm all cured!"

Grinning, Dr. Morris handed me the candy bowl. I scooped a square from the pile and removed the foil with my teeth.

"What can you tell me about the other places you've visited?" he asked, replacing the bowl under his desk.

"There was one place," I said. "Actually, I saw it the other day. While I was in group with Dr. Z."

"When your incident occurred?" Dr. Morris pulled a bonus chocolate from the desk stash and slid it my way.

"Yeah." I nodded, disrobing the chocolate like it was our third date. How could this sweet stuff be so delicious? "I went there right before I attacked Haily." I tried to picture the cold, dark cave I'd seen. Disappointed, I dropped the balled-up foil wrapper on the desk. "But I can't really remember anything about it. Sorry."

"Hmm." Dr. Morris tapped the stylus against the desk. "Maybe the Ocular will help you."

"What?" I looked up, but Dr. Morris was gone. The white walls of his office were replaced by sheets of holey sheet metal, and the man across from me wore a pair of strange goggles that stuck from his eyes like two mini cannons.

"I can't move." I heard my voice, but it hadn't left Erris' lips. I was still talking to Dr. Morris back at TIR. Only, my sight was here in the Wet World.

"I see Laura's world," Erris told the man in front of her. "She's in an office. There's a doctor there who looks a lot like you. Instead of your rags, he's wearing a purple tie."

We were swapping, our eyes glimpsing each other's world while our bodies remained at home.

Dr. Morris' voice echoed in the back of my mind, but I was too curious about what the man in the robotic eyewear was ordering Erris to do.

"Reach out, and grab my tie."

My arm jerked forward. The man in the goggles vanished, and my fingers were wrapped around Dr. Morris' purple necktie.

He let out an uncomfortable chuckle as he slipped his tie from my grasp, as surprised as I was.

"I didn't mean it!" I said, downright traumatized. "He—you—that guy ordered Erris to grab you!"

Dr. Morris was furiously scribbling onto the silver tablet. When he finally looked up, an excited, almost youthful smile had taken over his face. "Your turn," he said, his smile growing wider. "Make Erris grab his tie."

"I don't think he's wearing one." I didn't remember seeing a tie with his outfit. "Just a really dirty coat."

"Then grab his coat."

I crossed my ankles, brow furrowed as my eyes followed the stains on the floor. "I don't want to grab him," I said. "I don't even want to see him. I thought you said you could get rid of these visits?"

Dr. Morris' smile vanished, and I spotted the tiniest hint of irritation before he'd hidden it away. "You said you wanted to help us, Laura. Dr. Venkin made it seem like you were highly motivated."

"I *am* motivated. To get rid of the voices." I spread my hands over his desk, palms up like I was showing him all my cards. "That's what the plan is, after all."

Dr. Morris was quiet. When he spoke, it was to the tablet instead of me. "The plan may be more complicated than that." He twirled the stylus. "You see, Laura. I don't know if we can get rid of your visitors. Not without killing you."

13–ERRIS

The day before, Morris' office had held uncertainty. Today, the sight of the cold metal chair and strange Ocular hanging on the wall brought up new feelings.

And I didn't think they were all mine.

Lennox feared the Ocular—truly feared it in a way I'd never known Lennox to feel about anything. I couldn't be sure, but I thought the others feared it, too.

Morris' blinking penfocals brought me back to reality. "Erris, what do you see?"

Morris had kept me in front of the Ocular through the night, but he wouldn't tell me what he was looking for.

"White walls," I said. "And you."

His mouth fell open, and the incessant blinking of his penfocals stopped. "Me?"

"Yes," I said, squeezing my eyes tight against the throb in my leg.

"It was you, I'm sure of it—but you looked different. Cleaner. Like your white coat had never seen the mud."

Morris laughed, and the blink of the penfocal lenses

started again.

"If only," he said.

"What are you looking for?" I asked, hoping for a spot of kindness from the old man. "What do you want with the others?"

Morris interlaced his fingers. "One of them has the information we need to make the rain stop."

But how? This was twice now someone had brought up the idea of stopping the rains on Aquarius. How was I supposed to go about changing the weather?

There was a hum as the Ocular started again.

"Wait!" I cried, but it was too late. Morris was already changing. The sparse ring of white hair on his head filled out, and his penfocals became a regular pair of glasses. His stained suit turned into a clean white lab coat.

"I see Laura's world. She's in an office. There's a doctor there who looks a lot like you. Instead of your rags, he's wearing a purple tie."

Morris' damp breath brushed my ear. "Reach out and grab my tie."

My hand floated forward, and the last of Morris' dank office disappeared, replaced by the pristine white walls of Laura's hospital. The man in the robotic eyewear transformed, and my fingers wrapped around the tip of his purple tie and gave it a tug.

As my fingers clasped the tie, Dr. Morris and his white-walled office vanished from sight. I wasn't back in front of the Ocular; instead, I stood in the middle of a field full of colorful flowers. A girl with golden curls watched me from across the field.

Wisdom? Is that you?

Warmth flooded through me. The ache in my thigh was gone, and a glittery pink band-aid covered the wound.

Hello, Erris. Her toothy smile was infectious.

It looks different here, I said, glancing around. *Where are all the animals?*

They require a lot of energy.

Oh. I kicked at the ground, but the grass around my feet didn't budge. Every blade stood tall and vivid green. Wisdom's world had been like a playground for us once. I still remembered playing games of tag in this very field.

I haven't seen you since the flood.

Her voice was clear in my ear. *We made a promise.*

I kicked the ground again. It had been a stupid promise. One I hadn't kept. But did Wisdom know that? Did she know how often I'd visited the others over the years?

I missed you.

Wisdom smiled. She waved a hand, and the pink outline of a horse appeared at her side. A long tail flowed from the horse like a ribbon, and a regal golden horn grew from its head. *I've missed you too. But it's time for you to go back now.*

Why can't I stay? Wisdom's world held so much hope—even if it was an illusion.

Morris needs your help. Only you can stop the rain.

How? I wanted to know.

There was no time to protest before the meadow and all of its hope had disappeared. I was back at Morris' desk. The lens of his penfocals blinked excitedly. "Yes, Wisdom," he said, "That sounds like a great idea."

14-Lennox

On my third night outside the Hollow, I had snow hare for dinner.

The meat was tough, and I spent the evening picking fur from my teeth, but a decent meal was exactly what I needed to get my head straight. I followed the mountains, and the ancient waterfalls frozen in the cliff's side were all that remained of the river beneath my feet, forgotten under several feet of ice.

There was a deafening roar in the distance—the sound of house-sized chunks of ice breaking free from the mountainside and tumbling into the valley. It would be at least another day before I'd reach the sound and know if the dislodged ice had blocked my path. Dots of light blinked through the clouds, signaling the heat-seekers' constant patrol. The light was growing brighter. Closer.

I dove for the snowbank as the heat-seeker swooped low. Hot light erupted from the drone. I burrowed into the ice and pulled my legs up, narrowly avoiding the heat-seeker's blast. Not sensing any more heat, the drone moved on, returning to the cover of the clouds.

My ears strained for Crawlers. I wasn't just listening for them here. The men in dark uniforms were a threat to me in every world. Gleaners. Black Coats.

They had other names in the other worlds, too: Reapers. Breakers.

Their existence balanced out mine.

The snow hare left my belly satisfied and my body confident, so I risked a mental trip to the Wet World. As soon as I thought of Erris, I knew something was wrong.

Her mind was usually warm and comforting compared to the horrors in my head, but tonight, a war raged in Erris' thoughts.

I smelled a sickly sweet odor I recognized from my own world. I'd been in a small room then, and a man called Malicious had placed a heavy metal helmet over my head. He'd flipped a switch . . . and the stench had followed. It wasn't hair I smelled. It was human flesh. And then brain tissue. Malicious had been cooking my thoughts. I felt it here in the Wet World as Erris sat in front of a machine called the Ocular.

I recoiled, scurrying back to my body as quickly as I could. Once home, I curled up in the ice, arms wrapped around myself as tearless sobs racked through me. *Oh, Erris, I'm so sorry.*

My sobs kept me company through the night. I couldn't visit her anymore. Not like before. I could almost hear Wisdom in my ear, whispering *I told you so.*

If Morris had Erris in front of the Ocular, that meant he was searching for me. And he'd finally figured out where to look.

Both Erris and Laura called to me now. They didn't know; they were too blinded by their own lives to realize every gasp of pain they made was a scream in my ear. Usually, it was no problem for me to keep the voices out. But that all changed as soon as my dagger pierced Helectra's heart.

Thump, thump, thump.

My head shot up. Who was there?

Do you see them too?

Wisdom!

One wrong move, Lennox, and you'll end us all.

Why now? The calculations suggested we had years.

Years, Lennox?

A rush of icy wind blew over me. Wisdom was letting me feel my world. Reminding me of what the Ice Man was capable of.

You know the Dark World doesn't have years.

So, what do we do?

Keep one of them safe.

Thump, thump, thump. My heart was hammering now.

One?

My head spun. We were moving, but where was Wisdom taking me? Blinding white walls rose around me. *Morris is connected. He's Mal—*

I know who he is, I interrupted. *Which is why I don't trust him.*

You don't have to, Wisdom reminded me, *The others do. He'll push them together. Teach them how to jump. How to gain control.*

He'll break them.

Thump, thump, thump. They can handle it.

Can Laura handle it?

TIR's white walls dissolved. The young girl stood in the field, twirling golden ringlets around her fingertips. She snapped her fingers and the muted grass erupted into a field of colorful wildflowers. Butterflies and dragonflies rose from the flowers in mesmerizing patterns.

Wisdom was playing dress-up. Make-believe. *Stop looking like that,* I told her. *Arial's gone. Laura killed her.*

You killed her, Wisdom reminded me. *Ten years ago.*

I didn't forget what happened. I closed my eyes, but the girl's image was burned in my mind. *I kept my promise. I stayed away from the others, like you told me.*

She nodded. *Now, I need you to stay out of my way. There's no denying that my world has days and not years.*

I felt my hand twitch back home. I glimpsed the snow-frosted Dark World and pushed it back, irritated I'd let Wisdom influence me. I didn't know how long I could stay out in the cold without the Crawlers finding me—if the heat-seekers didn't first.

I'd been told my muscles rippled while I slept, flexing as

if I was practicing fighting maneuvers in my dreams. I'd spent so much of my life fighting, I didn't even worry about sleeping anymore. Not like the other Shadows did. If I were woken by a Crawler, I was confident I could crush his throat before fully reaching consciousness.

It was being here that scared me. Letting the others back in. Wisdom had cut me out, but I knew my work wasn't done. Erris needed me. Until this morning, I hadn't worried about our visits much. What was the worst that could happen to her already miserable life?

But the infection in her leg reminded me.

Wisdom reminded me.

And as I felt Erris' sorrow, having lost everything, I remembered there was still more to lose. As much as I loathed returning to the Abyss, stopping the Ice Man was the only chance any of us had.

As long as I was alive, he would keep coming for them.

Game on.

15-Laura

With each passing day, it became easier to visit the Wet World, and Dr. Morris was confident I would have full control of my ability before long. I practiced bouncing back and forth, jumping into Erris' mind and then mine again.

"Name?" I heard Dr. Morris say, even though my eyes were looking through the bars of Erris' cage.

"Erris."

"Safety of surroundings?"

I forced Erris' stiff neck left, then right. "No Gleaners," I said, pushing the words through her lips.

"Location?"

"Still in the cage."

It was always hard to read Dr. Morris' face when I returned to his office. Sometimes he looked nervous. Other times rather pleased. He never told me what it was he was searching for, and so far, I hadn't questioned him. I was just thankful someone believed me.

Being able to share my visions without judgment was a truly liberating feeling, but I feared I was doing nothing more than nailing up my coffin. Every secret I shared with Dr. Morris was potentially adding another day to my sentence at TIR. *Would* they ever let me out? *Could* they ever let me out?

I thought of Jessica's offer. If she ran from TIR and I wasn't with her, would I ever get another chance at freedom?

Rapidly approaching the end of June, we were experiencing a heatwave that just wouldn't quit. Every morning, we slathered ourselves in sunscreen and shuffled outside to enjoy the sun for exactly ten minutes. A few people complained about getting nasty sunburns, and soon the excursions were done away with in exchange for mornings in the air-conditioned rec room, watching *Star Trek* reruns and playing board games.

Jessica had ignored me for a week straight, but other friends had come to take her place. They were all surprised to learn of my daily meetings with Dr. Morris.

"He's so scary," said Evan, a boy who'd spent his childhood hospitalized for schizophrenic tendencies. "I only met with him once, but it was enough for me."

"What happened?" I asked, leaning close. It was as if everyone I met harbored some unseemly memory of Dr. Morris, though I'd yet to see anything but compassion myself.

Evan fingered the spikes of his gelled crew-cut. The tips were dyed Kool-Aid red, making him a dead-ringer for a woodpecker.

"He's just—I dunno. It's like since I visited that office, I've been having these dreams about him, you know? But it's not really him. It's someone else. He wears these weird goggles, and every time I'm there, he's doing these scary experiments."

"Yeah, he put me in chains," whispered Martha, pushing a red checker across the board we'd spread over the table. Martha was sweet, but she had the fashion sense of a color-blind toddler. Today she was boasting a ridiculous Minnie Mouse bow made from lime green craft ribbon.

"Chains, Martha? Really?" Evan tilted toward her, eyebrows dipped in a great Spock impression. "I think you might be exaggerating again." He turned to me. "She does this all the time. Martha's a chronic liar."

"Am not. You weren't there. You don't remember. Erris does though, don't you?"

I froze, the black checker in my hand hovering over the board like a flying saucer. "What did you call me?"

"I said you're running late to see Dr. Morris." Martha leaned toward me. "Are you okay, Laura? You look a little off."

I nodded as I slipped from my seat. "I'm fine. Just a bit seasick."

Martha and Evan swapped confused looks as I went to meet the White Coats by the door. The attendants always traveled in pairs here.

I passed matching doors differentiated by nameplates. Besides Dr. Morris and Dr. Venkin, the latter of whom I hadn't seen again in my time at TIR, I hadn't met any of the other doctors, and from what I'd gathered from my fellow patients, I seemed to be the only one with the legendary Dr. Morris as my primary psychiatrist.

Security guards in black coats stood outside every door, their faces somber. I hadn't witnessed a single violent outburst at TIR, but I could have sworn even more Black Coats were in the building now than when I arrived.

Dr. Morris was cleaning his glasses when I entered his office. He rose from his desk to greet me, slipping the oval spectacles back into place. "Laura! How are you today?"

I dropped into the chair, giving the familiar spot on my leg a good itch as I settled in. A week later and I still hadn't figured out why it was bothering me, although the nurses let me cover it with zinc oxide on days it was especially irritating.

I thanked Dr. Morris for the chocolate he passed me. There was always a square of my favorite dark chocolate waiting now.

Dr. Morris seemed like a good guy, but I knew better than to think the candy was anything more than a prop to earn my trust. I had made the mistake of believing Dr. Z loved me. We may have all been adopted by Dr. Venkin, but TIR was no family. I still desperately wanted my freedom. With three days until my eighteenth birthday, the only future waiting for me involved being restrained in some way, be it with bars or sedatives. If Dr. Morris couldn't stop the visitors, then it was time to figure out how to live my life with them.

I felt guilty as I stared at the desk. Part of me thought I owed Dr. Morris something. If not for his help harnessing my skills, I wasn't so sure I'd be confident about leaving. Even so, I preferred the rest of my learning happened outside these walls.

"I'm okay. I had another dream about Erris. You were there again, along with a few people from TIR."

"Who?" Dr. Morris asked, adjusting the camera.

"Martha and Evan."

He sat down and scribbled a note on his tablet. "What were they doing?"

"Just eating lunch. Martha said—well, she claimed—the doctors were doing experiments on her. Putting her in chains."

"Hmm." Dr. Morris gave the stylus a spin. "In the early days of psychiatric care, patients were often restrained as a precaution. Martha has been known to be volatile—" He caught himself, dropping the stylus into the pen cup and straightening his blue tie. "I didn't mean to disclose information about another patient."

I laughed. Dr. Morris may have answered to an ethical code, but the White Coats sure didn't. Get close enough to one and they'd tell you a hundred and one secrets about the other patients. "It's already forgotten," I said with a grin.

"Wonderful."

"So, any idea what's wrong with me?" I asked for the ninth day in a row.

"I have a theory. But I've got to test a few more things to be sure."

Dr. Morris pulled a small metal box from a drawer in his desk. "Today, we're going to try something different." The box reminded me of the charger an attendant at Clover Center used when the van's battery ran dry during a trip to the park.

"What is that? Are you going to jumpstart me?"

"Very astute." Dr. Morris smirked. "This is a unique machine; it was created by a rather famous man, and you won't find another one like it. I only bring it out for my favorite patients." Dr. Morris slipped the loops over my ears. He held his hands there, looking into my eyes for a moment.

"What? Do I have a zit or something?"

He chuckled. "No, I thought I saw something. Like your eyes changed colors. It must have been the light."

I only nodded. It probably was the light. But it wasn't the first time I'd heard about my irises changing color. According to my mother, they had changed several times when I was first born. The doctor said they'd gone from newborn blue to hazel to midnight black before settling on vivid lavender. The doctor had waved it off, saying he must've been so tired that he imagined it, but the nurses crowded me for hours, searching for any change.

Dr. Morris secured the earpieces.

"What will happen?" I asked.

He shrugged. His tone was cold and soulless, deprived of the warmth it had held moments before. "To be honest, I'm not sure. The effects are different for everyone. But what I'm hoping this will do is give you a little extra control. Put you more in Erris' shoes and less in your own."

"And what'll happen to her?"

He flipped a switch, and I was back on Rat Island, sitting in the hard metal chair in the other Morris' office. It had never happened in a blink of an eye like that before, and I hated the sensation, like an elevator coming to a sudden stop.

I didn't feel the usual ache in my skull, confirming I had Erris' body all to myself.

"Erris? Are you still with me?"

"Dr. Morris?" His glasses had been replaced by strange goggles like the top halves of two plastic water bottles, and the wiry ring of hair around his head was even more disheveled than usual. There was a decent possibility the man had just stuck his finger in a power outlet.

"I thought I lost you for a moment. You were saying

something about your eyes changing color?"

"I was?"

"Yes, when you were first born."

I turned my head. Erris' neck was stiff, but with enough concentration, I was able to look around the room. Focusing my thoughts, I wiggled Erris' fingers, finding none of the usual resistance. If I tried to stand, I knew Erris' legs would obey me.

Morris' office had sheet metal walls held together by rivets. There was no camera over his shoulder, but a strange lens, like a giant magnifying glass, was pointed at me.

"What's that?"

"The Ocular? It reads you. Erris, are you having trouble with your memory now?"

"Yes. I don't know what that is. I've never seen it before." The Ocular made me uneasy, but I wasn't sure why. Maybe it wasn't me who didn't like it. Maybe it was Erris.

Morris pursed his lips and reached under his desk. I expected to see the metal box again, but when he pulled his hands up, he was holding a pile of chains.

"What are those?"

"I'd like to do a reading—see if we can't get a glimpse of Laura."

"What?" He was looking for *me*? I eyed the chains warily. A set of thick cuffs hung from each end.

The old man darted forward, snapping the thick cuffs over my wrists. I tried to stand, realizing my legs were already shackled.

I heard buzzing, like when the big lights in the cafeteria first turned on at breakfast time. It was coming from the Ocular, which was glowing an eerie purple.

My head felt wrong. Sick. Hands were digging through me, searching the corners of my soul . . .

"Laura!" Dr. Morris shook me, and it took several seconds to blink away the other Morris' face. "Are you alright?" he asked.

I'd returned to TIR, but what just happened?

My smock was drenched in sweat, and I was embarrassed to admit I'd pissed myself. That was a first. "Something happened. I don't know. It was weird." I took a deep breath. Part of me still thought I was back with the other Morris. "I had an accident. I need to go to my room."

Dr. Morris watched me a moment, stylus between his fingers paused mid-twirl. "Sure, Laura. Take all the time you need."

16—ERRIS

I collapsed back in the metal chair, the bright light of the Ocular blinding my already weary eyes. The smell of sweet smoke hung in the air—a strange and unsettling byproduct of the Ocular.

"There's been a breakthrough!" Morris howled, pure ecstasy etched on his face.

"Please let me go back to my cage," I whispered. "I ain't got the strength to do this no more!"

An itch burned across my scalp, where the fleas had built their home in my dreads, but my hands lay shackled in my lap. Not that I had the strength to lift my arms, anyway. I'd barely eaten in the last week, other than the occasional raw fish filet a Gleaner would bring by. Whatever 'breakthrough' Morris discovered kept the both of us locked in his office for days.

He'd send me back to my cage whenever he wanted a break, and Laura would rip me from my rest, only long enough to plunge me into another Morris' chair.

Dr. Morris, Head of Research at the Tomlinson Institute of Research, introduced himself at our first meeting. That had been the end of the pleasantries. Every day since, the two Morrises played ball with me, batting me back and forth between Aquarius and Earth, both eager to find out who else they could gain access to inside my head.

I'd tried to be strong, doing my best not to betray the others, but if the venomous smile on Morris' face was any indication, I'd finally failed.

Morris shuffled around his desk. He was older than my folks—old enough to be my daddy's daddy—but today there was a skip to his step. The stupid old coot was downright giddy.

The swirling shapes in the Ocular taunted me. It was proof Lennox was here but avoiding me. She knew the torture Morris put me through and did nothing.

Only Wisdom answered me now. *I'm sorry I couldn't stop him.*

It's okay, Erris. You did good. Wisdom was the only constant in my life. I couldn't depend on food or someone to save my leg, but I could depend on Wisdom's friendly voice being there to greet me every morning.

Where is Lennox? I asked. *Why isn't she making me better?*

Irritation clouded my already desperate thoughts. *Lennox won't come back here. She's afraid of the Ocular.*

Well, so am I!

The large lens on the wall was quiet, but the purple shapes inside gathered like a rainstorm. More of my omens approaching. So many voices . . . but none would grace my ear.

I know it's hard, but things will get better once Morris finds the Dry World. Then, we'll stop the rain.

Morris helped me stand, and warm liquid slithered down my leg. Shame had abandoned me long ago, so I followed after him, not caring about the mess I'd left in his chair.

Dark clouds had settled over Rat Island. My senses were fried from the acrid sent of the Ocular, but the smell of rain was something impossible to forget on Aquarius. We lived the entirety of our lives in the dry days and weeks because when the rain came, there was no guarantee when it might leave.

I tried to imagine the Dry World, but I hadn't spoken to

the girl who lived there in ten years. Not since Wisdom had made us all promise.

Morris shoved me into my cage, and I collapsed on the ground, which was already damp from the rain. I curled into a ball, and my hands trailed down my body, pausing over the enflamed gash below my right hip. The stab wound that had appeared without warning the morning Hale died. The skin around the cut was bright red, and the wound was filled with oozing patches of yellow and green.

"It's gettin' worse!" I cried, pulling my shackled hand back.

Morris' stare lingered on my flesh. "It's infected, Erris. It's going to keep getting worse." He slammed the door shut and replaced the iron padlock they'd installed after my first escape attempt.

"Hold up!" I called as he turned away.

He swung back around. "Yes?"

"You found someone, right? You found Laura?"

He pursed his lips. "Perhaps."

"So, we're done? No more experiments? I can finally see my folks?"

Morris' lips twisted into the vile smile I despised so much. "No, Erris. We're far from done. Laura's not the only one we're looking for."

I watched him disappear down the trail.

Wisdom?

She was quiet. Probably back home playing with her unicorn. Why hadn't I gotten lucky with a world like that? All I got was a mud pit drowned in rain.

"Want some?"

I jumped, surprised by the red-haired girl who appeared at my side. Her freckled face was pressed to the bars as she slipped a rope of jerky my way.

"*Toughetter?*" I asked, teeth sinking into the tough rope. A mix of dried roots and berries, toughetter was considered a treat back on Fox Island. "Where'd you get this?" I asked suspiciously.

"A Gleaner," Jackie said, taking a bite of her own rope. "You can trade for just about anything 'round here." She pulled a pouch from her belt and emptied it of a few seashells and several playing dice. She held up the dice. "Wanna play?"

"No," I groaned. "I'm exhausted, I'd rather have the quiet, to be honest."

Jackie nodded. She rolled the dice and scooped them back up from the mud. "Morris is something, ain't he? The Raiders have pictures of him and the President all over our boats. The first thing we learned as kids was to watch out for those Gleaners' black sails."

"Holdouts, too," I said, smooshing my head back into my mud pillow. "I shoulda listened better."

Jackie let out a quiet chuckle. "Me too. You think he actually thinks one of us kids can stop the rain?"

"I can," I said. "I used to do it all the time."

"Sure, you did." Jackie grabbed the dice and slid them back into her pouch. "And I used to have a suntan."

She didn't have to believe me. It didn't matter if she did, anyway.

Warm rain pelted me, plastering my dreads to my face. Jackie scooched closer to my cage until her red curls were spilling through the bars.

I imagined a world without rain. A place covered in desert where storms no longer existed. My imagination was so real, I mistook the warm rain for the hot sun.

"Erris, look!"

I opened my eyes. Jackie stood outside the bars, hands lifted to the sky, warm sunlight basking her face.

17-Laura

After my morning in front of the Ocular, a pair of White Coats escorted me to the showers and then to my room so I could rest, but I couldn't shake the memory of Aquarius. What was Morris doing to Erris?

I'd barely settled under the covers when Jessica crawled out from beneath my bed.

"What the heck?" I flew from my bed, hand clutched to my chest. "You're going to give me a heart attack."

"Why weren't you at dinner?" Jessica asked, planting her butt on Ruth's bed before I could stop her. She leaped up just as fast. "Ew, it stinks over here!"

I was aware. If Ruth were a bird, she'd be a chickadee, not only because of her limited vocabulary, but because she was also a food hoarder. The White Coats had found piles of moldy sandwiches and hard rolls in her pillowcase the day before, but they hadn't yet discovered the cache in her bedframe.

I crossed my arms and glared. "Why do you care where I was? You've been ignoring me for a week."

"It's all part of the plan." Jessica slid a hand through her ruby locks. "The attendants can't know we're friends." She cast the door a nervous glance. "Sometimes I think they're on to me, like they know I'm planning an escape. We can't blow it now. My sister is almost ready for us."

I narrowed my eyes. "Who is your sister, anyway? I've never even heard her name. And how's she supposed to help us get out of here if she's locked up too?"

"She's got her ways," Jessica said with a wink. I hated how happy I was to see her after the way she ghosted me.

I paced a ring on the dirty floor. The attendants swore they cleaned weekly, but the grime beneath my feet suggested otherwise. "Are you sure this is a good idea? I mean, yeah, it sucks being locked up, but what are we going to do when we're outside? We don't even have a place to live. And that's another thing! Money. We're going to need jobs to pay rent."

"Hey! I'm offering to help you get a little freedom." Jessica glared. "I'd be more grateful if I were you."

I hated that I was second-guessing myself. Freedom was all I'd thought about growing up. I wanted out. But TIR offered me something freedom couldn't. Answers. And with all the strange stuff happening on Aquarius, answers were becoming more valuable than ever.

I sighed. It wasn't Jessica's fault I was so feisty. Every nerve in my body was on edge, as if Morris and his coke-bottle glasses were also hiding under my bed.

That thought didn't help to settle the unsure feeling in my gut. My only other option was to stay, and if I did, I'd be at the mercy of Dr. Morris. I wondered who would be the safer bet. Dr. Morris may be able to get answers, but he worked for an institution. What could Jessica possibly get out of helping me?

"I'm sorry," I said. "You're right. You're trying to get us out of here, and I've been a total jerk to you." My eyes fell to the floor. "I thought you'd forgotten about me." *Or hated me. Or realized what a spaz I am.* Goosebumps rose in hills on my arms as anxiety settled in.

Jessica reached out and stroked my hair. The caress

instantly calmed me, and I melted under her fingertips. Less people had voluntarily touched me than I had fingers on my hands, and I found I was a sucker for whatever human interaction she was willing to throw me. Embarrassment burned through me, and I pulled the knotted chunk of hair from her grasp.

"I like your hair," Jessica said. "It's pretty. And it smells like strawberries."

"Thanks." I slipped the strand behind my ear. Maybe I wouldn't cut my hair, after all. Should probably do a better job combing it though . . .

She laid a hand on my shoulder. "I would never forget about you, Laura. You just need to trust me. With your help, we'll have no problem getting out of here."

With my help? I wasn't sure how much I could do.

"Why me?" I asked. "Why don't you and your sister just sneak out by yourselves?"

Jessica flinched. "You don't want to go?"

"No, I do," I assured her. "It's just . . . you've been so nice to me." *With the exception of blowing me off for the last torturous week.* "I'm just wondering why you would want to risk taking me with you. You could have picked anyone."

Jessica perched on the corner of my bed. She lifted the thin sheet, rubbing the rough fabric back and forth between her fingers. "I chose you because of how you looked the day you arrived here."

I dropped down beside her. "What do you mean?"

She studied the sheet. "I thought you were like me. You saw these walls and couldn't wait to escape them." She didn't know how right she was. "I thought maybe you didn't want to be trapped anymore."

"I don't."

Jessica reached over, giving my hand a squeeze. "I know. So, let me save you."

At her words, my doubts shrunk back. They were still there, but their screams weren't nearly as loud. I imagined me and Jessica, even the mysterious sister. An apartment, a job, our own family. All the things the doctors had convinced me I could never have on my own. Suddenly, they didn't seem so impossible after all.

"Okay." My chin fell into a slight nod. "I'll go."

Jessica giggled, slipping her arm around my shoulder and giving it a tight squeeze. "Yay!" she whispered, pumping her fist victoriously in the air. "Trust me, Laura. It's going to be great. Everything you've ever dreamed of." She stood, tilting her head toward the door. "I better get going."

Ruth would be back from the rec room at any moment, and I had forgotten to get my night meds. So much for sleeping tonight.

"How do you keep getting in here?" I asked, following her to the door.

"The guard I told you about. He helps me get wherever I want."

Helps with breaking and entering? "Why?"

Jessica grinned. "Is there anywhere you want to go?"

I shook my head. I'd seen enough of TIR. "So, when are we leaving?" I asked.

"Tomorrow. I'll find you when it's time. Get ready, Laura. It's gonna be the best day of your life."

***

Jessica's words were still echoing through my mind several hours later—after I'd counted hundreds of sheep. I'd used sleeping pills for so long, my body didn't know how to fall asleep on its own anymore.

Finally, after the footsteps in the hallway had gone silent, the small room I shared with Ruth transformed into the flower-filled meadow. The little girl was busy brushing the tail of her unicorn.

I know you, don't I? I asked. The field hadn't had flowers before, and the unicorn was definitely new, but something about this place was so familiar.

The girl didn't hear me. She continued brushing the pink mare's golden tail, humming a song I recognized from another life.

You used to play with me. You were the one.

The girl looked up, but she didn't meet my eye. She was watching the black storm clouds swirling into a tornado in the distance.

I hurt you, I finally remembered. *The day my parents sent me to Clover Center.*

The unicorn disappeared, as did the girl's pretty dress and matching wide-brimmed hat. Her appearance turned haggard. Her clothes grew too small, becoming rumpled and dirty, and her golden curls tangled up like they'd never seen a brush. She glared at the swirling clouds overhead, but she didn't move.

You have to stay, Laura, she whispered in my ear. *Stay. Or you'll ruin everything.*

18 – Laura

My face was buried in the velvety plush of a pillow when I woke up, and I was surprised to find I was snuggling a stuffed pink unicorn with a golden tail.

"Is this yours, Ruth?" I looked over, but the bed across from me was empty.

I dropped the unicorn on her empty bed, the digital clock on the wall letting me know I was about to miss breakfast.

There was no line in the cafeteria, but most of the hot food was already gone, so I grabbed a banana and a blueberry muffin instead.

Jessica ignored me during chores and all through lessons, and soon I was back in Dr. Morris' office strapped to the awful machine. There was a blinding light on the other side, and I threw my hands up to protect my eyes from the Ocular.

My hands snapped back in surprise. I'd forgotten about the chains.

Aquarius' distinct scent of rain, sea salt, and rotting fish soaked into my pores as my eyes adjusted to the other Morris' lamp-lit office.

"How was it?" Morris asked.

"Are these totally necessary? My arms hurt." I lifted my wrists, giving the rusted chains a shake.

Morris adjusted his strange eyewear. "Maybe next time we can loosen the shackles. You know we have to be careful of Lennox, though."

"Who's Lennox?" The question slipped out before I considered it. I was just so damn curious. Between the icy cave and the little girl I kept seeing in my dreams, I was desperate to know who else was vacationing in my body. Still, I regretted my mistake. I wasn't sure why, but I suspected I needed him to think I was Erris.

Morris scribbled a note on a device that reminded me of an Etch-A-Sketch. I hadn't seen any computers or tablets in the Wet World—only water. "Erris, I have to say . . . I'm concerned about the memory loss. This is two days in a row."

"I'm fine. Just a little mixed up. It's probably that Ocular thing. What does it read me for anyway?"

"It reads your omens. Tells me how close the others are to the surface."

"You know about the others?"

Morris scribbled a few more words. "Yes. Laura and Lennox. You remember them, don't you?"

"I know Laura. But who is Lennox?"

Morris' eyebrows lifted. He sketched something else on the board and underlined it twice before dropping his pen. "Do you want to visit her?"

I nodded eagerly. "Yes. Very much."

He loosened the chains around my feet and helped me stand. "Follow me."

Morris led me through the door and out of the building he had his meetings with Erris in. A drizzling rain wet Rat Island, and the smell of human suffering wafted through the air where it mixed with the wails of prisoners. I shuffled past the cages, flinching as the chain links wore bruises deeper into my skin. A throbbing ache radiated from a wound on Erris' leg where my own phantom itch had been.

This wasn't the inconvenient tickle I'd gotten used to. The spot on Erris' thigh burned hot, and every step felt like a serrated knife was tearing through the wound.

The cages were full of kids, I realized. The oldest were younger than me, and the youngest barely walking. Every prisoner was nude, and most showed scars, burns, or missing fingers. How could a man who looked so much like my Dr. Morris cause pain like this?

We passed guard shacks and storage buildings, which all looked to be built from the remains of a shipping yard. They reminded me of the home Erris shared with her parents on Fox Island. A Conex box topped with barrels and pipes had been rigged up to divert the rain.

My mind was running wild. Who was this girl Morris was taking me to see? I thought of my earlier years when I'd dreamed of strange places—none of them covered in water. I always suspected that Erris and I weren't the only ones swapping minds, but another feeling was moving in, too.

Uncertainty. For the first time in my life, I was starting to get a grasp on the strange relationship I shared with Erris. What if I opened this door and there was no closing it? If this Lennox person was like me, someone who I could visit at will, could she do the same to me?

I faltered when I saw a flash of red hair in a cage to my left. The Raider girl. She was called Jackie here, but seeing Jessica's face brought a thousand more fears crashing in. If I was only scratching the surface of my problems, was now really the best time to be leaving TIR? What if I needed Dr. Morris now more than ever?

We were past the cage before she saw me, but all of my thoughts were on freeing her the way she had freed me. If only I could escape these chains.

We stopped at the edge of the island where the Gleaners' black-sailed boats were anchored for the night. "What do we do now?" I turned to Morris, seeing the same strange look on his face . . . just before he shoved me into the water.

I choked, spitting out mouthfuls of water as I tried to

swim. I'd never swum on Earth. My parents thought it was too dangerous.

If Erris were here, she would know how to control her limbs so we wouldn't sink into the deep, but she wasn't. She was back in Dr. Morris' office, doing whatever she did while I was away. Not that it would have been any use with the heavy chains around my hands and feet. Darkness swirled around me as my chest grew tight and I plummeted toward the bottom of the sea.

I sunk helplessly, a galaxy of stars distorting my vision as my body contorted painfully in the water. Seemed fitting I would die with all of the dignity of a mermaid in a straightjacket.

Opening my eyes, I found the familiar candy bowl perched on Dr. Morris' desk. I was back at TIR. I sucked in the sterile air, thankful as the pain in my chest faded. Dr. Morris' eyes were wide behind his oval glasses, and his face was frozen in the most confused look.

I looked down. I was soaked. Water dripped from my clothes, and around my wrists were chains.

***

It took about an hour to get the chains hacked off, and by then, I was dry. I passed Jessica in the hall on the way back to my room. She was huddled in a corner, her red bob barely visible behind Shannon and Gina, who shielded her with their bodies. I waved, but if they saw me, they pretended not to.

As the White Coats led me by, I overheard Evan from the huddle.

"Come on, Jackie, please. I don't want any more trouble. I gave you all I had." I stood on my tiptoes, spotting his woodpecker coif in the crowd.

"Call your parents," I heard Jessica say. "I need more money, or I'll have to tell Morris you've been dreaming again."

Evan exhaled a long sigh. "Yeah, Jackie. No problem," he said, scurrying away.

"Hey, Jackie, want to swing past the reading room?" Gina

asked, hurrying to position herself by Jessica's side.

Jessica beamed at the attendants escorting me. "Sure. We've got some time before I need to meet my sister."

I swung my head after her, mouth falling open in disbelief. "I thought her name was Jessica?" I asked the White Coat on my left.

She rolled her eyes. "It is. Jess is in for the long haul. She'll do whatever she can to get out of here. You can't believe anything that girl says."

19-Lennox

The snow never stopped. It came down in thicker and thicker chunks, as if it were taunting me. Like every night in the Dark World, the moon took cover behind clouds. Tonight, the sky was shimmering, and I lifted my eyes to watch. If my eyes were better, I'd be able to make out beautiful green lights dancing across the horizon.

It was a deception. Nothing was beautiful in the Dark World. Not since the Ice Man had his way.

I was close. I felt it in the arctic breeze and eerie quiet. Fade's cave was just on the other side of this valley. When I got there, we'd start working on the next part of our plan.

I'd wanted this to be the end, but Erris showed me that I was far from finished. No matter how I tried to hide from the others, my actions still affected them.

There was no retirement for a Shadow. Eventually, destiny came for all of us.

Yes, it was close now. More than the wind, it was the fear held deep in my bones that told me I was almost there. The Abyss called to me, warning me of my proximity to my birthplace. The Hollow served as my home for ten years, but before that, I'd had another home.

I shivered. *I know, I don't want to be here either,* I told myself.

My ears pricked. I couldn't place it. The snow made it hard to tell where the sound was coming from. A skitter? A snow hare? I tensed. The silence was broken by the slightest puff—the sound of a cold man exhaling. I couldn't see him, but if I had to guess, I'd place him a couple of hundred yards away.

I was so still, you'd wonder if my heart was beating while I listened. The shuffle of the boots. The brisk rubbing of gloves against his arms. It was no Crawler. The Ice Man kept his goons plenty warm.

But there was more. Another heartbeat racing—one I hadn't heard in ten years. I couldn't place it at first, but in gut-sinking horror, I realized . . . it was Laura.

20-Laura

I didn't see her at dinner, but as promised, Jessica showed up after dark.

"Peek-a-boo," she whispered in my ear. I hadn't fallen asleep that night, and there had been no twinges of Aquarius since Morris threw me in the ocean.

"You're here." I was more relieved than I thought I would be. Truth was, I'd expected Jessica to stand me up.

"Let's go," was all she said.

I sat up and glanced over at Ruth, a chickadee swaddled in the blankets of her nest. "Bye, Ruth. It's been nice getting to know you," I whispered sarcastically as I unwound myself from my own covers. In nearly two weeks, I hadn't heard more than a few terrified squeaks from the girl.

Jessica poked her head out the door. "It's clear. You have everything you need?"

I nodded, assuming 'everything I needed' was my ugly smock and the flimsy slippers they provided us with.

The hallway was conspicuously clear of guards and White Coats. Where was everyone? Usually, you'd hear a few shit-talking nurses or a whistling janitor at this time of night.

I took a breath. There was something I needed to ask, even if now wasn't the best time. "Earlier, I heard something weird. Somebody called you Jackie?"

"Oh, her?" Jessica waved it off. "That was my sister." Hurrying down the hall, she said, "She's meeting us up ahead."

Jackie was the elusive sister? It was like I was slipping off to Aquarius again. Nothing was making sense.

"Really?" I asked, struggling to keep up. "Do you have a twin? Because she looked just like you."

"Yeah. Now be quiet, we're almost there." She quickened her pace. We were heading straight for the front door.

"Won't someone see us?"

"The guard will take care of it." She stopped, swirling to face me. "But hey, Laura? I ran into a snag. Most of the time, I give the Black Coats money to do favors for me. But I couldn't get enough in time. My friend will still help us though if you do something else for him."

She started off again, and I hurried after her, not wanting to get caught out in the hall alone. I'd spent all day pacing my room, wondering how this night would go. I wasn't sure how well I could trust Jessica, but all of my doubts about leaving TIR had sunk into the ocean with Erris.

We reached the glass doors in front. I stopped as a man stepped from the shadows. I recognized him as the burly Black Coat Rowan.

I stuck my hand out, catching Jessica in the midsection. "Watch it!"

"This is the guard you were talking about? What exactly am I supposed to do for him?"

Jessica gave me a wink. "Oh, you know. Whatever comes naturally."

I flinched. *The hell did she say?*

Rowan's sleazy smile made my stomach turn.

"Hey Jackie, is this your friend? She's a cutie."

My eyes shot to the door. I didn't like it. I hadn't had a lot of experience with men—or trusting my gut, for that matter—but I knew I needed to get out of here fast.

"Hey, Rowan. Looking good," Jessica said, flashing him a playful grin. Was she flirting? "This is Laura, she's been dying to meet you."

I have?

"I don't like this," I said, taking a step back. My eyes darted around the lobby, but the only way out was through the glass door in front or back the way we'd come. Where the heck were all the guards? Most days, you couldn't take two steps through the building without spotting a Black Coat.

Rowan's jaw ticked. "Why does she keep calling you that? I thought your name was Jackie?"

Jessica waved him off. "Oh, Jessica's my sister."

My legs trembled, threatening to give out beneath me.

I tugged on her sleeve. "I don't know what you're thinking, but leave me out of it. I'm going back to my room."

"What's she talking about?" Rowan asked. His hand slid along his dark belt, and he glanced at a door beside the front desk. An employee bathroom? Utility closet? Room of shattered youth?

The truth came crashing down on me. Jessica wasn't my friend. I was nothing more to her than a way out the door.

I narrowed my eyes at Rowan. "I don't know what Jessica or Jackie or whatever the hell her name is, told you, but I'm not going to be a part of this *transaction*."

Rowan's excited grin vanished. "What are you saying? You want out? Cause that's just not gonna happen." His hand trailed to his holster. "I can't risk a tattletale."

I backed up, and Jessica's hands clutched the edge of my shirt. Her saccharine voice was poison in my ear. "He's right, you know. I need you to stay. Jessica needs you. You have to help us get out of here."

"You're Jessica!" I blurted in bewilderment.

She laughed, glancing around the room. "Uh, no. Jessica's my sister, remember?"

What in the actual hell? I turned to leave, blindsided when Rowan charged me. His shoulder caught me hard in the chest and I fought to catch my breath as I toppled backward ever so slowly. My right leg touched solid ground, and agonizing pain tore through my hip. I swung my left leg in an arc, striking Rowan's chest.

"Hey!" Rowan growled as he staggered back. I threw a punch, and he dodged it, swinging his fist at me in response. His movements lagged as if he was fighting in slow motion. I dropped, sweeping his feet from beneath him with a graceful slice of my leg. He crawled to his knees. "Where did she learn to fight like that?" he howled.

I was wondering the same thing.

Rowan jumped up, grabbing my shoulders and slamming me back against the desk. Pain flooded in, but I couldn't have stopped if I wanted to. I wasn't controlling myself anymore. Someone else was in charge now.

I leaped for him and wrapped my legs around his waist, feeling Jessica's nails dig into my arm. She was trying to drag me off him, but I was stronger—and I was angry.

"Help! We need help down here!" Jessica squealed. Alarms sounded, but I paid them no mind. A loud thumping sound pounded in my ears as I pushed Rowan's head back, not letting up until I heard his neck crack.

The thumping sound slowed to a stop.

Oh. Oh no. What had I just done? And how? My flimsy arms could barely crush a Pepsi can.

I fell with Rowan, using his still body to soften my landing.

His head smacked hard against the linoleum, mimicking the sound of someone smashing a watermelon. I scrambled up, losing my paper slippers to the sticky floor.

Footsteps pounded down the hall, and flashlight beams bounced off the walls as a herd of security guards busted into the lobby.

"You killed him! You killed him!" Jessica's shrieks were so annoying. I pushed past her, slipping through the blood that pooled around Rowan's busted skull as I struggled toward the door.

"Laura, stop!" I looked up, spotting Dr. Morris in his rumpled nightclothes among the gathering crowd.

I wanted to stop. I wanted to turn around and let them put me to sleep. But whoever was in control didn't. I broke through the door in a shattering explosion of glass, shaking away the shards like they were snowflakes.

I refused to look over my shoulder. The Black Coats were close, but not close enough for their tasers to reach me. It was different now, though. I was no longer a patient at TIR. Now I really was a murderer. It hadn't been my intention to kill Rowan, but there was no denying who was at fault now. If ever there was an excuse for the Black Coats to use the guns I suspected hid in their pant legs, it would be now.

Adrenaline pulsed through me. Every time guilt surged up for what I'd done to Rowan, it was quickly pushed back down by a desperate desire for survival.

Shouts met me outside, but the driveway was empty. Rowan must have arranged for the path to be clear for Jessica's escape, but the Black Coats were closing in on me from all sides now. As the first guard reached me, my leg flew up. I launched into the air and connected with his face, sending him sprawling into the crunchy grass.

The other Black Coats held back, scrambling to unholster their weapons before they dared come any closer.

I ran. I hadn't run since I was a kid. I had no sense of direction, and I had nowhere to go. There would be no running to Dawson and Amanda, and I didn't even know where my mother was. Jessica didn't have a sister. Not a real one, anyway. Why'd I have to be so desperate and gullible? Sure, she may have been nice enough when it benefited her, but if this was friendship, I was fine without it.

My body—and the strength running through it—was not my own. Whoever controlled my legs did a far better job than I, and I loped toward a cluster of trees at the edge of the property just as the first shot rang out. An iron fence surrounded TIR, no less than ten feet tall. I jumped, and the soft underside of my hands sank into the strips of barbed wire that topped the fence, but I hopped over it, barely feeling a sting before I rolled to the ground on the other side. In a crouch, my heart pounded as I weighed my options. Prison. That was my option now. Unless the Black Coats killed me first. The thought was oddly comforting because at least now I really did have a plan. I needed to get as far away from here as I could. I was back up and running in seconds. My right leg was stiff, and the itch I'd felt there had bloomed into full-blown fire, but I was stronger than I'd ever been as I raced from TIR.

As I ran, the streets turned to desert, and in the distance, I heard hooves.

Part Two

OUTSIDE

21-Violus

The Dry World — 2035

The Reapers were coming.

I could hear the snorts of the mutant horses and see the spiked helmets of the men who hunted me.

"Violus!"

I dropped to the sand at Mama's warning. I lost my bandana and scrambled to reclaim it before the desert sun could scorch my bald head.

"Here you are, Violus," Jessec said, snatching the patchwork bandana from the sand and tossing it my way. Her short ochre ringlets looked like a halo as she swung her scythe toward an approaching Reaper.

He darted aside, the textured heels of his boots helping him keep his footing in the sand. The weight of Jessec's scythe carried her forward. She dropped the weapon and rolled out of the way a half-second before she sliced herself.

The Reaper grabbed the weapon before Jessec could reach it. I yanked her back, but the tip of the blade was already cutting into her tunic. Blood spilled through the cloth, leaving the likeness of a red rose on her front.

No cry left her lips. The Reapers wanted our fear. Emotion was as rare as rain in the Dry World, and the first thing mamas taught their babies was not to cry.

Crying brought the Reapers.

Thwack! The Reaper stumbled as Mama's crossbow bolt struck his chest. He fell and his spiked helmet came to rest in the sand, resembling a cactus. Narrow and onyx in color, every spike was as long as my forearm. The helmets were cumbersome, but they kept out the dreams.

I stumbled as a rush of dizziness caused me to lose my footing. Jessec's tanned flesh paled before my eyes. Her brown eyes lightened, and the crop of red curls on her head grew down to her chest. Waking Dreams, now? While the Reapers were giving chase? I uttered a quick prayer to the Prophets, begging them to keep the dreams away.

We'd been traveling through Pacifica for over a week, and the dreams had tortured me ceaselessly. Lennox, Wisdom, Erris, Laura—my mind and my vision weren't safe from any of them. It seemed only I had honored the oath we'd made a decade before.

Jessec grabbed her scythe just as another Reaper arrived.

Mama raised her crossbow. *Thwack!* The Reaper slumped in his equimite's saddle and slid to the ground. Good job, Mama. She waved a sinewy arm before charging another Reaper.

The riderless equimite let out a low, soulful moan, mourning its rider. His head was that of a horse with a silky black mane and two blazing red eyes. Its legs bore stripes of black and brown, and a pair of humps on its back gave it the look of a camel. The equimite nudged at the fallen Reaper's spiked helmet.

I lay still, trying to hush my pounding heart as my eyes scanned the desert for Mama.

The equimite snorted, catching me in its scarlet stare. He gave a high and haunting wail. The sound carried in the wind, sending a chill through me. The equimite's claiming call. His way of telling the others I was his.

Hooves kicked furiously at the sand as the equimite charged me, its long legs bred to chase the Blessed Children through the desert. Dreamwalkers like me were worth a thousand drops of water.

I stood to run, but my legs were barely willing to hold my weight. Something was going on. Not just in the Dry World but somewhere else as well.

Flashes of buildings appeared as oases in the desert as another world mingled with my own. It was daytime in the Dry World, but overhead, the sky blinked on and off as the sun and moon fought for their place.

Shimmering structures made of glass and steel rose around me—buildings taller than I'd ever seen in the Dry World. The outlines of people appeared next. They drifted past like clouds, oblivious to the Reapers at my back.

"Move!" I cried, barreling past the people, who vanished like ghosts.

I tripped, crashing to the ground and feasting on a mouthful of sand.

"Mama!"

"I'm here, Violus!"

I couldn't see anything beyond my waking dreams.

"Violus!" A sharp pain struck my jaw as Jessec slapped me. She pulled back, preparing to smack me again.

I shook my head, finally clearing away the visions of buildings and strange people. "I'm back!" I said, sidestepping Jessec's swing. "That won't be necessary."

"Mama!" I let out a relieved sigh at the sight of her.

Her lanky arms looped around my waist, pulling me in tight. Geometric tattoos decorated her bronze scalp. The Mark of the Blessed.

Glancing over my shoulder, I saw that the Reapers and their equimites were gone. Instead of the midday sun, the sweet relief of multicolored twilight was flirting with the desert sky.

"What happened, Mama?" I asked, adjusting my raggedy bandana. "I lost time again. I saw buildings. Lots of them—more than ever before."

Mama thought for a moment. "Definitely Earth. Had to be. Nowhere else has many buildings left." She helped me sit and offered me a root from her pack.

I chewed the root, my dry tongue eagerly searching for any drop of water to distract my rumbling stomach. At night, temperatures plummeted on the Dry World, and if we were lucky, we could hunt the nocturnal xerocole, who would be out searching the sand for food in a few hours.

"I've been seeing Earth as well," Jessec said. She had tied a thick bandage around her waist to cover her blood rose wound.

"It could be a sign from the Prophets," Mama said, sitting down in the sand. "Best be thankful, anyway. We're out of Pacifica now, but it's still a day's journey before we reach Shade." She gestured toward Jessec. "Come, child. Let me fix your hair. Your markings are all overgrown."

Jessec settled in front of Mama, who took a long, thin blade from the pocket of her pantsuit and pulled one of Jessec's ochre curls taut. She cut it loose, repeating the process until I saw the black squares, triangles, and diamonds tattooed on Jessec's scalp. "There," Mama said when Jessec's head was as bald as mine. "Now you look like a proper Blessed Child. After the ceremony, you'll receive the name change that signals you are grown."

"Jessicus," Jessec said with an excited grin. "I can't wait to draw lots."

"Me neither," I agreed.

We were nomads, making our ceremonial trip to Dry Beds, the land of the Prophets. The tattoos on my head may have been the rings of a target out in the open desert, but I would risk the journey of a thousand miles to be in the presence of the Prophets. I only feared my waking dreams would prevent me from being considered for this year's ceremony. I was nigh eighteen and would be considered too old to draw lots next year. "Mama, why am I having so much trouble? I could hardly stay focused back there! The Reapers nearly got me before the ceremony."

Mama patted my thigh, offering me her best motherly smile. She sang me a song, the Prayer for Rain:

"Blessed Children roving every land,
Come heal together, hand-in-hand.
Beseech your hearts to bring the rain,
To wash the dust and heal our pain."

I settled in the sand, and Mama's song brought me peace after another hard day. She ran her hands over my naked scalp, her fingertips tracing the dark lines of ink.

"You get some rest now, Violus. We'll find Shade soon. He'll help you keep the others out. Until you need them, anyway."

22-Laura

I ran until I reached the city. Skyscrapers crowded together, and I tipped my head back, beholding a tower I thought may reach all the way to space.

I walked for hours, my hand alternating between the itch on my leg and the nagging cramp in my side. My bare feet ached, but the thin slippers I'd worn at TIR would have given my soles little padding, anyway.

Eventually, the tall buildings gave way to squat, dilapidated structures, and I found an alley to hide in for the night. Since the heatwave had started, the streets were busiest after dark, and despite the sirens I heard throughout the night, I kept my calm just enough to avoid drawing attention.

I found an old mattress tipped against the wall and curled beneath it, making myself as small as possible. I hadn't expected to sleep, but I did, and when the smell of the soiled mattress faded, it was replaced by a wave of heat and desert air so dry I was instantly thirsty.

***

"Violus, are you ready? The Reapers are nigh."

I opened my eyes and found that I was curled in a patch of dirt, a twisted shell of a tree the only thing to protect me from the sun overhead. It looked like every living thing had dried up, leaving only mounds of sand and cracked dirt. I scanned my surroundings. I didn't know this place. It sure didn't look like Aquarius.

"It's so hot," I grumbled, shielding the sun to make out the woman standing over me, already knowing it was my mother.

"Of course, it's hot. It hasn't rained in eighteen annuals."

"It hasn't?"

She leaned back and looked me over. She wore a flowing smock that tapered into two pant legs and sturdy boots laced up to her thighs. A rag was tied around her head, and her taut skin held a deep golden tan. She smiled, causing my heart to swell in my chest.

I felt a smile spread over my own face at the sight of her. I wanted to jump up and leap into her arms, but I remembered what had happened in Aquarius when Morris found out I wasn't really Erris.

"Are you well, Violus?" She kneeled beside me. "Do you want me to find you a Healer? I think we're close to one."

"No, no, I'm fine. Just confused I guess." I slipped my hand under the patchwork rags tied around my head, panicking at the feeling of smooth, hairless skin.

My mother squinted at me. Well . . . *Violus'* mother, but I'd call her mine as long as I could. "Did you have another dream? Nothing's changed, honey. We're still heading for Shade."

I glanced around. Besides the scrawny tree I'd slept beneath, there was only desert as far as I could see. "I don't see any shade around here."

She gave me a concerned once-over. "Let's go. There will be many Reapers out collecting bounties. They know the Blessed Children are traveling to the ceremony."

Reapers? I took the hand she offered, letting her pull me to my feet.

"Oh, great Prophets!" she said, crossing her eyes like she'd tasted an especially sour lemon. "Let our journey be guarded and overfilled with peace!"

A chuckle slipped through my lips at her twisted citrus "O" face, but my laugh was quickly shot down by the slap of a leather belt on my wrists.

"Ouch! Why'd you do that?"

Violus' mother glared at me. Stern and full of burning indignation, the look nearly lit my clothes on fire. "How dare you desecrate the Prophet's traveling blessing? Have you lost yourself completely, Violus?"

I shrank back, afraid she'd snap the belt on me again. Yeah, I have lost myself, I thought sarcastically. I wondered if it would blow this woman's cult-loving mind if I told her who I really was.

Her eyes softened, the burning glare thawing away. "I'm sorry for scaring you. Discipline is the blood and bones of the Blessed, Violus. You were taught better than to disrespect our traditions."

I faltered, surprised by her sudden change. My mother had changed too, at the rate of gale-force mood swings. This lady's words came from a place of love, though. Love seemed to ooze through her very pores.

"I apologize. It won't happen again," I said, hanging my head after she gave a satisfied nod and turned away. I would do my best to keep my attitude in check while I was here, I decided, wanting to keep this side of my mother as long as I could.

"Violus, you're awake." My blood ran cold at Jessica's voice. She was carrying a handful of rocks she dropped at my feet. Her skin was bronze, and tattoos covered a scalp that showed only a few shorn red hairs.

I wanted to scream. I wanted to throttle her. How dare this girl stand there looking so smug when she shared her face with a traitor.

"Thank you, Jessec. A wonderful offering." Violus' mother arranged the rocks into a circle.

Jessec wrapped a bandana made of rags around her head. "Shall we?" she asked, oblivious to the rage her face brought me.

We walked through the day, and I kept my mind off Rowan by enjoying the desert landscape. It was so different here than in Erris' Wet World. The sound of rain was constant in Aquarius, but the Dry World's eerie silence brought a peace I'd never known before.

Violus? I tried more than once, finding that both of our thoughts wanted to stay quiet.

The sun was burning hot, but I stayed surprisingly comfortable in my linen pantsuit and headscarf. The tall boots I wore kept my legs cool, and the textured soles saved me from sinking into the sand, although I often stumbled.

On occasion, Violus' mother would point out something on the horizon and we'd drop to the ground, waiting for the threat to pass.

When we rose again, it was always in order. Carolus, Jessec, and me last. Several times, they mentioned how "precious" I was, although I didn't know why.

Violus' body was weak. Pain tore through my stomach with such intensity that it was impossible to concentrate on anything else. I thought she might be sick—dying even—but I realized it was nothing more than hunger.

Real hunger.

I thought of Haily back at Clover Center; her wasted body and frequent dizzy spells. I had thought she was stupid many times. If she would have allowed anyone to see her without one of her trademark hoodies, she would have looked like the walking dead—and yet she continued to deny herself food, her desire for perfection slowly killing her.

Compassion was coming to me at the strangest of times. I'd always considered girls like Haily silly. Show-offs even. Crybabies only looking for attention. I understood now that she had to have been sick. Why else would someone starve themself on purpose? Every step was a blend of nausea and vertigo. I needed food. Truly needed it for the first time in my life, but my stomach felt so tight, I wondered if I'd be able to eat it if it was right in front of me.

We reached a village made up of disheveled homes shoved so close together they almost overlapped. Curls of melted paint hung from the walls, crisping in the heat.

"Stay low," Violus' mother warned. "And don't you forget your manners this time."

Two men with skin the color of rust guarded the wooden archway that served as the entrance to the village. "Carolus of Pacifica. Welcome back."

"Thank you, Darilus. Christophus."

Darilus stepped forward, taking my hand in his. "Lo, blessed be the Original Child."

"Yes," Christophus said, nodding his head excitedly. "Surely, Dry Beds will receive a glorious bounty from the Prophets with you here, Ms. Violus."

"Th-thanks," I muttered, cheeks hot. What a welcome.

We parted ways with Jessec just inside the gate. "See you at the drawing of lots," she said, before entering a hut.

People stood outside their huts sharpening sticks and beating dirt from rugs. Most were bald, with lines of interlinking squares and diamonds tattooed on their scalps, but a few men wore their hair in short braids that poked beneath scarves. The villagers all had deep tans or skin that was naturally the shade of copper, and no one stood under the sun without their heads covered.

A familiar man stepped from one of the boxy clay homes. He wore a flowing white robe covered in black squares and diamonds. As we approached, he threw his arms open wide. "Carolus, Violus! Welcome back to Dry Beds."

"Dawson?" His golden hair was chopped to uneven lengths and covered in rags. His skin was a dark bronze, and like Carolus, he was seriously emaciated.

He gaped at me. "Yes, Violus? Dawson, eh? That's an interesting nickname. Come, Amanus has prepared a feast for us."

"Amanus?" I blurted out. "As in *anus*?" I bit my lip to hold in the laugh. That was too good.

A concerned look flashed between Violus' parents.

"She's been acting strange for days," Carolus said. "I think her dreams are getting the better of her, Dawsonus."

Dawsonus peered into my eyes. "Hmm. Well, let's get inside. Perhaps a little food will help?"

It was nice to see that Violus' father didn't turn his back on her for acting weird.

I stumbled after Carolus, doing my best to wrap my mind around this strange new life.

I ducked into Dawsonus' hut, and found that Amanda was there. Her raven hair was shaved and her bald head tattooed in the same geometric designs that decorated Dawsonus' robe. A child sat at a small table, pieced together from tire rims and metal scraps. The boy was about five years old, a bandana tied around sandy hair that matched Dawsonus'. Huh, he didn't look like a baby raven after all.

"Welcome, Carolus." Amanus stood by the table and threw her leathery arms around Violus' mother. "Come, sit down!" she insisted, dragging a loaf of bread in front of her. At least I thought the gray lump was bread. Amanus turned to me, and I expected her to hug me too, but instead, she grabbed me by the shoulder and gave me a hard shake.

23 – Laura

Hey! Hey! You need to wake up. You can't sleep here."
I opened my eyes. I was back on Earth, curled under the dirty mattress in the alley.

"You need to get up. These guys are here for the mattress." The boy who was talking looked my age, with messy black hair, thick-rimmed glasses, and an untucked flannel shirt that had the sleeves cut off. He stood with his arms crossed. At his side stood two men in blue uniforms, a purring garbage truck behind them.

I crawled out, whispering, "Sorry." I shuffled to the sidewalk, hurrying out of the way as the grumbling workers hauled the old mattress off and the flannel guy returned inside.

I watched the rumbling truck drive away, remembering the sound of hooves from the night before. It was better than the other memories.

The memory of Rowan's breaking neck made my legs crumble. My palms were slick and my stomach was brewing. Another death on my conscience thanks to the visitors in my mind.

She saved you, I reminded myself. Rowan was going to hurt you.

But would I have done the same thing? If not for whoever possessed me last night, Rowan would probably still be alive.

I slipped down to the ground, planting my butt on the hot concrete and pulling my legs close to my body. Everything was numb. Now that I wasn't running from Black Coats or Reapers, all I could think about was the life I'd taken.

I'd gotten my freedom at the cost of someone else's.

What now? I needed to stay out of sight until I could find a way out of town. But where would I go? How long until TIR had my picture on the news? And if they caught me, then what?

There wasn't much around the alley but a few shops and a couple of makeshift shacks pieced together from flattened cardboard boxes. People huddled in the shacks, doing their best to avoid the relentless sun overhead.

"Hey, you! Girl!" called a balding woman stooped under one of the shelters.

"Yeah? What is it?" I asked, peeking out from between my knees.

She motioned me over. "You're a mess, child. Let me give you one of my shirts. I've got a few."

My eyes dropped to my smock, tie-dyed in Rowan's blood.

Flashes from the night before brought back the horrible memory of his death. I thought again of the strength that had coursed through my muscles. I was sure it hadn't been Erris, and it didn't seem likely that Violus would save me, either. So, who?

I hurried toward the woman, thankful for the break from the sun. It couldn't have been later than seven, and it was already scorching.

She gestured to a filthy pillow on the ground. "Sit there. I'll find ya something." I watched the woman rifle through a heap of trash bags. Deep lines covered her face, and she was missing several front teeth, but I couldn't be sure of her age.

Something told me she wasn't as old as she looked.

"Need pants?" she asked.

I shook my head. "Mine are okay. Just a shirt, and some shoes if you've got them."

"Here you go," she said, pulling a tank top displaying a sparkling American flag from the bag. "I don't have anywhere to wear this anymore, anyway." She dug through the bag again, coming up with a pair of worn flip-flops.

"Thanks." I slipped on the shoes, wincing as they rubbed against my fresh blisters. They were a size too big, but better than nothing. Next, I pulled the tank top through the gaping sleeve of my smock and shimmied around until I had gotten the tank fitted into place. I ripped off the smock and bunched it up.

"There's a trash bin over there." She pointed down the street and revealed a pock-marked arm. "Ah," she dropped her arm when she noticed I was staring. "I've had some struggles." Her glance fell to the smock still bunched in my hands. "And you?"

A shiver ran through me as the night before came crashing back. The stench of sweat and copper wafted up from the smock. How had I killed him? Haily was my age. My size. Rowan was a full-grown man. An armed one at that. And yet I escaped. I looked over my arms. My skin was smooth, and there was no evidence of the cuts I'd gotten bursting through the glass doors at TIR.

I stood up and walked on stilted legs toward the green garbage can at the end of the sidewalk.

"You're welcome!" the woman called after me in an annoyed tone.

I dumped the smock, burying it into the can as far as I could, my nostrils flaring at the offensive stink of old food and human waste. I considered throwing myself into the can next, so they'd take me away with the other trash.

My fingers gripped the edge of the can, and I heaved, puking last night's dinner up on my TIR uniform and creating a truly horrific specimen for any future DNA analysis. Holding my hair back, I spat until my pounding head drowned out the memory of the night before.

I surveyed the neighborhood. Most of the buildings were in need of a good paint job, and a few of the shops had boarded-up windows. Other buildings looked like they'd been built recently, and signs were posted on their doors warning of fines should anyone consider taking a nap on their front stoop.

A trail of sweat slithered down my neck as I made my way across the street. Why was it so damn hot?

I tipped my head, noticing a black Cadillac creeping down the road. The driver wore dark sunglasses, so I couldn't be sure, but I suspected he was watching me. The Cadillac passed and turned at the corner, but every cell in my body was on alert, making me desperate to get off the street.

I needed somewhere to think. Preferably somewhere with air-conditioning.

I found an open game store beside the alley I'd slept in and I stepped inside, where the ripe smell of old onion stew reminded me of the grungy boys back at TIR. Video game consoles were stacked in boxes, the games to accompany them lining the walls in rows. Board games were also for sale, and I spent several minutes perusing the display next to the front door before I realized someone was watching me.

"Can I help you find something?"

It was the man from the alley. He watched me the way Rowan had. Only this man's stare didn't make me sick to my stomach.

I turned away, wanting to get away from Rowan's memory before I hurled again. "I'm just looking around. I need a gift for my stepmother." Yeah right. The only gift I'd give Amanda was a swift kick in the Amanus.

"Hmm." His fingers tugged at his coarse beard. "I've got some copies of the classics in the back. You know *Clue*, *Monopoly* . . ."

"Actually, it's for a baby shower."

There was a jingle at the door as a freckled boy entered. The store clerk sighed, swinging his head between me and the new customer. "I'll be back," he mumbled.

He'd left me in front of an end cap displaying a new military game. A man in a black uniform was on the cover of the case. He looked just like Rowan.

Guilt taunted me from the depths of my stomach, which threatened to expel the last of its contents. What was I doing? Making small talk hours after killing a man with my bare hands. Who was I? Ted Bundy? My legs trembled, and I thought it best I move on before making a scene.

The store clerk returned with an arm full of board games. Again, he reminded me of Rowan—but different. Better. Instead of making me want to shrink in on myself, his stare made me feel . . . seen . . . as something other than a project.

A tingle brewed in my stomach at the memory of Rowan's leer; the way that same leer had morphed into the face of the Devil himself the night before.

"Do I know you?" the clerk asked, mercifully saving me from my thoughts. His eyebrows scrunched as he tried to remember.

"Nope," I said, with a shake of my head.

"Oh." He set the games down and fiddled with the earpiece of his glasses, gaze sneaking my way again. "Are you sure?" His eyes narrowed. "You were outside, weren't you? Sleeping in the alley?"

My cheeks burned. "Oh, sorry about that, I—" My words stopped short of my mouth. The air grew frigid, and my eyesight dimmed. Someone was pulling me loose, ripping me from my warm body, and casting me into the unknown.

My eyes re-adjusted to the game store. I could have only been gone for a second—if I'd left at all.

"Did I hurt you?" I spun around, thankful the shop looked intact. "Did she break anything?" I didn't know where I'd gone. It was too dark for me to make out much.

The clerk's mouth flopped open, working little O's like a gasping fish. "What just happened? Your eyes! They turned, like purple or something."

They did?

"You kept calling me 'Fade' and going on about some message, and I don't know; it was really weird . . . and I think you should leave." He swallowed hard and took a step away from me.

Poor guy. I'd clearly done a number on him.

My chin dropped into a nod. "Sure. Fine. I'll go."

I backed up and pushed through the door, hoping he'd stay freaked out long enough not to call the cops.

Turning toward the café, I realized it was too late. A patrol car sat in the lot. Red and blue lights flashed over the building, illuminating a server who was deep in conversation with an officer.

I heard sirens growing loud and heading for me. Another patrol car zoomed past, sliding into the lot. There were more, coming fast.

I tried to run, my legs screaming out with every step. The pain in my thigh was worse than ever. For a second, the restaurant disappeared, and the hot summer air turned cold.

I shuddered, realizing I stood on the brink of a cliff, teetering at the edge of a magnificent cavern that was illuminated by the heavenly green light of an aurora.

Two hands grabbed me tightly around the waist and jerked me back before I plummeted into the abyss.

I turned around, seeing the man from the game shop. He looked different—his bearded face, the dark goggles instead of glasses, the thick hides he wore on his back instead of flannel . . .

The clerk transformed again. His features filled out, and his goggles returned to the dark-rimmed frames he'd been wearing in the game store. I watched as his furs returned to flannel.

"Are you trying to get killed?" he asked, giving me a hard shake. "You just ran into traffic!"

I did? I stood on the street, inches from being mowed down by the ambulance that was rolling into the parking lot of the café.

"Hey! I need some help over here!" the clerk yelled, waving his arms to flag down an officer across the street.

The tingle in my gut spread, and a high-pitched voice erupted from my lips. "Please don't call them," the voice pleaded. "They'll kill me."

They will? Who? I tried to twist my neck, but whoever had moved into my body was locked on the man from the game store.

"The police. Please. I can explain. Just help me inside."

He glanced over my shoulder. "I don't think so. I'm not getting wrapped up in any batty business." He shot another look at the ambulance before turning back to his store.

"Wade!" the voice called in a high, childlike tone.

He stopped, turning slowly to face me. "How did you know my name?" he asked, raising an eyebrow.

The tingling moved through my body and down my right leg. I took a step toward him.

He held his hands up, scooting away. "Just stay there, okay. I'll yell for the cops if I have to."

A flood of information entered my brain, as if whoever worked my mind was downloading their knowledge into me.

"I know about the pirated movies," came the childlike voice again, more sinister than before. "And the music files, too. Shall we tell the police about that?"

Wade's eyes narrowed into a glare. "Are you blackmailing me?"

My head shook from side to side. "I'm only trying to stay alive. Can we please go back in?"

He glanced at the café across the street. "Promise you won't hurt me?"

I nodded again. Hopefully, whoever spoke for me was telling the truth.

"Come on," he sighed, motioning me through the door. I felt the tingles disappear as my mysterious visitor left.

"I'm so sorry about what happened out there," I said when we were inside.

Wade scooted back against a display of Marvel comics, keeping a healthy distance between our bodies. "After freaking out like you were possessed by a purple-eyed demon, running into traffic, and blackmailing me after I saved you . . . sorry sounds about right."

This guy was as fluent in sarcasm as I was.

"So, the police aren't here for me?"

"Obviously they *should* be," he muttered.

I couldn't get over the chilling words the child-like voice had said outside. Were the police really going to kill me or was that just a gambit to get me inside?

"Thanks for helping me. I'll leave, but please—I need to know why the cops are next door."

Wade let out a frustrated groan. He leaned over the counter and turned a knob on a slender black box that started playing snippets from a police radio.

"Scanner says an elderly man was having chest pains."

"Chest pains?" I crossed to the window, watching as an old man was loaded into the back of the ambulance outside. "So, they're not here for me?"

Wade shrugged. "Not this time."

Letting out a sigh of relief, I held out my hand. "I'm Laura, by the way. Thanks for helping me out back there."

He was still watching me like I might catch fire, but his hand inched toward mine. "Wade Rivers."

I studied the displays of books, movies, and games around me. Everything a man-child could want. "Nice place you've got here. Quite the collection."

"It's my life's work," he said, absent-mindedly scratching at his collar. "Say, what's your life's work? Why is it your eyes are changing colors, and all that? How about we *not* make any more small talk until I get some answers?"

"Color-changing contacts?" I tried.

Wade stared, obviously not buying it.

The truth was a fair request if I wanted him to help me. Even if all I was doing was convincing him not to throw me to the wolves outside.

"I ran away. I was staying at this place—an institute. Something happened there, and I had to get out." My fingertips clutched the sequins making up the American flag on my shirt. "A guard there wanted to hurt me, so I hurt him first. I had to." At the memory, a sob rose up in my throat, choking out as tears formed in my eyes. "I didn't want to," I said, my voice breaking with every word. "Not like that."

Wade's eyes, big and brown like a Labrador's, grew wide. He glanced at a thick black watch strapped to his wrist. "I barely get business this time of day anyway," he mumbled, crossing to the front door, where he flipped the open sign to 'closed' and dimmed the lights. He returned to his perch against the comics. "Are you dangerous, Laura?"

That was a loaded question if ever I'd heard one. "I don't think so," I said. Honesty had never done me any good before, but I needed someone to talk to. "The place I was at . . . it's for people who are different, people who are—"

"TIR?" he asked. "The research institute?"

"Yeah. How did you know?"

"I heard they were reopening on the news." Wade walked over to the counter where a display of superhero keychains hung next to the cash register. He climbed onto a stool and watched me with his chubby chin wedged between his hands. "There's been some weird rumors about that place over the years. They do all sorts of experiments on people's brains." He narrowed his eyes. "Is that what they did to you?"

"I guess. Mostly, it was just therapy. I've been in those kinds of places off and on my entire life."

"What's wrong with you?" Wade asked.

I bit at my lip, letting the rude question fester. "Nothing is wrong with me! It's more of an ability."

I studied Wade's expression for any change. Fear? Doubt? When he finally spoke again, I was surprised to see a smile toying with the corners of his lips. "You're a superhero. That's what happened when your eyes changed."

"Nothing's super about me. It's just this thing I can do."

He watched me expectantly.

"Sometimes, I hear voices. Or, talk in voices like what happened outside. It's like this other person sort of moves into my mind and—"

"Takes over?"

My jaw dropped. "You think I'm telling the truth?"

His shoulders bobbed in a shrug. "I mean, I don't know, honestly. But that trick you did with your eyes? And the way you knew my name and about the pirated movies and all that? That's the stuff of superheroes." His eyes ticked to mine. "Or villains."

I chuckled. "I'm guessing you think I'm the second one."

He shrugged again. "Heroes don't usually have to blackmail people to keep them from calling the cops."

I found a spot of wall to lean against. "Sorry about that. I swear it wasn't me. I don't know who it was, honestly."

Wade kept looking between me and the door. I wasn't sure if he wanted to kick me out or make a run for it himself. "Should ask them to wear nametags," he mumbled.

Funny guy. I recognized the way he used humor to distract himself. We'd discussed it in Dr. Z's group lots of times at Clover Center.

I shifted my weight. What the hell was I doing here? Who was that outside, and why had they blackmailed Wade? I was starting to miss Dr. Morris and his answers. Goosies ran down my arms. Why did I listen to Jessica? I should've stayed in bed last night. I'd be nice and comfy in Dr. Morris' air-conditioned office, snacking on a piece of chocolate while being treated like the most interesting person alive.

Instead, I was hiding out in a game store with a guy who clearly didn't want me here. I'd been a caged bird, a prisoner in a literal cuckoo's nest. I had my freedom, and now I was wishing I could go back.

But Rowan's death had ensured that wouldn't happen.

"Thanks for keeping me from being squished by that ambulance earlier," I said, knowing I didn't deserve to be saved.

He shrugged. "Bad business to have a casualty right outside."

I smirked. "I'm sure it was scary seeing me like that. I traumatized the kids in my group a few times."

Wade raised his eyebrows. "It was definitely the first time I've ever seen someone face swap. But the eye thing? That was pretty cool."

Cool? Maybe this guy was more psychotic than I was. I threw my hands on my hips the way my mother used to. I'd also watched Violus' Mama do it when I visited the Dry World. "It's not cool. It's terrifying."

His eyes softened. "Yeah, I suppose so. But I mean, you've got to be able to control it sometimes, right?"

"Not really. Most of the time, it's one of the others coming here. I haven't exactly mastered how to go anywhere else yet. Dr. Morris and I were working on it, but I hadn't been successful yet."

"Morris, huh?"

"You know him?"

"Name's just familiar." Wade pulled his glasses off and wiped them with the untucked portion of his shirt. "So, what's it like? In the other world?"

"You sure are interested." Not that I cared. I was thankful for the sanctuary from the police, however brief it may be. I met his warm brown Labrador eyes before the glasses settled back into place.

Wade grinned; his smile surprisingly pleasant amid the nest of facial hair. "I'm a nerd. I love the possibility of the supernatural being real." His gaze lingered on me, making us both blush. What was this? Why was this guy so cool? His eyes flicked to mine like he couldn't keep them away. My heart was pounding from the threat outside, but I realized whoever had forced him to let me in here must have been on to something. Being here with Wade almost felt safe.

Wade's cheeks flushed, and he turned away. I had embarrassed him, although I didn't understand how.

Stop it, I told myself, realizing I was being delusional. The only reason this guy was letting me stay here was because he was afraid of what I might do. It wasn't safe. For all I knew, I'd be getting a Darth Vader figurine to the skull the first time I turned my back.

Wade fiddled with the corner of his flannel, a disappointed frown playing at his lips.

"One place—Aquarius—it's like Earth, but covered in water."

His head snapped up. "Like *Water World?*"

"Exactly! My parents are there. Doctors. Friends. Only everyone looks a bit different than they are here. My *life's* different. There's another place too. A dry world. It's all covered in sand, and the grass is black and there are big scorch marks across the ground like something burned it."

"What do you think happened?"

"I don't know. I've only seen that place once that I can remember. Last night. Before, I only ever remember taking Erris' place."

"Erris? That's the one from the Aquarius?"

"Yeah, she's me, but from the Wet World. Violus is my name in the Dry World."

"And who's Fade?"

I shrugged. "No idea. Violus was looking for someone named Shade."

My thoughts were drifting back to Violus' mama and all the ways she reminded me of my own mother. I was thinking about my earliest memories when things were still good. Peaceful, even. I got caught up in the moment. I was falling again, but when I landed, I wasn't in the Dry World. Instead, I was somewhere unbelievably cold.

24-Lennox

My boots crunched in the hard snow, their echo deafened by my heavy breathing. I adjusted the furs hanging off of my back like a cape, pulling them tight.

I reached an icy bluff, tilting my head up, weak eyes looking for the dark smudge of an opening.

I jumped, reaching the lowest nook of the cliffside and grasping it with both hands before shimmying up. A cave was hidden on the ledge, only large enough to crawl through and protected from the heat-seekers by the stalactites that hung over the entrance.

The spiked pads on my gloves helped me grasp the ice as I squirmed through.

"Fade! Are you in here?" I called, crawling to my knees when the cave opened. A narrow tunnel led to a chamber hidden deep in the mountain. But if he was home, he already knew I was coming. I waved to the cameras I saw wedged in the ice. It was likely that Fade had installed plenty of sensors I couldn't see, too.

The chamber was lit by a handful of lanterns and large enough to house everything Fade needed on his nights outside the Abyss. A makeshift bed of furs in one corner, and whatever furniture he'd managed to free from the ice in the other. Filing cabinets and coffee makers and even a television, as he told me they were called.

Fade came here only for emergencies. The hike was dangerous, staked out by whatever predators found a way to survive the freeze, which hadn't been many.

The Crawlers were far worse. I would kill every Crawler that crossed my path, except one.

I found him in the middle of the cave. My childhood friend, who happened to work for the enemy. Unlike Helectra, I was confident Fade was on my side. Some bonds can't be faked.

Several tables had been shoved together, computers crowding every inch of them. Fade hid behind them, fingers rattling over a keyboard. He was huddled beneath layers of blankets, and only a tuft of bushy hair and his black-rimmed goggles showed.

"There you are! I was waiting for you to invite me in."

"Sorry," he mumbled, fingertips never slowing. "I just picked up a transmission. Someone's been trying to contact you."

I circled the computers and eagerly leaned in to read the message. They only came through in an emergency.

You changed the plan. Fix it.
—W.

"Wisdom's pissed," said Fade, giving me a knowing look. "Seems Laura's out of TIR, now."

I could still feel the guard's warm blood on my hands. The scars on my body could be a tally of every life I'd taken. But there was no remorse this time. That man was wild, and like a mother bear, I regretted nothing about protecting Laura.

"How are the kids?" I asked.

Fade gestured to one of the screens. A grainy black-and-white image showed an aerial view of the valley outside the Hollow. "It looks like everybody got out. The Crawlers finally breached the valley yesterday, and I didn't see them bring anyone out of the caves other than, you know . . ." His eyes fell to the table. "Helectra."

I sighed, watching the message blink on Fade's screen.

Dropping into the empty chair across from him, I kicked my boots up onto the table.

"Watch the monitors," he warned, fingers back on the keys. Fade's eyes appeared glued to the screen, but I sensed him watching me. His breathing was relaxed, but his heart erratic. "I'm glad you're safe," he said, earning a glare.

"Of course, I am. You know nothing can happen to me." I grabbed the steaming mug from his desk and drank the swill down in a few greedy gulps before slamming the empty mug back into the ice.

"That's fine," Fade said. "Coffee's not rare or anything."

"Your coffee's disgusting." I wiped my mouth with my furs.

"It's warm." Illuminated by screen light, I watched his eyes trail over me, heartbeat racing. Fade swallowed, and his lips parted as he prepared to say something.

Beep!

Fade's computer chirped, causing us both to jump. I picked at the claws on my gloves, distracting myself before the blush reached my cheeks.

"Wisdom again." Fade tilted the monitor. "It's an updated calculation."

I jerked upright, scooting closer so I could see. "That's what I was worried about," I said, exhaling as I got to my feet. "An apocalypse, just what I always wanted for my birthday."

"Two days," Fade said. "That's cutting it close. We'll have to get help."

A yell escaped my lips, and my fist shot toward the icy cave wall. I stopped short of hitting it, afraid of accidentally shattering someone else's hand too. Laura and Erris had enough to hate me for. Everyone had the right to hate me.

"About Helectra—" I started.

Fade raised a hand to silence me. "Thank you," he said.

"I don't blame you. I'm only thankful she wasn't here in my cave when the message came through."

I nodded, appreciating the out. In this cave, I didn't have to deal with judgment and regret.

But good things only last so long, and I had a mission to focus on.

She didn't know it yet, but Laura had finally come looking for me.

25–Laura

Are you with me Laura?"

A shiver ran through me, courtesy of the bone-chilling air I'd been pulled into. My chest grew tight, my teeth chattering as I forced out my words.

"Y-You know me?" My eyes were taking their time adjusting to the dark. Slowly, shapes formed. I tried to take a step forward but found that my boots were stuck in the ice.

"Yes. We've been trying to bring you here for a long time."

"Who has? W-where am I?"

It was so cold, I had to pick which words to use and which ones to keep in. Even breathing seemed to be a waste of precious energy.

The man the voice belonged to leaned into the flickering lamplight. I was surprised to find he could have been Wade's brother—a few premature wrinkles and even a frost of gray, but otherwise, they were twins. Only now we were in a freezing cave instead of the game shop. Spikes of ice stuck from frost-covered walls, and several stainless-steel tables were shoved together and piled with computers. These computers looked old, with boxy monitors and thick cables running between them.

"You're in Lennox's body in the Dark World. Do you know who I am?"

"Shade?"

He chuckled. He had heaps of blankets piled on, and I was jealous. I was so cold, it felt like every ounce of liquid in my body had crystallized. I was wearing a cape of furs, but it did nothing to keep out the chill. "I go by Fade here, actually. Shade's in the Dry World. Where Violus is."

"You've met Violus?"

"Yes, I've met all of you now. Apparently, I'm more of a people person than Lennox is. I think it's a little easier to process all of this wonky information when you can have some actual flesh to talk to, not just a voice in your head."

"You've known each other a while?" I asked. "I bet she's glad she has someone to share with."

He scoffed. "Lennox doesn't exactly share. She's as vulnerable and cuddly as a landmine, but that's part of what I love about her. We were only kids when we met in person. Lennox found me after she escaped the Abyss—that's what we call TIR here—but we were communicating for a long time before. She came back after she killed Helectra. No one would help her anymore. It's me and Lennox against the Ice Man now."

"Helectra? You mean Haily?" My mind was spinning, and I held out my hand to balance against the slick cave wall as a rush of dizziness came over me.

"I suppose so. It seems some worlds have similarities. Like names. I guess it's a lot different here than it is in the other places."

This Lennox person was responsible for Haily's death? "Why would she kill her?" A flicker of relief passed through me. I knew I hadn't been responsible, but still—the relief quickly drifted away. Haily was gone, and my hands had been the ones to do it.

Rage burned as I considered what Lennox had taken

from me.

"Helectra was a plant in our world. A Crawler. Her mission was so covert, even I didn't know. She was sent to the Hollow to be Lennox's friend, but really, the Ice Man needed something from Lennox. It was an accident. Haily wasn't supposed to die on Earth too. There's this effect called layering. You know how sometimes you only see things, but other times you might smell and hear what's around you, too?"

I nodded. "I've been practicing in the Wet World. The more I concentrate, the more control my body has over Erris.'"

"Exactly!" Fade said. "Helectra was so strong, Lennox had to use all the power she could to stop her. She didn't know what would happen."

"Power?"

"Lennox is the Crawlers' greatest achievement."

I remembered Rowan's death. The strength that ran through me. "These Crawlers, they're like doctors?"

Fade gave a curt nod. "I guess you'd call them that. We're more like scientists, actually."

"We?" I asked, surprised. "I assumed they were bad guys."

"The worst. Which is where you come in. Lennox and I need all of you if we're going to stop them from hurting anybody else." His eyes fell. "Helectra was a hard enough loss."

My mind was swirling. I'd barely gotten a grasp on Erris' life. I knew now that I hadn't imagined the others, but trying to find my place in the Dry World as Violus, and now here—a sharp twinge zigzagged between my eyes as if saying, "You're right; you can't handle this."

I took a deep breath, doing my best to ignore the migraine. "Haily—I mean Helectra. She was Lennox's friend?"

Fade's eyes fell. "She was *my* friend, too. And not that it's going to make you feel any better, but she put up a decent fight herself. I'm sure you felt what she did to your thigh."

My fingers traveled to the wound below my right hip. The scar tissue was thick beneath my fingers. No wonder it had been so itchy.

"This cut came from here?"

Fade nodded. "A stab wound that can cross dimensions. Pretty impressive. It's also pretty scary. It means our worlds are getting closer together."

Closer? I thought of the strange things I'd seen at TIR. The way the Wet World was blending with my own reality. The deranged Morris who mirrored the kind old man I'd worked with. What about Jessica and her so-called sister? Remembering the Raider girl, I wondered what else I had in common with the other patients at TIR.

Lennox got me out of there for some reason, so now what? A river of questions flowed through my head, but all I could say was, "It's so cold here." I couldn't think straight, and my teeth chattered torturously in my head. I hadn't visited the dentist often, but we had oral exams every year at Clover Center. Lennox's teeth hadn't seen a toothbrush in a long time, though, and I did my best to brace my jaw so the pain would settle.

"Cold, yeah." Fade chuckled. "Well, that's why we call it the Evernight. We haven't seen the sunshine in a couple of decades. Not since the Final Summer."

"Can-can I get a blanket, please?"

Fade shrugged his top layer off and handed me the rag. It smelled like a dead animal, but I was in no mood to complain. "Thanks," I said, pulling it as snug as I could around my shoulders. He crossed the room to a metal table where a single burner and a cast-iron kettle sat.

"What's that?"

"Coffee. They have coffee on Earth, don't they?"

"I hate it."

Fade pulled a saucer from under the table and poured a thick goopy liquid into the cup he handed me.

I took a sip. The coffee was twice as bitter as I remembered, but it was so warm; I thought it might have been the best gift I'd ever been given. My mother had bought me Barbies when I was little and then books later on when she got worried about the way I played with dolls. But this horrible drink was better. I swallowed down the strange flavoring he'd added—the texture of cottage cheese curds, yet sweet.

"What did you put in it?"

"Milk."

I choked, spitting liquid all over the frost-covered floors and showering the closest keyboard.

"Hey! Why'd you do that?" He threw his hands up, tossing his heap of blankets to the floor.

"It was chunky! You gave me rotten milk?"

Fade shrugged. "Sorry." He gave me a sheepish grin. "You probably don't want to know what kind of animal it came from either." I blanched, watching him collect his blankets from the ground. "Come on, we don't have time. I need Lennox back here where she belongs. The heat-seekers will find us if we take too long."

He read my look.

"They're these drones. They can sense body heat out on the ice and you make a whole lotta heat when you cross over."

"Cross over? Lennox can visit the other worlds? Like, on purpose?"

Fade chuckled, rubbing his gut, which was noticeably trimmer than Wade's. He was hungry, I could tell. I felt it in Lennox's belly, too. She'd eaten more recently than Violus had, but food was clearly scarce in this dark place.

"It's really risky, so she only does it when she needs to. When you ask her to."

"I've never asked anything from her. I never even knew this place existed!"

"You didn't know you were asking. You didn't understand enough. You're getting stronger, though. And the walls are getting thinner. Luckily, you've only had to deal with one at a time so far, but if the walls break, well, Lennox isn't so sure you'll be able to handle that."

I suspected she was right. "How many are there?"

"Six that I know of, but Lennox thinks there could be more. A lot more. Besides you two, there's Erris, Violus, and Wisdom. And Arial, but she's gone now . . ."

I recognized her name immediately. It was so long ago I barely remembered, but now her memory came slamming into me.

"What do you mean, gone?"

Fade's thick eyebrows furrowed behind his glasses. "There was an accident. You lost her early on."

"When we were eight." Arial. My imaginary friend. The one I killed.

Fade caught my eye and nodded. I hadn't imagined the fight after all.

"Does Lennox know what happened?"

Fade shook his head. "I don't think so. She never really wants to talk about it, anyway. Even when we were only swapping messages while she still lived in the Hollow." He looked around, desperate for a distraction. "Let's go. It's time to get you back."

"Wait!" I said, remembering one more question I needed answered before I could go. "Was it Lennox who took me over a little bit ago? Did she convince Wade to let me into his store?"

Fade's eyebrows raised in Wade's familiar surprised look. "No, I don't think so."

"Was it Erris? Violus?"

He shrugged. "I have no idea." He glanced at the nearest computer screen. "When you say 'convinced' what exactly do you mean?"

I thought for a moment. "I dunno. She, like, knew stuff about him. His name and whatnot. Private stuff about movies he'd stolen or something."

Fade sighed. "Sounds like Wisdom."

"Well, where is she?" I asked, but the blast of warm air I felt let me know I was already heading back home.

26-Lennox

I hated Earth, where everything smelled and the noise never stopped. Fade said it wasn't like this everywhere. There were quiet towns and fresh air somewhere outside of the city, but Laura hadn't been allowed there in a long time, so neither had I.

Laura's body was soft. She'd spent her life surrounded by soft things, all to protect her from me. Shame it hadn't worked.

Wade eyed me like I was a diseased rat he'd trapped in a cage in the hopes of an easy meal. But there was no such thing as an easy meal. Not in the Dark World.

"It's good to see you, Wade. I was afraid Laura moved on already."

"Who are you?" He was nervous. I could smell it on him, though my eyes barely worked. The sun that filtered in through the windows was hard on me, and I hoped the trip would be quick.

"My name is Lennox. I'm from a place called the Dark World. Laura called me here."

"Did she now?" Wade was damn near trembling, head whipping toward the door like he thought he actually had a chance to outrun me. Laura's body was weak, but it was my vessel. With just a thought, I could make her muscles as strong as mine.

"You should calm down," I warned him, running my fingers over a shelf holding tiny glass figurines. "Your weight and health suggest you could be prone to early heart attacks."

"Hey, Laura . . . uh, you in there?" he asked. "Please come out now."

"She's occupied." I could sense his unease from across the room. "And you don't need to worry about her. Laura's safe." I lifted a glass figurine from the shelf. "It's me who's dangerous." I squeezed my fist. The glass erupted in a muffled crunch, and a few drops of blood fell to the floor with the shards of broken glass.

He watched the broken glass fall to the floor. "Okay . . . So, how can I help you?"

Wade was slow and squishy, but I felt something at the sight of him—something Laura would likely feel too. Although clearly inferior, he was like Fade. A big dopey ball of warmth who could thaw our icy hearts.

Too bad Laura was gonna get him killed.

"You can help me by staying out of Laura's way," I said. "She's got a mission now; she needs to focus on finding Wisdom."

He lifted his hands. "I tried to give her the boot already. You're the one who made me let her back in. Thanks for the blackmail, by the way." The irritation in his eyes faded under my threatening look.

"What are you talking about? I haven't been in Laura's mind since last night."

He shrugged. "Well, someone threatened me. Brought up personal stuff about me and my search history."

So, Wisdom had been here after all? My curiosity leaped . . . along with my anxiety. Wisdom poking around behind my back meant things were really getting desperate. If I couldn't find a way to unite us soon, we'd come crashing together against our will. If that happened, everything I'd put the others through would be for nothing.

Wade leaned against a wall decorated with strange boxes. "What are those things?" I asked.

He followed my finger. "Video games. Do they not have X-Boxes where you're from?"

"We have ice. And cold."

"And dark," he said, failing to be humorous. His heart was racing. I watched his jaw tick and throat quiver. My senses were turned all the way up here, and although I was at a disadvantage in this world, I knew I was infinitely stronger than the strongest man here. The Ice Man had made sure of it.

"So . . ." Wade inhaled. "Laura called you here, huh? Any idea why?"

"She said she needed my help. There was some sort of trouble."

"And who is this Fade?"

"It's you, only where I'm from." I surveyed Wade's strange cave. He sure had a lot of X-Boxes. Were they for food or to burn for warmth? He wore a clunky watch on his wrist. Poor Earthling, still enslaved by a clock. "Fade is much more intelligent than you are."

Wade laughed, finally relaxing, if only a bit. "Is that so?"

"Yes. He's a computer hacker in the Dark World. He protects the Shadows from the Ice Man. Without him, I wouldn't risk coming here."

"How *do* you come here?" He leaned close. "Laura says she can't by herself."

"Wisdom taught us. She—" I took a step but lost my footing, stumbling forward into nothing and finding the firm ground again in Fade's icy cave.

"It worked," Fade said, helping me up. "We got her."

27-Laura

The warmth of the game shop sunk into my bones. It felt so good to be back. Wade watched me with a combination of intrigue and fear. Whatever he witnessed had changed him. Though I frightened him, I could tell he thought I was fascinating—the way the doctors had—but more importantly, he really did seem to believe me.

"It's me," I said, going over the checklist in my head. "Laura."

Glancing around Wade's shop, I checked "Location" and "Safety of Surroundings" off my list as well.

"Who was here?" I asked. "Was it Lennox?"

Wade nodded. "She was scary."

"I went there. To the Dark World. You were there too. We were in this ice cave, and you had all these computers. Your name was—"

"Fade?"

"Yeah." I nodded. "It was intense. I see why she's so scary. Did you learn anything? Fade didn't say much other than something about heat-seekers and somebody named

Wisdom."

"Lennox talked about Wisdom, too. Said you need to find her." Wade crossed to a coffee pot and poured me a cup. "Do you take milk?" he asked with a sideways glance.

I gagged, remembering the chunky goop Fade had poured me in the Dark World. "No, thanks."

Wade shrugged. "Lennox said this Wisdom person was who helped her figure out how to get here."

"Fade was talking about that, too. Saying the walls were getting thinner. We can only cross one at a time now, but they seem to think I'll have a head full of Lauras before long." The thought was intimidating. I rubbed the lingering ache on my forehead.

"Great." Wade sipped his coffee. "And what are you supposed to do about that?"

I shrugged. "No one's told me." I shivered at the idea of so many people having access to my mind. All of those unexplained blackouts and forgotten dreams were starting to make sense. But it was more than that. It meant that everything I'd ever been told was a lie—was *real*.

There was a knock at the door. Wade excused himself to tell the kid outside he was closed for the day. "What's it like? When you cross over?" he asked when he returned.

"It's usually like I'm falling . . . or falling asleep. I start to lose control here, and then suddenly, I'm somewhere else."

"Sounds like fun," Wade said with a hint of a grin. "Being able to explore another world? It's what fanboys like me live for."

"Fanboys?"

"Nerds, Trekkies, Too-Cool-to-Avoid-Wedgies-at-School . . . If it were me, I'd probably have a heyday with somebody else's life."

"It's not fun. It's terrifying. I think it's terrifying for them to come here too. That's why I start freaking out so bad while I'm having an—"

"Episode?"

"Yeah." I scoffed at "episode." It was far too

underwhelming a word for what I lived. My mind spun as I pictured the other worlds I'd visited. "I want to try something," I said. "Morris was teaching me how to visit Erris. But I wonder . . ."

Wade finished my thought for me. "You want to try to reach the others?"

I gave him a hopeful smile.

He sighed. "Okay. But Laura, if you lose it . . ."

I lifted my hand, showing my crossed fingers. "I'll do the best I can. If I lose control, call the cops over."

I didn't wait for his answer. I was thinking of the Dry World. Of Carolus, Dawsonus, and how happy Violus felt despite the danger she was in, even there. I started to fall—but this time, I held on. I dug my heels in and stayed put, keeping my focus on Wade. He watched my eyes, which were no doubt flickering between colors.

A tingle settled on my forehead. It was like a tickle—the kind you beg to stop. Almost painful. Flashes of people in white robes like Dawsonus had worn in the Dry World appeared around me. I squeezed my fists tight, digging my nails into my palm. Every thought I had focused on Wade and his eclectic collection of pop culture until the people faded into rows of shelves again.

I managed to hold on, but I wasn't alone. I had stayed on Earth, but someone else was here with me.

Where am I? My heart fluttered from her fear. My chest grew painfully tight, and I was afraid my heart couldn't handle the both of us. Using my thoughts, I did my best to calm her.

It's okay, Violus. I'm here.

Laura?

Wade leaned close. "Laura, are you alright?"

I drowned him out, picturing a comfy sofa. There was plenty of room on my sofa. If only Violus' thoughts would calm down. *I'm here with you, Violus. You're okay.*

"Laura's still here," Violus told Wade, "But I think I'm in control."

Yes.

"What's your name?" Wade asked.

"Violus," slid from between my lips.

"Do you know where you are?" Wade's eyes flickered, too. A dance between curiosity and unease.

"I believe this is the Green World. Earth. Laura lives here. Arial invited me to visit often when I was a youngling."

"Who is Arial?" Wade asked.

"She was from the windy place," Violus said. "Something happened there."

"Do you know what?" Wade pressed.

"Her planet broke, and she was trying to cross over so she could find a new home. She could leave hers whenever she wanted. Lennox said she was bad—that Arial wanted to take Laura's place so she could stay."

"So, Laura killed her." Wade let out a deep breath. "Whoa."

An emotion drifted through me. Regret . . . but with a kind of resigned understanding. Whatever happened all those years ago, I didn't think Violus blamed me.

My head bobbed up and down. "It was an accident," Violus said. "Laura didn't know. She's more vulnerable than the rest of us. That's why she crosses so easily. Lennox warned us to be careful of Laura. She's special. We need to make sure she stays safe no matter what."

Violus' voice grew weak as she returned to the Dry World. I drummed my fingers, feeling the taps against my leg.

"She needs to stay away," Violus' whispered before fading away, ". . . from the Reapers."

My mind became a stage ready for me to step up and take the lead, but instead, I tried something else.

Picturing Aquarius, I thought of Rat Island and the filthy cages where Erris lived.

I was in a place too dark to see, rocking slowly back and forth. I did my best to repeat what I had done before. I pictured Aquarius, but I kept myself on Earth.

"Laura, are you still with me?" Wade's voice cracked in terror. I wondered what he was seeing.

I'm here, I called, but nothing came out.

"Where is Morris?" Erris asked in a feeble voice. Something horrible had happened to her since the last time I visited Rat Island, but I didn't know what. The itch returned to my thigh, more intense than ever. A fiery blast of pain erupted there, and I felt malaise spread through my body.

Wade turned a dial on the wall, dimming the lights. "Morris isn't here. You're safe." I was thankful he was being kind. "What's your name?" he asked.

"Er-Erris," she answered, gnashing my teeth as she stuttered. "I ain't on Aquarius anymore, am I? This doesn't look like the Dark World."

"You're on planet Earth. Laura lives here."

"Laura?"

Erris, I'm here! Why couldn't she hear me?

Wade spoke up. "Laura's hoping to contact you all. She found Violus and Lennox . . ."

"And Wisdom?" Erris asked.

"Sure. Wisdom, too. But Laura needs help reaching her. Do you know where she lives?"

"She lives in the—"

We were moving. I didn't know who was going, me or her, but I got my answer when I opened my mouth and water flooded in.

Chains were shackled around my hands and feet, and my body jerked through the water as I struggled for the surface. My chest grew so tight, I was sure my lungs would pop when I was ripped free from the water and pulled face to face with Morris and his coke-bottle goggles.

"Ah," he said, his penfocal lens blinking furiously as he peered close. "Who do we have here?"

"Help me!" I sputtered. "Let me go!"

I was back on the muddy shores of Rat Island.

"You can't be Erris," Morris sneered. "Too much fight left in ya." He threw me to the ground. "Are you Lennox?" he demanded.

I landed hard on my ribs, but I was thankful to be out of

the grasp of the horrible man.

"I don't know who you're talking about!"

Morris gave me a hard kick to the gut, and I recoiled in on myself, tasting fish. The pain that radiated through my body was debilitating, and I knew I wouldn't have been able to stand if he'd allowed me to. An agonizing throb radiated from my right leg, and I feared what I may see if I looked at it.

Morris sneered. "I know you're new here, but it would do you some good to remember I have no patience for liars. Try that again, and you'll be back at the bottom of the ocean. Understand?"

I glared up at him and his stupid bottle-goggle glasses.

He pulled his leg back, ready to strike me again.

"Yes!" I spat. "I understand!"

"What's your name?"

I considered lying, but I didn't know what repercussions my insolence may have on Erris. "I'm Laura."

"What planet are you from?"

"Earth."

"The dry one?"

I shook my head.

"Is there rain there? Snow?"

I nodded. "Not for almost a year, though. We've been going through a rough drought."

He squeezed my collar. His breath had a strange acrid smell, like burning rubber. "It hasn't happened yet." It wasn't a question but a revelation. "Where do you live? The"—he searched for the word—"hospital, is it?"

"It's called TIR, where I'm from. The Tomlinson Institute of Research."

"Tomlinson, eh?" Morris stared off. "And what year do you go by there?"

It was a strange question, and I struggled to remember the answer, as it hadn't been of much importance at TIR. Pain tore through my body from the cuts and scars beneath my soaking clothing. I feared for Erris and what would happen when she came back. "It's 2035 on Earth. What year is it here?"

Morris watched me as if I was the dangerous one. "Same, but our calendar goes by 10 A.F. Ten years after the flood."

"What are you doing to Erris?"

His smile was ugly and inhuman. "We're not doing anything. Erris is a volunteer here."

I wasn't the only one this Morris scared. Every one of us thought this man to be a monster. Tingles danced on my skin, ghostly fingertips trying to drag me away from him. *I'm okay*, I thought, unsure who it was for.

"Why are you hurting her?"

He studied me, deciding if I was worthy of answers. It was hard to tell behind the blinking penfocals, but I thought the man a bit like me. He wanted answers too—was desperate for them—and that made me important . . . at least for now.

"To see what she knows," Morris said. "There's a whole lotta secrets trapped in your head, Laura, and the best ones require some twisting to get to. I've found my best patients have their breakthroughs when they experience great loss."

Morris grabbed my arm.

"Lennox is coming," I said. "She'll stop you."

Morris laughed. "Good. I'd love to talk to her. One of you has it. The key to stopping the rain."

With that, he shoved me into the chilly water. I didn't know what he was planning for me, but I wasn't willing to find out. I blocked out Morris' face, instead focusing on Wade back at the game shop. It worked, and within moments, I was in front of him, pleased to find I had my body to myself.

"It's me," I said, catching Wade's uncertain look. I'd stumbled back to Earth with all the wits of a drunk at 2 a.m.

The game shop seemed brighter—louder, even though the only noise came from the humming fluorescents and TVs. Those sounds had never bothered me before, but now they screamed so loudly, I had to cover my ears with my hands.

Wade looked ill. I knew it was me making him that way.

"Did you go there? To Aquarius? Erris was here. She seemed . . . off."

I lowered my hands, still wincing against the bright lights.

"She's being tortured in her world. Morris is dunking her in the water and who knows what else. I don't want to go back. I need to figure out what's going on. What do you know about TIR?"

Wade motioned for me to follow him around the counter. He bent his head, searching under the counter for something. Hopefully not a gun or a baseball bat.

Wade glanced at the door and pulled up the object he was hiding under the counter.

I let out a relieved sigh. Not a gun or a bat. It was a plastic file folder. Wade opened it and shook out the contents onto the countertop. Mostly magazine clippings and some computer printouts. I snatched up the scrap of paper on top of the pile, recognizing Dr. Venkin's face.

"Tomlinson Institute of Research established in 2010," I read. "It says here they specialize in brain disorders." I leafed through the pile. "What is all this?"

Wade blushed. "My collection." He gestured a hand around the shop full of superhero movies, comics, and video games. "I think this stuff is fascinating. These stories are fiction, but they're based on very real science. Who's to say superheroes can't exist in real life?" He shrugged. "If anyone's giving people super powers, it's TIR."

Wade picked up another page. "Tomlinson Institute of Research in deep trouble over controversial experiments. 'The Tomlinson Institute of Research has been under scrutiny for years for their peculiar experiments, many which critics insist to be illegal and worse, immoral, but this latest experiment may have gone too far.' "

I looked over the paper, reading the words myself. A picture showed a group of infants swaddled in striped blankets. They lay side by side in rigid bassinets.

"TIR's latest experiment—touted as an attempt to cross into other dimensions—has been labeled a massive failure by its investors, who have since pulled their funding from the project. Of the twelve infants involved in the experiments, only one is believed to have survived. The patient, known only as 'L' will be released to her parents with the hopes she'll be able to live a typical life outside the walls of the Institute."

Wade trailed off. "That's all it says. I guess a few of the doctors did some minor jail time, but it seems their legal team found all sorts of loopholes. Parental consent, waivers . . . blah, blah, blah. The next part just goes on about TIR's former experiments, which involved climate manipulation. Apparently, they got a lot of flak for that one too."

"What year was the article written?" I asked, already knowing the answer.

"2017."

"The year I was born." My words hung over the room like they were holding a heavy rain they couldn't wait to set loose. "They were attempting to reach another dimension, but why?"

Wade shrugged. "Because they're scientists. I get the curiosity. What I don't get is the babies."

"Me either. We'll have to wait until we get a chance to ask the others about it." I gave him a wink. "Or *you* will, next time they stop by."

We both stared at the counter. "Hey, Wade . . . I need to tell you something."

When he looked up, an excited grin was plastered on his face, like he thought I was about to tell him I had an invisible airplane or something.

"I've killed people."

Wade blinked. "*Multiple* people?"

I backed up, arms wide, to show him I was unarmed. "It was an accident. I-I didn't mean to."

"That's why you ran away," Wade finished for me. He smacked himself in the forehead, nearly knocking the glasses from his face. "Oh my God, I'm so stupid. Of course, you're a killer. Who ran away from a hospital that gives people superpowers?" He shook his head. "You *are* a villain."

There was a rattle at the door. I looked up, spotting a broad-shouldered man wearing dark sunglasses peering in.

Wade waved to the man. "Be right there!" he called, using his free hand to slide the clippings back into the file folder. He shoved it under the counter and walked around to unlock the door. Wade clicked his tongue, vision nailed to the floor. "Listen, Laura, I understand you're going through some messed up stuff, but I'm not sure how much help I can be. I mean, I've got some downloaded movies and games that I . . . well, I guess you already know about that, huh?" He finally met my eye. "TIR is no joke. They're looking to change the world but not in a good way. I'd rather not have the suits around here if you know what I mean. I've got customers to think of. I can't really keep the store closed all day . . ." He shifted uncomfortably, obviously not wanting to bring up the whole "afraid of me because I'm a murderer thing."

"Oh?" I understood. This wasn't his problem. What did I expect him to do for me, anyway? Reunite me with my sisters across the multiverse? What I was getting involved in was dangerous. *I* was dangerous. It was stupid to bring another potential victim into my life.

"Yeah, you're right." I decided to make things easy for him. "Sorry about everything," I mumbled, watching my dirty flip-flops so he wouldn't see the tears in my eyes. "And just so you know, it was self-defense."

Wade's eyebrows lifted, his expression frozen in place. "I'm sure it was." He shifted uncomfortably, so his shoes pointed me toward the door. "Well, if you ever need a copy of the old *Tomb Raider* . . ."

I laughed, even though I didn't have a clue what he was talking about. "Take it easy, Wade. Thanks for all the help."

I slipped out the door, doing my best not to look back. Wade didn't owe me a thing, but being alone felt lonelier than ever. My eyes were bleary—maybe from the saltwater Morris was plunging Erris in . . . or from the raindrops I'd felt back on Aquarius—but I suspected it was from the disappointment of losing someone else.

You just met him, I reminded myself. *He's not your mourning dove.*

I hurried away, almost barreling into the looming man outside who looked overdressed in his thick black coat.

It was nearly noon and people were huddled under the awnings to avoid the sizzling sun overhead. I darted across the street, slipping into the shadows whenever possible. I had nowhere to go. No transportation, and only the clothes I borrowed after I escaped from TIR. I stopped a few blocks from Wade's shop, realizing I was already lost. I spun, desperate for a glimpse of anything that could tell me where I was. Sweat dripped between my eyes, bringing a shiver as it slid down my back. The skin on my forehead was tight, suggesting a bad burn was already settling in.

Why was it 110° in June midmorning in Seattle?

I bolted across the street, narrowly avoiding more pedestrians. My heart was racing. *Where am I going?* I stopped, spinning in the middle of the sidewalk. Traffic signs and hand-written warnings plastered the neighborhood, but nothing pointed toward a bus stop or airport. *And I don't have any money!* I remembered, chest growing tight. People were staring, and a few of them took out their phones to start filming me.

That powerful feeling came over me again, like I'd been super-charged. Every person on the street became a target, and I sensed the heat of their bodies and heard the beat of their hearts. I could guess how fast that lanky man on the corner was capable of running and how high that little girl could jump. My surroundings became a battlefield and every passerby my contender.

My sight grew so weak, I could hardly see across the street. Even then, the sun was so bright on my eyes, I wanted to keep them closed.

"No!" I howled, refusing to let her have control. "Not this time."

We were a team, Lennox and me. For once, I wasn't cast aside. She wanted to hurt the people who gathered around me, jabbing their phones in my direction while they clamored to be the first to turn me in—but she let me stop her.

I had her strength. I felt it there, available to draw on whenever needed . . . seemingly my own. It was like the night before when Lennox killed Rowan and escaped TIR. Only now she was giving me some say.

"Did you see that?" a woman screamed. "What's going on with her face?"

"Her hair!"

"Were those scars there before?"

I wished I had a mirror so I could watch the show with the rest of them. Now Lennox's power rushed through me. She was letting me do whatever I wanted, but I didn't know what that was. I had more questions than before—and fewer answers than ever. I almost wanted a prison cell so I wouldn't have to make any more decisions, but I knew even if the police arrived, I'd inevitably end up back at TIR.

So, what now?

Lennox, can you hear me?

I'm here.

Her voice was solid. It almost tickled in my ear it was so real, but for a moment, I wondered if maybe I was slipping. What if I was nothing but a dangerous animal wandering the streets? Maybe TIR would be for the best.

No! Lennox cried. *Stay with me. Laura, you can do this!*

"What next?" I sobbed, glaring at the craning necks around me who risked their own sunburns to record my public unraveling.

We need to find a safe place from the Crawlers, where you can focus on contacting Wisdom. I think that's why she messaged me. She wants me to bring you to her.

Why are they after me?

Laura, we don't have time!

I held my ground. I had all the time in the world. "Why are the Crawlers after me?" I screamed, not caring that it was out loud and not in my head.

They work for TIR. They're here too. They'll take you back to the Ice Man.

Black Coats?

Yes!

The crowd was shrinking back, making way for the approaching sirens. I came to my senses long enough to turn and bolt down the nearest street.

Good, Lennox whispered. *Turn left up here. Stick to the side streets where there's more foot traffic.*

I dipped into an alley and squatted behind a trash can. Hopefully, the garbage truck had already been down here.

What are you doing now? Lennox demanded. *You don't need to relieve yourself.*

"I'm not!" I took a deep breath, concentrating on my thoughts instead. *I'm not going anywhere until you tell me what's going on.* I meant it. I had control over my demons for the first time in my life, and I was determined not to be the ventriloquist's dummy again.

There was silence on the other end, and I thought that maybe Lennox was gone. I felt a twinge of her impatience. *TIR—it's called something else where I'm from. There, Venkin is known as the Ice Man because he brought on the ice age. The sun hasn't shone on my planet since I was born. In the Dark World, I'm called a Shadow, one of the few born since the Final Summer. There's this group of his men who work further up. They serve the Ice Man by hunting down all the Shadows and bringing them back to the Abyss. Those are the Crawlers. Morris is the worst of them, so to the Shadows, he's known as Malicious. He's the Ice Man's greatest weapon besides me. He led the weather experiments and then later the experiments on the Shadows.*

And what are you and Fade up to?

Wisdom got us in touch. She taught me all about the Crawlers and the Abyss when I was just a kid. The Crawlers are everywhere. Wisdom calls them Breakers, and they're known as Reapers in the Dry World, but no matter where we go, someone's looking for us.

Why? I asked. *What do they want with us?*

They're searching for something. The trick to saving their worlds.

Saving them from what? The thought had only been for me, but Lennox heard it anyway.

What happened in my world . . . The ice age, the rain on Aquarius, Violus' droughts. The people at TIR are under the impression the Shadows are somehow responsible and therefore have the answer to stopping it.

Do we?

Uncertainty nipped at my thoughts. *I don't know,* Lennox whispered. *But Fade and I are trying. We need to find each other. We need to be united. It's the only way we can save the world.*

Now I'm saving the world?

What Fade and I are doing, Lennox said, voice so vulnerable I couldn't believe it was coming from her body, *is saving children. Kids just like you and me.*

My ears pricked, following the wave of sirens from a couple of blocks over. I swallowed, thinking of the story Wade read about the twelve babies at TIR.

Saving them from Morris?

Now I heard my own beating heart, slamming in my ears. *Whatever happens, you need to stay away from* the Crawlers.

Of course, I'm not going near them! The words were in my mind, only for Lennox, but they held such authority, I was surprised they hadn't screamed out of their own accord. *They'll lock me up! I killed people.* The words felt different now. *You killed people.* Yeah, that felt better. A peace trickled through me for the first time since Haily's death. I hadn't killed anyone at all.

Rage erupted. Dangerous rage. I wanted to hurt her now—make Lennox pay for what she'd put me through. How she'd ruined my life. The fiery, hot rage almost made me run out into traffic again.

I'm sorry! Barely a whimper, Lennox's words held enough pain to stop my rage, if only for a second. Sadness rose in the back of my mind and broke free from my lips in the form of a sob. *I'm so, so sorry.*

Lennox's emotion mixed with mine, nearly sending me to my knees. I couldn't stay mad at her just then because I understood my rage was nothing compared to how she hated herself.

I studied the pavement, contemplating what to do next. I needed off the street so I could find somewhere safe like Lennox said.

I thought of Wade. I'd only known him a short while, but if ever there'd been someone I felt safe with, it was—I shook my head. Whoa, whoa, whoa. Slow down there.

Dr. Z would tell me there were red flags all over my feelings of attachment. *I just met him,* I reminded myself. And I may never see him again.

Was it you? I asked Lennox when the sadness faded. *Did you get Wade to let me in? Know all that stuff about his computer?*

Irritation nagged at me as if I were disappointed in myself for my sudden insolence.

We need to get moving.

"No!" I blurted. "I'm not leaving until you tell me what's going on!"

Shh! My head tipped around the corner as Lennox checked our surroundings. We were alone. For now, at least. *It wasn't me!* she finally said, voice tense. *Sounds like Wisdom. I'd ask her, but she's avoiding me.*

Let's go find somewhere out of the heat and you can try for yourself.

I wanted to ask more, but another question took its place.

"What do you know about Arial?" I'd meant to think it, but the words popped out like they wanted to be said before I had a chance to chicken out.

A terrible sinking feeling stirred deep in my gut. Pain so overwhelming that the hate Lennox felt for herself over Haily's death was as warm as a tight embrace.

Arial was one of us. She lived in the Windy World. She and I were the strongest in the beginning. We had the most . . . power. We could cross over whenever we wanted. I think it was different at first. We could all be together, you know? But when we were born, we had to kind of work to get where we needed to be. I remember it . . . being in the dark and then in the light, and I knew, even then, that I wasn't alone. Even in my mother's womb, I felt you all there with me. I wanted to stay with you. We all did, but something tore us apart.

I almost remembered. Dr. Z, my parents, they'd all said it was impossible for someone to recall their infanthood like I could, but I swore I still remembered the day I was born. It was the last time I'd ever felt whole.

Arial didn't like where she was. There were storms all the time. Her parents died when we were barely walking, and she had to learn to be brave early like we all did.

Lennox's voice was sad, the words carrying the burden of her memories. It was new, being one with someone else's emotions. I'd sensed a fleeting smile or disappointment in Erris before, but this was different; it was . . . painful. Tears welled in my eyes, and I could no longer distinguish if they belonged to Lennox or not. Her pain infiltrated every inch of me, but I sensed there was so much more of it—so much I couldn't help her carry it all.

She went on, her voice a little more broken as every word crept out. *Arial realized she didn't have to stay in that scary place if she didn't want to, and she started coming to visit the rest of us. It was innocent enough at first, but she got greedy. She didn't want to go back after a while, and it affected us. We started to lose control over her. No one could keep her out anymore. She'd take our place, but she wouldn't send us to her world. She'd just trap us in our own minds while she did whatever she wanted.*

It was coming to me now. The memories were much sharper when Lennox was with me. I hadn't spoken a word for two straight months after my third birthday, although I'd been plenty chatty before. My mother dragged me to several visits with a speech therapist, who ironically enough, was at a loss for words about why I'd stopped talking. Now, I remembered, it hadn't been my silence at all. That was the year my imaginary friend came to stay with me. She couldn't talk yet. I wasn't sure why, but maybe she just didn't know how. I begged Arial to give me a little space—to let me have just a few words—but her presence in my mind had been as solid as a hand over my mouth.

Lennox had gone quiet, sharing the memory with me, but now she spoke again. *It was easy for me to cross too, so I followed her one time and I discovered something horrifying. She was here with you, just like I am, but she was trying to hurt you. She was trying to take your body forever. I stayed back; you couldn't handle both of us. You were so strong, Laura. You did such a good job keeping control. I took over just long enough to finish it. I didn't want you to have to remember something like that. My life had already been . . . well, things were never good for me, and I wanted life to be better for you, but Dawson walked in at that point. He saw something in us. I don't know what it was. At first, he thought you were hurting yourself. But then it was like he saw me—the real me—and it scared him.*

Lennox's words were bringing out a blur of memories I hadn't been able to make sense of for years. But I remembered the fight now. The look on Dawson's face . . . right before he had me hauled off to Clover Center.

He'd never stopped looking at me that way since. That was the night I'd really lost my father.

I tried to stay away after that, until the incident with Helectra, that is. When the Crawlers tried to send me to the Abyss, I knew I had to find a way to get back to you.

Why? I asked, drawing my knees to my chest and wrapping my arms around myself.

Because you're special, Laura.

I shook my head. *I don't know,* I whispered. *It sounds like being special is dangerous.*

The tingling between my eyes spread through my mind. Warm and comforting, I reveled in the mental hug. *I believe in you,* Lennox whispered. *I know you don't want anyone else to die. How about we start making up for the damage I've done? Help me free the Shadows.*

I don't know, I said. *I want to help the other kids, but how? Can't we just leave an anonymous tip with the cops?*

You don't get it, Laura! The Crawlers will never stop chasing you! They're watching our every move. They're already back with Wade . . .

She hadn't meant to say it. The words had slipped out, but I could tell—she didn't want me to know.

My head popped up. "What's wrong with Wade?"

Laura, you have to understand . . .

I snuck a peek around the building as the sirens faded. *Where do we go?* I asked.

There isn't time, Laura! The Crawlers will kill you!

No, I hissed. *You don't understand. I'm done letting you shove me around. There'll be no more blood on my hands because of you, Lennox.* I took a few defiant steps toward the crowd. *How do I get to Wade's shop from here?*

There was the sound of a long and defeated exhalation.

Go back that way, she said. *So we avoid the police.*

A map of the city fell over my eyes. It wasn't a real map with roads and buildings and stuff. This map was uniquely Lennox's, made up of every threatening heartbeat in the city. I saw the places to avoid—the areas where you could literally sense the evil in people's hearts. The streets appeared in my memory like flowing rivers, the threat of the cars urging us the other way.

Lennox gave me directions and I followed them back to the game store, stopping when I saw the black car sitting in front.

It's TIR. I'd recognized the Cadillac patrolling the neighborhood earlier. It was parked sideways, blocking the game shop from the street.

Don't stop, Lennox said. *They'll see us.* My chest was tugged in the Cadillac's direction, and I stumbled toward the car.

Lennox, I don't know about this. Maybe we should call the police.

And then we'll have dead cops on our hands. TIR is powerful, Laura. And they're not afraid to hide bodies, either. Isn't this what you wanted? For me to make amends? The tingling spread down, making its way into my legs. They grew strong as my muscles hardened. I ran . . . or Lennox did. Then, she dropped low so I could peer through the window. The "closed" sign was still up, and I glimpsed the top of Wade's head inside.

Someone will be on guard outside, Lennox said. *There! I hear him on the other side of the lot, by the food hut.*

It's called a café.

Whatever. There's a man inside pretending to be on his phone, but he's watching Wade's shop. We got lucky coming in from the alley or he would have seen us.

Is Wade going to be all right?

I don't know, Laura. We need to eliminate the bad guys first.

Eliminate? I thought we weren't going to hurt anyone else?

Crawlers don't count.

At Lennox's urging, I crept to the front door and felt the handle. Pulsing with her strength, my wrist flicked, ripping the metal handle from the door.

Nice trick.

Thanks. Now stay out of the way. I need to concentrate.

I obliged. I wasn't falling asleep this time. It was like a dip in a warm pool. Instead of trying to tread water, I let Lennox lead.

We entered the building, and Lennox headed for the counter. Wade faced me but was concentrating on the two meatheads from TIR, Glock-19s at their sides.

How did I know that? I wondered, realizing Lennox's knowledge about weapons had infiltrated my mind like a video game arsenal.

My vision dimmed as Lennox's eyes took over and I saw the men the way she did. Two targets in the middle of her narrow ring of sight.

Wait! I pleaded. *I don't want to kill anyone else.*

Lennox slowed, and I heard a series of ticks fill the room. They were heartbeats, and once I recognized that, it was easy to tell them apart. Creeping around the counter, my hand slipped around the neck of the closest man and squeezed until his body went slack beneath my arm.

You don't have to see the rest, Lennox said, right before she put me to sleep.

28-Lennox

L aura, what are you doing?" Wade howled. The folding chair the Crawlers had tied him to teetered back and forth as he struggled against the straps. If he didn't knock it off, he'd land right on his face.

I swung around, locking my lavender eyes on him. "I'm not Laura."

I heard a *click* and pivoted toward the remaining guard. He was shaking so hard, I was surprised he didn't drop the gun. I lifted my leg, crashing it down on his head. The man toppled from the chair and I scooped up his firearm.

I turned, pointing the gun at Wade.

"Lennox?" he gulped. "Did you just kill those guys?" His eyes lifted to the gun I held on him. "Are you going to kill *me?*"

I concentrated on the frantic rhythm of his heart and dropped the Glock to my side. It was an amateurish weapon compared to what the Crawlers carried in the Dark World, but the gun could still do plenty of damage to Laura.

"No," I hissed. "I'm not going to kill you. But it wasn't my choice. If not for Laura, you'd be one more pile of ashes in the Crawlers' incinerator."

His heartbeat quickened. "Laura came back for me?" I

couldn't see the blush on his cheeks, but I felt the rise in his body temperature. "Why would she do that?"

I sighed, finding the fragile game of human emotion exhausting. What did this guy care? Would he rather be dead?

"Because she feels guilty," I said, knowing too well. "She's risking her life making me come here instead of running for the far side of town, so in exchange . . . you're going to do something for her." It was infuriating that this was my only option. Why'd I have to have such a soft spot for Laura? I swore that girl was gonna get me killed too. If I didn't kill her first. "Laura needs somewhere to stay tonight. Somewhere *safe*," I clarified.

Wade's eyes were scanning me, taking in the scars that riddled my face from years of abuse at the hands of the Ice Man and his Crawlers. They'd made me damn near invincible. Most of my injuries faded easily, but the scars inflicted at my birth . . . those would never heal.

He swallowed hard. "Sure, Laura can stay here . . . or whatever." His eyes shot to the unconscious men heaped at my feet.

I slid my foot under the closest Crawler, flipping him onto his belly. "TIR" was sketched across the back of his black jacket. "They're not dead." I met Wade's unsure gaze. "Yet. But that's only because I made Laura a promise." I popped the magazine from the gun and stripped it to the barrel in seconds. I threw what was left against the wall with so much force it stuck in the drywall.

"I'm keeping this one," I told him, ripping another firearm from beneath the second Crawler.

Wade nodded, knowing I wasn't asking for his opinion.

"So, are you going to free me?" He wiggled against the straps.

I craned my neck. I could still see the third Crawler's form through the window of the food hut. *Café*, I reminded myself sarcastically. What a soft word. Everything on Earth was soft; crafted to please every sense. Not like in my world where the air stunk and it hurt to touch the ground.

"I'll let you go," I said, turning back to Wade. "But you and I need to chat first."

"I told you, Laura's welcome to stay all day. Maybe I'll even train her to use the cash register."

I caught the humor, but I had the smallest tingle of hope at the words. The idea of Laura getting to live a normal life someday? Those were the only dreams I looked forward to.

"That's not what I'm talking about." I plopped myself down at Wade's feet. "Do you think she's dangerous?" I asked.

He thought about it. "No. Not anymore."

My eyebrows lifted in surprise.

"It wasn't her at all, was it?" he asked. "It was you that killed those people. You're the reason she's on the run."

Bright guy.

My chin dipped into a curt nod. "Yes, it was. Every one of them. I did it to protect her." I nudged the Glock toward him. "And I'll do it again."

He let out an uncomfortable chuckle. "I'm not gonna hurt her. I'm way more afraid of her hurting me." He tilted his head to the side and added, "Actually, it's *you* I'm afraid of being hurt by."

"Good," I said, genuinely pleased he was willing to make this easy. "Laura needs help. Starting with somewhere safe to spend the night."

"My place is right down the street—"

I held up a hand to interrupt him. "No. The Crawlers will already be there. They're on to you. They saw her come in here."

"How do you know?"

"Because they wouldn't have been here if they didn't think you were important. So, do you have somewhere safe to stay tonight or not?"

His eyes rolled back as if they were checking the recesses of his mind for the answer. "Uh, yeah, actually. I think I know a place."

"Good. You'll go there immediately. As soon as I'm done here."

"Done with what?" his gaze trailed to the unconscious guards.

"Cleaning up this mess," I said, pulling myself to my feet.

Wade eyed the Glock I'd firmly planted in the drywall. "How did you do all that, anyway? I mean, you've got to be pretty freaking strong. You are a superhero, aren't you?" His voice brimmed with awe and terror, but the steadying rhythm of his heartbeat told me his panic was wearing off.

I lifted the gun again, nudging it toward my temple. "You see these scars? My eyes? This is what TIR did to me. They would have done worse if I'd let them. My superpowers you're so *impressed* by? That's the best of what those scientists did to me." I glanced at the Crawlers slumped at my feet. I heard the rhythm of another heartbeat coming close. Crawler number three. "Making me a killer was the worst."

The door to the game shop flew open. The Crawler filled the door, his gun pointed at me. I threw the gun in my hand, smacking the Crawler's weapon from his grasp. His gaze followed the gun in surprise. I tackled him, sending him sprawling backward. When I landed on top of him, I found his right hand and slapped it hard against the linoleum. There was a sickening sound as the bones in his hand shattered. I'd repeated the move with his left hand before the Crawler got a chance to cry out.

He let out a wail and lifted his hands, the fingers bent unnaturally in every direction like twisted tree branches.

He tried to stand. I stomped hard on his right foot and then the left, my mind concentrating on the spiked boots I wore back in the Dark World.

I hated being a killer, but Crawlers didn't count.

"Ahh!" the man roared, collapsing onto his knees.

I bent my knee into a strike, slamming the Crawler's face and casting him aside when his body went limp.

"No, he's not dead either," I said, answering Wade's unspoken question. Thankfully for precious Wade, I planned to keep my promise to Laura. "What have you got here? Any kind of office? Closet? Anywhere I can pin these guys until you can get Laura out of here?"

"Uh," Wade swung his head, taking in the mayhem I'd caused. "What will they do to my store?"

I gritted my teeth. "You won't have a store much longer if you don't help Laura, Wade." I gave him a threatening look, silently assuring him I would do the damage myself.

"Yeah, there's an office. Straight back."

I gave him a nod and wrestled the closest man from the floor. I dragged him through the aisles and found an unmarked door in the back of the store. I wrenched the door open, careful not to bust the lock before I shoved the man inside.

After I'd piled the other two on top of him, I freed Wade.

"Thanks," he mumbled, standing on shaky legs. He ran a hand through the mess of black hair on his head. "Those guys . . . they were really going to hurt Laura, weren't they?"

I nodded. "Yes, Wade. They'll do anything to get her back in TIR. They'll even kill her."

29 – Laura

That you, Laura?" Wade asked as the game shop came back into focus.

He looked shaken but alive. I didn't see the Black Coats around, and there was no sense of Lennox's presence in my mind.

I gave a shaky nod. "Lennox is gone. Are you okay?"

"She saved my life. You saved my life. Those suits . . . they were about to shoot me! They sure didn't look like doctors!"

"They're not. They're security. Lennox calls them Crawlers, but it's me that got you in danger. I'm so sorry, Wade."

He cast a wary look toward the back of the store. "Lennox said we've got about ten minutes until they start waking up, but we should leave in five anyway."

I followed his glance to the door at the back of the room.

"We?" I asked, raising a dubious eyebrow.

"I want to help."

Perplexed, my hand flew to my hip. "What changed?"

"Nothin'. I just want to help is all."

"Is that so?" I teased.

"Lennox made me," he admitted. "She's scary as heck. The way she . . . the way you. It was incredible. Like Samurai Superwoman."

I crossed my arms and gave him a playful wink. "You sound starstruck."

Wade tipped his head as he considered it. He gave me a lazy grin. "I mean, I don't want to creep you out or anything, but I don't think Buffy's my girl anymore."

Always jokes with this guy.

I narrowed my eyes. "I wouldn't recommend starting sentences with 'I don't want to creep you out', but yeah, Lennox is awesome."

He gave that uncomfortable chuckle I was beginning to find endearing. Come to think of it, it didn't smell so much like an onion in here, either.

I cringed. *Knock it off, Laura. Not the time. Definitely not the time.*

Wade shrugged. "Lennox said we needed to find Wisdom."

Thankful for the subject change, I eagerly leaned in. "Did she tell you how?"

"No." Wade scanned the ground. "She said you could figure it out." He was nervous. I didn't need Lennox's superhuman senses to know that.

"Did she say anything at all that might help me?"

"She said I needed to take care of you. That you were important." He glanced at the door where several canvas shopping bags were piled. "She also said we needed to get far from here. I guess more of those Crawler guys are after us."

"Us?"

"Yep. I told Lennox I'd keep you safe tonight."

I crossed my arms. "Hell to the N-O, Wade. I'm not letting you get involved. In fact, tomorrow, I'm going to see if I can scrape together enough cash for a bus ticket. Maybe a plane ticket. That way I can cross an ocean."

Wade glanced around the store nervously, lingering on each item as if he were taking a mental inventory. "Please, Laura, this place is everything I have. If she trashes my store, I'm done."

"Lennox?" I couldn't believe her. She helps me save Wade only to threaten him? What was it with these people and blackmail? I shook my head. "You're not coming with me."

Wade's eyebrows scrunched in worry. The game shop was nothing special. And I suspected business wouldn't be booming even if it was open. I noticed his sloven appearance, old shoes, cheap glasses. Wade was no slob. He was just an average guy, putting everything into his dream, which was clearly failing. Glancing down at the sparkling tank top I'd borrowed only confirmed I was in no position to judge, though.

"I'll make sure Lennox doesn't trash your shop," I told him. "But I'm serious. You don't have to help me."

Wade wrung his hands at his front. "I want to," he said. "I've been curious about what goes on in that place for years. Besides, Lennox told me how you made her come back here and save me. That was pretty cool."

"No, it wasn't. The only reason the Black Coats were here is because I decided to walk through your door this morning. You're in this mess because of me, and I'm not letting things get any messier!"

Wade stomped, lowering his voice to an angry whisper. The toddler move was the first time he'd reminded me of Dawson. "Laura, let me help you. Just for tonight. I mean, yeah, you almost got me killed. But you also came back before it happened for sure." He lowered his gaze. "Besides, what if those guys come after me again tonight? Might be good to have you and Lennox there." He raised an eyebrow, and I sighed, realizing he had a point. "Tomorrow, you, Lennox, and all your other . . . personalities . . . can get the hell out of my life."

His lips curled into a smug grin. Stupid guy was excited about being chased by trained assassins. A Dodo for sure.

"You look pleased."

He shrugged, smug grin turning playful. "I told you. I like drama."

I shook my head. "You must. I'd take anything to live a normal life—have parents to yell at, a bedroom door to slam."

"I'll have you 'round for Thanksgiving." Wade winked, reaching out a hand to help me up. "You and my folks can go wild. Right now, we need to get outta town."

I took his hand and stood, overcome by a sudden rush to the head.

"You okay?"

"Fine. Just woozy. My mind's been through a lot lately."

We left the shop and snuck around to the back of the building so we wouldn't be exposed in the parking lot.

"Don't you have a back door?"

"Piled up with deliveries."

Of course.

He caught my look and threw up his hands. "Well, turn me in to the fire marshal then."

We crossed through alleys cluttered with overflowing dumpsters and flattened cardboard. Wade stayed at my side, only stepping ahead to clear me a path.

"Chivalry's not dead."

The familiar blush crept over his face.

"Sorry, I don't have a car," Wade said, breathing heavily. "I could say that it's in the shop, or I left it at home to get some much-needed exercise, but the truth is the only new car I've ever owned got repo'd last week." He gave me an uncomfortable glance. "Games aren't selling so well lately."

I hung back, swiveling to face Wade. "Thank you for telling me that."

He raised his eyebrows. "Sure . . ."

I chuckled, startling him with a pat on the arm. "Sorry," I mumbled, unsure why I'd touched him. I rarely felt comfortable touching another human being, as I'd rarely been touched. "It's only, I've been sharing every weird thing in my life. I guess it's kind of nice to learn one of your dark secrets."

"Hmm." Wade lifted a mischievous finger to his lips as if

he were plotting something sinister. "Well, in that case, I peed the bed until I was ten, and for two months, I lied about having a broken leg so I could get out of my Boy Scout camp out."

"I'm sorry. What?"

"Three days of hiking and the acoustic murder of 'Kumbaya'? I think not."

"But why two months?"

Wade shrugged. "Well, the leg had to recover . . ."

I laughed again. A real, belly-bursting, tears-in-my-eyes-from-joy laugh. It caught both of us off guard. "You're funny," I said, noticing Wade's posture straightening beside me.

Wanting to stay off the grid of surveillance cameras, Wade grabbed us a couple of slices of pizza from a food truck, and we raced to see who could devour it first.

Pizza was so good.

The pizza they'd served us at Clover Center was square and crisp enough to chip a tooth, yet somehow still frozen in the middle. The pizza at TIR was at least shaped like a triangle, but the only kind they'd given us was covered in greasy cheese.

But freedom pizza? This was the most delicious, wonderful, totally-worth-melting-the-top-of-your-mouth food I'd had the privilege of eating. A huddle of pigeons gathered nearby, and I tossed them a couple chunks of crust in Haily's memory.

I didn't experience a second of joy without remembering what I'd done.

The sun fell as we crossed the city and the streets were crowded with people doing their shopping out of the heat of the day. Wade said most stores had switched their hours to improve business, as people didn't like to go out and risk getting scorched.

I didn't mind. I'd never been a fan of crowds, but now I loved the cover. Families laughed, and friends gossiped while they walked, but Wade and I slithered like polecats through the night, following the moon to a place we hoped the Crawlers hadn't found first.

Finally, we reached a tiny bungalow with an overgrown

front yard.

Wade circled the house, checking under every rock in the yard for a spare key.

"Whose place is this again?" I asked after he finally found the location of the key he'd clearly never been told about.

"An ex-classmate. He graduated last year. He's stationed in Texas now and hasn't been able to get a renter because of maintenance problems. No one's been here for months."

"Nice of you to check in on the place for him."

"Yeah, well, I probably should've checked in sooner." He fiddled with the lock and motioned for me to enter first. The lights didn't work, but a few stray moonbeams worked to illuminate our path.

"Hold on." Wade wrestled with something in his pocket, freeing a flashlight a moment later.

"You always carry that with you?" I asked. "Aren't we prepared?"

He shrugged, giving me a grin. "Well, yeah. Boy Scouts."

Wade led the way down the narrow hall. I eyed the moldy wallpaper with disgust, wondering if the smell of raw sewage had something to do with the lack of paying tenants. "This place looks like a hazard."

"It's the last place someone would look." The hall opened to a living room decorated with nothing more than a lumpy couch. "There are sleeping bags in the closet. We'll stay here tonight."

The pair of sleeping bags he found was an off-putting pea green color and smelled strongly of mildew. He handed me one and gestured to the couch. "That's you. I'll take the floor." He unrolled his bag and got to work on the stubborn zipper.

I curled up on the scratchy couch, pulling my knees tight to my chest. Wade sat the flashlight on the floor so that a white halo lit up the ceiling.

"This place is pretty gross."

Wade chuckled. "You're not wrong. I'm surprised the windows weren't boarded up."

The mildew stench drifted through my senses with every

rustle of my sleeping bag. I thought of Erris, whose life on Aquarius would have made her feel at home in this rotting house. I hoped she was okay with Morris, whatever he was doing to her.

"I gotta admit, it's still an upgrade from the cots at TIR."

"Hell, it's almost an upgrade from my apartment." Wade's grin was illuminated by the ghostly flashlight beam.

"I'm sure it's nice. At least it's yours."

Wade nodded. "I guess that's one way of looking at it. Actually, it was the only thing I could afford after my parents kicked me out. Grandpa left me the building the game shop is in, and my dad said I had to sell it or grow up and become a businessman like him. Obviously, I didn't grow up or become a businessman. I'm just a high school dropout with a bunch of cool crap everyone's already buying online. The whole reason I wanted a store was so I'd have someone else to play action figures with."

"At least you do what you love," I said. "My dad's also a businessman. He spent his fourteen-hour days bitching about how boring weather patterns were. All the man ever did was pore over weather forecasts from around the world. That was before the drought. Then, his fourteen-hour shifts turned to twenty-hour ones. I'd much prefer playing with action figures."

Wade rolled onto his belly and propped up on one elbow to face me. "Where are your parents?" he asked. "Does any family know what you're going through?"

I shook my head. "Nope. They cut me off a couple of weeks ago. When I was at Clover Center, there was this incident with Lennox. I was minding my own business one day, and then it was like I was knocked unconscious. When I woke up, I found out I killed someone. The same thing happened at TIR. That's why I ran."

The words poured out of me like a raging river. My body was heavy with secrets. My muscles ached carrying them. I hated being the only one who could see inside my mind.

"Lennox was protecting you," Wade offered. "The others seem to really care about you."

"Like sisters," I said. "They might care about me, but that doesn't change how they ruined my life. What I've done . . . it hurts so bad carrying that. All I ever wanted was to have a normal life, but I know what I deserve. I know why my family turned their backs on me. To protect themselves."

Wade's expression was soft. No twinges of judgment or fear. He was only listening.

I picked at the wiry fibers of the couch. "My parents never seemed happy, even when I was little. Mom battled her own issues—depression, anxiety—and it was always a sore spot in their marriage, something Dawson sort of put up with. I think he was just as eager to get rid of Mom as he was me."

"I'm sure that's not true —" Wade stopped, catching my doubtful look.

"Dawson always had a plan. He was going places. Places people like Mom and I wouldn't fit in. I guess he held some important job before I was born, and it always felt like he was trying to get back there. Back to his 'before' life that didn't involve us." I looked up and found Wade deep in thought. He caught my eye, and his chin jerked into a nod, urging me to continue. "I never had to wonder if my mom loved me. Even when she could barely get out of bed herself, she did everything she could to make sure I knew that." Until they sent me to Clover Center, that is. "But with Dawson . . . well, it kind of seemed like 'Dad' was a filthy word to him."

I cleared my throat, easing the tears back. I didn't like thinking about my parents this way. It was too soon. My cold heart was a dam, and if I let the feelings in now, there would be no holding the tears in.

Something warm slipped into my hand, and I looked up, seeing Wade's fingers twisted around mine. A tingle spread through me, almost like a bolt of electricity.

Wade's mouth fell open and he pulled his fingers free. "Yikes, did you feel that?" he asked, shaking his fingertips.

"Yeah," I whispered, watching my hand.

Wade exhaled, eyes shifting around the room. "So, what's next? What are you doing after all this? This morning, I found you sleeping in the alley. You can't go home, so what do you plan to do after all this?"

All this? I shook my head. I didn't even know what I'd be doing tomorrow. For all I knew, I'd be waking up at TIR, where Dr. Morris would tell me I'd imagined my little escape.

"No clue. I've thought about it before, sure, but I never really had any reason to make plans for my future. When the others . . . I mean, when the outbursts started getting worse and my parents decided I needed to go live at the hospital permanently . . . well, I sort of thought that meant I'd never get to live on my own. That I would always have to be at a hospital, or live with my parents or something, but then I thought, you know, since I'll be eighteen soon . . ." I trailed off. "But then Haily died. And Rowan. So no, I wasn't really planning to look for a place of my own." I went quiet then, busying myself with my own thoughts.

I didn't want to talk about it anymore. Not about the apartment listings I'd collected at Clover Center, or the secret talks Dr. Z and I had about what I would need to do to get released after I was a legal adult. I'd gotten my wish, and I was out of the institute, but I didn't know if I'd ever get the luxury of making plans again.

I studied the cobwebbed ceiling. "Thanks for helping me. I'm still sorry I got you involved."

He waved me off. "Don't worry about it. If it gets to be too much for me, I know where the door is."

There was that deflective humor again. Of course, I was worried about him. Haily and Rowan had been accidents, but now I was putting someone right in the crosshairs.

Don't forget about Arial, I thought, the name startling me even though I'd been the one to think it. I tried to remember her face, but it had been so long . . .

A series of blurred images hurtled through my mind; all I could remember of the last night I'd ever felt her presence.

"You okay?" Wade asked, pulling me from my thoughts. "It's been kind of a shitty day."

I scoffed. "You win the Understatement Award." After

everything she'd put me through, what else could Lennox want from me? This house was dusty and vermin-filled, but I'd sleep here every night before I'd willingly step foot in TIR again. "Hopefully, tomorrow, I'll find out more."

Wade nodded. He was facing the wall, but his gaze subtly slid my way. Suddenly, I felt silly in my stupid tank top with a sparkly red flag. What was I, a six-year-old at a Fourth of July parade? My cheeks burned as red as my shirt, and I was thankful the dark hid my embarrassment.

I'd never cared about clothes before. At the start of the day, I was just happy I was out of my TIR uniform. My mother never left her sweatpants, and the White Coats all wore . . . white coats, leaving Dr. Z as my sole fashion icon. But her clothes were beautiful and expensive. Reminding me of another problem. Money.

I'd need money for plane tickets, food, and clothes I wasn't embarrassed to be seen in. It wouldn't hurt to wear something more inconspicuous anyway.

I turned my head, realizing Wade's eyes were still on me.

"Do I make you nervous?" I asked, cueing Wade's uncomfortable laughter.

"A little," he admitted. "I'm not usually the kind of guy to sign up for a sleepover with a potential serial killer."

There was nothing 'potential' about it, I realized, feeling even crummier about bringing him into my ridiculous life. *I* was dangerous. I was a killer. There was no denying it anymore.

"I don't blame you," I said. "I also wouldn't blame you for peacing out in the middle of the night." Part of me hoped he would for his own sake, but the other part was terrified of waking up alone.

Wade slipped off his glasses and set them on the windowsill before shimmying down into the sleeping bag until only his face showed. "I'm staying here tonight. Hopefully, tomorrow we can part ways without Lennox coming for my store."

I groaned, hatred for Lennox deepening. "I promise I'll talk to her about that. Lennox will leave your place alone. I'm more worried about the Crawlers."

Wade's eyes went wide as he stared at the ceiling. "They're probably ransacking the action figure case now," he said, voice so sad you'd think he was actually seeing it. "Bye-bye, Boba Fett. Adios 1980s Ninja Turtles collection."

Remembering this was the man's business and not him recollecting his childhood bedroom, I tried to gather some sympathy. "I'm sure they ran right out of there without touching a thing. They just want me."

"Yeah, I'm sure you're right."

I lay down in my rumpled sleeping bag on a sofa that smelled only slightly better than the mattress I'd slept beneath the night before.

"Tomorrow, you can start resting easy again. But good luck getting any sleep tonight." I looked over, seeing Wade's eyes already fluttering shut.

The house was new to me, but the unfamiliar creaks in the walls soon faded to the back of my mind as the warmth of the night took over.

I guess it would be easier to sleep here than I'd thought.

30-ERRIS

I awoke, chained to the chair in Morris' office.

"Hello, Erris." I bolted upright at the new voice. My leg radiated a horrible aching pain that was now accompanied by a horrid smell. My lips were cracked and bleeding, and the chains around my wrists had worn the skin raw. A tall man stood at the door, his dark suit tight against a frame that would be considered heavy for anyone on Aquarius. He entered the room, sheet metal door smacking shut behind him. "Do you know who I am?"

I did, thanks to the hand-sketched wanted posters handed out among the Holdouts on Fox Island. "President Venkin," I said.

"Very good." He waddled toward me. "I wanted to see how you were feeling."

My leg throbbed at the question. "Still not dead."

"Do you remember how you got here?" President Venkin asked. He settled into the chair across from me and it groaned under his weight.

"Nope."

"A Gleaner caught your friend Jackie out of her cage. When he confronted her, you went wild and attacked him."

"I did?"

President Venkin's chin wobbled as he nodded. "He lived, luckily for you, and all the punishment Jackie received was a session in front of the Ocular. You and I are here to talk about something else."

I shifted in my seat, the pain in my leg making it hard to settle. "What?"

"When you were unconscious, you were calling out for your parents. They're here on Rat Island, aren't they?"

I nodded. "They were brought in last year. Dawson and Cici from Fox Island. They were medics for the old army. You know, pre-flood." The words slipped from my lips like drool. What had made me so chatty?

"Would you like to see them?" he asked. "I'll send a Gleaner to see if we can reunite your family."

I could see my folks? Eyes narrowing into a glare, I asked, "What do you want from me?"

"Only your loyalty. If you help me find Lennox, I'll do more than just reunite you and your parents. I'll free you from your service here, and the Gleaners will take your family to an island you can have all to yourselves."

"I'm not stupid. It's gonna hurt a lot if you're giving me an offer like that."

"I just want you to get some rest now, Erris. After that, we'll do another session with Morris."

"It's not working."

He drummed his fingers on the desk. "What do you need to make it work?"

I stretched my leg out so he could see the dark lines that spiraled from the oozing wound. "I'm dying. Maybe if I felt better, it would be easier."

President Venkin stood. He crossed to the door and opened it, whispering something to the Gleaner standing watch outside. Venkin returned, followed by a doctor in a white coat who carried an ivory case. Opening the case, he pulled out bandages, bottles, and a handful of fuzzy pills.

The doctor shoved the pills into my mouth, pushing the sticky wad back until my eyes bulged. He lifted a bottle to my lips, and a cool liquid slipped over my lips, causing them to tingle and burn.

There was a knock at the door and Venkin opened it to reveal the zit-faced Gleaner. He was sporting a new black eye, and several crooked stitches formed a jagged line across his face.

He reached out to grab me, bloodlust clear in his eyes. He didn't say a word, probably because of the wires holding his jaw together. Instead, the Gleaner pulled me through the door and shoved me down the path with the help of his baton.

It was a long and cold march back to my cage, and my lower back was covered in lumps and bruises long before I got there. If God was still up there watching over Aquarius, he'd decided to unleash a waterfall right on top of Rat Island tonight. Sometimes I thought he was watching over me, helping me out, telling me what I should do.

Other times, I thought I was losing my mind.

It hurt to walk, but oh lord, did I feel better. My mind was clear for the first time in weeks. Without the fever mucking up my head, I saw Rat Island under a new moon. Possibility lay on this island. A chance for change.

A girl watched me through the bars of her cage. She was maybe eight with hair as ratty as her clothes. Her dirty face morphed as the Gleaner pushed me by. Her features stayed mostly the same, but for a tick, her hair wasn't ratty. For the briefest second, her hair was long and tangled but clean. Then, she didn't have any hair at all. It fell right off her scalp, and the dome of her head was covered in strange shapes instead.

I didn't fret over the girl's hair, and neither did she because before I could squeal, it grew back.

The Gleaner locked me in my cage, and I squinted into the night, trying to change the appearances of the prisoners around me.

"You're back," whispered a frail voice.

Jackie slumped against my cage. Tonight, the light in her eyes was a little dimmer.

"How was the Ocular?" I asked. I hadn't decided which was worse, being dunked in the ocean or locked up in Morris' office.

"Horrible," Jackie whispered. "Why does it hurt so damn much?"

"Because the others are fighting," I told her. "They're afraid of Morris too."

"I saw my sister, Jessica," Jackie said. "Morris is torturing her, too. Every time I see her world, some doctors have got her hooked up to a machine." She lowered her voice, checking all around for Gleaners. "We're planning an escape," she said. "Soon, a Raider ship's gonna creep into dock, and then me and mine are getting off this damn island."

"Did you find the grumps?" I asked.

"Yeah," Jackie nodded. "On the other side of the hospital. The Gleaners walked me through there when I was done with Morris. There aren't as many of them, but I saw a few Raiders in cages too."

"Any Holdouts?"

Jackie shrugged. "Dunno. It's hard to tell who's who when they're all muddy like that." After a pause, she said, "but guess what I learned to do today?"

I tilted my head her way. Jackie held a hand out. Her palm pooled with a few drops of rain, and then the water evaporated into steam.

"The Dry World," she whispered. "Just like you showed me. I showed a few other kids, too. Your trick works, Erris."

I licked my lips, tongue lingering on every crack and blister. "That's good, Jackie. Morris will like that."

"Morris?" she scoffed. "I ain't showing Morris. I'm gonna teach the other Raiders. The power to control the weather? That's gonna give us a real chance against the Gleaners."

New thoughts were clouding my mind. A cramp flared between my eyes as a visitor settled in. *She's going to ruin things,*

Wisdom warned. *The Dry World is our leverage.*

Her presence brought a flood of warmth. The surrounding cages were buried in mud and fog, but when Wisdom was in my mind, they were almost . . . beautiful. The smell of human rot was replaced by the scent of spice cake. The gray drizzle of rain clouds became a quilt of color over my head. The birds were Pegasi pulling chariots of gold. It was a taste of the fantasy Wisdom lived in, and I wanted to stay there forever.

I shivered as the darkness returned to my thoughts. *Get her out of here.*

"Listen, Jackie," I said, scooching toward her. "I think you should go back to your cage. Quit showing off and keep your head low until the Raiders get here."

She frowned, and her pale fingers wrapped around the bars of my cage. "You sure? I thought you liked my company."

"We can't risk getting caught again. Besides, I need the rest."

Jackie nodded. She climbed to her feet and waved before slipping out of sight behind another cage.

Venkin wants more, I told Wisdom once Jackie was gone.

Then give it to him.

What if I can't? What if Lennox never comes back for me?

Then I'll save you.

The cool rain became warm sunshine, and the clouds turned to rainbows again.

But how? I asked. *You don't even have a body.*

Lightning streaked across the sky, illuminating the cages around me. *No, Erris, but I have so much more.*

Wisdom slipped from my thoughts, and I fell face-first into the mud, her fantasy fresh in my memory. Glaring at the pit Lennox had left me in, I knew I'd do anything to get back there.

The medicine would be wearing off soon. Would President Venkin give me more? What would I have to do to get it? When were he and Morris gonna make good on their promise and let me see my folks?

I went back to changing the prisoners around me. I imagined an Aquarius without rain. A place where the sun always shone and no one could remember the taste of fish.

No one changed, but after a while, the ugliest face I knew appeared before me.

"It's time, Erris," Morris said, the dumb bottles he wore over his eyes looking through me.

I was far from ready to go back to the dock at Prisoner's Point, but now my march was with a purpose.

As Morris plunged me into the cruelly cold ocean and the weight of the chains started to drag me down, I thought about my folks. I missed Daddy's long braids and perfect smile, Ma's embrace—

Then I thought about *her*. Her black hair and purple eyes . . . the oh-so cold place she'd told me bedtime tales about when we were kids.

I wasn't going to let her ignore me anymore.

I'm coming for you, Lennox.

31-Lennox

She's not ready, Lennox." Fade paced the cramped cave. "If we try to send Laura back in, they might break her."

We didn't have any more time. The walls were too thin. I saw Laura's world every time I closed my eyes now. Or Erris', or Violus' . . .

I crouched down, pushing my fur cape underneath me before I took a seat on the ice-covered chair in the corner of Fade's cave. "She's ready enough. We have to save Erris before she gets killed because of me, too. Morris is only torturing her because it makes a good a trap."

"Of course, it's a trap. But Laura cannot go in your place. What about Violus?"

I shook my head, catching a glimpse of my scarred face in the dark computer screen. My hair wasn't golden like the others. It was pitch black, iced with streaks of gray. My purple eyes looked wild among the scars on my face. If not for the bright lights Fade cast over our work table, I wouldn't have been able to see myself at all.

"Violus is happy. She has a family. I can't take them from her." Besides, who knew if she'd help? Violus was so wrapped up in the upcoming Rain Ceremony, it seemed she hardly remembered the rest of us. I admired her. Violus had never been scared. Certainly not of death. She would walk into the end with her head high and both shoulders back. Not crawling on her knees like me.

"I have to do it," I said.

"If you die, they *all* could," Fade reminded me.

I ignored him. I wasn't even sure if the Ice Man would let me die. Instead, I thought of the healing center where Violus and her parents were gathered with the man called Shade.

The hut was tiny but still bigger than the others in Dry Beds. Shade was addressing the group. His dark hair was trimmed into a hundred braids beneath his frayed straw hat. A group of bald children, all younger than Violus, were seated in front of Shade, their heads tattooed with geometric shapes.

I'd known what the shapes meant when I was little and Arial and I visited Violus more often. I made out the diamond penned on Violus' skull that stood for fertility. I knew it to be the fertility of the land, not of the body. All the children who would ever be born on the Dry World were gathering in healing centers just like this one. The Rain Ceremony would be soon.

Shade carried a wooden bowl and passed white twigs out to the children. They were already drawing lots. Every year they did this, choosing which children would participate in the annual Rain Ceremony.

This would be Violus' last year drawing lots. Years before, I'd waited for the verdict with bated breath . . . but not this time. Regardless of the stick she drew, I already knew what fate awaited Violus.

I saw the people I knew as Traitor and the Mistress. Dawson and Amanda . . . that's who they were to Laura, and no matter how they had betrayed her, she still loved them. I felt it deep inside, where she hid all of her most dangerous emotions.

I couldn't look at my father's face for too long. He'd sold me to the Crawlers early on in the Dark World. They still offered a reward for Shadows back then. Now, the Crawlers just killed those who protected us.

Leaving the Dry World behind, I skimmed over Erris, floating past like I belonged to the gathering rain clouds. She was back in her chains in the shallows of the ocean. My hand brushed the scarred wound on my thigh, my heart breaking at the damage I'd done to her. Erris was close to me. Through the years, all of them had worn my scars and felt my injuries at some point. But the infection I could feel spreading through Erris' body was a ticking bomb. Whether I had intended to or not, I'd hurt her. My heart plummeted into a pit of agony knowing I may very well kill her.

I didn't stay long; the Ocular would sense me there, and Morris would be on the hunt again. I wanted to kill him right then, but I couldn't. We weren't ready yet. And if something went wrong . . . well, Laura couldn't handle it on her own. None of us could.

I left Erris, zooming in on Laura instead. The change of worlds was as startling as plunging my head into a bucket of cold water. I was rusty, but this was what I'd been made for. I felt the hard ice of the Dark World beneath my feet. The spikes of my boots dug deep as my mind switched between worlds.

Laura was sleeping. She was on the run, scared and filled with uncertainty about what the next day would bring, but she felt peace, probably for the first time in her life. I would give anything to let her keep that sense of freedom.

Wade lay nearby, and although his eyes were closed, I sensed that he was awake. His heartbeat was in a frantic dance as his thoughts ran wild. It wasn't unease he was feeling, I suspected; instead, it seemed he was thinking of Laura. Worried for her, perhaps. Growing infatuated with her, definitely. It was as confusing for him as it would be for her. *She's too good for Wade*, I thought, knowing my disapproval was only because of my own romantic fate. I could never have my own Wade. "May you have one great friend over a thousand decent lovers," I whispered.

I took the plunge, somersaulting into Laura's mind, where I found she was looking for me, searching for the Dark World in her dreams. She was in a dim hallway. She passed doorways, pausing at each one and ducking her head in. It was how her mind tried to make sense of crossing over. I was proud of her. She was learning.

I could have called out to her, but I didn't. I wasn't the one she needed.

I crept up behind her, holding my breath as I fought to keep my thoughts focused. She couldn't know I was here. She couldn't get distracted.

Wisdom! I sang, my voice like that of a ghost in Laura's ear. A shadow of a whisper.

Laura stopped.

"Wisdom?" She turned to face me, but I was already gone.

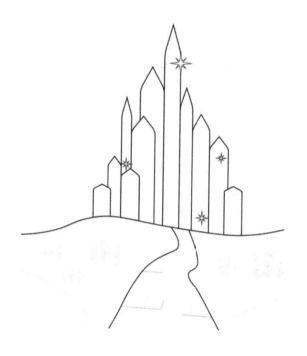

32-Wisdom

Wisdom's World — 2035

Some would call me a ghost. An apparition, a specter, a shadow lost to the night. A spirit doomed to haunt my world from the digital realm I'd been trapped in.

But the truth was, I still had a body. By whatever sick definition the Breakers had, I was alive.

Eighteen years old, but only in my mind.

I hid from them now, the black suits who eradicated all life on my planet. It started with an experiment like so many horrible things do.

The last time I had looked into my mother's eyes was when she put me in this box. It was dark here, like where Lennox lived, but this was my choice. At whim, I'd be living on the beach or in the city . . . or in a big castle on a hill. Cinderella's castle, I thought, imagining its steep towers and turrets. I'd have the room at the top—

I felt an icy shiver, although that was impossible. All of my feelings were at the mercy of ones and zeros now— whatever the technology I'd been imprisoned in could keep up with. For the truth was, a simulation could never replicate real life.

Some people do everything they can to escape reality, but me . . . I was desperate for it.

I felt the shiver again. I reveled in the discomfort, the pain of being cold. Lennox was right there, begging to come in, but I had no intention of letting her into my mind. This was my paradise, whereas Lennox had opted for Hell.

I imagined the sleepovers I'd have in my big princess castle. Violus would be there, along with Erris, and Arial— her memory was weak for the others, but I'd never forget.

The shiver came again, shaking the image of the castle from my thoughts so that I was alone in the dark. I heard voices, but they weren't in my mind. They were coming from right outside my box. The Breakers were close, so I ran. I didn't have feet to run on, but I pictured a road, putting as much distance between myself and the voices as I could.

I only stopped when I heard my name whispered in the dark.

33 –Laura

W isdom?"
Hello, Laura.

I could hardly call it a voice. It was more like an echo that started at one end of the abyss and reverberated across the room and right through my mind.

I can't see you.

There's nothing to see. I don't have a body like the rest of you. Her voice was high and tinny, almost like that of a child.

I remembered the voice from before. *You're the little girl from the field.*

Yes. I spun; the voice was to my left now. I thought she was only in my head and not in this hallway in my dreams, but it was hard to be sure.

How did you know that stuff about Wade? About the stolen movies and all that?

A child's giggle tickled my ear. *The world's a fool if they think the Internet keeps secrets.*

What did that mean? *You could like, see his search history or something?* I asked, sure I was reaching.

Yes, Laura. Something like that.

I had more questions but didn't know how long I would have with her. *Lennox told me I needed to find you.*

Yes. I've been searching for you for a long time. You were more difficult to visit than the others.

I was? Why?

In a lot of ways, you're stronger than the rest of us. It's easier for you to hide.

Even stronger than Lennox?

I thought I heard her chuckle, but it was probably my imagination. *Yes, even stronger than Lennox.*

I don't feel very strong.

No one ever expected you to be before. You just need practice.

I guess that's true. It was too dark to see. I tried to turn on the lights, but all I saw were shadows. One leaped from the wall and slithered past like a snake. *Where are you?* I asked. *What's it like there?*

The hair on my arms stood tall. I felt like Wisdom was standing right behind me, looking over my shoulder, ready to yell "boo!" I spun, but no one was there.

A light came on at the end of the hall. It blinked, threatening to go out. *Wait! Don't go!*

Relax, whispered Wisdom. *Pretend like you're falling asleep.*

Wisdom's world was unlike anything I could have prepared myself for. I shed my body and broke into a million streams of light before diving into the thick cables strung across the concrete floor.

We passed the place I understood to be her home—a box mounted to the wall. That was where her mind lived, yes, but it wasn't where it stayed.

Wisdom's world was wasted. Its bygone buildings had been reduced to rubble, which I zoomed over, following the serpentine path to a land of infinite possibilities. The real world lived in the grooves of this network, and I saw trees of every color, from blue cedars to violet firs.

Creatures danced around me, their fur glittering in shades of pink and purple. It was as if the vintage Lisa Frank notebook

I carried around as a small child had come to life.

A panda bear waved as we flew past, his fur deep plum instead of black. Puppies and kittens sauntered by, some standing taller than I was, their bodies adorned with brightly colored flowers. A bunny covered in green and turquoise tiger stripes hopped by carrying an Easter basket.

A neon moon and stars shone in the sky, as did the colorful shapes of planets with rings like Saturn. In the distance, I saw the outline of the *Starship Enterprise* and watched as dolphins leaped from glittering golden rivers beneath an emerald sunset. It was a place of monsters and elves, where cats had wings and unicorns were real.

But only here. Wisdom's mind was whatever she wanted, a portal to limitless imagination so vivid I smelled candy in the air. It had been forever since I tasted candy, other than Morris' chocolate bait, but here Wisdom ate it for breakfast, lunch, and dinner.

She lived in a literal dream, but a sense of haunting loneliness clouded my thoughts.

I asked, *Where is everyone?*

Wherever they want to be, the disembodied voice whispered in my ear. The world was fading, the technicolor images growing dim and gray. The green sky shattered overhead, and I was alone in a cold room. A refrigerator. The kind you could walk into like they had in the kitchen at TIR.

Metal boxes like freezers lined the room, glass doors in front displaying the sleeping bodies inside.

But really, this is where we are.

What happened here? I asked.

In my world, Venkin was known as the Vanquisher. Shortly after he unleashed his machine on us, 99% of our population was dead. This is all that's left of mankind. Our bodies wait here while our minds run free. We're waiting for someone to bring our world back.

I slowly walked past the pods on legs I only imagined.

How do you do it? I wondered. *How can you go wherever you want?*

Practice. And patience. Sometimes, it takes a while to get things right. That's why it took me so long to find you. I never really had anyone to teach me either.

But you can go anywhere?

Anywhere with lights or currents—anything like that.

I guess I'd found my computer hacker.

You were the one outside Wade's shop.

I needed you to be safe, Laura. You're very important to me.

My mother, I whispered, recognizing Carol's face frozen behind the glass. I saw Dawson and Amanda. There was Jessica, and beside her Shannon and Gina; even that creep Rowan had been preserved. No names were on the glass, but each had been sketched with a serial number.

I stopped, seeing Wade's familiar face staring back at me. *Wade's here?*

They all are. Everyone here . . . is a Shadow, like us.

Wade was like me? My heart pounded.

My gaze lingered on him. He looked so peaceful there, trapped in the ice.

Is this you? I asked when I reached the last pod in the line. The tube was mostly empty, being occupied by no more than a baby; the little girl was floating in clear liquid behind a metal plate etched with a row of numbers and the letter "L."

Yes. The Virus happened the year I was born. I was put here right away, but others got to age before the Vanquisher froze them. Only the people who worked in this building were spared.

We pulled out of the room and stood outside. It looked to be the only structure standing for miles. Above the door, a sign read, "Tomlinson Institute of Research."

TIR was in Wisdom's world too?

It's here. This place is the key. The Vanquisher's coming for you, Laura. For all of us. It's only a matter of time before Earth and every other world looks just like this.

What did they do here?

She didn't answer me, but she didn't have to. The wasteland of Wisdom's world changed before my eyes. I watched as towering buildings rose from the ashes and people filled the streets.

This isn't an illusion, she said. *It's a memory. The oldest one I have.*

A lively city appeared where total destruction had lain before. The sky overhead was a lovely blue, and there wasn't a cloud in sight.

But then, I heard a thunderclap so loud, I looked to the sky, expecting to see the Four Horsemen of the Apocalypse.

First, the wind picked up, and with it came rain. Snow started to fall from clouds that hadn't been there seconds before. It came down in the fattest flakes I'd ever seen, filling the streets and burying the people.

The snow stopped, and the air turned hot. I felt the heat so intensely on my skin, I knew I would be a sweaty mess when I woke up in my sleeping bag.

With the heat, the snow melted into a river.

What was left was a city molded by the crazy weather, but it still stood. It looked nothing like the wasteland Wisdom lived in now.

Venkin did this. He was trying to save his world, but in the end, he became the monster himself.

What happened next? How did your world become like this?

Wisdom zoomed in, and as we flew through the front doors like phantoms, the building changed. TIR was bigger and scarier than I'd ever seen it, and I knew I was seeing the Dark World because of the thick layer of frost on the linoleum. *Eighteen years ago*, Wisdom told me.

I saw a man I could only guess to be Morris, but he looked . . . different, somehow. His skin color was a bit off, his white hair wilder than ever. He was standing over a line of steel bassinets similar to those pictured in the article Wade showed me.

Wisdom brought us close, and I recognized her as soon as I glanced into the first bassinet. A tiny baby, hair pitch-black, eyes purple, and those scars . . .

This is Lennox's memory, Wisdom explained. *I like to hold on to it, to remember what I'm fighting for. Someone has to pay for what happened to my world.*

Morris bent over baby Lennox, a taser held in his hand.

"No!" I shouted, my voice stopping short in the mind I shared with Wisdom.

Morris' taser struck the tiny baby, who let out a heartbreaking scream. Again and again, he jabbed her until the cries no longer sounded human.

I squeezed my eyes shut, refusing to see more, but Wisdom pried them open, showing me a new room instead.

Clean white walls and the smell of bleach came with this new memory. I recognized it immediately as TIR, where a more familiar Dr. Morris examined a row of infants in matching bassinets. I couldn't see the children. I could only hear their screams.

This is from today. The experiments haven't stopped. They won't until Venkin gets all the answers he's looking for. They need you, Laura. Wisdom's voice was fading away. *We need you to go back to TIR. To save us.*

34-Violus

For eighteen annuals, I'd gathered with the other Blessed Children born in this part of the world, though I was the eldest. The others born my year had been chosen long ago, and the lingering drought ensured there were few younglings.

We gathered inside Shade's Healing Center, to avoid the roasting sun. The crowded gathering was necessary for the drawing of lots as there were few buildings that could house so many Blessed.

The day before the ceremony was a time for preparation and completing the necessary rituals to prepare the Blessed Children for the next year. If the rain came during a ceremony, it was the Prophets' belief it would stay, and there would be no more gatherings like these.

I spotted Jessec in a group of midlifings who gathered together on the far side of the hut. The midlifings laughed and shared excited whispers. Most Blessed Children would be chastised for displaying such rude behavior at a somber event, but the midlifings received a pass. They represented the fifteen to seventeen-year-olds, halfway through the predicted lifespan on the Dry World, who would be married off to Healers if their names were not drawn this annual.

My place was with the younglings I mentored. A girl named Domina sat beside me. She'd been in my group of younglings for every one of her eight years—for even the new ones could be chosen for the ceremony. If their parents drew lots for them, of course.

Domina was shaking nervously. Most children were ecstatic about the idea of being part of the historic Rain Ceremony. But sometimes, fear wriggled its way in before a Blessed Child's confidence could. I pulled Domina close, whispering encouragements in her ear.

Mama and I traveled from nearby, but the other children had traveled a great distance, and Reapers had captured many who would have been here to draw lots while on their way.

"I don't want to leave my mother," Domina said, gesturing toward the bald woman talking to Shade near the flap of the tent. "She's been very lonely since my father passed."

"Me neither." A young boy squished his chin into his hands. "I can't stand the thought of making Mama sad. My brother was chosen only an annual ago. I still hear her cries at night."

My eyebrows scrunched. It was disappointing to hear these youngling's parents had failed to prepare them for their duty.

"A necessary sacrifice," I told the younglings. "If you are chosen, your parents will mourn, yes. But then, they will rejoice! For a new generation will be built from your offering."

A few children smiled, but Domina's eyes were faraway and sad.

A heavy tension lay over the packed room, mingled with warm air and the scent of incense. The first activity was the Naming, and I recited a silent prayer for Jessec as she asked the Prophets to change her from Jessec to Jessecus.

Healer Shade lifted Jessecus' fist to the crowd. "Another dreamer." He dipped his head. "A Blessed like us."

A line of robed Healers took turns singing prayers and telling stories about Rain Ceremonies' past. The procession of tales seemed to take forever, and I was as restless as the younglings when it finally came time to draw lots.

"And with the drought came the Reapers." Shade wore a pair of spectacles pinned to a beaded chain around his neck. He read from one of the sacred tomes the Healers spent their lives collecting. "We all serve the Prophets, even the Reapers. Though they appear as a blemish in their design, we know this cannot be true. For as the wolf must keep the elk from overrunning the land, so the Reapers maintain the great balance."

My eyes were closed, hand squeezed tight in Mama's. I'd heard the story over and over, but I considered every reading a gift. I only knew what "wolves" and "elk" were from studying the ancient tomes. It was with these great stories I was able to imagine what my Dry World could be—and remember what it once was.

"Every annual, the Prophets release the Reapers from where they hide underground. Their existence ensures only those in the Prophets' favor survive." Shade held up a wooden bowl filled with slender white sticks. "Tonight, we'll find the Blessed Child the Prophets favor most."

Each child took their turn drawing from the bowl, all coming up with a chunk the size of my end finger. I held my breath on my turn, hand frozen over the bowl.

My heart slammed in the rhythm of a procession drum. My breathing was heavy, packed with the dread a lifetime of disappointment had brought. As I reached for the bowl, I thought of what waited for me if I wasn't chosen this year.

I glanced at Shade. His sacred duty was to prepare me for my part in the ceremony—whatever that may be—but Shade held another role in my life. If I wasn't selected this year, I'd be married off to the Healer of Mama's choice, in the hopes that my offspring would be the one to bring rain. Mama might have thought Shade a fine man, and I'm sure that he was—but I certainly didn't love him, and I had no plans for a union.

My fingers dug through the pile of little twigs, attempting to feel the length of each one. With no leads, I whispered a prayer to the Prophets and pulled a twig loose.

Shade's jaw hung slack, but he quickly pulled it back into place, and then . . . he smiled. He threw his hands up, turning to my parents in delight. My father and Amanus beamed, their little son clapping for me excitedly.

I looked down. My fingers were wrapped around a slender white twig twice the length of the others.

"I-I've been chosen!" I said, joy rising through my bare feet and traveling all the way through me. "Praise the Prophets!"

I kneeled in front of Mama. Her leathery hands were at her mouth, and tears showed around her eyes, but when Mama pulled her hands back, I saw they were happy tears. "Oh, Violus," she whispered, grabbing hold of me tight. "I'm so proud."

Not every face in the room was happy. Nor their tears. The Blessed Children, all hopeful, would be greatly disappointed they hadn't been chosen. They had all studied, learning the ways and the stories as I did. But their disappointment would not sway my excitement. For their years were few, and at the next ceremony, the Prophets would have other plans for me.

It was hard to concentrate. There was a painful nudge in my mind. It started as a little headache, annoying but harmless, but quickly erupted into a ruthless inferno that threatened to consume my skull.

A scream escaped from my lips, and I fell, grasping my face with both hands. I felt as if I was being torn apart cell by cell, and although my mouth was open wide, my screams were far away, echoing from another world.

The dark room turned bright, and the tall gray buildings of Earth appeared. Snow was falling hard on them, piling high in the streets until I couldn't see the buildings at all.

The snow started to melt, and for a moment, the roofs of

the buildings showed. Then, the air grew warm and chunks of ice—big as boulders—tumbled away, crashing to the ground and smashing the people below. The air was hot . . . so hot all of the snow melted at once. I heard a thunderous crash and looked up, seeing a wall of water rushing down the street.

In horror, I watched as the water washed all of the people away.

"Violus! Violus!"

Someone shook me awake. I lay on the floor of the little adobe hut. My hand flew to my right thigh, where a lingering pain ached from a phantom wound. My skin felt hot there, but the pain soon faded, leaving nothing but a scar.

My clothes were soaked through with sweat, and my heart was pounding out an unsteady rhythm.

"I saw rain!" I cried, allowing Shade to pull me to my feet.

At my words, a gasp traveled through the room. The Healers came closer, surrounding me there within the small hut.

"Oh, Violus, that's wonderful!" Shade pulled me close, his strong arms tightening around me. He slid a hand over my bald head. "I knew you were ready. 'Tis a sign when you can find the Wet World."

Had I though? What I saw . . . It was different from the places I visited in my waking dreams. I hadn't crossed over. I had experienced a premonition.

I turned away from Shade, clutching my hands nervously at my sides. My stomach quivered, and I felt a great gaping emptiness there. Hunger pains. I bent, clutching at my gut. I'd gone hungry most of my life. Barely any food could be found in the Dry World. It was why the few villages that remained had settled so far apart. But after the waking dreams, I always became painfully aware of my ravishing hunger. It was the only thing I truly despised about my calling.

Shade stepped forward, humming a tune. The other Healers hummed the melody with him, and their haunting song spread through me, filling the void in my stomach, easing the worry in my heart.

I blinked, letting my eyes adjust to the flickering candles that illuminated the hut.

Shade reached out, taking my hands in his. "I know you can do this. So do the Prophets; that's why they chose you." His hands squeezed tighter around mine. "It will only work if you are prepared. Are you ready to fulfill your destiny, Violus?"

I thought about the year before and my disappointment about not being chosen for the Rain Ceremony. This was everything I ever wanted. To be special.

"Yes, Healer Shade. I'm ready. I've been waiting for this all of my life."

A twinge of disappointment flared up in the back of my mind. Disappointment so distant, I knew it could only be from someone else.

So, you've made your choice. I heard her distinct voice among my own thoughts. She wasn't asking. She knew my heart as well as I did. *I don't blame you. In the end, we'll all have to choose which world to save.*

35–Laura

Wade hadn't woken yet, and I sat watching him sleep for a long while. Sunlight burned through the windows, highlighting the patches of facial hair that covered his face and neck. I still hadn't figured out what kind of bird he would be. A robin? A sea bird? Perhaps a sparrow of some sort?

I'd barely slept past sunrise for as long as I could remember. The places I lived were always filled with the clamor of attendants first thing in the morning when their coffee was fresh and they hadn't grown to hate the day yet.

Wade looked like he would have no problem sleeping through the day, and I gave him a soft kick to get things moving.

He squirmed in his sleeping bag but didn't rouse. "Wade!" I jabbed him again. This time, he rolled, releasing an audible fart that made him grin with pride in his sleep.

"Disgusting," I said, grinning too. I got up and roamed while he slept. Mice had gotten to the pantry, and I didn't dare check the fridge, as there was no power in the house, anyway.

I felt rested, like I'd experienced the kind of sleep impossible to get in a place like TIR or Clover Center. It was a miracle I'd gotten any sleep, as Baby Lennox's shrill screams were still ringing in my ears.

I'd tried not to think of Dr. Morris much since my escape. I had plenty else to worry about. But now, I couldn't stop thinking about him—the crazy penfocaled Morris who tortured Erris back on Rat Island and now the terrifying version of him that Lennox grew up with. And Wisdom wanted to send me back to him.

I parted the dusty blinds and wiped the grime from my fingertips before peering through. A black and white police car cruised by, and panic rose in my gut. The screams were back; they were getting louder—

"There you are," Wade said, causing me to jump away from the window.

I turned, surprised at the subtle happiness that crept in at the sight of him. "Hey, I was starting to worry about you." I snuck another glimpse through the blinds, seeing the cruiser was gone. It was a big city. Of course, I was going to see police. I really would drive myself crazy if I got paranoid about every passing copper. I wondered if Venkin had put me on the news yet.

Wade chuckled. "I like my beauty sleep."

Self-conscious, I ran a hand through my own messy hair. "I think I could have used some more."

His cheeks flushed hot pink, and his mouth fell open and then closed again.

"Am I embarrassing you?" I flashed him a smirk.

He avoided my eye. "I just don't hang out with cute girls too often. Especially not ones with superhuman personalities living inside of them."

I snorted. "Is that what you think about me?" I asked in surprise. I turned away before my face was as pink as his. Wade didn't need to know how rare compliments were for me.

He raised an eyebrow. "Would you prefer I considered

you a murderer?" Wade was joking, but the words stung. He noticed. "Oh, I'm sorry Laura. You know I didn't mean—"

I waved him off and glanced through the blinds again. "We should get going."

"Oh? Do we have a plan now?"

I nodded. "I visited Wisdom last night. She told me what we need to do."

I expected Wade to question me—ask about Wisdom's world or my dreams—but he didn't. He pulled a thin wallet from his pocket and flipped it open, revealing the few crumpled bills inside, and saying the words every girl loves to hear. "Mind if we get something to eat first?"

***

After breakfast, Wade and I set up in the local library. I loved the musty smell of books here, where dust had been allowed to accumulate. The books I'd read at Clover Center were stored in air-tight totes, only a case at a time brought out for us to choose from. "There were fewer messes that way," Dr. Z had said.

Wade's laptop was propped open in front of him, and his fingers flying over the keys.

I studied his pasty face and dark mop of hair, following the trail of curls under his collar.

"I got it!" I said, earning a confused look from Wade. "I can't believe I didn't see it before! You're obviously an emperor penguin."

He paused. "Huh?"

"If you were a bird, you'd be an emperor penguin, it's so simple."

"If I were a bird?" he raised an eyebrow.

"Sorry, it's this thing I've done since I was a kid. It's like my way of remembering people . . . and their quirks."

"And I'm . . ."

"An emperor penguin."

"Huh." He nodded. "Why, exactly?"

"No real reason. Your shape, your demeanor . . ."

He flinched.

"No! It's a good thing," I assured him. "I love penguins."

"Oh." Wade looked pleased. He typed something on his laptop, then turned the screen my way to reveal a picture of a Surakav, better known as the hummingbird that changes color every second. "Then this is you."

I laughed, appreciating the similarities. "It's true. You never know who I'll be second to second."

He only shook his head, returning his gaze to the screen in front of him.

Wade had checked out a guest computer for me, and I stared at the waiting search bar, my index finger hovering over the letter "T."

"T-O-M-L," I whispered to myself, my own clumsy fingers stabbing awkwardly at the keys.

This is going to take forever. I looked around the warm room, where everyone from college students to vagrants were taking advantage of the free air conditioning. The fans overhead rattled loudly, signaling it was only a matter of time before the cooling unit gave out completely.

I watched a girl of about eight as she played with a stack of dominoes at the table across from us. Her clothes were baggy and outdated, and her frizzy ponytail suggested that her hair hadn't received a good combing in a while.

A woman I assumed to be her mother sat beside her; her hands jumpy as she filled out paperwork. I studied the little girl's face, wondering if I'd ever visited the library with my own mother.

I couldn't remember if I had, but a long-lost memory came to me that I had visited the library before, as Violus.

As I watched the little girl stand the dominoes on end, she began to change. The room shifted, and the sunlight filtering through the windows went dark as night took over on the Dry World.

I was in a large building on Dry Beds. Rusted ladders were mounted on the walls, replacing the library's bookshelves.

The rungs were heaped with books bound in leather, and although I couldn't make out the embossed spines, I already knew them to be history books. The Blessed studied the history of more than just their own world, and as my thoughts merged with Violus', I sensed that plenty of the tomes in the room contained stories about Earth's past as well.

The little girl's ratty ponytail was gone and her bald head covered by the same makeshift bandana the rest of the people in the room wore. The dominoes had disappeared, and instead, she twirled a little twig in her hand, a sad look on her face.

Her mother leaned in. "It's all right, Domina. Perhaps next year you will be chosen for the ceremony?"

Domina wiped a tear that wiggled from the corner of her eye. "I know, Mama."

I stood up as Violus went to speak to the girl. She settled next to Domina and took her chin in her hand. "Domina, are you unhappy that I was chosen instead of you?"

"Of course not, Violus. You deserve this! It's only that I wish I could help as well. I feel like I'm ready." She lowered her eyes. "Although not quite ready to leave Mama."

"I've waited a long time to be chosen. I studied for many years."

Domina gave a somber nod. "I know."

My arm wrapped around Domina's shoulders. "And I spent many Rain Ceremonies crying because I hadn't been chosen. But someday, all of the Blessed Children will do their part." My mouth opened and Violus began to sing a song I hadn't heard since I was a child.

"Blessed Children roving every land,
Come heal together, hand-in-hand.
Beseech your hearts to bring the rain,
To wash the dust and heal our pain."

Someone gripped my shoulders. "Laura!"

I opened my eyes; I had dozed off. I glanced over at the table where the little girl was watching me with her mouth open wide, her dominoes scattered all over the floor.

Wade's hand was still gripping my shoulder. "Um, Laura. You were just singing to this young lady."

My hand shot to my mouth. "Oh my gosh, I'm so sorry."

The girl's mother looked horrified. She tugged on her daughter's arm, pulling her toward the exit. *My singing voice must be horrible.* The girl stayed frozen, watching me with eyes far too wise for her age.

"That song! Mommy, I've heard it before!"

Her mother cast me an angry glare and dragged her out the door, muttering, "Shut it, Dominique! I told you not to talk like that."

The other patrons in the library gaped at me.

I mumbled another apology as I tried to disappear behind the slim laptop monitor.

Wade glanced around, tilting his screen toward me when the onlookers returned to their books. Apparently, spontaneous musicals weren't too out of the norm around here.

"I've been through the website twice. I don't know what Wisdom thinks we're going to find at TIR, but short of turning you in at the front gate, I have no idea how we're gonna get in."

I slumped back in my seat. "I went to the Dry World. I saw that girl and her mom there, that's why I started singing."

"Was I there?"

I raised an eyebrow at him. "I don't know. Would you be jealous if you weren't?" I teased, holding my smile.

He sighed dramatically. "You know I would be."

I let the grin break free.

"Well, you weren't there. Not that I saw, anyway. Violus and that girl were discussing something—some sort of ceremony the little girl had been chosen for."

A *ding!* sounded from my computer. I looked down to see a yellow envelope flashing on the screen.

Wade scooted closer. "That's weird. Who would be messaging you?"

"No idea." I opened the message, finding a single word:

Run.

I hadn't seen the Black Coats arrive. I scanned the room,

noticing several new faces blocking the library exits. A few were facing outward, making sure nobody else came in. Their dark jackets read "TIR" in silver letters across the back.

I reached under the table to clasp Wade's clammy hand and squeezed tight, watching as the nearest Black Coat approached. Her fingers twitched at her hip, and I suspected she was fingering a gun handle.

"Laura?" she asked.

I opened my mouth, but Wade interrupted. "Never heard of her," he mumbled, eyes glued to the laptop screen.

The guard held back. "Excuse me?"

Wade turned with an impatient huff. "You're looking for someone named Laura? Well, we've never heard of her." He swiveled back to the screen.

I bit my lip, trying my hardest to focus on my own screen. My leg bounced like crazy beneath the table, and my sweat mixed with Wade's where our fingers were still entangled.

The lights were blinking overhead. I was having a hard time staying grounded, but I wouldn't let the others pull me away now that I was so close to freedom.

The TIR guard glanced between us. She looked over her shoulder, where another guard was checking their phone, probably looking for my picture. It had been a while since I'd had a picture taken. Maybe they wouldn't recognize me?

I tried to relax. I thought of Lennox, but only of her face. I'd only seen her reflection once, but I could imagine it well enough.

The guard stepped closer, her own phone in her hand now.

"Miss, you need to come with me. You're—" she stopped. "Hey, did you have those scars a minute ago?" Her eyes narrowed. "And your hair . . ."

Wade's mouth was dangling open. He snapped it shut. "How dare you! My girlfriend was born like this! Now get the hell out of here or I'll call the real cops on you." He started gathering his stuff while the confused guard stared on. "Come on, let's go."

I stood, stopped by a rush to the head. My skull ached. The lights grew bright and hummed so loud I had to put my hands over my ears.

"It's her!" a Black Coat cried. "She's changing again!"

The woman reached for me, and Wade cocked his fist back, swiveling to sock the male guard behind her instead. "I don't hit girls!" he explained when he saw my bewildered look.

"Well, I do," I threw my fist, catching the older lady in the cheek. She staggered back but quickly recovered. My fighting skills were seriously lacking without Lennox.

The guard's fist connected with my nose, and black spots took over my vision.

"Little help, Wade?" I called.

Wade responded with a grunt as he grappled with the male guard, who was clearly winning.

The Black Coats were closing in on us. Hands gripped my shoulders; I saw the flash of cuffs.

I tried to kick out, but my foot was caught by a Black Coat who gave it a rough tug. I thought of Lennox as I fell, but when my head slammed against the linoleum floor, I was still on Earth.

"Lennox!" I screamed out loud.

I tried to get to my feet but was stopped by the force of the full-grown man as he collapsed on top of me. I saw stars as all of the Black Coat's weight crushed down on my chest.

I gasped and wheezed but couldn't scream. *I can't breathe.* I smelled the man's dirty hair and the stink of his pits as he wriggled over me, slowly squeezing the life from my lungs.

Stop! Let me up!

My fingertips flailed, but he didn't acknowledge the little slaps against his arms as I tried to tap out.

"Get off her you mammoth!" Wade cried "You're gonna hurt her!"

He was. He was killing me.

Panicked screams erupted as library patrons clamored to figure out what was going on.

"Is this girl under arrest?" asked a voice I recognized to belong to the librarian we'd met on the way in. "You don't look like police officers."

I was losing consciousness fast. I was desperate for air and knew I was seconds from being drowned by some guard's B.O.—what a way to die.

The Black Coat who was crushing me turned to her. "Ma'am, we've got the situation under control." When he lifted his head, I took the opportunity to slam my skull against his jaw. The guard yelped and rolled off me.

I climbed to my feet, struggling to stay upright as the room began to spin. "Wade!"

He stepped forward, catching me before I hit the ground again. Then, he dropped me in the closest chair. He grabbed a book from the table and chucked it at another Black Coat, smacking the guard in the face.

We both froze at the sound of a gun being cocked.

"Stop right there," said a deep voice. "I don't know who you are, but you're not police. Step away from the young lady." The Black Coats circled. I looked back at my savior, a graying man in bifocals who had a faded flame tattoo poking out from under his sleeve.

He pointed his gun at the nearest Black Coat. "I'm well trained to use this," he said, his voice steady. "I'm sure you're trained with your weapons too, but I've got mine out." He glanced between me and Wade, who was glaring at the Black Coats like a chihuahua growling at a pit bull from behind its owner.

"We don't want any trouble, Old Timer." The Black Coat stepped toward us, hands raised. "But that little girl you're protecting is wanted for murder."

"In that case, call the cops. But I'm giving her a head start whether you like it or not." He turned to me and nudged his head toward the door. "So, what are you waiting for?"

36-Violus

A haunting quiet hung over the atheneum, where dozens of Blessed Children gathered to study the Prophets' sacred tomes in anticipation of the Rain Ceremony. I had come as soon as I left Shade's Healing Center, excited to read through the almanacs of years past. Part of the ritual included reciting the details of major storms that had happened in the past in the hopes the memories would stimulate the clouds. There were no operating hours in the atheneum, which was open to the Blessed at all hours of the day.

I was more at home here than I ever had been in Dawsonus' hut or any village I stayed at with Mama. These tomes were full of culture and heritage—a piece of the world that had existed before the droughts.

I rubbed the little white twig between my fingers. I hadn't let it be all eve, and it was nearly broken in half. Eighteen annuals old . . . and finally chosen.

My thoughts were interrupted by a loud bang at the atheneum doors. The wooden doors burst open, startling the Blessed Children bent over candle-lit tables.

"Reapers!" cried the Healer Shade, his face pale. "You must run, Violus! Hide! Now!"

Domina looked up at her mother. "Mama?"

"It's all right, let's go. Down to the ossuaries." Domina's mother caught my eye. "You first, Violus."

I stood on unsteady legs, surveying the surrounding shelves. "The tomes!"

The children were in hysterics. They scurried after their parents, following the Healers below ground.

I scrambled to the nearest shelf and pulled down an armful of leather-bound tomes before hurrying after the others. "Father!" I called, spotting him in the crowd.

"Violus, hurry. To the front of the line!" Father called. The group of scared children stood waiting, honoring me even now.

Shade shoved past, catching my elbow in his arm and dragging me along. "Move! Move it, child!" he yelled, pushing Domina aside so he could throw me through the narrow doorway where I lost the armful of books.

The sound of splitting wood erupted behind me as the Reapers made their way through the atheneum doors.

"Domina, where are you?" I spotted Domina's mama pushing her way through the chaos as we clamored for the ossuaries below ground. The frantic woman grasped my arm. "Have you seen my daughter?"

My mouth struggled to form words as I was washed along in the sea of bodies. "She's back there!" I cried as someone tugged me down the stone steps.

Behind me echoed screams and cries. The wails of the dying and the lamenting call of those who mourned those who were already dead.

I broke free from Shade and took off back through the crowd, darting around people as they desperately fled. I struggled against the flow, stopping at once when I entered the atheneum.

My gaze flickered around the room. Broken bodies laid

over the tables, crossbow bolts sticking from their backs. The ancient tomes were piled on the ground, grave markers for the unfortunate souls who had lingered behind to save them.

A few Healers held off the Reapers. Some swung bats, and I saw one wielding a scythe. The Reapers towered over the smaller Healers, the intimidating spikes on their onyx helmets brushing the ceiling. Each Reaper came armed, and though never much for violence myself, I longed to get my hands on Mama's crossbow to help even the fight.

My attention broke from the standoff when I heard a sob in the corner. "Mama!" Domina wailed, clutching her mother's blood-stained tunic over her like a shield.

"Violus, watch out!" Shade screamed from the doorway.

Thunk!

I swiveled to see the Reaper's crossbow bolt cemented in the wood paneling inches from my head.

Thunk! Even closer.

"No!" Domina sobbed, pushing her mother's body aside. "Not the Chosen One!"

Time stopped. I watched in horror as Domina leaped to her feet. She rushed toward me, her body moving slowly as the seconds ticked by like hours.

The scream hadn't even left my lips when the little girl staggered in front of me, face frozen in surprise.

Shade's hands slid beneath my armpits. He lifted me into the air, turning and tossing me down the steps before I had a chance to watch Domina's body fall. I tumbled down, gasping as my ribs were battered by the stone walls.

Shade closed the doors behind us, plunging the stairwell into darkness. He dropped the drawbar into place just as something heavy slammed against the door, threatening to bust it from its hinges.

"Stupid girl!" Shade screamed, grabbing the back of my tunic and hauling me down the dark steps toward the amber glow of candlelight.

"Violus!" Father stepped from the shadows, an equally disappointed look on his face. "How could you be so foolish and run off like that?"

Shade shook me by the collar. "You risk the life of the

Chosen One to save some little girl? May the Prophets' wrath forgive you for your impertinence!"

Some little girl? Anger welled up inside me at the insensitive remark. The Prophets' wrath be damned. The day before, I was no different than that little girl. Now, I was alive and Domina wasn't. All because a stick had decided I was "chosen."

I didn't have long to dwell on it, disturbed by the rattling door at the top of the steps. The smell of smoke leaked through the cracks and wafted down the stairs.

"The tomes!" I cried, turning back. Father gave me a hard shove forward, and Shade held my arm tightly. The two men I trusted dragging me toward the city of bones.

Cries met me at the end of the tunnel, where the Blessed Children hurried to light the torches mounted on the ossuary walls. The Healers led us through the winding tunnels. We marched toward an opening somewhere on the other side where we could only hope the Reapers weren't already waiting.

Sorrow filled my heart over Domina's death, but I wouldn't voice my agony. I wouldn't share my doubts.

When the tunnel forked in five directions, the crowd split up. I was pulled right, with Shade on one side and my father on the other as they marched on, never letting me stumble.

Screams echoed through the stone tunnels as the Reapers made their way into the ossuaries. The screams hushed as the Reapers lay waste to whoever was unfortunate enough to be caught in the tunnel they chose to storm first.

We passed little windows carved into the walls, revealing ancient piles of bones. I never looked back, even as screams started up again somewhere to my left.

I was the Chosen One. I was all that stood between life and an entire generation reduced to bones.

At least that was what I had always been told.

37–ERRIS

I woke with a start. I was curled in a ball on the ground, my clothes soaked through with mud, rain, and piss.

"Violus!" I called out, clutching my arms and rubbing them vigorously, although it brought me no warmth or comfort.

I lay back in my bed of mud, letting the dreams fade away. Violus was being hunted in my dreams. I hadn't dreamed of her since I was a girl, but in the last couple of days, I had lived through her eyes every time I went to sleep.

Violus had been chosen for her ceremony, and my dreams revolved around her preparations. I didn't know if it was because of my fever, or because of Morris' breakthroughs, but I'd barely held onto consciousness all day.

"Hey, you girl," a voice hissed through the bars of my cage. "Yer the one Morris has been courting, aren't ya?" My fevered gaze traveled upward. I didn't recognize the older man who watched me, but I did recognize the red flames inked on his forearm. He was a Raider.

My first instinct was to shrink back. Everything Daddy,

Cici, and Instructor Zera had ever told me reinforced my belief that the Raiders were bad. Thieves. Pirates.

"Entitled Pricks who think they're above the law," Daddy had called them. "Why can't they just pick an island and hold onto it like the rest of us?"

I wasn't so sure now, though. All I saw was a man outside my cage who knew how to sail a boat.

"Ain't nobody courting me," I said. "'Specially not Morris."

"Aye," the Raider said, watching me a long while. "That girl, Jackie. She told me to come get ya. Said ya looked to be in bad shape, and I'd say she's right. You look like death, little girl."

I felt that way too. My hand drifted over the white-hot sore on my leg, too tender for me to touch.

I heard a clink and looked up to see the padlock fall to the mud. The Raider pulled the cage door open. He bent down, scooping me up and helping me stand.

He didn't say another word, and I was happy because every step I took on my injured leg made me want to scream out. The short break that President Venkin's pills had given me made it all the worse when the pain inevitably returned. Prisoners called out as we weaved past the cages. Some asked to be freed, while others tried to alert the guards.

Too broken to care, I let their voices fade into the back of my weary mind.

A flash of red hair darted past me when we reached Prisoner's Point.

"Hiya," Jackie said, giving me an overenthusiastic wave.

I merely nodded, not wanting to exert myself further.

Jackie wrapped her arm around me and dragged me toward a waiting ship. The Raider man followed behind us, dousing the dock with the contents of a watering can.

The stench of kerosene mixed with the rain as I thought of my folks and the life we'd shared on Fox Island with the people I'd called friends. People like Zera and Hale.

I considered breaking free of Jackie and using the last of

my strength to go find my folks wherever they were being kept. I didn't even know if they were still alive. I didn't even know if they were still on Rat Island.

Flames spread over the dock, melting boards into the sea. "Daddy!" I called, sure I spotted him through the fire.

"Hush, Erris!" Jackie cried.

"Ma!" There she was, standing in the flames right next to Daddy. I had to be imagining it. It was only the fever. Some part of my mind knew this, but my voice wouldn't stop calling out.

Shapes were shouting from the far side of the burning dock.

I waved my free arm. "Daddy! I promise I ain't gonna leave without you!"

Jackie gave me a hard shake. "Shut yer mouth, you dingbat! Those ain't your folks, they're Gleaners comin' to fight the fire."

Gleaners! I came to my senses, realizing there might not be an opportunity like this again. Venkin wanted proof I was loyal. Well, this was my chance.

"Over here!" I howled, shaking my shackles over my head. "Raiders! They're making a getaway!"

"What are you doing?" Jackie dropped me with a frustrated scream.

Her scream turned to a gasp as the Gleaner's arrow stuck in her in the chest. Her body went rigid, and she tumbled from the dock and slipped into the water.

"No!" The Raider man howled, shoving me aside as he dove after her.

My feet slid over the kerosene-soaked dock, and I tumbled into the icy sea. *What had I done?* I didn't fight as I sunk toward the bottom of the ocean. Instead, I let my mouth open wide, welcoming the peace the water offered.

The weight of my betrayal filled me like lead, squeezing my lungs as tight as the crushing water.

Something swam past, and as my vision faded, I made out a black coat. A pair of arms wrapped around my stomach.

Higher and higher I went until I broke free of the water. He squeezed tight, forcing the water from my lungs.

I was thrown back on the muddy bank as my vision returned. The sopping mane of the black-eyed Gleaner hung over me, his rank smell soaking through my nostrils, even past the smoke and rain.

"Can't have you dying on us yet," he hissed. "President Venkin's got another deal for ya."

38-Lennox

I was dreaming of Arial. Wisdom taught me how to keep the memories away, but when it came to these memories . . . well, it just didn't feel right to bury them.

I was small in my dream. Five, probably. I was in a field, watching a twister rip across the ground. Lightning tore through the dark clouds, and cold rain drenched me, but I never looked away.

The force of the wind's screams hit like a wall, the pressure causing my ears to pop like fireworks. I smashed my hands flat against my ears, but the popping didn't stop.

"Arial, we need to run. The storm's gonna get us!"

No, Lennox, I heard her say, the small sweet voice I remembered so well. *The storm will never get me.*

The twister was getting close. There were no buildings left for it to destroy—no people left for it to kill. There was only me and Arial.

I was scared, but Arial wasn't. I couldn't recall her ever being frightened.

She wrapped her arms around herself, and I felt the hug soak all the way into my soul.

"Lennox!"

"What is it, Arial?" I asked, watching as the magnificent twister unraveled in the breeze. The winds stopped. The air was calm. A silence settled over the Windy World, and I knew that if I were to shout, my cry would be heard for miles—if anyone was left to hear it.

"Lennox!"

"It's not me. Laura's calling you. She wants you to come play."

"I don't want to."

"She needs you, Lennox. She's hurting."

"I don't want to go," I repeated, my own young voice cracking. "I don't want to hurt. I want to stay with you . . ."

"Lennox!" I opened my eyes, finding Fade leaning over me. My hand was wrapped around his collar and I released the fabric, allowing him to straighten up.

"Sorry," I mumbled, sitting up and squinting into the dark. "I was dreaming."

He nodded. "I could tell. Firestarter's almost here."

I stood, using the ice-painted wall to steady myself as a rush of dizziness took over and I glimpsed a brightly-lit room filled with bookshelves. *That's weird.*

I staggered across the room to a peephole Fade had melted in the ice. He handed me a pair of heat-sensing glasses. Looking through, I saw the hunched back of an old man making his way through the barren snowfield toward the abandoned lookout tower Fade and I had set up in. The spot was out in the open but only a day's journey to the Abyss.

I turned back, seeing Fade bent over the laptop in the corner. "How do you manage to keep those things working?"

"The computers?" Fade asked, eyes on the screen and fingers a blur. "It's my superpower." He winked at me. I felt a flutter at the flash of his face I saw behind his grizzled beard and heap of blankets. I pushed the butterflies down until they stopped stirring.

Feelings coursed through me at Fade's every glance. His touch—even his smell—drove me mad. But as with everything else, my feelings were just going to get someone hurt. Fade's parents had protected him—found him a place amongst the Crawlers early in life. It was nothing like what my family put me through. So far, I'd been the biggest risk in Fade's life.

A shallow hole had been dug in the snow that carpeted the floor. We patched the hole in the ceiling with packed ice and insulated the room with every spare pelt we could find. I kneeled beside the hole, busying myself melting snow into drinking water, and had a full pail when I heard Firestarter's signal below.

Fade poked his hand through the peephole and gestured for Firestarter to come up. By the time the old man had scaled the tower and climbed inside, half the pail of water was already frozen.

Firestarter didn't speak. Once he'd been a scientist, but his conscience had gotten the best of him, and the Crawlers had cut out his tongue before letting him leave the Abyss. He simply nodded to each of us and accepted the mug of water I offered before settling behind Fade's computer. I could see faded orange flames licking his wrist when his sleeve pulled away from his gloves.

Firestarter's face was lined with wrinkles and tufts of white hair poked from his hood, but his fingertips danced over the keys even faster than Fade's.

"Tomorrow," Fade said with a nod, reading over Firestarter's shoulder. "That's when we need to make our move. We want to stay as in sync with Laura as possible. We don't go back to the Abyss until she does."

A twinge. I still hadn't decided if I was sending Laura back to the Abyss. At the moment, I was more tempted to sneak onto a cargo ship and sail her off to an island somewhere. But Laura wasn't the only Shadow whose fate was in my hands. The others were out of time, too.

Beep.

We all froze as if someone had pushed the pause button on the old VCR back at Fade's ice cave.

"Go, Fade," I ordered.

"Maybe it's a false—"

Beep!

I pointed toward the ground. "Go."

Fade swallowed hard and nodded. He typed something into the laptop and slammed it shut. "A warning for Laura. Just in case." He climbed into the divot we'd carved in the center of the floor and jumped, stomping his heavy feet against the ice until a hole opened up beneath him, swallowing him into the ground.

I heard a muffled *thud!* when he landed at the bottom of the tunnel.

When he was gone, I kicked snow over the opening and ran my hand over it until the floor was smooth again.

Firestarter kept watch at the peephole. He held up a hand, showing me four fingers. Four Crawlers.

Beep!

Firestarter's glance slid to the beeping laptop.

Dammit. It would be weeks before Fade could get another one working. Hopefully, our mission would be complete before then. Or we'd be dead. I sighed and grabbed the laptop. I bent the screen back as far as it would go until the screen broke loose from the keyboard. I lifted it, slamming the bottom half against Fade's frost-covered desk until the computer was a pile of busted chunks, which I proceeded to bury in the snow. Firestarter was willing to make the sacrifice, but the Crawlers couldn't know Fade was here. They still thought he was on their side.

A hum filled the sky, and floodlights filtered through the patched roof as the heat-seekers circled overhead.

Lennox! I heard Laura's panicked cry in the back of my mind. She was in trouble, too.

Firestarter was still standing at the peephole. His back was rigid and tense, and when I focused on the sound of his heartbeats, they proved erratic.

"Firestarter?" He wouldn't turn to meet my stare. "What's going on?"

He stuck his hand through the peephole, flashing another signal. But it wasn't for me; it was for the Crawlers.

He'd set us up.

Lennox! I heard Laura cry again. I hadn't checked the messages before destroying Fade's computer. I had no idea how long she'd been trying to reach me. My skin felt hot, burning almost, and Erris and Violus' screams reached me next.

Sorry, you guys are going to have to be on your own for a little while.

The ceiling ripped away, and floodlights soaked the room, causing me to shrink back as the harsh light assaulted my eyes. Malicious had kept me in that dark box for so long; he still knew my greatest weakness.

I tried to cover my eyes, but nothing would keep the light out. The others' fear ricocheted through me. *Lennox, please!* Laura whispered. My mind flashed to a room filled with books, and I did everything I could to push her away.

Boom!

There was an eruption outside, and the lookout tower gave a threatening shake that sent me staggering back.

The humming grew louder, and I searched the blinding light for the source of the sound. I ducked out of the way just as a heat-seeker barreled through the hole in the roof. I swung my arm out of pure instinct, batting the drone away before the glowing laser light hit me. There was a scream as a beam of light struck Firestarter instead. He yelped, slapping uselessly at the flames that popped up where the laser had hit him. Good. That's what he got for being a traitor.

I grabbed hold of the little drone and chucked it through the peephole. I looked down, seeing the four Crawlers in black snowsuits already scaling the tower.

Their suits were clunky. They were fitted with lightweight padding to protect them from the grueling temperatures, and the bulges around their legs held deadly weapons. The Crawlers were moving slow, but once they got the red dot of their guns on me, I'd be done.

I faced Firestarter. "Did you sell us out?" I yelled over the hum. Another heat-seeker was coming in fast.

"Help me!" he mouthed as the flames traveled up his arms.

I shoved Firestarter into the snow, collapsing on top of him in the place Fade had disappeared through. I heaped snow over us until both of our bodies were covered, but Firestarter's head was still exposed.

He let out a muffled scream as he was struck again.

I yanked him down with me and domed the snow over our heads. "Do you want to stay down here?"

Firestarter nodded furiously.

"Did you sell Fade out?"

Firestarter paused. He shook his head once.

"Just me?"

He nodded.

Good. At least Fade still had a chance.

I straightened up, bracing my feet on either side of the hole so my knees created an "M." I slipped my arms around Firestarter's waist and hoisted him over my head, breaking free of the makeshift igloo. Firestarter went limp as the heat-seeker's beam finished him.

I stomped, feeling the snow shift under me. I jumped again, and the snow gave way a few more inches.

I saw light as someone pulled Firestarter's body loose from the hole. He was replaced a second later by the black mask of a Crawler. "I found the Shadow!" The Crawler called over his shoulder.

I reached up and grabbed the Crawler's shoulders, giving him my sweetest smile. "Yeah, you did, Big Boy." I stomped again, knocking the last of the snow free from the hole. I dropped into the narrow tunnel, pulling the Crawler with me.

The three-story fall went fast with the Crawler's heavy body. Once, there had been a ladder in the tunnel, but it was entombed in the ice long ago. I landed in the crater Fade had left at the base of the tower. The full weight of the Crawler's body fell on me, crushing my chest and squeezing the breath from my body. I groaned, choking on my blood.

The Crawler climbed off me and I felt the air return to

my lungs.

"You're okay, Lennox," I heard Arial say. "You're strong."

I don't want to be. I want to go with you.

Get up, Lennox. It wasn't Arial, after all. It was Wisdom.

"You all right down there?" someone yelled from above.

I was being pulled to my feet. "I've got her," the Crawler lifted his head, calling up to his buddy. "I'll meet you down—"

I was strong. I remembered now.

I slid my hand over his cheek and slipped two fingers into his mouth. I jerked my arm, slamming the man's skull against the wall of the icy tunnel. I shook my fingers loose. He collapsed at my feet and didn't get back up.

"Man down!" I called, fidgeting with the trapdoor. I tore it open and stumbled out into the snow tunnel Fade and I had dug the night before. I shut the door behind me, unsure which way the Crawlers planned to follow.

There was a thump on the other side. *Oh, goody.*

I was hurt, but I could move, which meant I could fight.

The door burst open and the first Crawler stumbled after me. "Where you going, Shadow?"

I wrapped my arms around his neck, pulling him toward me as I brought my right knee up in a hard jab to the throat. His hands flew to his neck, and he staggered back, gasping for air.

Where were the other two? I spun and ran from the tower. The Crawler lumbered after me, yelling for me to stop in strangled whispers.

The hum grew louder. The heat-seekers were hot on my trail. Something smashed through the wall of the snow tunnel, and I stopped, watching as the hatchet broke through again. It stuck in the ice, and the Crawler outside struggled to pull it free. I grabbed the ax handle and wrestled it from his hand.

He was only confused for a moment. I swung the hatchet back on him, catching him in the right arm.

"Ahh!" he screamed, falling to the snow, his remaining

hand shaking over the mangled remains of his arm.

I stuck my head through the opening the hatchet had created, spotting the last Crawler heading my way.

A pair of hands slipped around my waist, and I spun to see the man still in the tunnel with me. He gasped, struggling to force words from his damaged larynx.

"Yes, yes, what is it?" I asked, feigning interest. I swung my right arm, my clenched fist delivering a finishing blow to the weak spot in his neck.

He fell back, and I stepped out of the way just as the remaining Crawler broke through. I continued down the tunnel, the heat-seekers' hum growing louder as they swarmed outside. It would be seconds before they found their way into the tunnel.

The Crawler was right behind me—exactly what I wanted.

"Where you think you're going, Shadow?"

I stopped. I'd reached the end of the tunnel. I faced the Crawler and took a testing step back.

"Come and see."

He started for me, and I jumped out of the way before he stepped onto the hidden opening. The snow vanished beneath his feet, and the Crawler didn't even have time to scream before he was sucked into the ground. I leaped over the pit, staying just out of reach of the heat-seekers.

I followed the sound of Fade's heart, wondering who else had betrayed me.

39-Violus

Come on, Violus. Up through here." Shade's hand dangled from the lighted opening above my head. A group of children ambled up the ladder in my wake, allowing Father and Shade to pull them free. The ossuary tunnels were quiet below.

We had walked circles through the ossuaries through the night. It had taken hours to lose the Reapers who hunted me. When we finally had, we were down to only my father and Shade, as well as a handful of Blessed Children.

The tunnel led back to Shade's Healing Center in Dry Beds. He opened the hatch door first, checking the path before motioning the rest of us out.

"I'll take care of the other children," Shade told my father. "Dawsonus, you take Violus home now. She needs to get some rest before we leave for the Rain Ceremony."

Father placed his hand on Shade's shoulder. "May the Prophets bless you."

The words stayed with me as I stumbled free of the hut, my mind in a haze, filled with the horrors I had witnessed in the ossuaries.

Father held my hand as we meandered through adobe and clay structures that were arranged in a spiral marketplace in the center of the village.

The streets were on alert, but even the events at the atheneum couldn't dampen the excited buzz the ceremony brought. What was wrong with them? I wondered, shaking my head, though it did nothing to help the dizzy feeling. Healers memorialized the dead by etching names into rocks with chalk, but they did so with a hum, and the irony wasn't lost. If my sacrifice achieved rain, the memorials would be washed away.

My sight was blurry. I tried to gaze at the wares the vendors were peddling, but I couldn't even make out the features of the vendors' faces against their gold or red or brown skin. Music floated through the market as a band played a lively tune.

"A stark and weary candlelight
travels in the desert night.
Journey to the miracle sight
if you dare to accomp'ny me
to the Rain Ceremony.
The Prophets' call is in the air
fauna march in matching pairs,
the Blessed Children everywhere
sing 'O please choose me,'
'What a happy lad I'd be!'
'O please choose me,'
'What a happy lass I'll be!'"

"We're nearly home," said Father, squeezing my hand. "Amanus will have a feast ready. Your mama will want to hug you plenty too. You've got a big day coming up."

I blanched, still reeling over the image of the rocky path of gravestones the Healers had laid. "I want to skip the procession tonight," I said, eyes forward so I couldn't see Father's disappointed look.

"Violus, it's important to the people. You know how much you anticipate the procession every year. It's encouraging for the younglings to give the Chosen One a proper send-off."

"Encouraging?" I spat. "Do you not recall what happened back there?" My legs crumbled. My head spun. "How can you go on like nothing changed? Lives were lost!"

"You're dehydrated, Violus. You know that was only a sacrifice. Sometimes, the Prophets require them."

"I'll take no water," I vowed. As the Chosen One, I could approach any vendor for water and they'd give me their entire supply without pause. The precious drops were currency, and any one of us would spend our bank if it meant the next generation wouldn't go thirsty. I now understood that "sacrifice" was only a word we were taught to make it easier. The children had no say in the matter.

I'd been raised to believe that being chosen was a gift. That being a Blessed Child was something special. But doubt had settled into my gut like hardened clay. I was starting to realize that "special" meant something very different to the people on the Dry World.

"What if I can't bring back the rain?" I asked, causing Father to stumble.

"Excuse me?" He dropped my hand and swung to face me. "Violus, you know you cannot say such things. All of Dry Beds is counting on you. All of planet Earth is counting on you. If you fail tomorrow, we are another year closer to death."

We broke free of the maze of vendors and started across a barren field. Manmade caves had been built from stones on either side of the field, serving as entrances to the underground stables that hid beneath Dry Beds. Several animals had been brought out, and the handlers brushed and beaded the golden fur of sheepe, goatens, and müle in preparation for this evening's procession.

I snuck a look at Father, whose face was solemn as he walked, gaze fixed, hands in the pocket of his Healers' robes. "Do you ever think . . . I mean . . . maybe the Rain Ceremony's just a waste of time. Maybe the Dry World is going to burn up anyway."

Father let out an angry huff. He pulled his hands from his pockets and clenched his fists at his sides. "Violus, knock it off now. You stop talking like that."

You're right, you know, a voice whispered in my ear. *Lennox and I have been telling you that for years.*

Not now, Wisdom.

Then when? The end is coming sooner than Lennox thought. Too soon for you and me.

I bit into my lip. Anger welled inside me. It wasn't supposed to be like this. I wasn't supposed to be having doubts so close to the Ceremony.

I'm thinking about stepping aside, I admitted. *I don't think my heart is pure enough for this annual's Rain Ceremony.*

You have to do it, Wisdom said. *You know you're the one the Prophets have been waiting for. You're "L." The Last Original Child. The Reapers will go away once you've succeeded.*

Can I come stay with you? I asked. *After the Ceremony, can I finally visit your world?*

I heard a rhythm in the back of my mind—like a beating heart or a ticking clock.

I wish you could, Violus. I wish you all could. But you know that's not what Lennox decided. Wisdom's voice grew quiet. *Besides, I don't have anywhere for you to stay. The Breakers are coming to my world soon.*

I had forgotten the others had their own problems to deal with. A tingling sensation spread through my limbs as Wisdom's calming presence settled over me, bringing with it a cool breeze and the sensation of a full stomach. *I know it's hard,* she whispered, *but it'll all be over soon.*

40-Lennox

Fade and I found a snowbank to sleep in that night. Fade's pack was loaded with a couple of small shovels, and we dug into the bank until we'd cleared enough room for the both of us to lie straight.

We were hot and sweaty under our layers of insulated clothing and furs, and it was a miracle we hadn't caught the attention of the heat-seekers.

"Something's wrong," I said when the work was done.

Fade's head spun. "You think Crawlers are near?"

"Not here, but what about what happened with the others? I understand how the Crawlers found us so fast, but Laura?" I climbed into the hole we'd left in the snowbank. "How did they find her?"

Fade wiggled in after me. "If the Black Coats aren't tracking her, then there's only one other explanation. Someone else is letting them know where she is."

"That's impossible. Wisdom's watching all of us."

Fade shrugged. "Maybe Laura's got a chip or something. We'll have to wait and see where she runs into them next."

Fade pulled a small lantern from his pack and I peeled off my furs, draping them over the snow to make a bed for the night. My chest was tight, my skin hot and sticky. It may have been from shoveling snow, but I suspected I was close to one of the others. I slid my leather top down around my shoulders to get some air.

A heartbeat started up at the rate of a freight train, and my eyes shot to Fade, who was watching me from his own bed of furs.

"Knock it off," I hissed, slipping the fabric back over my skin.

Fade didn't care about my scars—or the fact I woke up screaming damn near every night. Every time I let him set his eyes on me for long enough, I heard his racing heart.

And it broke mine.

"I'm going to sleep," I said, settling into the stiff fur and squeezing my eyes tight. He knew I wasn't sleeping, but Fade didn't push it. He merely lay back in his own bed and closed his eyes.

Fade was lucky. We would've grown up in the Abyss together if his father hadn't been a Crawler. But Fade had been saved from the experiments reserved for the Shadows, merely trained to perform the experiments. The Crawlers had no idea he'd really been sneaking kids out of the Abyss and into the Hollow. Helectra knew, but it seemed there were a few secrets she'd been willing to keep.

Eyes closed; my mind started to wander. Tomorrow was the day. Our one and only chance to free the Shadows before there wouldn't be enough of us left to save them.

As Fade's face disappeared from my thoughts, Wade's face appeared. He and Laura were back in the decrepit old house they'd slept in the night before. Like Fade, Wade was pretending to be asleep—as was Laura, who was really just staring at the ceiling.

I was about to get her attention when someone settled into my mind, pulling me out of the Green World and back into my pile of furs.

You can't stop, can you? hissed the baby voice I knew so well. *Three deaths on Laura's conscience because of you.*

Wisdom, I thought you were avoiding me.

Erris is suffering. They wouldn't have felt that stab wound if you'd just listened.

Helectra and her Shadows still would have died.

Even so, Wisdom said, her girlish voice grating on my ears. *We'd be healthier. Besides, Laura wouldn't have gone to TIR if not for her killing Helectra. She might have been celebrating her release from Clover Center tomorrow instead of helping us.*

I had no doubt what Laura would've picked if given the chance.

Do we absolutely need them to get back into the Abyss? We're sure there's no way I can do this alone? I thought of Laura back at the house. My gaze rolled toward Wade as Laura snuck another glance at him. She could hardly keep from staring at the guy.

Everything will fall apart if we're not all on board. Wisdom sounded annoyed. Hard not to be when you know you're inches from death's door. I could hear her heart rate pulsing all the way from the little refrigeration unit they kept her body in.

It won't be easy. They've already had to sacrifice so much. Wisdom didn't say a word, leaving her heartbeat booming like thunder in my ears. *It's time*, she finally said, her voice a strike of lightning.

Laura was first. She imagined the other worlds as doors in a hallway, but it was easier for me. I didn't have to poke around and guess where someone like me might be. If I imagined trees or water or sand, there was sure to be a world there.

I pictured Wade's face again, and then I was seeing it through Laura's eyes.

Laura, I said, tearing her from her thoughts.

Lennox, is that you? What's going on?

I felt Wisdom's presence here with us, but she was holding back, keeping her focus on her own world as not to overload Laura.

Nothing's wrong. Close your eyes. Focus on your breathing.

As Laura's heartbeat fell into a steady rhythm, I went looking for Violus. I found her lying on a sleeping mat in the corner of her father and Amanus' hut. Her face was sticky with tears, throat sore and raw. Violus' thoughts were bleary, faded, not quite clear enough to hear. She was experiencing loss—the pain of suffering and death that racked through her with every sob was a sensation I knew intimately from my own life.

Violus, I whispered, thoughts reaching out like a set of hands that scooped her up. There was no resistance—none of the strength I'd come to know from her. Whatever Violus had experienced left her a shell of the girl I'd known all my life.

I pulled Violus' consciousness into Laura's body with me. Unlike Wisdom, who floated above us like a ghost, Violus crashed into Laura with so much force that Laura wiggled in her sleeping bag. Laura's thoughts had been filled with curiosity and anxiety seconds before, but as soon as Violus' mind touched ours, a deep and unbearable sadness took over that I could do nothing to control.

I wanted to ask Violus what horrors she'd seen, but every second we spent together was putting the others at risk. Their bodies would be left vulnerable for the duration of our meeting, which meant none of us were safe. The Crawlers prowled at every corner as if they knew Wisdom's plan and wanted to capture me before I had a chance to return to the Abyss on my own terms.

Next, I found Erris. Getting her would be the riskiest of all, as Morris would be quick to snatch me up if the Ocular gave him any hint I'd stepped foot in his world.

As if preparing for a dive, I took a deep breath and leaped. The room Laura slept in became the muddy shores of Rat Island just long enough for me to pull Erris' mind from the arms of the Gleaner who was wrestling her toward the towering ivory building only a few in the Wet World would ever see inside.

Erris was sick and broken too, and her mind bounced against Violus' as they each tried to flee Laura's world.

Earth was harsh for the others. Noises were different here, smells somehow more intense. My world existed in a state of survival and every step into the Green World, where food and warmth were plentiful, human interaction encouraged, love celebrated . . . it was far from easy for me, and I suspected it was difficult for the others too. Earth was a miserable pit of a planet and still somehow better in every way than any other place I'd visited.

Except for the Shadows like Laura.

Hatred bubbled up in me, threatening to spew like the boiling cast iron back in Fade's cave. There was no funneling this hatred, as it was solely for me. If not for the other Shadows locked away in the Abyss, I'd have rather thrown myself from a clifftop than force Laura back through the doors of TIR.

But sacrifices were going to be made. Wisdom knew it as well as I did. Tomorrow, I'd need something precious from every one of them.

Can everyone hear me?

"Wisdom?" asked Laura. She said it out loud, causing Wade to roll toward her excitedly.

It's me. Wisdom's voice was no longer a crack of lightning. Now it was soft as falling snow. Each of us was weaker here; Wisdom, and I worked to hold the others back, only letting enough of their consciousness into Laura's body to hear what needed to be said. Their heartbeats were quiet mumbles, far away in their own worlds.

Everyone's here? Erris asked, frail voice almost dreamy in her delirious state. *How can that be? Won't it kill—*

We'll only be here a second, interrupted Wisdom. *Just long enough for everyone to understand what they need to do.*

I concentrated on Laura, feeling the dampness of her palms and quiver in her throat. *I don't know about this,* she said.

I could no longer see through her eyes, my mind too full of the others' presence. They all would be seeing the same darkness I was; no human body was made to carry five minds.

Wisdom didn't waste her words. A flash of light erupted, giving way to a fuzzy image being streamed from the camcorder in Dr. Morris' office. Dr. Morris sat at his desk, where Wisdom watched him through the lens of his camcorder. Jumping anywhere that wasn't a body was a skill

Wisdom alone possessed, and one that made her invaluable to Fade's and my mission. We were looking at the back of Dr. Morris' head, which was covered in a smattering of liver spots and wiry white hair. Beyond him sat the girl Laura knew as Jessica.

The image crispened until I could see that Jessica's wrists were in shackles. Jessica wasn't sick. Like she'd told Laura, the kids at TIR weren't suffering from the usual afflictions found in the human mind. They were Shadows—too broken by Morris to know what world they were standing in from one moment to the next.

Dr. Morris hunched over his little machine, a crude box that looked like it had been torn from ancient times. Bolts of electricity shot from the contraption, causing Jessica to convulse until she slumped in her seat. She was still for a few seconds, and then she started to rock back and forth, screaming. Her eyes were wild—the same shade of purple as mine.

Dr. Morris had reached the Dark World.

Jessica's screams cut short, a line of dark liquid crept from the corner of her lips, and then she fell from her seat, hitting the floor with a horrific thud.

For a while, Dr. Morris didn't move. He just stared at the still body on the floor.

Finally, he lifted the phone from his desk.

"Dr. Venkin? I'm afraid we've lost another one. Yes, same as the others. We only got through a few seconds before she was gone." Morris was silent as he listened to the voice on the other end of the line. "Yes, sir. I agree that finding Laura appears to be our only option."

Dr. Morris hung up the phone. He turned, staring straight into the camera before it went dark. There was silence, followed by the echo of Laura's beating heart.

41-Laura

I couldn't catch my breath. The video from Dr. Morris' office replayed in a horrifying loop. I knew the others were still here in my mind, Wade just inches away from me, but I was very much back in that office watching Jessica die. Was that what Morris was doing to me? What would have happened if he succeeded?

I can't go back, I said. *I won't. I'm getting out of town first thing in the morning.*

Laura, you have to. It was Erris. Her presence made my mind feel slow and loopy. The room was dim before, but every time Erris spoke, I got a rush to the head. *Wisdom and Lennox . . . they'll keep you safe, but all of us gotta help.*

What do you need us to do? I asked.

Pleased, Wisdom's baby voice turned chipper. *Lennox will be first*, she said, loud and clear as the others' presence faded to the recesses of my mind. *As soon as she's inside, Laura will sneak into TIR with our help.*

Sneak in? I interrupted, wondering if they were oblivious to the patrolling Black Coats. *How am I supposed to do that?*

Lennox answered. *All you need to do is get to the fence. We'll help you break in after dark.*

And then what? Again, I watched Jessica tumble from her chair.

Wisdom's high voice pulled me back. *Erris, you'll find a way to Morris. Anything. Tell him Lennox wants to talk to him if that's what it takes.* To me, she said, *Laura, once you're inside, you'll need to make your way to Dr. Morris' office. Once everyone is in place, I can access Morris' tapes. We'll need that footage to get Morris and Venkin put away.*

I tried to imagine old hoot owl Dr. Morris locked in a cage. And Venkin? What part did he have in all this?

Why can't we just tell the police? I asked. *Figure out a way to get the cops involved without me having to be the one to collect the evidence.*

You have to, Laura! Wisdom insisted. *It's the only way. If any one of us refuses to help, we risk all of our worlds dying.*

Please, Lennox begged. *I know you hate me for what you went through growing up. For what happened with Arial, Haily, and Rowan. You're right, Laura; you don't owe me a thing. None of you do. But the Shadows still back at the Abyss? The kids locked up at TIR? They don't deserve this either. And now Morris knows one thing for sure. You're the only way he's going to get to me. If I can get in front of Malicious, I'll end all the Morrises in one fell swoop. The experiments will have to stop. And then the Shadows can start to heal.*

I was barely listening to Lennox. I was watching Dr. Morris zap Jessica, seeing that strange blue-skinned man torture Baby Lennox. She said it herself. I didn't owe her a thing, but she had saved my life. More than once. Something evil was happening at TIR, and I realized that I couldn't stand by and do nothing.

I'll get you to the fence, I said. *But that's all I'm promising. You can get your own footage, and I'm not going anywhere near Morris.*

Thank you, said Lennox. But somewhere in the back of my mind dwelled intense disappointment.

42–ERRIS

What was this place the Gleaners had brought me to? I couldn't smell the ocean from here—or the rain—and my nostrils flared from the stench of antiseptic, which was dripping from every surface in the room. The walls were covered with mirrors, and an amber lamp flickered from the ceiling, illuminating stainless steel furniture and a few cardboard boxes ruined by the rain. A light blinked from a corner, and it caught my attention because of the simple fact I hadn't seen anything resembling a camera on Aquarius since the flood.

The man in the white jacket arrived again with his little ivory case. He pulled a heap of bandages and creams from the kit and then forced another handful of sticky pills down my throat.

My vision came and went in the following hours I dipped in and out of consciousness. Whatever the man gave me was helping, and after a while, my fever finally broke.

Saving me said nothing about the value of my life. Morris just didn't want me to die because he hadn't gotten what he needed from me yet.

I opened my eyes and found two men looming over me. Tall and fat President Venkin in his bulging pinstriped suit and decrepit old Morris with his creepy penfocals.

"There's a camera," I said, pointing out the blinking light.

President Venkin gave it a glance. "Yes, I still have a few set up across Aquarius. Helps me keep an eye on things."

"I thought they didn't work?"

Venkin's lips curled into a smile beneath his black mustache. "Rat Island is full of Aquarius' most brilliant scientists. We have people that can make most anything work if I need it bad enough."

Morris leaned back; arms crossed in front of him. His penfocals blinked. "What did you see?"

I pictured Daddy's face clearly for the first time in over a week, as if the fever had been keeping the memory of my folks from me. "What about our deal?" I asked, pulling myself upright.

"I haven't forgotten," President Venkin said, giving his mustache a twirl. "As soon as you give me what I want, you'll board a boat with your folks and get a Gleaner-escort to a lovely little island where you can live in peace."

I closed my eyes, trying to avoid the memory of Jackie's last moments—the way she had screamed and how her body had moved. *Ain't gonna be me*, I told myself. I'm not dying on Rat Island. Not like that.

I'd betrayed the Raiders, gotten Jackie killed—whatever I'd become, it was far from special, and there was no turning back now. Wisdom was right. It was time to start looking out for myself.

"They're coming," I said, mind my made up. "Lennox, Laura, all of them. You'll get the Dry World. And anything else you want."

Part Three

THE ABYSS

43 –Laura

My head was pounding when I woke up. The combined presence of the others left me with a terrible hangover, and nasty burned coffee was the first thing I wanted when I awoke. Maybe a caffeine overdose would help with the headache, though. If only caffeine could do something about the memory of Jessica's death.

As the morning sunlight tickled my cheeks, I remembered—today was my birthday.

Happy Birthday to me.

"Hey, Wade, wanna check out that coffee cart down the street?" I leaned over the side of the couch. The faded wood floor was bare. Wade and the rumpled sleeping bag he'd slept in the night before were gone.

"Wade?" I shoved my sleeping bag to the ground and sat up. "Wade, are you here?" I whispered, afraid of alerting bogeymen. What I really feared was calling out and not hearing an answer.

I kicked the sleeping bag aside and went to search the house. The kitchen was empty. The small bathroom only held a toilet, sink, and tub. No Wade. He wasn't in the bedroom. He wasn't in the front or back yard. I opened the closet and found Wade's sleeping bag curled up inside.

I lay down on the living room floor, nibbling chunks of flesh from my lip to keep from sobbing. Of course, Wade left. I'd expected it—wanted it—but oh, I missed his face.

Dawson, my mother, Dr. Z . . . everyone in my life left me, once they saw who I was. Only Venkin and Dr. Morris wanted me.

I crawled to my feet and shuffled across the room. My hair was pasted to the back of my head like a nest, and I hadn't bathed in . . . days. Maybe that was what chased Wade away. I pushed through the door, halting on the front stoop when I was overcome by the sensation I was being watched.

It was hard to tell who the spy might be, as it looked like every car in the neighborhood had been replaced by a black Cadillac.

Shoving through the gate, I ducked behind the closest car. I peeked inside but didn't see a driver. I stayed low, using the cars parked along the road for cover.

Was I being paranoid, or were the Crawlers here? My every sense was on alert, every shrub a potential threat. I so badly wanted Wade here to tell me I was imagining things, but I knew those were selfish wants. This dangerous life was my problem, and the best thing I could do for Wade was let him walk away.

The suspicious feeling drifted over me again. I was sure someone was watching me. I dropped, spotting a dark figure in the driver's seat of the closest Cadillac. The driver shifted my way.

A man in a black jacket stepped from the car across the street.

"Laura?" he asked, lowering his sunglasses. Down the street, door after door opened. I kicked off my flip-flops, running on bare feet that were still sore from my TIR escape.

Had Wade sold me out?

I darted across yellow lawns, shoving through any fence

that looked like it wouldn't resist me. My legs cramped, and my chest tightened, but I stayed ahead. The Black Coats were weighed down by their cargo pants and bulky jackets, and I imagined many of them were panting under the hot sun.

I found a place to hide by accident. My feet caught on a coil of garden hose, sending me sprawling across a gravel pathway and rolling toward a leaning shed. I crawled in the direction of the shed, but instead of going in, I curled up on a crumbling woodpile hidden between the back wall of the shed and the wooden fence.

As soon as my feet were under me, a Black Coat was shuffling toward the shed. He ripped the door open and searched inside, mumbling profanities when he left a few moments later. When he was gone, I shimmied over the fence and made my escape through the neighboring yard.

What now?

Lennox!

Wisdom!

Anyone!

No answer.

I reached the end of the sidewalk and bolted across the street, realizing I'd ended up on the same block as the coffee cart. I spotted a familiar man on the corner. Wade had his head down as he balanced a tray holding two coffee cups and a couple of pastry bags.

Wade hadn't left me; he'd just gone for breakfast. My heart swelled. Joy returned to my broken spirit. I wanted to scream out and wave him down, but I held off when a black Cadillac pulled to a stop, blocking my view. I heard a door open and shut, then a squeal of wheels as the Cadillac shot down the road.

I looked over. Wade was gone, leaving a pile of bags and coffee spilled across the sidewalk.

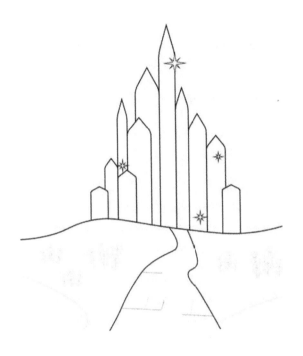

44-Wisdom

Rain poured over the field I stood in, soaking my favorite hat. I couldn't remember where it had come from. I'd woken up one day, and it had been there, waiting for me. It was only after I slipped it on my head that someone told me its story.

That was our mother's hat. She hadn't said the words, but they were very clear in my mind.

My name is L, I told her, *but Lennox calls me Wisdom.*

I don't know my name, said the little girl.

Maybe I can find one for you, I said, thinking it over. I leaped from my mind, thinking of the green place Lennox had shown me. A girl lived there in the Green World, and I landed in Laura's mind, where I swam in her dreams and dug through her deepest memories.

I jumped back to the white-walled box I called home. The

little girl with the blonde curls was waiting.

Squeezing my eyes, I pictured Laura's pink bedroom. When my eyes opened, my white walls were covered in pink wallpaper decorated with colorful flowers and sparkling animals.

Arial should be your name, I told the girl. *Laura will like that.*

Who's Laura? she asked.

She's one of us. A sister. I took Arial's hand, and my bedroom faded into her world. We stood in an empty field. Rain poured, lightning cracked, and I saw a swirling tornado close by. *You don't have to live here*, I said. *You can stay with her. I'll teach you. I can teach you how to use all of them.*

The rain stopped, but tears still soaked my cheeks.

Arial had been gone for ten years now, and Lennox left me nothing but the void. I imagined the wide-brimmed hat on my head and felt the weight as it disappeared. I ran my hand through my golden curls and brushed my fingertips across the front of my pretty sundress.

All of it was an illusion. I had no idea what I might look like, so instead, I dressed like Arial, my long-lost companion in the void.

Sometimes, it was quiet in the void. Other times, I heard voices.

These weren't the voices of Arial, Lennox, or any of the others I'd heard since the day I was born. These were the voices of the men who would kill me. In the end, they'd kill every one of us.

"There's nothing viable left," they'd say on my worst days. "We're diverting power away from the machine."

I'd come to understand these words over the years, thanks to my dear friend Arial, who'd shown me the secrets Lennox wanted to keep. If anyone preferred illusion, it was Lennox.

Some of us were realists. Lennox forced us to be.

"The machine" these men discussed was the very thing responsible for ending all life in my world. The Vanquisher of Mankind's horrible invention that changed the climate one day and killed off all plant and animal life the next. Much like the machine used to bury Lennox's world in ice.

As for "nothing viable?" That was me. The tiny baby preserved behind glass. Left to grow up in virtual reality.

The void changed. The transition was clunky and slower than normal because the men outside were right. My life support was draining energy from the machine. A choice would come for the Vanquisher—his creation, or me.

Lennox saw Arial as a threat, but I understood she was merely trying to survive. She took because she had to. Every one of us would be forced to make the same decision, and it was all Lennox's fault. Our only chance was to get Laura back where she belonged.

Lennox would resist when she realized my true intentions, and that was exactly what I wanted.

I imagined a desk. A rolling chair appeared, as did a hot pink computer. The monitor was large and boxy like the kind I'd seen Fade use. I sat at the desk and typed out a message. An address. The location of an abandoned house on the outskirts of Seattle.

When my message was sent, I stood up from the desk, and the computer vanished, just as more storm clouds rolled in.

"Rain's back," I said, watching the void change.

Lightning struck in the distance, but the air smelled sweet as cake.

45–ERRIS

"Happy Birthday, Erris."

I smiled, reaching out to grab the little spice cake Morris brought me.

"You'll have to excuse the crumbles. It's a bit dry."

I was already shoving the last bite into my mouth. "It's amazing," I said, scooping up the pieces that rolled away.

"And your birthday present? Is it everything you expected?"

"Are you kidding? It's incredible!"

Morris laughed, penfocal lens blinking. The eyewear didn't give me the creeps anymore. Wisdom had helped me view Morris as a mentor—a grandfather almost. Someone who actually wanted to help me, unlike Lennox and the others. "You have enough room here?" he asked.

I stood, gesturing around the modest kitchen. Half the linoleum was rotten, and the cabinets and appliances had been gutted, but a few plates and cups had been left behind. "My own apartment? I didn't even know a place like this existed on Rat Island. Actually, I didn't think there was anything like this left in all of Aquarius!"

"Only for the Gleaners," Morris said, standing up as well. "President Venkin's plan will work, Erris, and you'll be glad you chose our side." I glanced at the fresh scar on my wrist. A tattoo of a blue wave, large enough to cover my tally marks.

"What will happen to the kids?" I asked, leading Morris into the living room, which had been wallpapered in mildew and furnished with a pile of plastic crates.

"You let us worry about that, Erris. You focus on getting rested now. Your life is about to get a lot busier. You have your first raid in the morning."

"Fox Island," I said with a nod. "I see President Venkin is still testing me."

"He wants to be sure you're loyal," Morris assured me. "Do your job like you did last night, and there won't be any problems."

Betraying Jackie and getting her killed was only part of my job, right?

I bid Morris farewell. When I heard the deadbolt lock on the other side, I retreated to the window that overlooked the island. Storm clouds were gathered as usual, but it was strange viewing them from the safety of my new home. I couldn't smell the rain. I didn't feel the excitement in the air. All I saw was a field of mud, cages covering the ground like landmines. These were grump cages, not the cages full of children I'd been housed in at Prisoner's Point.

If President Venkin considered kids prisoners, what did he think of grumps? How did he treat the folks who'd raised us, teaching us to be Raiders and Holdouts?

Soon, I'd see for myself. I was finally going to be reunited with Daddy and Ma. My legs were shaking as I stepped away from the window. What would Daddy think when he looked me in the eye? What would Ma say? Would they know the way I'd crumbled under Morris' torture, forgetting all about the soldier I once was?

My new apartment was located in the same abandoned hospital Morris' office was housed in. The Gleaners had given me a brief tour of the cafeteria, offices, and apartments, and I was surprised to find the Gleaners even had a library . . . but the books were so dusty, I doubted anyone had been in there in a long while.

I drew a bath. The water smelled like sulfur and was a brownish color. Pink rings wrapped around the tub, but I was too weary to bother scrubbing it. I wasn't afraid of filth. The mud and muck were more home to me than this cavernous apartment lit by amber light and serviced by running water.

When the tub was full, I tore the black uniform from my body and climbed into the warm water. An air vent hung over the tub, covered in nasty sludge I thought would plop into the water at any second.

Lennox, can you hear me? I asked, sliding deeper into the tub until only my face was showing. *If you're there, I really need you. I need to know I have a friend.*

She's not coming, Wisdom answered instead. *I told you, the others are avoiding you. They won't forgive you for how you betrayed them, Erris. We only have each other.*

Knowing she was right, I leaned back and let my face slip beneath the water.

46-Laura

I'd spent over an hour crouched in the bushes outside TIR, celebrating my eighteenth birthday alone and covered in thorns.

The date meant nothing to me at this point, but I was well aware of its irony. Two weeks ago, I couldn't wait to get away from TIR. Now, I was turning myself in.

I would have run if I had any sense left in me. So, what if I didn't have any money? Maybe I couldn't get a plane ticket yet, but if I could lay low long enough, I was sure I could make enough for the bus.

But every time I stepped away from the fence, I thought of Wade. I hadn't seen any Black Coats since they'd taken him, meaning Wade hadn't told them where I was. He hadn't abandoned me, and I wasn't planning to leave him alone with the Black Coats, either.

Would Morris hurt him like he hurt Jessica?

How could I let Wade get taken? He didn't deserve to be here. Wade was as responsible for me as a puppet was for the hand shoved up its ass. He'd been there for me, and I had every intention of saving him from Dr. Morris' crusty clutches.

I leaped, trying to grasp the top of the fence, but my hands barely scraped halfway up. I'd tried summoning Lennox and even attempted to cross into the Dark World, but I remained on my own. What help could I be if I couldn't even get into the building? I closed my eyes and imagined Aquarius, but whenever I thought of Erris, all I got was a nagging ache in my temple.

I thought of Violus instead. I felt the hot sun on the Dry World, warmer than the sun shining on me if it were possible, but it was hard to see anything with her either.

Squeezing my eyes tighter, I imagined rainbows and unicorns.

Laura?

I jumped, surprised by the voice in my head. "Lennox?" I whispered, rolling my eyes when I remembered I could save my words.

No, it's me, Wisdom.

Great, I let out a relieved breath, not realizing how long I'd been holding it. *I could use some help.*

The bushes around me started to sparkle. Most of the shrubs were dead, but now fruit grew from the plants, and I saw a single bush overflowing with apples, bananas, strawberries, and kiwis.

I'm jealous. I'd do anything for your power.

Wisdom made a tense, high-pitched sound I realized was supposed to be a laugh. *No, you wouldn't. What's wrong, Laura? Where's Wade?*

Wade's gone! The Black Coats picked him up a couple of hours ago. I can't get a hold of anybody!

The others are fine, Wisdom said. *They're doing what they should be. You can't reach them because they don't want you to. The others are gaining power too, Laura. You have to respect people's bodies. You can't bounce around whenever you want to.*

I imagined her standing there with her hand perched on her hip like my mother as she lectured me.

My legs flexed, and I leaped for the fence again, but then,

I was flying, being sucked through the multiverse by Wisdom.

She'd brought me back to her Candyland world of colorful playgrounds and mythical pets. I saw a field of grass that smelled sweet like sugar. But as I stood there, the world began to rot. It melted and distorted around me, and all the joy was changed to terror. I sensed someone was hunting me on a primal level. Someone was coming. They were going to hurt me. They were going to hurt all of us.

Please, Laura. Wisdom's high voice was at my ear now instead of in my mind. I looked over, expecting to see her flying alongside me, but all I saw were streams of light. *Things are getting worse. The Vanquisher of Mankind wants to end us. He wants to pull the plug on all the world and let us fall into the black forever. We need you, Laura . . .*

In a blast of light, I was on Earth. I stood on the other side of the fence, and Wisdom was gone.

Thinking of Wade, I made a beeline for the front door, which was still boarded up from the night I'd broken through the glass. Would they hurt him? I wondered. If Morris dares to put that machine on him . . .

I marched across the crunchy lawn, waving my hands overhead while I screamed, "Hey! Come and get me!" at the top of my lungs.

With a groan, one of the boarded-up doors pushed open, and a guard in a black coat appeared.

Sneering, he pulled out a pair of cuffs. "Laura, was it?"

TIR was bigger and colder now than it had ever been. When I entered the doors this time, there was no doubt it was as a prisoner.

The Black Coat dragged me down the hall, ignoring my questions about Wade.

I was left alone in a room with bars over every opening— even the heater vents. The silence was suffocating, so I filled the void in my mind with screams. Why had I come here? Was I truly insane? What if I'd imagined it all along and had done nothing more than put myself back in the care of Dr. Morris and his experiments? What if he wasn't nice anymore?

Finally, someone spoke.

Laura, are you alright?

Wisdom, I'm scared. Where's Wade?

He's on the other side of the building.

How do you know? I couldn't stop blaming myself for ever letting Wade step foot in here.

I saw him through the camera. My mind's not tied to a body, remember?

Right. I remembered the streams of light I'd seen in Wisdom's world.

Are they hurting him?

No, he's okay. They only used him to get you here. Focus, I have to show you something.

My mind was changing. I wasn't crossing over. Wisdom was just settling in. It was nice having her there, and I appreciated the warmth her presence brought. My limbs felt weak, and I dropped onto the metal bed, wincing as my tailbone hit the hard frame. The Black Coats had taken the mattress and everything else. They hadn't even left me a lightbulb. The only light in the room came from the red numbers on the digital clock on the wall.

With Wisdom, I didn't need light. My legs felt useless, but my mind was the strongest it had ever been. I watched as the details of the room came into focus. I saw studs through the wall and differences in the texture of the paint. I heard voices outside, maybe on the far side of the building. I sensed the pulsing electricity in the air and the rush of water through the pipes. Suddenly, I knew the building better than my own body.

I struggled to stand as Wisdom and I found our balance. My strength and her mind. She didn't speak, but I didn't need her to. She was a part of me, and I saw her plan clearly. I jumped but not high enough to reach the ceiling vent. Wisdom retreated, and the room went dark again as I leaped, inches higher than before but still not high enough.

We need Lennox.

She's busy, answered Wisdom.

Then we'll have to wait. It's no use. I won't make it on my own.

There's no time! You have to get to the others!

I wasn't sure who she was referring to, but I didn't have long to wonder. Wisdom took over. I expected to retreat into the depths of my mind, but she was taking me somewhere else.

My clothes soaked through as the room filled with water. There was light above, but Erris couldn't reach it. Her chest was tight, her sight blurry and dim.

The light was beckoning to me. Just a little further.

I'd never played an instrument, but we'd watched an orchestra once at Clover Center. Most of the girls had complained about the noise and tried to get the White Coats to turn it off, but not me. I watched the conductor, mesmerized by the movements of his arms as he blended a hundred instruments into a single melody.

That was how I thought of it as we scrambled for our places in Erris' mind. We needed her water, my freedom, and Wisdom there to make sure we all stayed in rhythm. I tuned Wisdom out, confident she was still with us. I pushed aside Erris' desperation and concentrated on only one goal. The surface.

My mind was two. I stood on my tiptoes in one world and swam in another. In a single moment, two worlds became one.

The storage room at TIR filled with water, a flood originating from my very imagination.

My fingertips grasped the vent, but it didn't budge.

In a flash, the vent changed. Black sludge appeared over the grates of the vent, which was now hanging haphazardly from the ceiling.

What?

It's Erris' world! Wisdom said, answering my question. *Don't get distracted while you're pulling matter through the multiverse. She's almost there!*

The water rose over my head, and I took a final gasp of air before my hands clutched the loose grate. I gave it a yank and pulled the vent cover free.

Good job, Wisdom whispered. I peered through the gaping

hole where the cover had been torn away and watched the water recede into the ground.

How?

You're learning. Come on, keep moving.

It was strange crawling through the vent while Wisdom and I fought to keep our places. Sometimes we slipped, and I caught the whir of the ventilator keeping her alive or a glimpse of her melting dream world. Then, it would go dark, and I'd think I'd lost her completely.

At last, there was a stripe of light in the shadows, and I stopped in the middle of it, seeing a white-walled room below.

Here. This is what I wanted to show you. Wisdom's voice was weak. She was fading. *There's someone down there.*

A doctor paced the room, checking in on patients strapped to cots. I could only see their feet through the vent, and I ducked low, smooshing my face against the filthy grate to get a better look.

Wait, Wisdom whispered. *It's not time yet.*

47-ERRIS

I was crouched in the air duct overlooking the bathtub I'd been submerged in seconds before. Water filled the room all the way to the vent, and I watched as the water drained back into the tub until every drop was gone. How the heck did I get here? I lifted a hand to cover my mouth, but it didn't do much to keep the overpowering smell of mildew out. Clearly, no one had been in these vents for a while.

I kept crawling, stopping when I heard voices below. I was careful not to let my face touch the grating, which was thick with black slime.

I saw filing cabinets and plush chairs with chunks missing from the cushions where the rats had fed on them. Instead of a desk, the center of the room held a metal table, where a little girl lay.

A slender man in a white coat hunched over the girl. He had long dreads like Daddy. I couldn't see what he was doing with his hands, but I could see the little table at his side. It was covered in rusty saws and black-crusted machete blades.

The little girl let out a horrible scream as she tried to

squirm away.

A rotund figure appeared in the doorway, and the doctor stepped away from the table.

"She was stubborn, but like you said, Morris found a way to get to her." President Venkin's voice sounded distorted through the vent and I wouldn't have recognized it if I couldn't link it to his horrible face.

I peered at the child strapped to the table. That girl was giving Morris trouble? What was she up to?

"Erris?" the doctor asked. "I'm surprised."

Intrigued, I pressed my nose against the grate. The smell of mildew crept into my nostrils, and it took all my will not to sneeze.

The floor creaked as President Venkin crossed the room. "Do you know why Erris is so important to us here on Rat Island?"

"Because of her omens?" the mysterious doctor guessed.

President Venkin gave a slight nod.

The omens? Morris had called the shadows he saw in the Ocular "omens." I knew what he saw weren't shadows at all; they were the others.

"Morris has met with dozens of children like her. Many claim to see other worlds. But none of them have visited the worlds she has."

Which worlds? The only thing Morris seemed to be interested in was stopping the rain.

"She is talented," agreed the doctor. "It's why we worked so hard to keep her safe. We even changed her name. Cici wanted to name her "Elle" you know, but it would have been so obvious who she really was."

Huh? What were they talking about? My mind swirled, and I didn't know if it was due to the moldy vent or a visitor in my head.

"Where are you looking now?" the doctor asked, his scratchy voice barely audible through the vent.

"Has she ever mentioned a place called the Dark World?"

"Where Lennox is from?"

I pushed my face so close, I tasted the black slime clinging to the grate.

President Venkin nodded. "That's right. We're sure that's the one we're looking for, though to be honest, there's somewhere else we're more interested in now. She has valuable information. Calculations we can use to our benefit."

What? For days, Morris had been tossing me in the water as bait. Now Lennox wasn't even the one they were looking for?

"I don't understand," the doctor said.

"No, you wouldn't," President Venkin agreed. "They don't tell you Holdouts much, do they?"

Confusion battered me like pounding rain. What were they talking about?

"What do you know about Wisdom?" Venkin asked the doctor.

I perched over the nasty grate, my face lined with black ooze from the sludge on the vent. Exhaustion screamed out from every cell of my body that wasn't already brimming with anger—or confusion.

"Now you want Wisdom?" asked the mysterious doctor who stood across from President Venkin. "And not Lennox?"

"Well, it's not so much that *we* want *her*." President Venkin smiled, his teeth pristine despite the squalor he'd left his people to rot in. Worldwide floods, war, and lack of food and medication were just a few of the problems that tormented Aquarius over the years. The Gleaners had been the worst plague. The fresh tattoo on my wrist throbbed. I belonged to that plague now. "It's more that she has something we need."

A stubborn streak rose up in me. I didn't feel any hints that the others might be with me. For all I knew, this defiance was mine alone.

"I won't do it," I whispered. "Kill me if you want, but I ain't gonna hand over Wisdom."

There was a rap at the door, and the little girl on the table twitched. "Ah, good, Morris, come in," President Venkin called.

I twisted my neck to make out the man at the door. "Sir, there you are," Morris stopped, spotting the doctor. He turned to Venkin. "Sir, I need to speak with you"—he glanced at the man in white again—"in private." The doctor nodded to President Venkin before he left the room.

"I'm surprised you trust him," Morris said when the doctor was gone.

"He's never let me down before," said Venkin. "Unlike *someone*. So, tell me, Morris, what is it you want?"

"Well, it's the girl. I sent a Gleaner to retrieve her, but it seems she's disappeared."

I leaned close to listen, all my weight balanced on the rotten grate. In a flash, the drywall buckled beneath me and the grate gave way in an explosion of dust and black drywall. I crashed to the floor, where Morris was quick to yank me to my feet.

"How the hell did you get up there?" he demanded, slamming me down in a holey chair.

"Never mind that, Morris. She's here now, aren't you, Erris?"

"But she snuck out of the apartment!" Morris roared, swinging his head between me and the hole in the ceiling.

I ignored them, drawn to the girl on the examination table. Her eyes were glazed over, and her irises flashed between colors. What could she be seeing? Desert? Tundra? A room padded by white walls?

"What are you doing to her?" I asked.

Morris' penfocals went wild, lenses blinking in a fury. "You know what we're doing, stupid child. We're ending the rain." He grabbed a pile of chains from the medical cart and slapped them over my wrists.

The little girl on the table hardly moved. Her breathing was so slow. "What if I don't want to anymore?" I asked, jaw pushed out defiantly.

President Venkin chuckled from his seat at the desk. "You will if you want to see your folks."

Unless you already killed them.

"Where are they?" I demanded. "You're not hurting 'em are you?"

Morris sighed. "Erris, your parents are with the other lab rats. They're part of the rain experiments."

My folks were being experimented on, too? A shiver shook through me. Was there an Ocular pointed at Daddy and Ma at this very moment?

A grin curled across President Venkin's face. "Yes, Erris, at least someone in your family is being cooperative."

Since when did anyone on Rat Island consider Holdouts cooperative?

President Venkin turned to me. "Erris, tell you what. If you connect us with Wisdom, we'll go get your parents right now."

I squirmed against the new set of chains I'd been given. "You're pokin' and proddin' people without their permission. You're hurting me!" I thought of the infection Morris left to fester for weeks. "Tryin' to kill me. Now I find out you're doing the same thing to my folks, and you're callin' it cooperation?"

I pictured poor Daddy in shackles, and Ma pent up in a cage. It was damn cruel.

Morris shook his head with a chuckle. "I think you misunderstood. Your parents are not being experimented on."

"They're not?"

"Erris, your parents are doctors. They *do* the experiments." Morris leaned toward me, lines around his lips deepening. "Your mother and father volunteered to come work for us here on Rat Island."

My mind was spinning round and round like the little top I used to play with.

I shook my head. "No . . . no." That can't be true. "They wouldn't."

There was another knock at the door, and a dark-haired woman arrived in a Gleaner's uniform. *Amanda*, I remembered from Laura's life. I didn't know the woman enough to hate her like Laura did, but a boiling rage erupted at the sight of the man trailing behind her.

The doctor President Venkin had been talking to minutes before.

His braids had been washed and trimmed and his dingy white garbs replaced by a crisp ivory lab outfit. "Erris?" His eyes went wide. "Is that you, baby girl? It's been forever."

"Daddy?" I whispered, a stream of tears making an exodus from the corners of my eyes. "Are you okay?" I glanced at Morris. "They're saying such awful things about you."

I tried to stand, remembering they'd shackled my arms and legs.

Daddy smiled, and my heart swelled at the sight until I realized he wasn't looking at me. "President Venkin, we've got good news. A dozen children from Prisoner's Point are saying they can access the Dry World now. They must not have much longer."

48-Lennox

Nothing ever goes according to plan.

Fade and I were huddled outside the iced-over remains of a barbed-wire fence.

"It's the only way," Fade said. "Laura's already inside."

"Why didn't she wait?" I closed my eyes, trying to concentrate on Laura's thoughts. "We went over it three times last night. Wait for the signal!"

Fade sighed. He knew I was stalling. "Lennox—"

"What?"

"You have to let me go in."

I shook my head. "It's not happening, Fade. I can't risk you getting killed . . . again."

He reached out and grabbed my hands.

I ripped them from his grasp. "What are you doing?" I hissed.

Ignoring me, Fade took my hand again. "I'm touching you, Lennox. Snap my neck if you hate it so much, but I will not let another lifetime pass without feeling your skin."

My mouth fell open. My heart was racing, my legs

trembling. Fade was out of his mind! Both of our body temperatures were rising, and the patrolling heat-seekers would sense us soon. I tried to pull my hand free, but he squeezed tighter.

Relaxing, I let my fingertips melt into his. This was insanity. We were risking more than our own lives playing this foolish game. I couldn't love, and I didn't want to be loved in return. It hurt too damn much.

"Fade, I've gotta go. If I'm not back in an hour, then assume I failed."

"Are you sure anything will change?" Fade asked. "What if the Ice Man isn't even who you're looking for?"

"I have to start somewhere," I said. "And I really want to hurt him."

"Then what? Are you planning to kill every Venkin in the multiverse?"

"Isn't that what he's trying to do to me? He wants to make sure things end his way, but I'm not going to let that happen."

"What *will* happen if you succeed?" Fade asked. "Do we have any clue about what kind of effect it's going to have on the others?"

I didn't answer. I didn't know what to say. I'd spent every day wondering that very thing myself.

What was I about to do to them?

Sirens mounted in the distance and a hum filled the air.

"Looks like we're going with my plan, after all." Fade tightened his grip around my wrists and dragged me toward a gate that had been frozen in place long ago.

"Fade!" I yanked my hand, but his grip tightened.

"I've got her!" he called, using his free hand to wave down the Crawlers on watch.

The Abyss was as horrifying as I remembered. The Crawlers dragged me down a long hallway. Screams echoed around me, and I didn't know how far away the Shadows who made them were. I was surprised they still screamed at all, honestly.

Fade marched beside me down the snow-frosted hall. He didn't make a peep, not to scream or cry. To them, he looked like a good little soldier bringing me in. His march was sure—head up, shoulders back. Looking straight ahead, his bluff was so convincing that I almost believed he'd be walking back out of here.

They left me in a vast cavern I remembered too well as the place I was born. Fade was gone. A line of Crawlers stood guard, waiting for the moment Malicious summoned me.

I jumped. The spikes on my wrists caught the slick wall, and I wiggled up, alternating the spikes in my heels with those on my gloves until I reached the ledge. The heat-seekers zoomed for me, but I was already running.

Crawlers scaled the wall behind me, and I heard their groans as they pulled themselves over the ledge and their boots landed on the loft.

Every heartbeat pounded in my ears. I heard the subtle shifts—the tensing of breath and the lull in the beat when they'd pause to aim their guns.

I avoided most of the shots . . . but not all.

I bit into my lip, willing myself to stay focused. I did my best to absorb the wounds, terrified of what might happen to Laura and the others if I lost control.

Instead of bullets, the Crawlers used bits of shrapnel as ammunition. A Crawler aimed a shotgun at me, but it might have been glass or pebbles that came out of it. I cried out as the shrapnel punctured my shin and vanished, leaving nothing but a scar. Soon, the scar would be gone too, but I'd always feel the pain.

I was on an upper story of the building—not that I would have known that if the path wasn't so well burned into my mind. Frost was thick on the walls, and bears roared from cages deep in the belly of the Abyss. The haunted, tortured screams of the living Shadows never ceased. I used them, pretending they were cheering me on. I would bring justice to those children if it was the last thing I did.

I jumped the railing. The Ice Man's office was close.

Something in my memory sensed him nearby and begged me to run the other way.

Crawlers carried flamethrowers through the halls, melting doors free from the ice. They came through every day, which I knew because although the sun still hid somewhere in the sky, it was never enough to keep the frost away for long.

The Shadow's screams assaulted my mind like an unholy choir. I climbed another wall, finding a fresh tunnel in the ice— just wide enough to crawl through. The tunnel was a path for the heat-seekers, and I squirmed through as quickly as I could, knowing they'd be back again soon.

Holding my breath, I counted the heartbeats below me. Most were erratic and racing. Those belonged to the Shadows. The ones with evil so strong I could sense it through the ice . . . well, those belonged to Crawlers.

I waited several minutes until the strongest heartbeats had left the room and a relative relief had spread through the prisoners. I lay on my belly and gave the compacted ice beneath me a hard jab, barely containing my scream when the fragile bones in my elbow shattered.

I lay on the ice, panting until I was strong enough to ignore the shards of glass shooting through my arm. I braced my elbow in my hand, fighting to hold on to consciousness. Dipping my head through the opening, I saw children strapped to the icy walls by iron shackles. Helmets were clamped over their heads, giving the Ice Man answers to whatever he wanted.

The stronger ones bristled at my presence. They were somewhere else, watching another world, but knew someone was here who should not be. The Crawlers would be alerted about the disturbance, and the heat-seekers would arrive in minutes.

A metal panel covered in buttons was affixed to the far wall, and I made my way over to it, smashing the buttons with my spiked palms. Across the Abyss, alarms started.

I pushed through the heavy door with my stronger arm and came face to face with Malicious. The man was hardly even human anymore. He more resembled the bears with his clumps of white hair. Veins bulged from his bluish skin, and the thick goggles he wore made him look like a giant bug.

He adjusted his goggles. "Hello, Lennox."

I didn't struggle as he clamped cuffs over my wrists and pulled me down the hall behind him. He jerked on my injured arm, only causing me to bite further into my aching lip, unwilling to show the man a glimmer of my weakness.

"Did you know it was me?" I asked him.

"Of course, I did," he said, pulling me past windows that glimpsed into the horrors of the Abyss. Crawlers worked under strained light, poking at their victims with whatever crude tools the ice left for them. "We keep track of all the Shadows."

"Not me. Not until I let you."

Malicious laughed. "Sure. You tell yourself that, Lennox. You pretend we didn't know about the caves and the hideouts. We've had men on you since the day your mother took you out of here. You didn't squat in a hole in the ice without me knowing about it."

"If that's true, then why didn't you just come for me?"

"Because you're doing what we want simply by being alive. It would have been a waste of resources to try and bring you back against your will. Besides, it's not like you can go anywhere."

I scoffed. "Can't I?" I flexed my wrists, popping the cuffs. Malicious dropped my hands and stood back with a smug look on his face. There were roars. They were loud—and they were close.

"Would you like to see the bears?" he asked.

I felt the scars on my body as vividly as when they were new. I remembered my father creeping into the cage and leaving me on the floor long before I could walk. My mother had broken in and saved me before the bear made a meal of me, but I never forgot my father's intention.

"I wasn't going to let them kill her," the traitor told my mother. "I was only testing her. Malicious thinks she's strong, and I do too. She might be the one. You have to let her go."

They had, and it had been easier for them after that.

When the Crawlers started coming for us. Every scar on my body remembered my parents' betrayal. Eventually, my mother had run with me, but the place she left me had hardly been better. My years of freedom were only a pastime. I was always going to end up back here.

Pictures of the Ice Man were frozen into the walls, relics of a world past. I squeezed my eyes shut and followed Malicious, all my strength pouring into the steps I took. After tonight, I never wanted to be strong again.

49-Violus

I rode on the back of a mastodon nigh as tall as Father's hut, clinging to its dense golden fur. It was another creature bred in the chambers beneath the Prophets' Healing Center, like the Reapers' equimine. The animals they created required little sustenance and could survive even the hottest days. Shade rode on the back of his own mastodon, leading a procession of animals that marched in pairs.

Even a creature as big as a mastodon required little water, but still, the Healers only brought the animals above ground once an annual. The day of the Rain Ceremony. Shade smiled and waved happily to the cheering crowds, but I couldn't bear to cast them a glance. Blessed Children were missing from the crowd, as were a handful of Healers, but the people celebrated anyway, shockingly oblivious to those who had been lost in the ossuaries. Our only purpose was to serve the Prophets and obey the tomes they had provided us, the secret for rain.

As younglings, we'd been taught that these men knew what was best, but I no longer saw the Prophets through the eyes of a youngling. I now understood that my world was ill, plagued by a sickness encouraged by people like my own mother and father. Lennox had warned me of ignoring my instincts, but I never listened. I followed blindly. And my ignorance had gotten Domina killed. It had gotten them all killed.

My stomach flopped as the events in the atheneum came flooding back. The sounds of lives cut short—the rotten stench of blood in the heat.

I nigh vomited, and I straightened up on the great animal's back, careful not to send myself toppling from the mastodon's saddle. Doubts nagged at my mind, and I begged the Prophets to take them from me. All I'd ever known was that the Healers protected the children. They shared their scarce food with us. Their precious drinking water, too. They kept us safe from the Reapers . . . I let the thought trail off.

What about the children in the ossuaries? Seemed to me the Healers had only been interested in protecting one child then.

Me. The Chosen One. The Healer's sacrificial lamb.

My blasphemous thoughts were interrupted by a flare of pain in my elbow. I cupped the phantom ache, feeling it quickly fade away. My first instinct was to call out—to beg for the Prophets' forgiveness for my lacking faith—but I didn't.

I saw Mama's smiling face in the crowd. She beamed at me, but all I saw were the shapes on her head. The promise she made to dedicate her life to bringing back the rain. Father and Amanus were there, and their little son, too. His head would be shaved soon. He would take the vow and, with it, the tattoos as soon as he was old enough to read. I would call him "brother" in another life, but here, he was nothing but an offering.

All of the children born since the drought had been raised for a single purpose. The only reason the survivors in the Dry World kept anyone alive was the hope they would someday bring back the rain.

***

"Violus, you must stay focused."

I glanced up at Shade, shaking away the remnants of the waking dream I'd been having. For a second, I saw dark rain clouds over the Dry World, but then they were gone, once more revealing the scorching desert wasteland Shade and I trudged through.

My family had remained in the village at Shade's insistence. This was a journey for me alone.

"I *am* focused."

"You're dallying. You have to snap out of it. Your mind will slip."

The only thing that had "slipped" was my confidence. "I'm nervous," I said.

"About what? Seeing the Prophets again? That's silly."

"My experiences with them haven't been as pleasant as yours," I reminded Shade. "Don't forget the Prophet Morrus kept me in a box for weeks."

"Maybe you deserved it." Shade was teasing, trying to distract me from the warning in my heart.

"Even so, I'd rather not have been the one chosen."

"*You* chose this, remember, Violus? Besides, we draw lots," Shade called back. "It could have just as easily been one of the other Blessed Children."

He spotted a wilted bud in the cracked soil and scooped it up. He took a hefty bite of the flower and offered me the rest. I ate greedily, unapologetic about my lack of manners. I hadn't had decent food since we'd left Pacifica and although I didn't want to be rude to Amanus, I hardly considered the meal she'd provided in Dry Beds a "feast."
"Thanks," I mumbled when I'd swallowed down the bitter greenery. Well, *brownery*. Nothing here was green.

Shade marched on, and I watched his bandana sway as we walked.

"Could you tell me the story?" I asked. "About how I was

born? Mama said you know it well."

"Aye," he said, glancing over his shoulder. "It was my study."

"She doesn't like to tell me anymore."

"Maybe there's a reason for that. Suppose she wouldn't like me telling you?"

"Please!" I begged. "She wouldn't mind. She just says she has grown weary of the tale."

The truth was, I hadn't asked Mama about my birth since I was a youngling, but something about this journey was making me desperate. Desperate to know who I was before I was the Chosen One.

Shade nodded. He adjusted his tunic and glanced around. I didn't bother to look. I knew there weren't any Reapers nearby because they would have already tagged me if that were the case. The Reapers didn't care about rain—only collecting a bounty. They would rather all the Blessed Children were gone, so the earth could burn away to nothing.

"You were born at the place we're going. The Prophets' Healing Center. You were one of twelve children birthed there that year."

"Is it true my father worked with the Prophets? He never speaks of it."

"Aye. Amanus too. It was where your parents met, and all the Healers agreed it would be the best place for you to stay."

"Because of my dreams?"

Shade stopped for a moment and shook his head before continuing. "Because you were special, Violus. You were blessings, all of you."

"How did the other Original Children die? Mama doesn't like to tell me that part." I was the remaining Original. The last child born the year the drought had started.

"Well, I don't want to, either!" Shade said, throwing his hands in the air. "They were special. But they couldn't stay here."

"Why not?" I looked around, taking in a world of deserts

and salt flats and burned fields. A world destroyed by man at the command of the Prophets.

Weather experiments first . . . and then the animals . . . and then the people. There had been little the Prophets hadn't found to interfere with.

Shade slowed. He paused, turning to face me. "I don't know. It's a mystery even to the Healers."

"What happened next?" I pressed.

He sighed and swung back around. Dunes peaked into pyramids on either side of us, and I struggled to match his stride.

"Wait up!"

"I don't know if I want to talk about this anymore," Shade said. "Now my head's getting all foggy."

"Is not. Don't change the subject on me now." I caught up to him as the corrugated metal walls surrounding The Prophets' Healing Center came into view. The setting sun painted a glorious mural of gold, rust, and violet.

Shade cleared his throat, turning to face me once more. "After the other children . . . well, Dawsonus and Carolus were free to go home after that. They took you, and things were well enough until—"

"Until the Reapers came and Carolus took me to Pacifica to finish my studies," I finished for him.

"I thought this was *my* story to tell."

"Is it?" I asked, raising an eyebrow.

"I guess the Prophets found out there was still some value in that noggin of yours. Plus, other children were born after the rain stopped."

"The Blessed."

Shade nodded. "Your mother changed your name."

"Laurus to Violus," I added for him.

"Yes. She thought you would fare better against the Reapers if they didn't know you were an Original."

I took a deep breath, a lifetime of curiosities culminating in one unasked question. "What happens to the chosen?"

Shade pointed to the scrapped-together structure in front

of us. "Every year, they return to the place they were born."

"And me? What happens next?"

Shade's finger trailed to the sun, which hadn't allowed the clouds to gather in eighteen years. "Next, you steal the rain back."

He turned, sensing I was no longer following him. "Violus?"

I was on my knees, my face buried in my hands. I looked up, unable to hold back the tears.

"What if I can't do it, Shade? I don't want to die!"

50 – Laura

When the White Coat was gone, I dropped through the vent, with only Wisdom's frail voice to keep me company. Pain surged through my knees when I landed, but I brushed it off when I saw the children strapped to cots around me. Their eyes were closed, but their chests moved in rhythm thanks to the ventilators.

They varied in age, but all wore the yellowed uniform that stated they belonged to the Tomlinson Institute of Research. They had been shaved bald, and thick gauze bandages were wrapped around their heads.

What's happening to them?

The experiments, Wisdom answered. *This is what the White Coats do.*

It was like something out of a black and white sci-fi movie. I expected a boxy robot to burst through the door at any moment, right beside a hunch-backed medical assistant wielding a dripping syringe.

Was I here? I asked, already knowing the answer.

Yes, said Wisdom. *We all were at one point. We're close to where we were born.*

What are they doing to these kids?

They're looking for answers about what went wrong.

My curiosity was cut short by a sudden pain that ripped through my arm and dropped me to the ground. I gripped my arm where it felt like the tip of my elbow had been busted loose.

I cried out before I could help myself.

It's Lennox.

I could hardly hear Wisdom. She was almost gone.

She's hurt.

I didn't think Lennox got hurt. I cradled my elbow, rocking it to the rhythm of my throbbing pain.

Of course she does. She's human still. They made her body tough, but . . . she's still got her limits.

I shook the pain away the best I could, wondering what to do next. Wade was here somewhere. I needed to make sure he was okay. He was only here because of me.

Where are they keeping Wade?

Don't worry about him, Wisdom said. *Lennox will take care of it. You need to find Morris.*

Morris? *How can he help me? I thought we were looking for tapes?*

I reached for the doorknob, feeling it pull away as someone jerked the door open from the other side.

"Laura," Dr. Morris said, a sickly sweet smile on his lips. "Welcome home."

"Dr. Morris!"

"Laura, you need to come with me. You're in a lot of trouble."

"Me? What about you? What did you do to Jessica?"

He cocked his head to the side. "Jessica's resting," he said.

"She's not resting; she's dead. I saw it myself." *What do I do, Wisdom?*

Silence.

Wisdom was gone, and my mind was my own— something I'd longed for all my life but hated now. As hard as it was to admit, I was getting lonely without the voices in my head.

Two Black Coats appeared behind Dr. Morris. The closest threw cuffs on me and dragged me down the hall. My wrists were sore, but I was glad the pain in my elbow had dulled. I hoped Lennox was okay, whatever she was up to.

We were in a hallway I'd never seen before. We passed unmarked metal doors with the unmistakable sounds of screams and cries behind them. Dr. Morris never slowed, and my questions about what caused the terrible sounds I heard were never answered.

Several photographs and framed newspaper clippings were mounted on the wall. I hung back, noticing an article titled "Research Institute Ends Controversial Climate Study." My attention had been caught by the familiar couple who stood with a group of scientists beside Dr. Morris and Dr. Venkin. Her dark hair was shorter then, but there was no mistaking Amanda's bird-like face, and there beside her was . . . my father.

Dr. Morris led me to his office, where Venkin was already waiting in the chair.

"Hello again, Laura."

He was too-tall, too-thin. Like someone had taken a normal man and stretched his limbs as far as they would go.

I plopped into the open chair, ignoring the chocolate on the desk. "My father worked here?" I asked neither man in particular.

Dr. Morris dipped his chin into a nod so low only the tops of his oval glasses showed. I didn't see him as a wise old owl anymore. He was a cassowary. The most dangerous bird in the world.

"They worked in climate research," said Dr. Venkin, pushing his chair back. "Dawson was one of our best scientists."

"But what about my mom? Why didn't anyone ever mention this chapter of my life to me?"

Dr. Venkin nodded. "Your parents met here. In fact, you were born here."

"I was?" I'd always been told I was born at the private hospital across town. I swung my head from Morris to Venkin. "What else are you keeping from me?"

Dr. Venkin exhaled, and I smelled the menthol mouthwash on his breath. "It's probably time you hear the story."

Wisdom? Nothing. *Lennox?* I thought of her. Her icy home, her scars, her mysterious purple eyes—but she stayed silent.

"Tell me the story."

Venkin grabbed the chocolate from the desk. He unwrapped it and ran the morsel across his top lip like he was applying lip balm. "About twenty years ago, TIR specialized in climate research and manipulation. Do you know what that means?" He nibbled at the corner of the chocolate.

Nauseated by watching Venkin eat, I studied the camera behind him instead. "Dawson worked for a company that focused on climate trends. He's working for the Environmental Protection Agency now."

I never understood what Dawson did when I was a kid. My mother told me he was like a living Farmer's Almanac. He studied weather events from the past to try to predict the storms of the future.

"Yes, your father was one of the men assigned to the project. Basically, we were attempting to manipulate the weather to improve growing seasons. It was noble work. We sought to bring rain to the desert and cut back precipitation in parts of the world where it's difficult to grow grains. At the same time, we were progressing with other kinds of research.

Our climate trials were good for the most part, but as time went on, we began to notice changes in the trends. Have you heard of the butterfly effect?"

He didn't wait for me to answer.

"Things were fine in the beginning—a few months of rain, a longer-than-average summer—but over time, things started to change. The rain lasted longer and longer or never came at all."

I thought of the Dry World, where it had barely rained in two decades.

"Dawson met a woman here," Dr. Venkin continued. "She was a volunteer. They came from all over the world—people no one claimed who were willing to be a part of our studies in exchange for a place to call home."

I shifted at the words, remembering the day Venkin had brought me to this place.

"You were born here. We wanted to keep your father's affair private, and we never planned to let you leave TIR. Especially after we discovered your . . . anomaly. You were born an only child, yes, but when the doctors were tending to your mother, they detected multiple heartbeats early on. A DNA sample at birth would confirm it. Six different strands were collected that day. Every new test confirmed what your father and my doctors had grown to suspect. Multiple heartbeats. Distinct brainwaves. We couldn't even get the same thumbprint off you twice. You may have been one body, Laura, but you were connected to many minds. We received anonymous tips about other pregnant women who shared characteristics with your mother. We brought them in, finding their children had the same anomalies." Dr. Venkin shrugged. "Unfortunately, those children didn't last long."

Dr. Morris finally spoke. "Their minds couldn't handle the magnitude of the work I was doing."

Venkin shook his head in disappointment. "We were forced to scrap our entire project. Your parents took you home, but we kept an eye on you."

Anger boiled inside me. Had Lennox known this all along? Had the others? Was I the only one left in the dark about our origins?

Venkin continued, "Our research was blending. Our case studies were becoming realities somewhere . . . else. We started getting weird emails. Messages from other Dr. Venkins and Dr. Morrises who claimed they had met similar children. None of us knew how, but our climate experiments were becoming real life. A girl named Erris who lived on a planet covered in water claimed she dreamed about you. A slave girl in an arctic world who they discovered could cross over at will and had a penchant for haunting the others . . ."

"She doesn't haunt us," I interrupted. "She helps us."

Dr. Venkin chuckled. "Ten years ago, I received the most interesting phone call from your father. TIR was barely recovering from our last scandal, but his news would give me the drive to make our facility what it is today. Dawson said he'd watched you try to hurt yourself. That your face became covered in scars. Your eyes glowed purple, and the evil he saw in them was so intense he would never trust you again. Your mother protested, of course, insisting you were only pretending, but it was easy enough to remind the courts of her history."

"My mother wanted to keep me home?"

"Sure," Venkin said, "but your father wanted to bring you back to us. If your mother got custody, she would've never let you in here again."

"You've been destroying my life since the beginning!" I was outraged! Horrified! How could someone be capable of such egregious manipulation?

And Dr. Morris? "Did you know about this?" I asked him. "Were you lying to me all along?"

His eyes were bright and his face giddy as he spoke. "I'm doing what's necessary for science. You and I, will save the world, Laura."

"Many worlds," Dr. Venkin said when he'd swallowed down the last of the chocolate. "While we were scrambling to make sense of the multiverse we'd somehow stumbled upon, you girls were growing stronger. Closer. A Dr. Morris from the planet Aquarius sent word that he'd discovered something with his Ocular. Looking at the children through the device, he claimed he could see shadows that weren't there. 'Omens' he called them. The stronger of an omen he saw, the easier it was for his patients to cross over. He brought the others to his world to study, sometimes sending his own patients away for a while. He was convinced the key was there somewhere. That whatever went wrong and made the rain stay so long could be undone if he found the right shadow. He thought you children were born with the ability to change our very world."

"You think it will work?" I asked. I was having trouble staying focused. I was so tired. A sharp pain erupted in my chest as if my heart was trying to break free. And where was Lennox? Her silence was maddening.

"Aquarius wasn't the only planet. They all inevitably concluded that the secret was hidden somewhere in the children born at TIR. More specifically, the first child, "L." You're hunted on the other worlds because the scientists are right. You *are* the cause of their distress. Somehow, you created their worlds with your very mind."

"I'm imagining them?" I asked.

He eyed me. "You know that's not true."

I did. I'd experienced too much real pain and fear to let myself pretend it was a fantasy. But that sure would have been easier.

Dr. Morris circled the desk and planted himself at Venkin's side. He looked like a parrot perched on his shoulder. "I think we should try something new." He reached under his desk to retrieve the metal box and held the earpieces out to me.

"Experiments? You're not going to call the cops?"

"Why would we do that?" Dr. Morris asked.

I slammed my fist against the desk. "Because I'm a murderer!" What was with these people?

"Yes, Laura. That seems to be true no matter where we find you."

He jammed the attachments over my lobes and threw the switch before I had a second to realize what was happening.

It was a freefall—a leap into the unknown. I dreaded finding myself in Aquarius, tied up in front of the Ocular or chained beneath the sea, but when I landed, I was in the Dry World.

Desert. Everywhere I looked. I scanned the multicolored sky and couldn't even see a bird.

"Wade!" I called in relief, spotting his form hanging over me.

He flinched. "What did you say?"

Shade. That was his name here.

"Where are we?" I asked. I was kneeling in front of a building half-buried in the sand. The ivory structure was bleached bright white by the sun. The manicured lawn had been replaced by dirt, and not a speck of green could be seen from the bushes I remembered outside. Strange animals gathered on the dirt lawn as if they were preparing to board an ark. Camels and llamas, even an antelope, all smaller than the ones I'd seen when I visited the zoo with my mother as a child . . . and all watching me with glowing red eyes. I blanched at the sight of a towering, hair-covered mastodon nearby.

"Is this TIR? What's with all the animals?" Shade held back and looked deep into my eyes. "Who are you?" he growled, freeing a knife from his baggy trousers and holding it to my neck. "Where's Violus?"

"It's me, Laura! I'm from Earth! Dr. Morris sent me."

Shade dropped the blade. "Laura, huh? At least that explains the foolish things you've been saying. This Morris sent you? How?"

I climbed to my feet, still shaking from my encounter in Dr. Morris' office. I shrugged. "Some kind of machine. Like you'd use to jump a car."

Shade stared.

"You don't have cars?" I guessed, realizing I hadn't seen any.

He shook his head. "There's no one to make or fix them anymore."

"Well, it's this like this electrical thing . . ." I sighed at his blank look. "You guys are living in the Stone Age, aren't you?"

"It seems we are." He glanced at the looming building. "I wonder how long she'll be gone?"

"I don't know. I'm in as much of a hurry to get back as you are to get me out of here." I surveyed the strange animals. "Although, the menagerie is interesting."

"They're part of the ceremony." Shade was growing impatient with me. "You could see for yourself, but we can't go in without Violus."

"I'm offended," I said, doing my best to lighten the mood.

"You may think this is a joke, but I'm late. Without Violus, we can't make our request for rain."

I eyed the barren land. "Hmm. You think you'll get it?"

Shade's jaw clenched in defiance, and he set his eyes on mine. "We must try."

I decided to drop my attitude. This wasn't my world. It wasn't my life in question. "Is there any way I can help while I'm here?"

"You can go back to your own body."

This version of Wade was the least likable one I'd met by far.

"That's not so easy. I'm stuck here until Morris brings me back."

"Sounds like you haven't been training too hard. Your parents must not care for you as much in your world."

The words stung. He couldn't have known how hard of a blow it was, but I held my tongue. "I guess not. What would Violus do now?"

"She would show me some respect, first of all—" Shade's mouth fell open as he spotted something in the distance. "Reapers."

I turned. A caravan of horses ran toward us, kicking up a cloud of dust behind them. As the horses neared, I saw they were unlike any horses on Earth. They had tiny heads, brown and black bodies striped like zebras, and humps on their backs like camels.

"What are those things they're riding?" I whispered.

Shade let out a frustrated growl. "Equimites! Their breed is unique to the Dry World. Now shut up! Don't you know how much danger you're in?"

Obviously, I didn't. I shot Shade a glare and watched the equimites approach. The riders on their backs wore sleeveless black suits and helmets with sharp spikes protruding from them.

The equimites stopped feet from us, and the lead rider jumped down.

Shade stepped between us. "You can't take her! You have no right today! We're here for the ceremony!"

The Reaper sneered. "How's being a fanatic working out for you, Healer? Eighteen years without a successful Rain Ceremony. Your life would be better spent killing these abominations than honoring them."

The Reaper pulled his helmet loose and let it fall to his side. I recognized him as Rowan, the TIR guard Lennox had saved me from.

Rowanus pointed to me. "Sacrificing her won't change a thing. Nothing's gonna save the world. The sun's just going to keep getting hotter until we're all scorched from this miserable earth." His eyes slid over me. "When you kill them, at least you feel a few drops of rain."

Sacrifice? What was he talking about?

Our standoff was interrupted by the blast of a trumpet. The sound carried across the desert, and when it hit my ears, a feeling of horror washed over me.

The Reapers stopped, their heads all whipping in the direction of the call. Rowanus gestured to the others, before returning his helmet and climbing back onto the equimite. "Next annual," he promised.

Shade grabbed hold of my collar and hauled me toward the building, away from the Reapers who held their ground. Why weren't they chasing me?

Shade broke through the doors of the Prophets' Healing Center, and I shrunk back at the sound of cheers. The ceiling had been torn free of the building, allowing the ruthless sun to beat down on an arena that had been erected where the institute once stood. Children, all younger than me, paced in cages, surrounded by stands holding more people than I'd seen in all of the Dry World. They all wore the white robes of Healers.

Shade wasn't leading me anymore. He was pushing me. The crowd went wild when I entered the stadium and took my place in the center cage.

It was only then that I understood what the Rain Ceremony was.

51-Violus

I couldn't move, but I could see. Shade threw me into a cage barely taller than I was. Laura was in control. Everything about her—her thoughts, her breathing, her cries—were stronger than mine. I should have been comforted by her presence, but instead, I felt disappointment. I had waited all my life to be the Chosen One, and now, I wouldn't even star in my own sacrifice.

The smell of sunbaked animal feces filled the air, and a haunting chorus echoed through the cavernous room, singing the Prayer for Rain.

"Blessed Children roving every land . . ."

I retreated into my mind, wishing my ears would close up and keep the wretched sounds away. Laura swung my head in panic, taking in the crowds of Healers from every village left on the Dry World.

I remembered when Father had brought me to witness

my first Rain Ceremony at the age of eight. I sat at the very front, enraptured by the circus of animals and strange rituals the Healers performed. That was the last year Arial was with me. Lennox had come to watch as well, causing me to fidget non-stop during the ceremony. Lennox was inconsolable and kept trying to force me from the stands so she could run out and save the Chosen One, a little girl of only four that year.

Father had given me a stern lecture about respect and obedience.

"You need to be still, Violus. The Ceremony won't work if we're not all concentrating."

Arial, on the other hand, had been riveted.

Do you think they can do it? she whispered. *Do you think they can really bring the Wet World here?*

Of course not, Lennox told her. *Like Wisdom said, the only way to change the weather is to find a new world.*

Mama told me it will work; I had said then. *She says the Prophets have been studying. They know how to fix things now.*

There's no fixing the things they've done, Lennox said sullenly. *They'll only make things worse.*

Arial spoke up. *What is studying? I don't understand.* Arial never understood the things we did. She was all alone in the Windy World. She had no one to teach her any better.

It's what the Crawlers do, came Lennox's cold reply. *It's poking and prodding and pushing your limits until you want to die.*

Arial had been quiet for a long time while we watched that year's procession play out.

I watched now as a line of animals trotted in front of the stands. These animals were a show of confidence. The Prophets never let us eat them, even during the driest years. They existed only as a reminder of the Prophets' capability to give and take life. Two mastodons trailed behind, mounted by the Prophets Venkus and Morrus. The men wore golden robes instead of white, and the shapes on their robes were etched in red instead of black. I didn't know, but I had a horrible suspicion the shapes were drawn in blood. Tall and lean, Venkus wore his hair in sleek black braids. The older Prophet, Morrus, rode with a hunched back and had no more hair to carry braids, so he wore a golden headscarf instead.

The people in the crowd cheered at the Prophet's arrival—and so did the children shackled in cages. They would be safe this year. Only the Chosen One would be expected to make the sacrifice.

The Prayer for Rain grew louder and louder. The Healers in the stands were almost giddy. Laura scanned the crowd. Something was keeping me from hearing her thoughts, but if I had to guess, I'd say she was looking for Shade. My eyes bounced over the ceremonial bowl being passed through the crowd. Healers from all over the world had brought their rain sacrifice in little vials, doing everything they could to keep the water from drying up before the ceremony.

Laura found Shade and I watched as he poured his own vial into the brass bowl before passing it on. Another Healer signing my death warrant.

Venkus and Morrus dismounted the mastodons and took their place in front of the crowd.

"Blessed!" Venkus called, a smile of rotten teeth darkening his face. "Let us summon the Wet World!"

The crowd cheered. They continued to sing the Prayer for Rain, but the melody had changed. It was no longer comforting; it was manic. Every word the crowd sang was rife with the call of bloodlust.

"Blessed Children roving every land,
Come to heal, hand-in-hand . . ."

The ground started to rumble in an earthquake that nearly shook me from my feet. Screams sounded around me as the Blessed Children grew frightened and the voices who visited their minds arrived to help them stay calm.

What if they left? I remembered Arial asking, all those years before. *What if the Chosen One goes to the Wet World instead?*

Arial, we've talked about this, Lennox had said in a somber tone. *We only get to keep the world we were born into. No matter what it asks of you.*

I hadn't joined their conversation. I was too eager to find

out what would happen next.

Now that I knew, I felt peace. This was why they'd raised me. All they'd ever trained me for. Like it or not, I knew the destiny that awaited me.

My life of hiding would be over soon. My gaze rolled over the other cages. But what about them?

52–Laura

"Violus!" I screamed out loud and in my head. "Lennox! Wisdom!"

The ground rumbled beneath me, knocking me from my feet and sending the crowd into a frenzy. "Erris!" I sobbed, tears flowing down my face. Again, I looked for Shade, but I couldn't tell him apart in the sea of white robes.

The kids in the surrounding cages were screaming too, but their screams were almost excited.

Not me. Terror convulsed through me like a stampede. It was so powerful I thought it might knock me off my feet. I might have died of terror right then. That was if these "Healers" didn't kill me first.

I saw two of the monstrous mastodons covered in fine tan fur out of the corner of my eye. Dr. Venkin and Dr. Morris rode in on the beasts, and I hadn't yet lost hope the animals might trample the men to death.

There was no such luck, though. Venkin took his seat in the crowd. Other than his black braids and the set of teeth that matched them, Venkin looked much the same as he did in my world.

Morris, however, walked with his back so bent, you would have thought his spine had been broken in half. I imagined his x-ray, which would probably look like an upside-down "V."

The ground finally stopped shaking, and I rose to my feet, unwilling to die on my knees. I gave the crowd a contemptuous glare. They were a murmuration of starlings with the shrieks of koels. I shook my head—how could I be thinking of birds now?

Dr. Morris—whoever he was here—collected a brass bowl from a man in the stands. He turned to me, a look of great anticipation on his face.

"Help me," I sobbed, not even caring who answered now.

But I knew who would come. She had always been the one to save me. "Lennox," I whispered. "If ever you were going to do me a favor, now would be the time."

And then, when I needed her the most, she didn't let me down.

I'm here, Laura.

53-Lennox

Lennox, are you still with me?"

My blood boiled at Malicious' voice.

"It hurts," I whispered.

"Yes, but you're a strong girl. You'll be all right."

"The others won't be."

"It's okay. You'll be stronger without them."

I was strapped to the metal table in Malicious' chambers, an iron helmet clamped over my head. The same helmet my mother had worn when she brought me into this world. Malicious stood in front of a panel covered in little switches he threw at will, sending volts of electricity through me every few minutes.

It wouldn't kill me, unfortunately. He was right. I was far too strong. Sometimes I wondered if the Ice Man had only made me so strong so that he would be the only one who could break me.

Wisdom told me that my strength was a blessing, but here in Malicious' torture lab, there was no denying my curse.

"Where are you sending me?" I asked.

"I'm deciding. I can't find Laura. I think perhaps she's out."

I almost thought of her, but I stopped myself. I needed

to protect her however I could.

"Are you trying to block me?" Malicious asked with a disappointed *tsk*.

"I'm doing my job."

"You're a Shadow, Lennox. You already failed at your job."

I glared, causing him to retaliate with another painful jolt. I was ready for it. I braced myself, keeping my jaw tense so my teeth wouldn't shatter if I bit down. When Malicious flipped the switch, I broke free of my shackles and reached out, grabbing Malicious by the face. His expression froze, and he convulsed under my grip until foamy white vomit spilled from his mouth. I shoved him aside, throwing the restraints to the ground before climbing onto what remained of Malicious' desk, buried in the ice. I jumped as high as I could, punching the compacted snow in the ceiling. Pain tore through my elbow, but I ignored it, jumping again and giving the snow over my head another hard shove. I repeated the move over and over until my right arm was useless and tears of frustration streaked my face.

At last, the ice broke loose, and I jumped out of the way as a mountain of snow came tumbling from the ceiling vent. I crawled up and burrowed my way as far as I could into the ductwork. I was exhausted, so I didn't make it far, but it would do.

I curled up and searched for Laura, finding her in the Dry World. She was in the large stadium that had once been TIR, surrounded by children in cages. Shadows. Laura was in the main cage, the one that held the annual Rain Ceremony's sacrifice. The people in the Dry World were zealots, willing to believe and do almost anything to bring the rain back.

I remembered witnessing the sick tradition once with Violus. Out of all the bad days I'd seen, it was still one of the worst. I made myself a promise that day, and I'd done everything I could to keep the others from harm since then.

Laura wasn't alone. I sensed Violus there as well, pushed to the back by some unseen force. Someone was keeping them apart.

The Prophet Morrus was approaching Violus' cage, and I saw the thin man, Venkus, up in the stands. The Ice Man. The one who had taken the sun from my world and the rain from this one. The Vanquisher of Mankind.

Laura, I called when I'd settled in her mind.

Lennox, is that you? I've never been so happy in all my life.

Laura, you need to get out of here.

I can't, I'm trapped. Dr. Morris is keeping me here.

Violus is here too. We'll get killed if we stay.

What can I do? Laura whispered, her voice scared. *I'm not strong enough to fight him.*

Morrus carried a bowl of water in his hands. The sacred liquid the Healers had been collecting for months in preparation for the ceremony.

They'll drown you, Laura. That's how it works. They choose a child and put them in the water. They think it will bring back the rain.

That's stupid!

They're trying to summon Erris. We need to go—now. Morrus was almost to the cage.

Laura wasn't strong enough, but I was.

I kicked out, imagining I still wore my spiked heels as Violus' boot connected with the lock. The lock erupted, and the door flew open, surprising Morrus when the bowl was knocked from his hands. He let out a wail, hands following after the vessel. It crashed, leaving a ring of mud where the bowl landed.

Morrus scraped at the dirt, stuffing clumps of the mud between his cracked lips.

I spun into a roundhouse, but Violus' body was too frail. My skin felt hot, my breathing forced. Instead of striking, I shoved Morrus into the dirt.

The kids, Violus murmured.

There were far too many cages for me to free everyone.

I can't.

Violus' strength surged through me. I reached down and grabbed the heavy bowl, crashing it down hard on Morrus' head. Healers poured from the stands, but I made a beeline for the Prophet with the slick black braids sitting in front.

"Help! Help me, you fools!" Prophet Venkus cried. My eyes scanned for a weapon, finding nothing but an empty glass vial. I plucked it up and crushed the glass in my hand.

I dropped the handful of glass, only needing a single shard. I flicked my hand across Prophet Venkus' neck, slicing his throat in a fluid motion.

A sharp pain flared from between my shoulder blades, and Violus let out a gasp. I turned, seeing Shade holding the blade.

I leaped from Violus' body, pulling both of the others with me. Someone's heart was beating too fast. I searched, desperate to find somewhere to go before I lost one of them.

Thunder boomed. The multicolored twilight was gone and replaced by dark storm clouds. A tingle of excitement spread through the crowd, forcing the Healers to halt their chase, instead turning their heads toward the heavens.

And as Violus slipped from her body, rain started to fall on the Dry World.

I'd only felt a few drops before I was back on Earth.

I opened my eyes. We were in Laura's body, and Dr. Morris was watching her face with great fascination.

Where am I? Violus whimpered.

The Green World, I told her. *With Laura.*

But the Ceremony . . . it worked!

Erris must be here now, I said. *Laura, are you alright?*

Good enough. Thanks for getting me out of there.

There's still work to do.

I leaped up, surprising Dr. Morris when I crawled over the desk.

I squeezed his neck, summoning as much of the strength from Laura's intact elbow as I could.

Morris' eyes bulged as he fought me. I felt his trimmed fingernails brushing uselessly against my arms as he tried to gasp out a plea for help. His eyes rolled back, and his body went slack under my grip.

He was alive but would give us a head start. Morris may have been a headcase in the Dark World, but Laura didn't need any more death on her conscience.

I broke through the door. Laura knew this building better than I did, but it was hard to focus on her mind with Violus' anxiety running wild. I pushed Violus back, ignoring her protests.

It was the hardest for Violus to cross over into such an alien world; she was used to a very different kind of violence.

We ran down the hall, past pictures of scientists and children. I turned left, whipping around again, when I heard Laura yell, *Right!*

Smashing through the door, I pushed Laura's legs as fast as they would go. She would be hurting tomorrow, but it was better than being dead.

I started to recognize things, and my mind flashed to the icy halls of the Abyss. I kept my focus, careful not to accidentally send us to the crawl space above Malicious' chambers. I wondered if the heat-seekers had found me yet but was confident I'd know if they had.

I pushed through another door, finding the kitchen. I slowed, cautious of unsuspecting attendants preparing lunch. The kitchen was empty now, though. I darted around shiny metal counters, searching for another door before the kitchen attendants got back from their break.

The cafeteria's that way! Laura warned. *Take the side door.*

The door swung open, putting us face-to-face with a squishy-nosed Crawler in a black coat. I dropped, expecting another shrapnel-flinging weapon in his hands.

I've got this one, I heard Laura say.

My fist shot forward, striking the Black Coat upside the head.

Kick his shin, Violus offered.

I gave him a rough kick and shoved him back against the stainless-steel counter. I grabbed a pot from the stove, feeling the weight of at least three people behind it as I swung.

The Black Coat stumbled and then slumped to the

ground.

I ripped the door open, feeling someone fading into the back of my mind. Exhaustion radiated from deep within me. I stayed focused on my escape. I needed to get out of here, but where was Wade?

I pounded down the hall, glimpsing the front doors just as the alarms started.

My legs were wobbly, growing weaker with every step. A sharp pain radiated from the center of my back, and I prayed my legs would make it all the way to the door.

A Reaper is coming! Violus warned, a strange gurgle in her voice.

I turned to face the security guard. "Stop right there!" he yelled, raising a taser on me.

No, not a taser.

The sound of a shot echoing through the lobby was amplified in my ears.

I staggered back but didn't fall. My hand brushed my stomach. I couldn't find a wound, although the sweet, copper taste of blood was filling my mouth.

The guard watched me with tremendous confusion, stunned that I was still standing. I pushed past him. We were almost outside—almost free—but everything felt wrong.

Something was draining from me, but I didn't know what. I stopped, no longer caring about the guard.

Laura?

I'm here.

Violus?

A sob rose up and broke free of my lips, and the tears were close behind. *Violus, answer me.*

She's gone, Lennox.

My stilted legs moved in slow motion. The door was right there but another world away.

I can't do it, I whispered, crumbling to the floor as sleep took over.

54—ERRIS

There were alarms. I couldn't place them. Were they in my world or the dark one? I didn't even know where I was until Morris pulled me loose.

"Erris, what did you see?"

The Ocular was bright, and I threw my hands up to shield my eyes.

Morris leaned over and dimmed the light before turning back to me. "What did you learn? Did their ceremony work?"

"She's gone," I said, falling forward onto the desk. I was just so tired. Daddy had carried me back to Morris' office.

"Who?" Morris shook me back and forth. "Who's gone? Which one?"

"Violus," I choked out, holding back tears. "They killed her to make it rain! The others couldn't feel me, but I saw everything."

I felt empty, as if someone had broken a seal deep within me and all my energy was seeping out.

"Violus," Morris glanced at President Venkin, who was standing by the door. "She was from the Dry World."

"What does that mean?" President Venkin asked. "Are we too late? If it rained there, why don't we have the sun?"

"There's still a chance to repeat the ceremony with Laura," said Morris. "But Erris has to act now."

"I don't want to!" I pleaded. "Not again."

"This will be the last session, Erris," I heard a haunting voice say.

My breath caught. I turned my head, seeing Daddy by the door.

"I'm here now too, Erris." My Ma. Standing there at Morris' side. Encouraging him. "We know it's hard, but it's so important, sweetheart. You can save all of Aquarius. You just have to be stronger than the others. Take the sunshine back from them."

"No," I gasped. My mind was thick with fog, and I struggled to understand.

I knew the perfect melody of my Ma's laugh and every callous the ropes had worn into Daddy's hands, but the two people who watched me now were nothing more than strangers. Worse, they were traitors.

Gleaners like me.

"Why are you here?" I asked, my own hoarse voice unfamiliar.

Ma came close. She laid her head on the desk, inches from mine, her golden hair spilling over the desk. It was clean. It even smelled like strawberries. How many baths had she taken while I lived in ruins back on Fox Island?

"Why didn't you ever come for me?"

Ma shook her head. "Your abilities . . . they're special. We didn't understand before, but the Holdouts were wrong. Morris' work . . . it's important. *You're* important. The other worlds you see? They're stealing what's ours. Without them, we'll have sun—maybe even snow. We'll grow food across the whole planet again. You need to take control. Push the others out. It's the only way to keep the rain away."

"You lied," I whispered. "You're Gleaners."

Ma ran a hand over my dreadlocks. I hadn't soaked them in the tub long enough to rinse out the filth. "For you," she assured me. "President Venkin makes a good deal with anyone who'll help him. He promised us freedom, a little island of our own. With fruit trees," she added with a giggle.

The same promise he'd made me.

"You taught me to keep my mouth shut," I reminded Daddy. "Told me not to tell the Gleaners what I can do."

"Well, I thought you would, Erris," said Daddy. "Part of me was hopin' you'd escape. Can't blame me for wanting my baby girl to have a normal life."

"This is your normal." Ma said, nuzzling close. "You were made for great things, Erris. I knew Morris could help you. That's why I arranged for you to join me here 'stead of going to the gallows."

"You knew I was here?" I asked, mortified. "Your Daddy and I were planning to come see you soon, Erris. We really were."

"Well, why didn't ya?"

"We were busy." Her eyes slid toward President Venkin. "You get rewarded for working hard around here."

What kind of rewards had the president offered? What could have possibly made my folks knowingly leave me in the hands of a man like Morris?

"Steak," Ma whispered, a twinkle in her eye. "Bacon. Lettuce that don't have any rotten parts on it." The corners of her mouth curled upward. "Sometimes, he even lets us watch old movies on TV."

My voice cracked. "TV?" I said, the full force of my folks' betrayal sinking in. "You left me with that monster so you could *watch TV*? Made me betray the other prisoners . . ." Betray my friends.

I shook my head, wishing God would take the truth back. I didn't want to know. If I hadn't abandoned Jackie, she'd still be here. I might be safe on some floating Raider city now. Maybe there really were fruit trees nearby.

My folks were watching me, expecting me to be a good soldier and do as I was told so they could get back to the luxuries Venkin bribed them with.

Abandonment and loss were a normal part of a Shadow's life, I realized now.

"What about him?" I asked, tilting my chin toward Morris. The ooze that dripped from the seam of his penfocals looked spoiled, with chunks of brown falling from the eyewear.

Daddy appeared on my left. He leaned in so close, the salty smell of his breath tickled my nostrils. "He's here to make sure we don't let you fail."

I heard the buzz of the Ocular start up again. Morris was getting ready to send me back, but I wasn't ready. I would never be ready.

Ma lifted my chin. "Go get the others, Erris. Find them, and bring them back. Bring back our rain."

As soon as the spots left by the Ocular's bright light cleared, I leaped from my chair and charged Morris.

I'd been a prisoner for too long. At last, I remembered what I really was.

A soldier.

I slipped my shackled wrists around Morris' neck and slammed his face into the desk. Daddy darted toward me, but I stepped to the side, causing him to stagger past. I pivoted, smashing my shackles into the Ocular instead.

For a second, I was glued in place—and then a shock shot through me, its force lifting me from my feet and slamming me hard against Morris' desk. I couldn't see. I didn't know if it was from the Ocular's shock or something else, but I felt hands grab me. Hands wrapped around my legs, wrists, and waist, lifting me into the air.

"Get the door!" Morris yelled.

Warm rain showered down on me. Pain throbbed through my body from the shock and I wondered if my vision would ever return.

"The Ocular! What are we going to do now?" President Venkin asked, his voice high and panicked. "How will Wisdom help us?"

"Forget Wisdom!" Morris muttered. "Hopefully, we'll

have better luck with one of the other brats."

"But she said she could help us! What about the deal she offered?"

I spun through the air. Morris was carrying me, but I doubted he could have packed me like this alone.

"She's going to have to find somewhere else," Morris said. "There won't be anywhere for her to stay here."

"No, please!" I heard my Ma cry. "Give Erris another chance! We don't need the Ocular. The other kids didn't need it!"

A hand grasped my arm. "She can use her mind! I know she can!" Daddy sobbed. "Oh, Erris, why do you have to be so defiant?" I was jerked to the ground by my ankles, and the back of my head bounced hard against the ground, painting my face with a cold spray of mud on impact.

"No!" Ma wailed. "What are you doing to her?"

There was a *splash!* as I was pulled through the mud and Ma's cries grew faint. Morris had me all to himself now. I smelled the salt of the ocean heavy in the air. We were close to shore.

I was thankful I'd lost my sight when I felt Morris' hot breath on my neck. "I could've forgiven you for hurting me," Morris whispered as he pulled me upright. "But the Ocular . . . that was precious. Thanks to you, all of Aquarius will drown."

I tilted my cheek toward the sky, feeling the unmistakable warmth of sunlight. I held onto the sensation, going so far as to imagine I was back on the Dry World. Violus was gone, but for a few seconds, I brought the desert to Aquarius, and the pounding rain stopped.

Across the island, I heard cheers.

"Thanks to me?" I used the last of my strength to lift my shackled hands into the air. Morris tried to back away from me, but I dropped my hands, looping the chains around his neck for the second time that day. I wouldn't need a third.

Morris squirmed, his body writhing against me as he tried to flee. I pushed him back, shoving him toward the smell of salt.

"Help me!" he wailed. "Get her off me!"

I shoved him again, sending us both staggering into the water. Morris tried to overpower me, but unlike him, I had nothing left to lose. Water splashed my feet and soaked my pant legs as we stumbled further into the waves.

"Hurry up, she's gonna kill me!"

Shouts surrounded me. I had no idea if I was still going the right way, but I didn't stop. I pushed Morris deeper into the water, pulling the chains tight around his neck. I toppled with him, taking a final gasp of salty air before we both plummeted into the ocean.

Morris' body jerked. His nails scraped at me as my weight pushed him further down.

I laid there until Morris stopped moving. My lungs screamed for air and my eyes bulged in my skull, but I wasn't worried about saving myself anymore.

I thought of Laura and Lennox back where I'd left them in the Dark World, and I jumped.

55-Laura

My eyelids were pried open, and a blinding light was directed at my face. I tried to force my eyelids closed again but found they were held by duct tape.

Lennox was quiet. There was a gaping hole inside where Violus had been—a hole that I knew we both felt. Grief didn't begin to describe the pain. A part of me had been cut away like a limb, and just as people talked about feeling the loss of an arm or a leg long after it was gone, something felt like Violus was still hiding in the back of my mind somewhere. Or maybe she'd gone back home?

But then I remembered that nothing was waiting for her there.

There won't be any more ceremonies, was all Lennox said.

Dr. Venkin leaned in. "You are remarkable, Laura." His words held the hope of a death sentence.

"Something's wrong inside." I tasted blood. Was it mine? Or Violus'?

"A world disconnected." Dr. Morris kneeled beside me. "You won't see the Dry World anymore. And checking the local weather stations confirms no change in temperatures. It appears Violet wasn't the key to saving Earth."

"Violus," I corrected him. "What do you mean, her world disconnected?"

It means she's dead, Lennox said. Sadness swelled, and a few tears brushed my cheek.

Dr. Morris leaned in and pricked my finger with a needle I hadn't seen him holding. It stung, but I was far too tired to complain. It was only a little blood. He returned to his desk and shuffled through the drawers until he found an empty microscope slide.

"Why didn't I feel the gunshot?" I asked.

Dr. Venkin answered, "Your body regenerated using a trick called layering."

Dr. Morris nodded excitedly. He held the slide up, illuminating the drop of red blood under the light. "If I were to evaluate this, I suspect I'd find three different strands of DNA. But what would your brain scans reveal? How many are with you now, Laura?"

"Only one."

"Yes, I see." He placed the slide into an envelope and dropped it in the filing cabinet. "It's fascinating, really. We've witnessed other patients heal from cuts and burns by summoning their omens. But a bullet wound?" He turned to Venkin. "Do you know what this will mean for the medical field? Almost limitless regeneration is going to be an incredibly valuable industry."

Dr. Venkin's face lit up like he was already counting dollars.

"But I don't even know what I did!" I wanted to stomp my foot. Right on Venkin's face.

"You didn't do anything," Dr. Venkin said, finger curling around his mustache in a most villainous way.

"That shot would have killed you if not for your ability to layer. A normal human would have never survived such a wound. You lost someone, yes. But you'll be stronger without her. Won't she Lennox?"

Lennox squirmed, recoiling into my mind.

"What are you planning to do with the other kids?" I asked. "Will you shoot them too?"

Dr. Morris met my eye, not a drop of emotion left. "If I have to."

Dr. Venkin let out a low *tsk*. "Stop it now, Dr. Morris. Of course, we don't want to hurt any more of our children. It's a waste of resources anyway. The kids in this building aren't the ones we need. The true cure to our world's problems hides deep in the Abyss."

"The Dark World?"

"We kept our eyes on you, Laura, because we knew the original would break through eventually."

What are they talking about, Lennox? She was avoiding me. I felt the chill of the Dark World, but Lennox was silent.

"I'm not the original?" My head swung between Venkin and Morris. A cassowary and a shrike—a pair of butchers.

Dr. Morris spoke. "In the beginning, we thought we were the first, but we discovered the experiments started somewhere else. You're nothing more than a side-effect like the rest of them. You only exist because of Lennox."

Is that true? I wasn't asking the doctors.

Yes. Lennox's voice was so fragile, I would have thought she was one of the others. *My planet had an obsession with how the world would end. We were so caught up in avoiding the apocalypse that Venkin's machine, meant to warn us about the dangers our planet might face, ended up creating them. Every prediction became a self-fulfilling prophecy. Plagues, unstable weather... Whatever the machine thought of, became a reality. But not our reality.*

We started dreaming about places that mirrored our own. The purpose of the Shadows is to try to find out what went wrong. Your world, Laura ... it's the only one that has a chance, but— She was cut off and when she spoke again, it was hardly a whisper. *They found me.*

Lennox? I closed my eyes and searched for her, but she'd locked me out.

When I opened my eyes, the machine was waiting on Dr.

Morris' desk.

"I'd love a piece of chocolate, instead."

Dr. Morris spat in my face. I jerked my head back in disgust.

Before I could recover, he was slipping the earpieces into place. "Tell Lennox she needs to stop hiding." Dr. Morris threw the switch, and I woke up in the Dark World.

The Crawlers' hands were on my body. They pulled me loose from the crawlspace and shoved me down the hall toward the smell of rancid meat and roars I thought belonged to bears. For a brief second, I was relieved. It would be over soon, and I'd be back with Violus and Arial. We'd be sisters, as we always should have been.

But that wasn't how it worked. Venkin called it layering, but Lennox's scarred body told the truth. Every cut, burn, and gunshot had traveled through this flesh.

Get out of here, Laura. Save yourself.

We entered what I assumed to be an office. Every surface was wreathed in thick frost. Beneath the frost, I saw Morris' desk as well as a computer and a phone—his life preserved from before he became Malicious. I knew the other man who watched me had to be Dr. Venkin, but I wouldn't have recognized him here. His skin was wrong—pale blue and covered in fine white hair like that of an animal.

The men wore thick goggles, but I guessed their eyes were as weak as Lennox's on the other side.

"We got one," growled another man. Fade was hunched over an ancient computer I figured was the only one in the building that still worked. "Erris is close; she's being forced through."

"Good," Morris said. I tried to remember what Lennox called him, but her thoughts were so weak, I barely remembered her name.

I'm sorry, Laura, she said. So small, so fragile.
Pain flared in my skull as someone forced their way in. I tried to lift my hands, finding them strapped to my side.

Erris' thoughts joined mine, but they were fleeting and erratic, and I didn't know how long she would hang on. The room flashed through worlds. Ice melted from the walls until water pooled around my knees, only to drain away just as quickly. I was out of control.

"I've got Erris," Fade said, regret thick in his voice. "But they're not stable. I don't know how long Lennox can hold on."

"Others lasted longer. Lennox is strong. Unbreakable even. She'll be fine." Malicious. That was his name. "Besides, if she disconnects, it'll simply restart the machine. The others may die off, but with Lennox, it's just another chance to find out what went wrong."

"Who's left?" asked the blue-faced Venkin. The Ice Man lived up to his name.

"Wisdom," Fade answered. "She might already be gone. The Breakers are almost done there. I'm looking, but we'll have to be careful or I'll lose her while trying to pull her in."

I started to think of Wisdom's colorful world, but I felt something fall over me. Like when my mother draped a blanket across me in the days she still tucked me in. *Don't make it easier. Fade's trying to keep her out. He's still on our side.* I expected Lennox, but it was Erris who spoke. *Venkin's machine is too unstable,* she whispered. *We'll be gone soon, Laura, I'm already sinking on the other side. You were so brave. You tried so hard.*

"Where is she?" Malicious demanded. "Where's Wisdom?"

"I found her," Fade said. "She's with *me*."

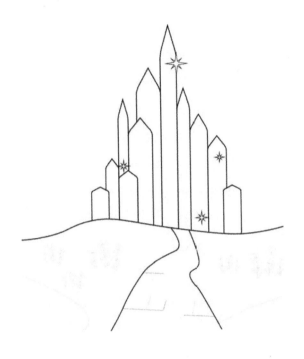

56-Wisdom

All I saw was black. The black turned to gray and then to white. From the white, a million shades of color erupted as little pixels.

At my command, the colors came together, settling into the beautiful Land of Oz. I lay in a field of wildflowers, looking up at the looming Emerald City.

I stretched the arms and legs built from my imagination. I looked like Laura. With another thought, I became Erris, complete with hazel eyes and dread-locked hair and the tattoo of a blue wave on her wrist. I flexed, becoming Lennox next. I ran a hand over my face to feel the rugged scars. When I lifted my hand, a pink hand-held mirror appeared in it.

I studied Lennox's lavender eyes. Her ratty black hair melted away, and the dark lines of tattooed squares and triangles appeared over my bald head.

At the sight of Violus, I let out a sob. I dropped the mirror to my side, slamming it against the ground until the broken instrument finally grew weary of my abuse and vanished.

First Arial. Now Violus.

I rolled onto my front, beating my fist against the ground in a flurry until it, too, disappeared.

I forced myself to my feet and followed the yellow brick road away from the Emerald City.

This had been Laura's favorite place once. I knew it somehow, even if she never told me herself.

I shook my head, allowing Laura's sandy blonde hair to grow again.

I looked to the sky, where the swirling green clouds had turned burgundy. A winged fox swooped low and turned into a dragon. He roared, and a blast of flames erupted from his mouth. Peeking over my shoulder, I saw the Wizard's green castle was gone.

A shiver ran through me.

"Arial?" I called. For a second, a girl appeared. Her curly golden hair had been wind-blown into a knotty mess. She watched me for a moment before darting into the trees. "Violus, is that you?" I asked when another girl appeared, young and bald, a kind smile on her face.

She didn't answer, and soon she, too, disappeared into the forest.

They weren't real. Like everything else in my life, I only imagined them.

Over the years, Lennox had helped me piece together my life like the puzzle it was. She taught me about the others and told me what she knew about what happened to my world. Venkin's machine, the famines, the plagues that spread over my Earth, killing billions. How it all came from TIR, and only the people who lived within the institute's walls were preserved. And how the man known to me as the Vanquisher of Mankind was responsible for worldwide death and destruction on a multitude of worlds.

The rest I'd been forced to figure out on my own.

Eventually, I learned how to use the wires that led out of my world to my benefit. Then, I helped Lennox figure out her own world. I got her in contact with Fade, who had an in with the Crawlers, and together the three of us had learned every secret Venkin, Morris, and the Crawlers had been keeping from the rest of the world. Several worlds, actually.

That was when I started reaching out to the people in power. My messages brought worlds together. Until Lennox broke us apart.

A unicorn stepped from the trees and came to feed from my hand. Today, its body was white and its mane and tail were braided in my favorite shades of pink, purple, and turquoise.

The unicorn was startled away by voices. I wondered who they belonged to—whose world I was close to stepping into. As the voices got louder, I realized they were from my own world.

A rip appeared in the red sky, and I leaped toward it, flying through the air until the hole in the sky became a screen.

I saw a message from Fade: **Wisdom, get out now!**

I waved a hand, and the message vanished. Instead, I imagined I was the surveillance camera blinking on the wall. My body floated in the tank outside.

"This is the last one," said a man in a black hazmat suit.

"Ah, she's only a baby," said another.

"Says here it's her birthday. What a shame she never got to spend a day in the real world."

The second man shook his head. "I can't believe Venkin's ready to jump ship. What will happen to us?"

I watched my beautiful home and beloved pets melt away at the hands of the Breakers who pulled the plug on me like I was nothing more than a number.

"Who knows whether anyone's still conscious in there," I heard one of the men say before they tore apart the tiny box that held my universe. My friends were gone, as was my family. I never had a chance to connect with them on my planet, but I knew them from other lives, and I mourned my parents when their life support ended just the same.

They couldn't keep me here. My body may fade away in the physical world, but that little box on the wall couldn't hold me prisoner. I'd been sneaking away all my life.

It was over. My world was as good as dead. I zoomed through the cables, searching for a way out. My body became light as I shot through the air and landed in a digital thermometer mounted on the wall. I couldn't see or hear a thing. All I could feel here was the heat of the room.

It was all I needed; my mind filled in the rest. I saw the pods of people, the light that had illuminated their suspended bodies now dark.

I dove into the depths of my dying mind. Searching . . . searching, desperate for a light on the other side.

When I landed, I was surprised to find I wasn't alone.

"Let me out of here!" Wade screamed, banging on the metal door. We were in a supply room, far from where Laura was being held in Dr. Venkin's office.

I'd made my temporary home in a surveillance camera, where I could see but couldn't communicate.

Wade! I tried, forcing my thoughts on him.

He kept shouting for the guards to free him. I did my best to wait him out, but there was so little time. Who knew how long I could exist without a body? The Crawlers had trapped the others, and I knew if I dared to set foot in Laura or Erris now, I'd be sent to the Dark World just as fast.

That couldn't happen yet. I needed more time.

"Wade!"

I searched the room, looking for a way to get his attention. There. I dove for a digital clock mounted on the wall no one had bothered to reset after the last power outage. It displayed 12:00 in flashing red text.

My hope waned. What if the power went out now? What would happen to me then? I didn't have time to worry about it. I got to work on the LED display, rearranging the little dots of red light into a message.

Wade searched the empty room as if he expected a window

to magically appear in the wall. A stream of curse words fell from his mouth—a waterfall of expletives—and I waited patiently for his eyes to find me.

"WSDM," he said, seeing my message. "Wisdom?"

YES.

"It's you! Are you here to rescue me? Do you know where Laura is?"

I flashed the "YES" message twice.

MORIS, I wrote, distorting the two dots in the center of the digital display so it appeared as an "R."

"She's with Morris?"

I rearranged the lights again.

LNNX.

"Linx? Oh! She's with Lennox?" Disappointment crept into his gaze. "She left me?"

Had Wade always been this dim? This was going to be harder than I thought.

NO, I wrote. **HERE. MORIS.**

"Does she need help?" he asked.

YES.

"From me? I'm a little stuck."

DOOR.

He yanked on the handle, but the door didn't budge.

LOKR.

He turned to the blue utility locker in the corner and tried it. "It's locked." He glanced around until he spotted a key ring hanging above the closet door. He jumped up and yanked the key ring down. He pulled aside a key and used it to force open the flimsy metal door of the locker.

"It's cleaning supplies. Rodent poison. The keys are useless, too. All the doors are automated now. They have readers."

He rifled through the supplies. "Wait a second. I think I've got something. He held up a little black box.

RATS?

"Yeah, it's one of those electric mouse traps. It kills them with currents." Wade flipped the trap over, revealing the fastener on the back. He wrapped the little device around the door handle. When he turned it on, a high-pitched hum filled the room.

BACK, I warned.

Wade pressed himself against the wall just as I jumped into the trap. I tried to take Lennox's advice and make myself as strong as I could. There was a *pop!* as the box exploded. I escaped just in time and heard ringing when I leaped back into the clock.

Wade stuck his head out the door, seeing the hall was clear. "Now what?"

WATCH.

He stared at the clock as if it was going to perform for him, and I flexed, making the digital watch on his wrist to beep. He glanced down. "Oh, there you are."

I'd never had eyes to roll—not ones I could control anyway—and this was the first time I missed it.

Wade's wristwatch had the ability to display the date, and I was thankful for the chance to extend my vocabulary.

MORRIS.
NOW.
HURRY.
And he did.

57-Lennox

It was crowded in my head with both Laura and Erris, and I wondered how long Malicious was planning to keep us in the Dark World.

I sensed a commotion but didn't know if the glimmer came from Laura's world or Erris'. The icy walls of Malicious' chambers melted away, and I returned to Dr. Morris' office back on Earth. Wade burst through the door, holding a Glock I recognized from the TIR guards who had hassled him at the game shop. He must have taken down a Black Coat. *Way to go, Wade.*

Laura? Erris?

We're here, Erris answered.

Wisdom? I asked when I sensed another presence.

Yep.

You've got this, Lennox, Laura said.

They lingered in the back of my mind, but I could recall them anytime I needed to.

I broke free of everything. The restraints on my wrists and the ones in my head. I jumped up, charging Morris first.

The box! Erris cried.

I scooped up Dr. Morris' strange electrical device and

slammed it against the wall with all my strength.

Dr. Morris let out a primal scream and grabbed me by the throat. The humanity fled his eyes as he throttled the life from me. My thoughts poured into protecting the others, but someone was resisting me. I was shoved aside as one of the others took my place, sacrificing her neck for mine.

"Erris, no!"

A gasp escaped my lips as the soul-wrenching despair flooded in.

It was as if I stood up too fast—like all my blood drained away—and I was nothing more than a shell racked with pain.

Hot, then cold, my body was going into shock.

"That's not possible!" Morris said, swinging his head from Dr. Venkin to me. "You should be dead!"

Dr. Venkin stepped in front of him. "I told you, you've got to kill Lennox! As long as she's in there, the girl is invincible!"

"Yes," I said. "Come and get me."

I shoved Laura to the edge of my mind, bringing the fight back to the Dark World.

"Erris is dead!" I told Fade.

The glint of tears covered his face. He already knew.

He gave me a final goodbye look that told me what a lifetime of words couldn't have. "I'm sorry we failed." He loved me I knew at that moment, finally admitting to myself that I loved him too. Maybe it would be different in the next life.

Malicious saw the look pass between us. "Did the Shadow and the Crawler fall in love?" he asked, bemused.

"I'll find you," I promised Fade, hoping he'd remember me in the next world. "I'll always find you."

My heart stopped as Malicious swung his arm, ending Fade's life in the drop of a blade, simply because he meant something to me.

Blood boiled up. It wasn't just mine. They were with me here, teetering between my Earth and Laura's. Laura leaped for Malicious, wrapping my legs around him and shimmying up him like a monkey scales a tree. He screamed as the spikes in my boots dug into his flesh, but she didn't stop. My head slammed against his and intense pain rocked through me—pain I knew we all felt. Blood covered my eyes, and I didn't know if it belonged to me or Malicious.

A queasy feeling sloshed in my gut, and I toppled over, taking Malicious' slack form with me.

I turned to the quivering Ice Man in the corner. "Venkin," I hissed, pouncing on him. Following Laura's lead, I pummeled his face with the spikes on my gloves. His heart began to race beneath his heavy layers. Blood sprayed my face and splashed to the ground, turning the snow crimson. I held Venkin in my hands, listening to his heartbeat quiet to nothing as his body temperature plummeted.

I waited for something to happen. The dark sky to turn bright or the apocalypse to come. But it didn't; and in horror, I realized the Ice Man wasn't the original after all. He was nothing but a Shadow.

My maker was still out there. Which meant he wasn't done looking for me.

The Ice Man was gone here, but it wasn't the end of Venkin. Like me, he was a special kind of strong. But where in the multiverse might he be hiding?

I forced the door open and fled the massacre, making my way toward the screams of the Shadows.

Arial.

Violus.

Erris.

And all the others. Would Laura forgive me once she knew the truth? Once she realized the magnitude of the curse I'd marked her with?

I ducked, dodging shots and slashes, but my legs were heavy, my mind sore. I desperately longed for sleep that would never come.

Venkin would hunt me forever. Until every mistake was undone.

Unless I found him first.

Crawlers yelled, and the heat-seekers swooped low over

my head. The drones struck me with beams of light hot enough to melt ice, which was exactly what I wanted.

Laura's gasps and cries escaped my lips. I couldn't keep her from the pain anymore. I needed her.

I dove for the control panel, and it burst into flames as it was struck by the heat-seeker's beam. The ventilators fell silent and scared cries started up.

"What's happening?" the Shadows asked as they tried to make sense of where they were. It was almost cruel, I thought, taking them away from their dreams and plunging them into the real world. There was no alternative. The experiments couldn't go on any longer. I wouldn't allow it.

"Run!" I screamed. Heartbeats roared, and the Shadows cast me panicked looks before they fled the room, their visitors urging them on. The Dark World would be cruel outside the Abyss, but these children had been built to survive far worse than the end of the world. Plus, with the Ice Man gone, they may have a real chance to live their lives. No matter how fleeting they may be.

There were more heat-seekers coming, and I waited for them to set their sights on me before dodging, risking the injuries for the chance the heat-seekers would burn me a usable path. I dove into the heat-seeker tunnel I'd used earlier, letting the drones follow me.

Though the pain was unbearable, I no longer cared. I'd seen many other worlds . . . but only one worth saving. I swayed back and forth as I crawled so the heat-seekers' beams shot past me and melted the snow, little bits at a time. The others were quiet, doing their best to let me keep my energy.

I found the end of the tunnel and rolled loose, landing on the snow-packed floor in the middle of a circle of Crawlers who pointed their flamethrowers at me.

Don't worry, I told the others. *We've got this.*

There was silence on the other side. Something was wrong.

58 –Laura

*L*ennox!" I tried to scream out a warning, but someone was muffling me. "*What are you doing? She's in trouble!*"

Someone was pulling me away. I glimpsed the icy tunnel of the Dark World and Dr. Morris' office on Earth, but we kept falling . . . all the way to Wisdom's world.

I expected the candy land, but all I saw was desolation. A lone building stood with its roof on fire.

This is all that's left of my world, Wisdom said. *Even our bodies are gone now.*

What will you do? I asked.

How long could Wisdom survive without a body? And where would she go?

As her thoughts mixed with mine, her plan became clear, and I realized that like Arial, Wisdom wanted to take my place.

I felt a shiver, closely followed by Lennox's voice. My vision dimmed as I glimpsed the Dark World.

Wisdom! Laura! Are you there? Lennox spun in circles, eyeing the Crawlers' weapons and the flames that leaped from them. The heat-seekers slowed, gathering to watch her as well.

"Stop!" Wisdom's voice rose. "Venkin needs me alive."

***

"Wisdom! Why are you doing this?"

She'd dragged us back to Earth. I was in Dr. Venkin's office, held to a chair by the strongest restraints the Black Coats could find. Beside me, Wade watched the doctors discuss us in whispers over Venkin's desk. I saw the Glock he'd stolen hanging from Venkin's hip.

I felt a yank at my scalp, like someone had pulled my hair. *I showed you what she did to me.*

It wasn't Lennox! It was Venkin, remember? The Vanquisher of Mankind?

Yes. Wisdom's voice was no longer sweet and childlike. She'd matured to a full-grown predator. *Venkin is responsible for the machine, but it was Lennox who decided to play God.*

That's not true!

Isn't it, Laura? You don't know anything, do you? She let you stay oblivious. The rest of us had to deal with the repercussions of Lennox's existence a lot sooner. After a while, you grow to resent a person.

What are you talking about? Your life is a dream! You can create whatever you want.

Wrong, Laura. I distracted myself with rainbows and glitter because I was left with nothing but a breathing tube and a box! Wisdom's memories were soaking through me, filling me with all the loneliness she'd felt over the years.

There's got to be another way. There's enough room for all of us! You can, I don't know, jump between our worlds or something.

Wisdom scoffed. *You honestly think Lennox would let me stay? I'm dangerous. Selfish. It didn't play out well when I suggested Arial try it, and it won't for me either. Plus, it doesn't work that way. Even Lennox's body couldn't handle two of us for a lifetime. Eventually, one of you will give out.*

You sent Arial to hurt me?

I was desperate to feel something, Laura. I begged Lennox to save my world instead. We never would have grown old. We could have been friends forever, and there would have been room for all of us there. But no, she insisted it was you.

I'm sorry, Wisdom, but she must have had a reason. Go save Lennox! Ask her for yourself.

The Crawlers are already taking Lennox to the bears.

But you said we needed her alive!

Not her, Laura. You. If I have to live out the rest of my life in one of your worlds . . . well, like Lennox said, yours is a better choice. Besides, I'm doing you a favor.

How do you figure?

Have you been outside lately? Where the sun burns so hot, most stores don't open until after dark? Is this the Earth of your childhood, Laura? Or does it seem more like the Dry World?

She was lying. She had to be. *What do you mean?*

Those other worlds, the ones the rest of us belong to? The Dry World, the Wet World, the stormy place, my AI planet, or Lennox's Dark World . . . one of them is coming. Maybe something worse. Venkin's experiments didn't avoid your planet; it just hasn't happened yet, and if the weather report is any indication, it's coming faster than you think. Wouldn't it be nice to be free of all this? To sleep through the drought in the eternal slumber? Come on, let me be Laura now.

Never. I jumped, all of my thoughts on Lennox and her Dark World. Wisdom was right; she was with the bears.

The body I leaped into laid in strips across the icy floor. Through Lennox's remaining eye, I made out the monstrous form of some grotesque cousin of the polar bears I'd seen pictures of as a child. The fur had been white once, but now it was so soaked in Lennox's blood you would have thought the animal was born red. The putrid stench was revolting, and I couldn't be sure whether it came from the animal or myself. These "bears" must have been another of Malicious' experiments.

Agonizing pain tore through me, like every molecule in my body was being squeezed tight.

Why did you come back? Lennox whispered, struggling for breath.

You would have for me.

I'm sorry I failed, she said. *But I can try again.*

How?

It's my fault. The experiments are because of me. Every time Venkin kills me, he creates another world. A fresh chance he calls it, but only I know the cost.

You're his machine.

I counted. Me, Erris, Violus, Wisdom, Arial. *You've been through this five times already?* I realized in horror.

For just a second, Lennox let me feel the weight of her scars. The people she'd loved, the family she'd lost. *No,* she said. *I've been here thousands of times.*

A sob escaped my lips as she slipped from me. *Will I ever see you again?* I asked.

I don't know, she said, the last of her thoughts drifting away, *But I'll try to come back.*

I stayed with her while she faded away—until she was finally free of her pain.

But *my* pain was excruciating. The loss I'd felt today was nothing compared to Lennox's scars, but in a way, I understood her. I missed the days of being unaware of the betrayal in my own body. Back when I'd just barely quit referring to the voices in my head as invisible friends. They were strangers to me—something scary I wanted to do away with. It would have been easier if I could remember them that way, instead of as friends.

I was weaker than I had felt in my life without her, but I was glad she was with the others. I was glad she was free of her burdens.

As Lennox drained from me, my mind grew sharper and my body sure. For once, I knew I couldn't be pulled away again.

I leaped back to Earth, surprising Wisdom, who was busy trying to convince Venkin to free her binds. I threw myself over her, using my mind to smother hers.

Dr. Morris gave me a sick smile. "Wisdom. It's a privilege to have you with us." He slid a chocolate across the desk.

"I can't wait to help," I said in my best Wisdom impression.

I feigned reaching for the candy but grabbed the crystal pen cup instead.

"It's Laura!" blurted my traitorous lips, and my eyes met Dr. Morris' before I smashed the crystal dish over his head. He slumped over the desk, and this time, I didn't know if he would get back up.

"Laura, please," Venkin whispered. His eyes grew dark. "Come on, Wisdom, take her!"

She tried. I felt her wrestling with my mind, trying to grab a hold of my thoughts with her very being. She was smarter, but I was stronger. I shoved her back and leaped for Venkin, stopping short when he pulled the gun from his hip and held it up to me with shaky arms.

I considered my options. Venkin was clearly uncomfortable with the gun, but I would be, too. Sadness swelled inside me at the thought of her. What would Lennox do?

Fight for what's right.

I grabbed the gun from Venkin, shocked by my own tenacity. I held it to his face, setting a look of determination on my own.

Venkin raised his hands. "Be civil here. You don't want to go out a murderer."

I jabbed the gun toward him, insisting I didn't mind. "Open the door!" I yelled.

Venkin pulled the door open, and I waved him out before slamming the door in his face and locking it behind him.

"You're a badass!" Wade exclaimed. His gaze fell to Morris. "But why are we still in here?"

I bent down and loosened his restraints.

"The others are gone. It's only me and Wisdom now." He opened his mouth to console me, but I cut him off. "Wisdom works for Venkin now. She's trying to take my place."

Wade stood and cleared the ropes away. "Whoa. What are we gonna do?"

I reached out and grabbed his face, running my hand over

his scruffy beard. Things had turned out different than I expected, but the truth was I'd found freedom—if only for a couple of days. "Thank you for your help. You've been the best friend I ever had, Wade. Well, outside my own head anyway," I added with a grin.

Wade rolled his eyes. "Dammit, Laura." He faltered, uncertainty lingering on his face.

And then he kissed me. The first and best kiss I ever had—probably the last.

I pulled away, heart racing in my chest. Damn this stupid, awkward penguin. How dare he make me so soft.

"Get out, Wade. People have to know what's going on here. Someone needs to make sure the kids are safe if this doesn't work."

The tingling in my scalp intensified as Wisdom grew stronger. She would overpower me soon.

"If what doesn't work? Laura, what are you doing?"

I kissed him again, shoving him away just as Wisdom broke loose. There was only one option left. It was a no-win scenario. A Kobayashi Maru. As Wisdom took control, I turned the gun on myself . . . and pulled the trigger.

59 – Alone

There were screams. It was the only thing to penetrate the dark, but when I finally saw the light again, my mind was my own.

The light came and went, fading in rhythm with the sound of Wade's voice. He was speaking to someone. Who? No one else was here. Had I failed? Maybe the shot hadn't been fatal after all.

I opened my eyes.

"Laura!" Wade leaped for me, a cell phone grasped in his hands. "There are kids here. Lots of them. Dr. Venkin is torturing them. One of the patients was protecting herself and killed a doctor. Yeah, that's right. Okay, we'll wait right here until the police arrive."

✳✳✳

There were sirens. I fell in and out of consciousness, but every time I woke, Wade's reassuring voice was there in my ear. They took me. I was loaded onto a gurney, as was

Dr. Morris. A blanket had been draped over his head, and the paramedics hauled him into a separate ambulance than mine. As the sirens faded, I remembered the uneaten chocolate still on his desk.

***

There were voices. I looked up and saw Wade bent over me. Ringing phones echoed through the halls of a place I recognized to be a hospital.

"Welcome back," Wade whispered, brushing his lips along my hairline. "I've been worried about you."

"Me too." I struggled to sit up, seeing the TV in my room was playing the news.

"Tomlison Institute of Research is to be shut down after the latest string of scandals," a reporter said. "Dr. Venkin, head of the Research Center, which studies everything from climate change to behavioral disorders, has been placed under arrest for a long list of crimes including child abduction and endangerment. Police found dozens of children kept in hazardous conditions inside the Institute being tortured and used for TIR's strange research. Dr. Venkin claims he is the legal guardian of each of the almost one hundred children, but Family Services is prepared to testify that not one of those adoptions could be considered legal in any court . . ."

Wade snapped off the TV. "Are you nervous?" he asked. "About the real world?"

"It's always been real. Only now I don't have to look at it from inside padded walls."

He nodded.

"Although I am nervous about testifying."

"You'll be fine," Wade assured me. "You've received tons of letters, you know."

"The nurses told me. They said they were thank you notes from the kids. I take it their foster families helped them."

"Everything will be okay. Morris was a monster. There's plenty of evidence of that."

I nodded. One more trial to go.

"They're going to put Venkin and those doctors away for a long time," I said. "I still can't believe everything that's happened." My hand trailed over the bandages that covered my stomach. Every time I shifted, the wound screamed out and threatened to tear the stitches like they were still new. "I know weeks have passed, but I still feel them, you know?" I closed my eyes, but I hadn't seen anything since the incident at TIR. "It's hard to be alone now."

Wade took my hand. "You're not alone, Laura. I visit you every morning."

I grinned. "It's almost like you like me," I teased.

His playful smile turned serious. "Laura, I—"

"Ahem." We were interrupted by a clearing throat. Amanda stood by the door, wearing a knit sweater that strained over her belly. "Hello, Laura," she said, cheeks pink as she watched the floor.

"That the stepmom?" Wade whispered, narrowing his eyes on her. He crossed his arms like he was my personal bouncer.

"It's okay," I told him. "I'll be fine."

"I'll be right outside if you need me," Wade said, before slipping out the door without giving Amanda another glance.

"Sorry about him," I said after he left. "He's just protective."

"That's great," Amanda said. She took a few cautious steps into the room. "I'm glad you found someone who cares about you like that. You really deserve it, Laura."

I do?

"Your father's not coming," she said. "He's not—"

"Capable of human emotion?" I finished. Big surprise.

"Exactly." She laughed. "Dawson's kind of a vulture, actually." Amanda plopped into the empty chair beside my bed. Her discomfort was palpable as she wrung her hands in her lap.

"So . . . why are you here?" I finally asked. For once, I didn't see her as the beak nose and pile of black hair that stole my father. Her eyes were red and her makeup smeared. I saw a few grays in her beautiful raven hair and her laugh lines had turned into wrinkles. Amanda was human, just like me.

"Because I'm sorry about what happened to you," she said. "I was blind to what a pawn your father had become. His work is important, but—" She stopped, glancing at the digital clock on the wall. She stood up from the chair and ran a hand over her sweater to smooth it. She reached into her purse and pulled out a picture of a sonogram. "Your baby brother," Amanda said, patting her belly. "Only a few weeks left."

I took the picture and studied the blurry smudge of a baby. "I bet he'll look like Dawson," I said. At least he didn't look like a newborn raven. I handed the picture back. "I think you'll be a good mom, Amanda." After a deep breath, I added. "You already are one. I'm sorry I've been so hard on you. It means a lot to me that you came here."

Amanda gasped, and I thought I even saw a couple of tears wet her cheeks.

She glanced at the clock again. When she spoke, her voice was low and urgent. "Be careful, Laura," she warned. "I know Nikola Venkin is locked up, but he won't stay that way. TIR's connections are . . . *powerful.*"

She waved to the nurse, who entered to check my vitals. "Take care, Laura," Amanda said. After a pause, she reached out to give my hand a squeeze. "We always loved you, no matter what. I know it doesn't seem that way, but there's still so much you don't understand."

She left me with the nurse, who changed my bandages and loaded me up with a new batch of sleeping aids. I already felt the seds working, and Amanda's strange warning drifted to the back of my mind.

I caught a glimpse of the clock on the wall before I slipped back to sleep. Instead of numbers, the red text spelled **WSDM**.

***

After nearly two months in the hospital, my physician declared me healed, and a psychiatrist labeled me sane, stating she hadn't seen any of the symptoms I'd been institutionalized for in my youth. I was eighteen now and old enough to consent, so they had no choice but to release me on my own.

Wade had visited me every day, and he pushed the wheelchair to the front door of the hospital the day I was released.

He took my hand, thanking the nurse who wheeled the chair away.

We stepped out from the awning that hung over the hospital's entrance and started walking toward a waiting car. I wrapped my hands around my arms, glancing at the thick black clouds that hung in the sky. "It looks like the drought is over."

Wade glanced up. "Yep. Now we're just waiting for the rain."

I thought of Erris and reached my hand out to catch a drop, finding it wasn't rain at all—it was snow.

ACKNOWLEDGMENTS

Jake, thank you for investing in me, loving me always, and being the greatest support I could ask for. I hope to always be as big of a cheerleader for you as you've been to me.

Lillian, Elianna, and Talia, thank you for your encouragement, your patience, and your snuggles. I chase my dreams for you, and I can't wait to watch each of you chase your dreams someday, too. You are my biggest accomplishments in life.

Thank you, Mom, for introducing me to reading and being my biggest fan from the start. I love you forever. Thank you, Dad. Although you never held my book in your hands, I know you'll be reading every word in Heaven.

To my second mom and dad, Dottie and Kevin, and my awesome sister-in-law, Desirae, as well as everyone else in my big, marvelous extended family. Thank you for being so supportive. I love you all.

Thank you, Shiloah, for not making me feel like a terrible friend all those times I abandoned you so that I could write, and thank you, Kendra, for wanting to be one of my first readers since forever.

To the amazing team at Midnight Tide Publishing, thank you for taking me under your wing and making me a part of your family.

A huge thanks to Lucie and Maxwell for catching my grammar mistakes, teaching me the difference between UK and US spelling, and double-checking my bird facts. I can't wait to show you what's in store for Laura next.

And to the beta readers, editors, and artists who made Laura's story so much better. See you again soon.

ABOUT THE AUTHOR

 H. R. Truelove lives with her family in the beautiful Pacific Northwest.
She developed a thirst for reading during her long bus rides to school, and has been writing poetry, song lyrics, and short stories most of her life.

H. R. Truelove can be found across social media @authorhrtruelove or you can join her newsletter at www.hannahtruelove.com.

ALSO BY H. R. TRUELOVE

Alter Trilogy:

Alter Book One
Alter Book Two (2022)

MORE BOOKS YOU'LL LOVE

If you enjoyed this story, please consider leaving a review.
Then, check out more titles from Midnight Tide Publishing.

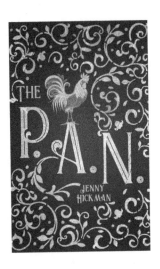

The P.A.N. by Jenny Hickman

Since her parents were killed, Vivienne has always felt ungrounded, shuffled through the foster care system. Just when liberation finally seems possible—days before her eighteenth birthday—Vivienne is hospitalized with symptoms no one can explain. The doctors may be puzzled, but Deacon, her mysterious new friend, claims she has an active Nevergene. His far-fetched diagnosis comes with a warning: she is about to become an involuntary test subject for Humanitarian Organization for Order and Knowledge—or H.O.O.K. Vivienne can either escape to Neverland's Kensington Academy and learn to fly (Did he really just say fly?) or risk sticking around to become a human lab rat. But accepting a place among The P.A.N. means Vivienne must abandon her life and foster family to safeguard their secrets and hide in Neverland's shadows… forever.

Full Trilogy Available Now

Magic Mutant Nightmare Girl
by Erin Grammar

Holly Roads uses Harajuku fashion to distract herself from tragedy. Her magical girl aesthetic makes her feel beautiful-and it keeps the world at arm's length. She's an island of one, until advice from an amateur psychic expands her universe. A midnight detour ends with her vs. exploding mutants in the heart of San Francisco. Brush with destiny? Check. Waking up with blue blood, emotions gone haywire, and terrifying strength that starts ripping her wardrobe to shreds? Totally not cute. Hunting monsters with a hot new partner and his unlikely family of mad scientists? Way more than she bargained for.

Available Now